Reluctant Witch

Reluctant
Witch

☽ ✱ ☾

Melissa Marr

Ⓑ
BRAMBLE
TOR PUBLISHING GROUP | NEW YORK

RELUCTANT WITCH

Copyright © 2025 by Melissa Marr

Designed by Jen Edwards

A Bramble Book
Published by Tom Doherty Associates / Tor Publishing Group
120 Broadway
New York, NY 10271

www.torpublishinggroup.com

Bramble™ is a trademark of Macmillan Publishing Group, LLC.

The Library of Congress Cataloging-in-Publication Data is available upon request.

ISBN 978-1-250-88415-2 (trade paperback)
ISBN 978-1-250-88416-9 (ebook)

Our books may be purchased in bulk for promotional, educational, or business use. Please contact your local bookseller or the Macmillan Corporate and Premium Sales Department at 1-800-221-7945, extension 5442, or by email at MacmillanSpecialMarkets@macmillan.com.

First Edition: 2025

Printed in the United States of America

0 9 8 7 6 5 4 3 2 1

To the scientists, researchers, doctors, and various medical personnel out there who create the magic that keeps so many of us alive. I know you all claim it's "science," but your potions and pills feel a lot like magic from where I stand. Whatever you call it, thank you from my whole family for what you do. I am alive because of you.

Reluctant Witch

1

Prospero

Prospero fled to her study after retrieving Ellie from the nonmagical world. All the Victorian witch could think of was the venomous way Ellie had called her a "lying bitch" before Prospero erased Ellie's memories of escaping Crenshaw.

Now, Ellie thought they chose to be wed. She remembered a hand-fasting that had never happened.

"Is something bothering you?" Ellie asked gently, glancing over at her as they walked toward the castle.

"I am tired." Prospero opted not to lie outright.

And overwhelmed and not sure how to fix . . . anything. Not the rift. Not my life. Not this sham marriage.

Ellie's expression tightened. "Something between *us* is wrong."

Prospero gestured at the front door of the castle as they approached, and it opened like an invitation. "You cannot—"

"Bullshit. I know this sour face of yours is about you and me!" Ellie gestured with one hand as she snapped at Prospero. "You're keeping secrets."

Prospero tucked her wife's other hand into the fold of her arm and all but marched her toward the room Ellie *thought* was hers. Ellie had moved out of her actual room when she escaped from Crenshaw. Too much evidence waited there, although the headmaster refused to throw it all away.

"You're making a spectacle of us," Prospero murmured softly.

"You have no idea what sort of 'spectacle' I could make." Ellie's voice thrummed with a threat.

Prospero looked around as they hurried through the castle. The hall was nearly empty now that the student class had been trimmed some. Those not staying had been siphoned of their magic, and the rest were free to roam the village.

"Here we are. Safe and sound." Prospero gestured at the door to the student lodging. After a pause, she flicked her fingers, and the door opened at her unspoken command. "I'll leave you in your home, and—"

"Seriously? We're *married*."

"But you're still a student." Prospero stepped back, evading the door and the unspoken threat of being alone with Ellie. "Students live in the castle."

Prospero crossed her arms over her chest. Until Ellie escaped Crenshaw, they'd been building something real—but then everything fell apart. She was not going to manage this ruse well.

Ellie stepped closer. "Find time for us."

She tilted her head up in an obvious request. Instead of the kiss Ellie clearly expected, Prospero lifted Ellie's hand to her lips and kissed the air above her knuckles. *No touching. No kissing. And certainly absolutely nothing* else.

Ellie scowled. "Surely the headmaster wouldn't object to—"

"He is busy with his bride and the students and dozens of things," Prospero explained lightly. Those details, of course, were *all* true. They were not the whole truth, however. One learned to twist words when overt lies were not options. "We had last night, Ellie—"

"Right. The night I fell asleep waiting for you?" Ellie snapped. "Exactly the honeymoon I dreamed of."

"You know who I am, Ellie. I have obligations to Crenshaw."

Ellie frowned. "I'm not sure why I married you."

"I see." Prospero flinched. She'd made Ellie's memory alteration in a crude manner, leaving behind their few date-like moments but erasing the meeting with the Congress of Magic, the escape, anything with Maggie or Monahan. There hadn't been time to sort through each memory slowly when Ellie's aunt, the headmaster, the other escapee, and Monahan were all present.

With such massive deletions, the brain would fill in the gaps with conclusions. However, in barely a day, Ellie was already questioning the parts left behind after Prospero's crude memory erasures.

"I feel like I should have met the headmaster's wife." Ellie frowned. "She's a remedial witch, too, right? Margie? Same group as me?"

"*Maggie*. Maybe you didn't notice her. There are hundreds of witches who didn't catch your attention." Prospero stepped back, giving Ellie more space.

"I noticed *you*." Ellie flashed a flirtatious smile at her and reached out to catch Prospero's hand. "What if you stayed in my room tonight? Remind me why I'm your wife."

Prospero's morals recoiled.

Ellie tugged on her hand, pulling her off-balance. Ellie, the same woman who said she'd rather die than be a witch, would not want *any* affection from Prospero. And she certainly wouldn't want to be *married* to her.

Prospero sounded every bit the uptight Victorian she had once been as she retorted, "Truly, I must go—"

Any further words died as Ellie leaned forward and kissed her to silence.

Prospero's lips parted reluctantly as Ellie pulled her closer. Prospero's good sense considered fleeing at the feel of the woman she *wanted* becoming pliant and very eager to stay in her arms.

Which I don't deserve.

Prospero detangled herself. "Good night, Ellie."

Then she turned and walked away. Apparently, she couldn't trust herself to kiss Ellie—not if she was to be tangentially ethical.

No more kisses.

No more anything.

After she left Ellie, Prospero strode through the castle hall and into the main foyer. A few witches gave her curious looks, and some of the staff looked away as if she were a monster they had stumbled upon. She straightened her spine and exited the front of the castle to head toward Lord Scylla's home.

Scylla was one of the few witches she was likely to call a *friend*. They had no subterfuge between them, so it was no surprise to receive her summons that morning. When Scylla's door drifted open, Prospero found herself in one of the most nondescript spaces in all of Crenshaw. The room was what Scylla called "open concept"—which as far as Prospero could see meant empty. No interior walls dividing rooms. Minimal furniture. From any position, a person could see everything other than the toilet and washing area.

And what Prospero saw was Cassandra, madam and seer of Crenshaw, sitting there waiting. Until recently, she was one of Prospero's most trusted allies. Since Cass was in Scylla's home, Prospero realized that the decision to meet *here* was a strategic move. Cassandra was banned from so much as approaching Prospero's house, but here at Scylla's home, there was no such edict.

"Why?"

Lord Scylla gave Prospero a look that was somewhere between "are you serious" and "don't push me." She lifted her chin in a regal way. "Because we are friends, even though you are irritated with her."

Amusement simmered under the grumbling admonishment. Scylla was a striking woman, one of the few who dressed in what had been called "men's clothes" before Prospero became a witch. Unlike Prospero, who preferred her suits to all other options, Scylla favored casual trousers and blouses when at home. Her throat was even bare at the moment.

Prospero glanced at Cassandra before returning her focus to the bottle of some strange liqueur that a hob had deposited earlier. "She deceived me."

"I *managed* your moods, P." Cassandra lifted the bottle and poured three glasses half-full of a dark red liquid that looked almost too thick to drink.

Aside from the exasperation in that brief statement, Cassandra was uncommonly subdued, as if she was trying to match her mood to Prospero's temper. The usually vivacious seer was . . . dimmed. Typically, Cass was a bundle of motion and joy, so much so that her plain hair and plain features were transformed into Mona Lisa beauty. She was voluptuous, energetic, and most residents of Crenshaw found her irresistible.

"Ellie *has* to be in Crenshaw or . . . things go wrong." Cassandra pronounced this in the way that she said all things, as if she were infallible.

"Then maybe you shouldn't have put her in peril," Prospero snapped. She tossed back the cherry-tasting syrup, not sure if the taste or the burn was worse.

"Look." Scylla pointed at one woman and then the other. "I need you to hush your mouth for a moment, and I need to know exactly what *you* know that you aren't telling P, and both of you need to check the attitude."

Cassandra smothered a smile. "Without Elleanor Brandeau, Prospero will die." Then she shrugged. "And without Prospero, we lose. *Magic* dies. We all die."

"Well, fuck," Scylla muttered.

For a moment, they all sat in silence.

Then Cass looked at Prospero. "You are upset, but I wouldn't change a thing. You *matter* to me."

Prospero opened her mouth to reply, but Cass held up her hand.

"But this is also about our home. Our *people*. Without you, Scylla dies. I don't know how or why or when, but she dies." Cass shot a sympathetic look at their friend, emptied her glass, and continued, "Then Walt. Sondre. Me. All I could see was a field of dead. Familiar and unfamiliar witches . . . and the only way to stop it is to protect *you*. And that meant bringing Elleanor here. So I won't apologize for the things I did to bring your wife to our world."

Then she stood, dipped in an odd little curtsy toward Scylla, pivoted, and walked away.

"I hate prophecies." Scylla grabbed the bottle with one hand and shoved the third, still-full glass toward Prospero.

"She could have told me. Or you . . ." Prospero scowled in the general direction of Cassandra's departure. "Cass keeps everything to herself and—"

"Pot, kettle," Scylla said lightly. "You are nothing but secrets in a well-cut suit, P."

"Oh, fine. We need a plan, then." Prospero sighed. "I don't see how I'm to be responsible for keeping everyone alive, though."

"Well, step one was having your wife here. That's done."

"You know it's not that simple."

"We have to talk to Walt."

"And Sondre," Prospero added. For a moment, the weight of it all slammed into her. She felt like she'd lived for Crenshaw since she became a witch well over a century ago. When would it be her turn to live for something else?

For love.

For happiness.

Scylla lifted the bottle, tilting it to clink gently against Prospero's glass. "To none of us dying."

2

Ellie

Ellie stood in her room in the castle, not entirely sure what she was supposed to do now. She'd not made friends with any of her classmates since she had been focused on her new relationship. Honestly, Ellie was embarrassed by how little she remembered of the school and her time in it. She knew no names, although she did know her way around. She remembered hobs, wee magical beings who popped in and out of existence. She remembered the infirmary and the doctor there. She recalled snippets of classes. She had a hazy memory of voices in hallways.

And a car . . . going . . . somewhere.

Was that the accident when her magic awakened? Or something else?

Ellie scowled. She was worried about how jumbled her mind seemed. Had she not slept enough? Was this a side effect of magical usage? Was it just the lack of the internet, smart phones, or even newspapers? How was she to keep track of time without the constant reminders on a device that never left her reach? *Or television or streaming shows or a job?* Everything that had been commonplace in establishing a linear sense of time within her life was gone. Her routines were gone. Her technology was gone.

Ellie made a mental note to talk to someone—she wasn't sure whom yet—about whether or not there were calendars in Crenshaw. At the least, she wanted a sense of tracking time. Once she knew *when* it was, maybe her memory would get back in order.

A *tap-tap-tap* on the door interrupted Ellie's musings.

"Ellie?" Hestia's voice identified her arrival before she opened the door. She sounded strong, and Ellie was grateful that she'd decided to come to Crenshaw, too.

Ellie paused, staring at her aunt. "Why did you come here?"

"To visit you . . . ?" Hestia stepped past her and made her way into Ellie's rather undecorated, nondescript room. For reasons Ellie couldn't explain, she knew that all the rooms looked like hers initially. She couldn't recall *whose* room she'd visited, though.

"Yes, but why did you come to Crenshaw?" Ellie clarified.

"To be with you. Lady Prospero thought it was important." Hestia scowled. "Maybe to heal up my body after that surgery . . . ? I remember surgery, and then being here. Again. I think Prospero is . . . *was* my friend. She rescued me, sent me back to you a long time ago."

"You gave up magic to raise me." Ellie felt her eyes fill with tears.

"No regrets about surrendering my magic, El, but I will admit that I feel a little sad now that I remember that I used to be a witch. I dreamed of being here, you know. Considered seeing a talking doctor because of the dreams." Hestia dropped a small twig on the floor and looked at Ellie. "I want a rocker like at home."

Ellie let her magic roll out of her body and started to reshape that bit of wood into a chair with elegant spiral rockers. In a few moments, a bentwood rocking chair sat gleaming in the low light filtering into the room. Instead of the cane back and seat on the one at home in Ligonier, this one had lightly woven twigs, as if they had been soaked and thatched together.

Hestia let out a deep sigh and settled herself into the chair. "I want to go home, lovey. I'll miss you, but . . . let me go home."

"*What?*"

"I can visit you. I know witches can't stay over there in the regular world, but if they're letting me come here now, they'd let me visit you." Hestia stared at her, rather reminiscent of arguments over the years that had sometimes erupted into loud words. "I don't want to live here."

Ellie flopped onto her bed, feeling like someone had just taken her down at the knees. "Did something happen?"

Hestia stared out the locked window briefly before saying, "I don't belong here, Ellie. I remember enough about magic to miss it, to miss Crenshaw, to miss the witch I got to having feelings for once upon a time." She met Ellie's gaze and added, "But this isn't my place now any more than my old farmhouse was *your* place."

"So what are you going to do? Just . . . live over there alone?" Ellie had made so many decisions to avoid that very thing. She remembered *that* quite clearly. "I planned to take care of you."

"I know you did. Now, I need you to go talk to Walt about the rules. That cagey old man is hiding things. In my younger days, I was ready to move in with him, you know? Maybe be a wife. Then I had to choose between being your auntie or staying here as a witch and wife. I chose you."

Ellie felt tears on her cheeks now. No longer threatening, they were spilling down her face like a small river. "I'm sorry."

"Pishposh. I'd choose you every time, Ellie. Being able to act like your parent all these years was one of the best parts of my life." Hestia held a hand out toward Ellie, who moved to sit on the floor beside her feet as she'd done often as girl. "But this is *your* world now, Ellie, and I don't have a place here. I'll grow older, and they all won't. You won't. I had extra time before I was siphoned. That's enough."

"I can't . . . you . . . what if they could give you some of your magic back? Is that a thing?"

"No."

"But I don't want to lose you. Without magic, you'll get older and . . ." Ellie couldn't even say the words. She felt like a child every time she so much as considered the loss of her remaining parental figure.

"That's what people do. Get older. Die. The trick is to live a good life first, a full life, adventure." Hestia touched her shoulder gently. "You stayed there with me long past when it was time to have your own life. You refused to move on, which isn't what I want for you. I think being a witch is forcing you to move on like you *should*."

"I was content," Ellie protested.

"I want you to be more than content. Be *happy*. Be *fulfilled*." Hestia gave her a gentle smile.

They had this argument so often that it was one Ellie couldn't counter. Not really. She *did* want more out of life, but she didn't know how to have that sort of future.

Especially when Prospero is rejecting me.

"You have a place here, a woman who makes your eyes sparkle, and I want to go home. Back to my farmhouse. Back to my books and television, and maybe get some chickens." Hestia laughed briefly. "And a goat. I always wanted a goat. They've been bothering me to teach a few history classes over at the high school. Maybe I ought to do that."

Ellie sat there, silent as her aunt stroked her hair like she was a child. She knew she was clinging to Hestia, endangering her or trapping her if she stayed here. The rift spewed toxic air that would sicken Hestia if she went outside, so she was forced to stay inside the castle. That didn't mean Ellie wanted to be apart from her.

"If you could change anything in your life, what would it be?" Ellie asked. "Usual rules."

The "rules" to their game had always been that they never mentioned Ellie's parents' deaths. The game, Ellie now realized, might have been a side effect of the magic Hestia once had.

"Fuck the rules," Hestia said. "I never wanted to wish your parents to stay alive. When your time is up, it's up, but I used to wish *they* were witches instead. I used to imagine that they were swept away to Crenshaw, and I was given *you* instead. It felt like a fair trade, a child to raise rather than magic. You were the prize, not a burden. I hope you know that, Ellie."

"You wanted kids?"

"Eventually. Then I was a witch. No kids for witches. Then I was with you. I would've taken a dozen of you, lovey. A house full of grumpy kids who thought they knew everything." Hestia grew silent then. "But my life has been amazing, El. I want it back. Tell them you are fine with letting me leave."

Ellie laid her head on Hestia's lap. "You'll visit."

"I will."

"And bring me books to give Prospero and books for me and—"

"You can count on it." Hestia sniffed. "I always thought you would move out sooner or later, but it feels so sudden. I'll need to find a chicken sitter sooner than I'd planned."

"We . . . *you* don't have chickens."

"Yet. Maybe I'll find me a nice young man who bakes. I did get used to those morning scones of yours." Hestia smiled down at her. "When I visit . . ."

"I'll make you scones. It's a plan." Ellie sat upright. "Okay, so we have a plan. How do we get it sorted out?"

"Atta girl! No time like the present. I suppose we talk to Walter. Explain that I am going home, but I'll be visiting sometimes. You can send Prospero or Walt to fetch me." Hestia straightened her sweater as if she were readying herself for a battle of wits. She had always liked to look polished before she went to debate anyone.

"Why don't I go talk to him?" Ellie offered. She had a few questions for the chief witch anyhow.

Hestia gave her a look. "Be careful. Use the fact that he liked me if you need to, but don't mistake him for harmless. He's older than dirt and as wily as a snake."

Ellie shivered at the tone in Hestia's voice.

3

Maggie

"I'm too fucking old to be a student again," Maggie grumbled as she shoved open the door to the suite of rooms she shared with Sondre and Craig. The rooms were nice, especially now that the eggy scent—from whatever toxic leak there had been—was not *as* extreme. The water was still vaguely sulfurous, but it didn't permeate everything. If they stayed inside, they could even keep Craig safe-ish.

"Nice mouth, Mom." Craig glanced up from *The History of Houses in Crenshaw,* the textbook that Maggie had been unable to find that morning. He was nestled on a cowhide-patterned sofa that was comfortable if a bit odd.

Maggie snatched her book out of his hands. "Do you know that Sir Alarick, witch of petty nonsense, made me write actual lines today for forgetting this? *Lines.* I'm a gods-blessed lawyer, and I wrote lines."

Her son looked as unsympathetic as only a teenager could be. "Poor thing. I'm a hostage in a castle with no social media, no sports, no . . . available girls."

His pause was just long enough that Maggie narrowed her eyes. "What did you do?"

He shrugged and popped a cube of yellow cheese in his mouth. The hobs delivered him snack plates like he was a young god.

"Craig." Maggie's hands went to her hips. She closed her eyes, counting, and then started, "It's dangerous out there and—"

The door slammed, and as Maggie opened her eyes, she realized that her son was gone. She grabbed the door to jerk it open and follow, but arms wrapped around her from behind.

"Let the boy go. I have hobs minding him. He won't get out of the castle again today." Sondre's voice was a soothing rumble.

"Do I want to ask?" Maggie leaned back into Sondre's embrace.

"Probably not."

She turned around, still in the circle of his arms. "And yet . . . I am."

"Don't overreact," Sondre said, hands dropping to her butt.

"Not a great start."

"I like your curves, Maggie. It's an excellent start. No kid at home. No interruptions and—"

"Sondre." She didn't disagree with him, but she wasn't going to be distracted just then. Her son was her top priority and had been since she decided to carry and birth him.

Her new husband sighed. "Craig climbed out a window and found his way to the village." His voice had that skipping-a-few-details tone.

Despite logic, she prompted, "*And?*"

"And the madam refused him service," Sondre finished with an air of finality. "He's a boy, Maggie. He's lonely. It's normal."

"Horny is different than lonely," she corrected, although she could see an argument that sometimes they felt like the same thing.

"Is it, though?" Sondre said gently. "He was a young athlete, surrounded by adoring young women . . ."

Maggie paused at the things implied but not said. Sondre's tone hinted that he might know things about her son's life that she didn't. On one hand, she was grateful that they were talking instead of yelling. On the other, she cringed at the thought of her baby boy being quite *that* grown-up.

When had that happened?

Being here where there was literally not a soul near his age was a complication she hadn't thought about. All she'd wanted was to get him away from her ex, Craig's father, and Sondre told her that she'd had quite the plan to do so—a plan she didn't recall at all and he wasn't explaining.

After a few moments of struggling with mom-guilt and mom-denials, she asked, "Was I wrong to bring him to Crenshaw?"

"It's safer than with the man who tried to murder you both." Sondre lifted her up, and her legs automatically wrapped around him. He carried her like that over to the sofa and sat. She was on his lap, knees on either side of him. It was far more distracting than mere words and an embrace.

And he knows it.

Maggie rested her head against his, her cheek against his temple. "I was between two bad options. I'm afraid he thinks I chose you over him."

"He thinks you chose your safety and a new life over the danger of being with Leon. We talked." Sondre ran a hand soothingly up her back. "He *is* lonely, though."

"So what do I do? If I send him back . . . if I let him choose that . . . what if he chooses that? Then he's in danger and—"

"What about your relatives?"

Maggie thought about her extended family. Her cousin Hector was probably the person she trusted the most, but he trafficked in white- *and* blue-collar crime. He took great care of his assorted offspring and baby mamas, but if Leon found out Craig was with Hector, he'd have Hector arrested and still end up with custody of Craig. Maggie shook her head. "No."

"What if Craig could go somewhere with other teens?" Sondre's voice had an odd edge to it.

Maggie leaned back and stared at him. "Somewhere he'd be safe?"

"Boarding school."

"Under a false identity? Like he could visit on holidays?" Maggie wriggled in Sondre's lap.

"Woman," he groaned. "You can't squirm like that and expect me to stay focused on talking."

Maggie's cheeks flamed. "Sorry, I got excited and—"

"Me too." He kissed her briefly. "Maybe we could continue this conversation later? I'd need to consult the chief witch to be sure there were no issues moving between worlds. He's not magical, so there is no logical objection."

As much as Maggie wanted to take advantage of their privacy, she said, "Magical chemistry in less than fifteen minutes . . ."

Sondre looked at the clock that hung on the wall somewhere behind her, and she knew he was calculating. She couldn't fault his logic. Whatever else they were, Maggie knew they were incredibly compatible naked.

"You *could* teleport me to class . . ." she suggested.

In the next moment, they were both naked, and Sondre's mouth was on hers. *Magic is amazing.* Being a parent always meant that quickies were on the menu more often than leisurely days, but with magic . . . with Sondre . . . even a quickie would be satisfying.

Maggie ground down on him as his tongue darted into her mouth and his arms tightened around her. With one hand cupping her ass, Sondre lifted her so she was on her knees in a wide straddle. The position meant he could cover first one and then the other nipple with his mouth.

"No time for that," she breathed out.

He frowned and kissed both breasts almost mournfully. "I'll be back for you later."

And Maggie laughed at the oddness of the fact that she was certain he was speaking to her breasts, not to her directly. She shifted her knees as he positioned himself, and she lowered onto him with a satisfied moan. Even though this wasn't anywhere near the first time, Maggie still marveled at the way her body felt with him inside her.

Almost too much.

For a moment, she paused, adjusting, and he made eye contact to ask, "Too sudden? Need—"

"A little," Maggie admitted sheepishly as Sondre murmured a spell for magical lubrication. The sensation made her breathe out, "Better."

Sondre preened a little, and Maggie laughed again. She was sure that sex *could* be serious, but there was something incredibly freeing in having a lover who approached intimacy with a sense that it was sheer fun.

"I love when you laugh," he said, looking at her with undeniable fondness. It did something to her when he looked at her that way, nudged a forgotten memory of their first meeting, as if she could summon her erased memory by will alone.

Maggie shoved the thought away and said, "Hips."

"Yes, dear." His hands gripped her hips tight enough to bruise as he steadied her, and she took control.

Together they found a rhythm that would satisfy both of them.

But after several moments, she noticed that he was glancing at the clock again. "It's okay if I . . . don't," she started.

"No, it's not." Sondre shifted one hand from her hip to the juncture of her thighs and helped speed things along with his talented fingers. "*Never* okay if you aren't satisfied."

"Oh . . . kay . . . oh . . . *there.*"

Sondre's mouth curved in a smile that made her grateful that he was stubborn on this topic. Maggie wasn't sure how long they'd been together. She knew there was some degree of magic involved in that lack of clarity—because he'd told her so. However, she knew with certainty that she'd never been left unsatisfied.

"Oh, I . . . *like* . . . you," she whispered. It wasn't love yet, but whatever this was between them, it was good.

"You do?" Sondre teased.

"Yes. Fuck, *yes.*" The throbbing pleasure built toward something more than mere magic as the combination of his fingers and the thickness of him had her wanting to say more than that she *liked* him.

He followed her orgasm with his own, and they stayed there, breathing heavily and entwined. Then he rested his forehead against her shoulder and said, "Luckily, I like you, too, wife."

A part of Maggie ached for something more than "like," but they had a good companionship and consistently orgasmic sex. It was a lot more than she ever expected to have again. She was safe, cherished, and satisfied. Her son was safe because of Sondre, too.

I still want more. Greedy woman that I am.

"I want to love you," Maggie whispered. "I want to know everything. Know it. Not just have you tell me about it . . ."

"Maybe you will." Sondre's voice was just as quiet. "We haven't known each other very long. Remember? I told you that. . . ."

She nodded. "No one can know I know that, though."

"That's right." He smiled at her. "Because the only way I can keep you and Craig safe is?"

"No one knows what you told me, and I never ever talk to Elleanor Brandeau," Maggie repeated dutifully.

"Other than that?"

This time, Maggie grinned. "Nothing. I'm not obligated to like you, love you, obey you, or fuck you." She tightened her internal muscles until Sondre's expression darkened into lust again. "But I want some of that . . . maybe everything but the obeying."

"Me too, Maggie. Me too." He brushed his lips across hers and then pinched her ass cheek. "But right now? You're going to be late if you don't get dressed."

He lifted her to her feet.

"You'd think being married to the headmaster would have perks," she grumbled as she bent down to grab her jeans.

Sondre swatted her ass. "It does."

When she glanced at him, she saw that he'd already magicked his own clothes back on. She, however, was left naked and dressing herself as he watched. Maggie gestured between them. "Not fair."

"Perk for me," he said mildly.

By the time he teleported her to outside the classroom, Maggie was still smiling. *I think I could love him, but even if I don't, this is pretty damn good, too.*

4
Ellie

That evening, Ellie found herself walking toward the Congress of Magic. It was, in part, a way to escape the castle. Classes that day had been fine, but Ellie was not sure why *she* had to take them. She was obviously staying in Crenshaw and knew what her magical strength was. Why did she still need to attend remedial magic school? And why did she have to stay in the castle?

Ellie walked toward the town center, knowing that either hobs, students, or witches watched her every move. The forest that reached out toward her like sentient branches made something uneasy crawl up her spine. That discomfort blossomed when an older witch stepped out of the shadows. The witch had once-red hair that had developed white streaks, and her gaze had the sort of glint that made Ellie scan her surroundings.

"Looking for your friends?" Agnes, Lady of the House of Grendel, thunked the end of her staff onto the ground with what seemed excessive force as she stared at Ellie. Two witches waited a few yards back, like guards. The first was a witch with a long, thin braid. He smelled of skunk and sweat, even from here.

The second was a witch she'd met previously. Jenn. She'd seemed recently arrived, maybe a few decades at most, and she had that pinched face of someone who was perpetually sending her food back or asking for a manager.

Ellie watched a third witch sidle up to a tree, still within the shadows. All she could tell was that he had a more masculine form. As Ellie watched, she saw at least a dozen more people moving in and among the shadows.

Glancing back at Agnes, she asked, "Meeting of the New Economists?"

Agnes narrowed her gaze. "You're quite an unusual witch. Braver than you ought to be, all things considered."

"Well, *that* feels like a threat." Ellie saw a hob pop into existence and vanish just as quickly. She didn't recognize the hob from here, but someone's spy had gone to report. "Are you threatening me, Lady Grendel?"

"Not as daft as you look." Agnes scanned the area. "All alone then?"

Ellie shrugged. She stared into the shadows. Easily twenty witches lurked there. Even with her increasing control of her magic, Ellie was incredibly outnumbered. Within the dark of the wood, shapes shifted as if there were more people than she wanted to face even with help. All told there were less than a hundred New Economists, and like any group, there were probably true believers and hangers-on who were there for other reasons. Those details had been glossed over in one of her classes, in a lecture on the history of Crenshaw. Even Prospero wasn't very forthcoming. She mentioned a few names in a "stay clear of these witches" way.

The male witch Ellie had initially noticed ducked behind a tree, hiding his face. Ellie tried to see him. Anyone who wanted to *hide* their affiliation with the radical group was someone she ought to identify for Prospero. It wasn't as if Prospero was going to attack them. For all her talk of being dangerous, she was a woman with an ethical code. Unprovoked violence was the stuff of villains, true monsters, the sort of person who once made Prospero bleed and nearly die. She was not randomly violent.

Although she would be livid that I was here in danger. . . .

"As much as I'd love to stay for your little bonfire party, I have places to be." Ellie tried to step around Agnes, but the elder witch swung her staff out like a barrier. The end of it tapped against Ellie's stomach just hard enough to be uncomfortable but not with the force of a strike.

"You are too bold for your own good."

Ellie smiled. "I can reshape the world at my will. It makes a girl feel all confident."

"Imagine what you could do over in the real world." Agnes adopted a cajoling tone. "How powerful you'd be . . ."

"I don't crave *power*," Ellie said lightly. "Everything I could want is right here. Love, happiness, a place I belong."

Laughter rang out from the trees, and Ellie flinched internally. She was well aware that her own desires were simple to some people. She wanted a grand romance, happiness, peace, and knowledge. Crenshaw offered everything she could want.

Like a fairy tale! Well, it will be once I fix whatever is bothering Prospero, get Hestia home, and patch the rift. Ellie smiled at the absurdity of her thoughts. The thing was that it all felt possible.

Because I am a witch. Isn't that power enough?

She looked up and Agnes caught her gaze, and for a moment, Ellie couldn't look away. Something was wrong. Fear started to bubble inside Ellie, rising up in her throat as if choking her.

"Little lost lamb," Agnes murmured. "Ready to be turned on the spit, are you?"

"What is going on here?" Prospero's voice came from behind Ellie.

Ellie stumbled as Agnes pulled her gaze away, freeing Ellie from her hold. Any trickle of fear Ellie had been considering vanished. She glanced back over her shoulder to where Prospero had just popped into sight.

"I was out for a walk," Ellie said in a wavering voice. "I hoped you were free, but I ran into—"

"Grendel." Prospero stared into the woods as if taking names and faces into memory. "Rather suspect to be clustered in the forest, wouldn't you say?"

"Picnics are quite popular," Agnes said dryly.

"If you have to hide what you're doing, isn't that indicative of it being unwise?" Prospero asked, stepping slightly in front of Ellie as she spoke.

"Hey!" Ellie whispered loudly.

Prospero's left hand reached back as if to grab hers, so Ellie twined their fingers together.

"Blocking her from my view? Where's the trust?" Agnes taunted.

"Do not mistake my patience for kindness, Grendel." Prospero sounded like every dark threat given form. "Stay away from my wife."

"Your *wife*?" Agnes laughed, but she kept her eyes cast low. Both women were apparently able to use their magic if eye contact was present.

Ellie thought about that moment of terror. *What magic is hers? What would've happened if Prospero hadn't arrived?*

"She is mine to protect." Prospero didn't look away from Agnes, as if she felt no fear or threat. They were outnumbered, but even now, she didn't back down. It did interesting things to Ellie's libido.

Agnes shook her head and turned away, disappearing into the group in the woods where shadowed bodies all vanished deeper into the darkness.

"The rift is that way," Ellie said quietly.

"They know." Prospero sounded thoroughly exhausted. "They know exactly where it is. I'm not sure how they did it but . . ."

Of course it is their doing.

It occurred to Ellie then that the conflict between the two factions was one that was unreconcilable. The New Economists sought power for themselves. The Traditionalists sought peace and equality for every witch. There was no possible compromise between those two positions.

When one group wants the other's oppression, both sides are not equal at all. How can you compromise when the opposition wants to take away your life, safety, or health?

For a moment, she stood, hand in Prospero's, and thought about the impossible situation that faced Crenshaw. Ellie was not yet required to sit on the Congress of Magic, and for a tremulous moment, she was incredible grateful for that. How was she to speak to witches like Agnes who were blinded by greed?

Then Prospero pivoted and said, "What in the name of all that's holy were you *thinking*?"

5

Prospero

"Are you *trying* to kill me?" Prospero asked Ellie in a barely there whisper once she had dragged her safely into her arms. "Is that what your throwing yourself into danger at every turn is designed to do? Simply press me into panic until my heart stops?"

Ellie paused, as if weighing the question. That stung. Hell, everything about Ellie stung today. This falling-in-love business was terrible. "You say that as if there were other dangerous acts. . . ."

I should have known better. I cannot let these feelings continue. The last woman Prospero had loved was murdered because Prospero had loved her. *I don't deserve Ellie, either.*

"Come on." Prospero jerked Ellie into her arms and teleported them home. Maybe she held her tighter than she strictly needed. Maybe she buried her face in Ellie's hair. Prospero was weak where Ellie was concerned.

Ellie slipped her arms around Prospero like she had no intention of letting go. "Perhaps you ought to let me live *in our house* if you're going to overreact every time I talk to a w—"

"She's not simply 'a witch,' Elleanor, and you know that." Prospero tried to step back, but Ellie held on to her waist. "She would take you from me, from Crenshaw. Doom all of us to—"

"*Doom* you?" Ellie smiled as if there were a joke to be made in devastation. "Surely, nothing quite so dire?"

Prospero sighed, forcibly pulling away this time. "Actually, exactly that dire. You know there was a prophecy."

Ellie stepped around her and put the kettle on the stove. "You need tea. You're all . . ." She gestured at her. "*Emotional.*"

"She can evoke things, Ellie. If she holds your gaze, she'll pull up fears—"

"Yes, I figured that out what with the terror and trembling." Ellie's voice quavered briefly, and Prospero realized that she was not as calm as she was appearing.

"Are you . . . well?" Prospero stared at her, taking in her blanched expression and cupping the edge of her face gently. Whatever memory Agnes had started summoning was a raw one. "She's not to use her magic outside of the Congress."

"And we all know that witches are great at rule-following," Ellie muttered. "Except you. You are inordinately good at it."

"You might be surprised," Prospero confessed.

Ellie lifted her chin, gaze falling to Prospero's lips. "What are you hiding from me, Prospero?"

Everything, Prospero answered in her mind silently. Aloud she only said, "You have a habit of endangering yourself."

"Interesting. I don't recall that." Ellie frowned. "I remember you in my library at home. A car accident. Snakes of asphalt. Classes. Seeing you naked . . . and then being here."

"Yes. Fine, but—"

"Things are missing." Ellie crossed her arms. "You . . . fucked around in my head. That's it. That's why you are withholding affection. You feel *guilty,* don't you?"

"That's not the topic at hand. Your rash actions—"

"I am not a child, Prospero. Do not speak to me as if I am." Ellie moved closer. "Stop lying to me. Stop pushing me away."

"Could we argue another time? All I am asking is that you avoid danger. That's not a huge request." Prospero stepped around her because if not, she was in danger of doing something foolish. She wasn't sure whether that foolishness was kissing Ellie or confessing. Either was a bad idea. In her chilliest, most rational voice, Prospero said, "I would prefer you stay safely at the castle where you are protected and out of potential peril."

"What I want doesn't matter?" Ellie's voice was seething now. "I understand that you are . . . older, but I am your equal here. As your wife. As a head of house. You do not tell me where I may go. You do not make the rules for my body *or* my life. Am I clear?"

Prospero pivoted and took her hand. "Things are complicated, and—"

"I. Don't. Care." Ellie stared at her, holding her gaze brazenly.

No one did that. Most witches acted as if prolonged eye contact was a dare to her to slip into their minds and alter things. Of course, Ellie thought Prospero was unable to do so. Maybe it was just her directness.

"Perhaps I could . . . talk to the chief witch? Ask if I could answer a few questions."

"You can, or I will." Ellie was brazen in her temper, and the thought of letting her too close to Walt made Prospero almost as tense as seeing her with Agnes. "Either way, I will know what you have done to my mind. I will find out my answers, and I think you are underestimating my temper if you expect that to go easily for him or you if I don't like the answers."

"I will talk to him."

"Hestia is moving home, by the way. Tell him that, too." Ellie gave her a tight smile. "I should get some of my wishes heard."

Prospero blinked at her. "I thought you wanted Hestia to live here."

"I do, but *she* wants to go home." Ellie gave Prospero a pointed look. "People respect the wishes of those they love. If *she* wants to go home, that's her choice. Just like if for some mad reason I wanted to go back . . ." She paused and frowned, and Prospero wondered if she was remembering something. Then Ellie continued, "If I wanted to go back to Ligonier, you would respect that."

"I hear you." Prospero added the tea and hot water to the teapot. She could not let Ellie leave, but only one of them knew that.

She wants to leave me. Prospero flinched at the thought. *Even after I erased her escape from memory, she still thinks to leave me.*

Ellie shook her head. "I am not interested in playing games like some child. I want to be with you, and you are *mine*. So either admit you want me or tell me you don't. Life's too short for games."

"Life's rather long for witches," Prospero said, trying to avoid the question.

She silently poured the tea.

"I know you're hiding things, but you cannot pretend that I am simply a remedial witch trying to find my place." Ellie put her hand on Prospero's. "I *know* where I belong."

"Well, it's not in the woods confronting my enemies."

"All the more reason to keep me close, then." Ellie gave her a smug smile. "She was afraid of me. Not as much as she was of you, but she didn't want me to dislike her or dismiss her."

"That doesn't make me feel better," Prospero admitted.

Ellie shrugged. "Maybe fear will make her rethink her actions."

Prospero shook her head. "I doubt that. The New Economists want power. It's a greed that is at odds with our way of life . . . and there's no solution. We can't just kill witches for their vices."

"Have you suggested it?"

Prospero looked away. "In anger? Yes. It sets a dangerous precedent, though. If you are on the side of *good,* should you be the one to strike? Shouldn't you try to appeal to their reason? To find an answer that isn't as violent?"

"So you do nothing?"

Prospero's inevitable answer felt weak, but she couldn't sanction violence for something a witch *might* do. "We *try* to broker peace. We let them meet, and we hear their grievances in Congress." Prospero sighed. She stared into her teacup as if there were solutions hidden in the tea leaves at the bottom. "I don't have an answer."

Ellie looked worried. "Would you like me to talk to the chief witch? Tell him about their gathering and talk to him about ideas?"

"No." Prospero smiled. "But I would like you to remember that you were right. I was pushing you away, and that endangered you."

Ellie nodded. "I could stay. We could have a bath and—"

"I need to speak to Walt. Right now." Prospero stood and moved away from the table. "Urgently."

Ellie rolled her eyes. "Coward."

Prospero knew she wasn't *technically* running away from Ellie, but it was a close thing. She paused outside the front door, collected her wits, and teleported to Walt's house. His hob, Grish, whisked open the door before she could knock. "He was expecting you."

And Prospero went into the chief witch's home a little more confidently. She stood in the tiny kitchen. There was often something comforting about Walt's home, but tonight it did little to ease Prospero's worry.

Walt came out of the depths of his house with a grumbling noise. "If someone else had the stones to be chief witch, I'd be working on my knitting tonight."

"They are plotting something," Prospero announced without preamble.

"What, though?"

"I don't know." She rubbed her forehead as if she could rub the stress away. "Are we too patient? Too lenient? *Should* we strike them first?"

Maybe she just needed to hear the validation, or maybe she was doubting herself. She waited as Walt stared at her. After a moment, he said the very thing that made her certain he was the right choice for his current position. "War has no place in Crenshaw. You know that. We all agreed to that. We are few, and though we squabble—"

"This isn't a squabble, Walt."

"Did they hurt your woman?"

"No, but . . . I feel it. Something is coming. They're meeting. They created the rift that poisons us. We all know that!" She paced the small space while she talked, wanting to be talked down or set loose. Maybe that was the crux of why anyone landed on her short list of friends and loved ones: they told her the rules. After a few centuries of meddling with people's minds, Prospero sometimes doubted her own judgment.

Which is why that *is my magic.* Magic was based on a critical character trait; of that she was certain. And her ability to compartmentalize and hide her own memories, to question her recall or judgment, to ask confounding questions had manifested as mental magic.

"So we attack because we *think* they are going to do something else?" His voice was gentle, but it did the trick. Prospero felt herself relax. She lowered her shoulders from the tense position where they'd been raised.

"What if it's worse than the rift?" she asked in a small voice.

"Then we deal with it. We can't strike out against Agnes and her lot because of something they might do. You know that. Thoughts and talk are not crimes." Walt gestured to the worn chair he always offered her. It was currently draped in a lemon-and-puce-colored knitted blanket.

"Even after your patches, the rift is killing witches. Our witches are *dying* while we try to reason with their greed and . . . I feel helpless," Prospero confessed.

He nodded. "I know you do. I do, too."

"I want to *do* something," she added.

"That's your youth talking." Walt sank into his chair.

"I'm an old lady! A hundred plus isn't *young*."

"Ha! Talk to me when you add another century to that." Walt looked at her, meeting her eyes the way few people did. "What else had you rattled tonight?"

"Ellie has questions. She's upset that I'm rejecting her and—"

"Why reject her? You like the chit." Walt gave her an odd look.

"She thinks we're married—"

"You had relations before that." Walt leveled a confused gaze at her. "She's only attractive when she's not yours?"

Prospero sighed. "If she doesn't remember, she can't really say she wants to—"

"She is saying it, if I understand correctly." Walt frowned. "You're looking for trouble where it doesn't need to be. You were both boneheads. Romance the girl. Leave the past in the past, and keep her safe. Why does it need to be complicated?"

"*Your* age is showing." Prospero shook her head. "I want to tell her the truth."

He tugged his beard. "Which truth? The one where we all die if she's not with you? The one where she got the best of you over there?"

"Walt—"

"No. Don't try your wiles on me, woman. You broke the rules for her." He shook a finger at her. "You can tell her you had a fight. You can tell her I ordered you to erase it. You can even tell her that she is all that stands between you and death. You will not tell her she fled Crenshaw. Do that, and we're back to more damn trouble. Can you imagine if the girl joined Aggie?"

Prospero felt like she was deflating. "I think that was why Aggie talked to her tonight."

"Well, there you go. Kiss your woman until she's obedient, and keep her away from the enemy. Problem solved."

Every so often, Prospero could see the truth of how different eras had mindsets that simply clung to them. Walt came from an era when women were objects to be controlled, and while he had evolved to a degree, she realized in such moments that he saw her as his equal, manlike in his mind, and his "wisdom" on dealing with Ellie was flawed.

Kiss Ellie to compliance? To obedience? The thought was laughable. Prospero would try to talk to her without breaking the chief witch's rules, and she would hope that whatever was coming from the New Economists wasn't as bad as she feared.

How bad could it be?

6

Sondre

Sondre stared forlornly into the pot of tea he'd magicked up. That was what the teen called it: "Magicked up." The teapot, obviously, was not filled with tea. Between Maggie's escape, capture, and the arrival of her son, Sondre had wished that he could simply stay perpetually inebriated.

Probably a bad plan, Sondre admitted as another yell came from his once-peaceful home.

"I don't know who you think you are," Craig yelled as he stomped into the room.

"The headmaster of the College of Remedial Magic," Sondre said mildly.

"Well, I'm not a witch or a student, so . . . piss off." Craig crossed his arms over his chest and glared.

No hitting children. Not even a tap. Sondre repeated the mantra to himself for the dozenth time that day.

"What exactly is the drama now?" Sondre tried to remember that his acerbic tone was fine for students but not his son.

"I am sick of being trapped in here."

"It's dangerous outside the castle, Craig," Maggie said, voice pulled tight as if the strain of parenthood and the pressure of her magic combined to make her chest constrict.

"So send me back."

One of the hobs popped into the room, appearing out of thin air as they were wont to do. "Perhaps some toys for the young mast—"

"I'm not a *child*," Craig yelled. All the boy did the last few days was yell.

The air is less dangerous this week.

"Fine. You want to go out? Let's go out." Sondre stood. "Maggie, you have class. I'll sort this out."

"If you're both sure?" Maggie said.

"Go to class, Mom." Craig bent down to kiss his mother's cheek, suddenly sweeter when Maggie's voice took on that fragile-glass note. "I'm safe with him. You know that."

He was, but it felt good to hear Craig acknowledge that truth all the same. Sondre wished the boy could yell less frequently, but in all, he'd had an abrupt adjustment—like all witches—but without the salve of having magic. Craig was in a brand-new world with new people, new rules, new everything. It had to be challenging for him.

Once the door closed behind her, Sondre turned his most menacing stare at the younger, male version of his new bride. "Let's take a proper tour of the village."

"*Really?*"

The trace of hope in the boy's voice was enough to make Sondre wonder for the 337th time if there really was ever that much joy in the experience of being a witch. Witches lived for centuries, but that was all spent locked away in the tiny hamlet of Crenshaw. Maybe it was the fact that Sondre himself was approaching a century of life, or maybe guilt ate away at joy.

Whatever the cause, Sondre felt a smile slip out.

"Yes, really. If you get sick, though, your mother will be devastated, so you'll wear a mask." Sondre went over to the cupboard and pulled out a gas mask he'd had fashioned for the boy. "No breathing poison."

"Is this really necessary?" Craig lifted the bulky black contraption.

It looked like a relic, something as old as Sondre, but thanks to magic it was as good as new. The fabricating witch, Ellie, had created several of them for the boy and her aunt—and a few spares for witches who were low in magical reserves.

"Better isn't the same as gone. I promise you that when it's over, you can stop wearing it." Sondre wasn't going to budge on this. The toxin that was slowly seeping into the village made things stink of sulfur, and the gaseous air killed any witch whose magical levels weren't high enough to repair the constant damage from the poison.

"Fine." Craig sulked.

"If we go inside anywhere the air's not bad, you can take it off." Sondre paused and, feeling rather like leaning into the dad thing, added, "It's like a condom. They're always a good idea unless you're one-hundred-percent sure you're safe."

Craig stared back at him, blinking. "Are we going to have a birds-and-bees talk?"

"I don't know. Do you need one?" Sondre frowned briefly. "I can explain things unless you need details on sex with men. I know a guy though who—"

The rest of Sondre's words were lost under Craig's laugh.

"You still aren't my real dad, and I don't know if I like you," Craig said when he stopped laughing. "You're not a total tool, though."

"I'll add that to my next job interview. 'Not a total tool.'" Sondre rolled his eyes. "You're not the worst thing that's ever happened in my life, either."

"What is?"

Sondre gave him an assessing look and decided to be blunt. "Bit by a rattlesnake? Became a witch? Couldn't see my family again? It was all part of the same thing, I guess."

"Sounds pretty bad."

"It was. I hated losing everything and everyone who mattered. My plans. My friends. My brother." Sondre pointed to the door.

"I feel like you're doing that I-can-relate thing old people do," Craig muttered.

"Nah. I can't relate. I lost everyone. *You* got to keep part of your family. The best part," Sondre pointed out.

"Rather not think about how great you think my mother is. I heard you the other night. Scar a kid." Craig's cheeks were red, and Sondre reminded himself that for all the difficulty, the teen boy was dealing fairly well.

"Sorry you heard. She's happy, though. Having you here and having someone treat her like the amazing woman she is."

"*Still* not okay thinking about you and her," Craig stressed. He sighed, glanced over at Sondre, and added, "But yeah, she is. My dad was an ass, tried to take her to court, just . . . awful. Plus, he tried to kill us in the accident. She thinks I don't know, so she doesn't talk to me about it, but I'm not stupid. Rather kill me than pay child support. What a dad, huh?"

"Might be easier on her if you were stupid." Sondre shoved open the main door to the castle. "Mask."

Craig fixed the awkward contraption over his face as the two were headed out of the castle intentionally—which was an improvement on the few times when Sondre had to find and retrieve the boy.

Sondre was weighing what to say about the fact that the kid's father tried to have him killed. Over the decades here, Sondre had seen his share of bad situations, but it never got easier to find the words of comfort.

"I don't have anything to do here," Craig blurted a few steps later. "It's not like I'm trying to start trouble for Mom. I'm just so fucking bored. No school. No one but old people to talk to. No TV. No games. No anything."

"So what are we to do?" Sondre asked, grateful that the murderous-bastard-is-your-father conversation was paused. Talking to the teen calmly was the only way he could deal with Craig. Honestly, in most cases the answer was just talk to the new witch like a *person*. That worked on teenagers, too, apparently.

They walked along the path that stretched from castle to village.

"I was thinking I could join one of the sports houses," Craig mused, scuffing his feet in the dry ground as they walked. "I mean, I can't do magic, but there are plenty of sports that are nonmagic."

"Does your mother know your plan?"

"Sort of," Craig evaded. "She said that since I'm not magical, I don't need a house, but I can't just . . . do nothing. That's all I do. Nothing."

"And break rules," Sondre muttered.

"You'd have liked my mom before I came along," Craig said. "I'm not supposed to know, but she was not really a rule follower either."

She still isn't. Sondre considered saying it. If Maggie had been following the rules that governed Crenshaw, Craig wouldn't be here. Instead, Sondre only said, "You don't say."

Craig leveled a surprisingly mature look at him. "Do you blame her? What would *you* do if you had no responsibilities?"

"Not blaming your mom. If I wasn't headmaster—or a married man—I'd pretty much drink and get laid," Sondre said. "That was a lot of what I did when I arrived here . . . hmm, roughly seventy years ago."

"So you get it." Craig looked back at the path. "I'm bored. I can't go to your magic college. I don't have friends. I love my mom and all, and it's not like I want to go back to live with *him,* but . . ."

"What if there was another option?"

"There's a *third* place?"

"Maybe." Sondre had been trying to be patient, but the choice was obvious. "If I can convince the Congress, we could look at sending you to a boarding school back in the nonmagical world."

"Could I still see Mom?"

"Yes."

"She'd miss me." Craig looked up at him. "And if you don't treat her well—"

"My vow, a *magical* one, that I will put her happiness above all else."

Craig gave him a long serious stare. "You love her, huh?"

"I do." Sondre pointed at Craig sternly. "But that's between me and her. Stop being such a pain in the ass, and I'll discuss the boarding-school idea with your mom."

"Deal." Craig smirked. "If you do, I won't complain that you failed to ask me for her hand in marriage."

Sondre guffawed. "Well, if you behave, I won't tell *her* that you were discussing her like she's property."

Craig's eyes widened briefly before he smiled. "You're made for her."

I do hope so, Sondre thought. Whether or not he'd meant to, he was fairly sure he and Maggie were as close to perfectly matched as he could even dream of finding.

7
Scylla

Each day before the sun rose over Crenshaw, Scylla patrolled the barrier. As she made her way through the predawn streets of Crenshaw, the residents of her tiny magical village were asleep, so the world seemed silent, as if she were the only person alive. That was exceptionally untrue, of course. The houses in Crenshaw were often *overfilled* with witches, and in the distance, Crenshaw Castle squatted like a perpetual reminder that things here were not quite like other places. But in this moment, Scylla had the welcome illusion of solitude.

She looked back at the path toward the edge of the magical town where she'd lived for over a century now. The moon was half-full, so there was enough light to turn her path silvered. Not a soul had passed her so far.

As she turned to the gravel-and-dirt path that twisted into the dark wood, she saw a few badgers creeping up behind a chicken.

Scylla pointedly glared at them. "Not a good idea."

One of the badgers flipped her off, and Scylla flung a spell-loaded stone at the furry menace. The spell stone hit the badger's side, and the little beast fell sound asleep. The rest of his partners in crime scattered while the thieving badger slept off his attempted crime.

Badgers, like the rest of the citizens, were given food allowances. There was no need to *murder* a chicken. The hens were for sustainable egg production, *not* meat. In general, Crenshaw aimed to be a peaceful community. No killing animals. The one exception had been the fish, but now the fish were polluted. The badgers, unfortunately, were those citizens who had trouble following rules in the first place. If they were law-abiding, they would be human. Crimes were addressed by a period of time sentenced to life as a badger. Even then, being a badger didn't mean that they were left without essential resources or even caged. They were simply . . . in an alternate shape. The punishment was primarily in the lack of human activities.

One of the badgers stopped beside a nearby well and glared back at her.

"Go on," Scylla told them. "Scoot."

The others scurried away toward wherever badgers slept or clustered. At night, they were typically at the tavern, but there was a house where the badgers could all go. Witches weren't trying to deprive the criminal element of shelter.

Until the political factions formed, Crenshaw was a peaceful community, but then a hundred citizens started agitating to return and "seize power" in the nonmagical world—even though magic was simply not compatible with that world. *Everyone* knew that. They might not know why, but they knew the law: No one moved between the worlds other than those who went to retrieve either new witches or provisions. Both were quick trips, rarely over a full hour. *That* was the law, and no matter how much the New Economists argued that the law needed changed, Scylla knew better.

Some rules of magic were immutable. Every witch had a natural magical affinity—one revealed during their time as a remedial witch— drawn from innate character traits. There were magics, basic self-healing and teleportation, that most witches could handle, but the critical magic was whatever trait manifested as their unique skill. Every witch had one, and they were grouped together in houses based around those traits.

Scylla's affinity was illusion, so much so that she had grown into her power more and more. Some of her illusions even *felt* solid at a brief touch. She was the witch in charge of House Scylla—which meant her "job" was managing all significant illusions. Her house's primary responsibility was making sure that Crenshaw was thoroughly hidden from nonwitchy eyes. Obviously, she wasn't excused from noticing other areas that needed attention.

Scylla made a mental note to mention the badger unrest to the chief witch. *Maybe badgering isn't enough.* The witches who were sentenced to badgering were often repeat offenders. That was a problem for the next Congress of Magic meeting.

For now, she continued into the woods. The moonlight illuminated the dirt path that wound from the village to the shadows of the forest. Beyond that was her goal: the barrier to the nonmagical world. The path to the barrier was one Scylla suspected she could walk with eyes closed.

Something inside her seemed to relax when she eventually stood in front of the barrier that was an extension of her magic. Checking the barrier had long since ceased being a duty and become a moment where the world reduced to magic and silence. The trail she followed was a path toward that spot where her magic met itself.

As she walked closer, the magic inside her skin thrummed in tune with the magic that created the barrier that hid Crenshaw.

She saw no shadows in the dim light following her as she charted the path into the woods. No branches cracked to alert her to unwelcome companions deep in the woods. All was as it should be. The only thing of note was the soft slither of ferns as they brushed against her boots. It was a familiar feeling, a telltale sign that she was nearing the edge of Crenshaw's territory. Here was where the magic of the barrier began, *her* magic, *her* creation.

Despite appearances, the wall that protected Crenshaw wasn't solid. If it were, it would mean they were cut off from supplies. The barrier was an illusion with repelling magic woven into it. Nonmagical people would see a slick mountain face lined with briars. Scylla saw the truth: there was no mountain, no briars, nothing at all. Her magic maintained the illusion for Crenshaw. It protected the nonmagical from wandering into the city of witches. It protected the witches from discovery.

A whisper from the dark said, "Foolish Scylla."

"Hello?" Her hand went to the dagger on her hip. Being confident in one's security did not come with carelessness. Since she'd nearly died so many years ago—which was the way all witches discovered their magic—Scylla had carried at least one weapon on her at all times. It felt foolish some days, but not today.

Scylla looked around and saw nothing but shadows. "Is someone here?" Had she imagined that whisper?

Her hand stayed loosely on the hilt of the dagger she wore on her right hip. All she'd used it for in years was cutting an errant branch or bit of twine, but she, like most witches in Crenshaw, was increasingly aware of the conflict between the two political factions—the New Economists who wanted witches to return to the nonmagical world and the Traditionalists who thought that was a terrible plan. To date, that conflict had mostly been petty magic and angry words.

There was the rift, of course, with its seeping ooze of poison into their home, but no *individual* had been targeted. If one witch were, the common belief was that Prospero—the most vocal of the Traditionalist witches—would be the logical target. Perhaps Walter, acting chief witch, would be targeted. Lord Scylla, the head of House Scylla, had no reason to believe that she was a likely mark.

But within the next few steps, something caught her around the ankles. In the next moment, Scylla was trussed at the ankles, suspended wrong side up over the forest floor and clutching her dagger with the intent of sawing through the snare currently cutting into her skin.

"Utter bullshit," she muttered. Louder she said, "A bad idea. That's what *this* is."

A hunter's trap ought not be in the woods near the barrier. The guards could be injured or—

Where were *the barrier guards?*

"Hello?" she called out, trying to remember which members of the community were on patrol.

Is it better to saw at the snare or prepare to defend myself?

Scylla gripped the hilt of her dagger, peering into the darkness for the whisperer as she spun in almost a full circle from the rope around her ankles. *Is this more pettiness or is there an attack forthcoming?*

Someone would come to her aid. She just had to stall until they found her. Louder now, she yelled, "Who's on patrol?"

As she tried to recall the roster, she twisted on the trapline. No one had appeared or spoken, and since bound women were easier targets than she had any intention of being, Scylla decided that freeing herself was the wisest next step.

With a strain she felt in every inch of her abdominal muscles, she folded nearly in half, bent upward in the most unpleasant sit-up ever, and sliced the rope around her ankles.

She rolled to her feet as she dropped to the forest floor with a *whump,* scattering leaves and other detritus. She had several spell-loaded stones in one hand. They weren't fatal spells, just more of the sort she'd tossed at the badger. In the other was her dagger.

Scylla scanned the dimly lit area. "Show yourself."

Several witches appeared: the town stoner, Jaysen, stood beside Agnes. Slightly in front of them was a witch, Jenn, who hadn't the sense that God gave a turnip. She was one of those perpetually unhappy people who complained nonstop about everything. In reality, she was the exact opposite of the perpetually cheerful Jaysen, who always seemed to either be getting high or sleeping off his highs.

"Agnes . . . what are you doing?" Scylla stared at the witch she'd traded barbs with at Congress for decades.

Agnes looked uncertain. She glanced behind her at a witch who remained hidden. Then she told Jenn, "Just do it."

"Do what?" Scylla glared at them. As far as she could recall, Jenn and Jaysen were both so low-level in magic that they could be returned to the Barbarian Lands easily. She met both their gazes. "Go home. All of you."

Aggie said, "That's the plan, isn't it?"

"Hey, Scylla?" a raspy voice said. A fist hit her from behind. "You should've stayed up there until we left."

She turned, and hot fire speared through her back and into her belly. She felt the pain before she heard the rifle. A bullet lodged deep in her gut.

"You *shot* me?" Scylla managed to say. Pain radiated in so many directions that she couldn't say where she'd been shot.

Neither Jenn nor Jaysen held the gun. Aggie didn't either.

Who pulled the trigger? She struggled to find the witch responsible. Owning or using guns was unheard-of in Crenshaw aside from the guards, who only carried them at the barrier, where they watched for any cougar or bear that might wander into Crenshaw. Animals saw through illusion in a way that humans didn't. Sometimes, that meant needing to carry a weapon for safety on the rare occasion that magic wasn't deterrent enough, but shooting another *witch*? Not in Crenshaw. Not ever in the history of the town.

Until now, Scylla amended, trying to push to her feet.

"You picked the wrong side," a voice—*Aggie*—said. The head of House Grendel had her trusty staff in hand, and Scylla cried out as it slammed into her stomach. The impact of the club-like stick added more agony to the waves of pain already rolling over her. "Stay down."

Scylla pressed her hands against her belly, as if she could keep the blood inside.

"It's not personal," Jaysen whispered. "We were just getting you out of the way, dude."

"This wasn't the plan," Jenn muttered.

"It was a hope of *mine,* though." A man's voice was close enough that Scylla could smell fetid breath, a mix of vomit and alcohol. "Never did like you. That felt *good.*"

Him. He was the one with the gun.

Nearby, Agnes laughed. The old witch was one of the few people in Crenshaw who would still let slip her racism, her homophobia, her hatred for other faiths or any other difference. Today, though, Scylla could do no more than scowl at the old bitch. Later, if she healed, there would be words to say and charges to bring.

Right now, Scylla simply needed to not die.

Despite the very real danger of antagonism from her attackers, her mouth still managed to say, "Fuck you."

But Aggie and the others were gone by then, and Scylla was left dying on the leaf-strewn ground. With each beat of her heart, each stream of blood around her fingers, Scylla felt her magic retract into her skin, drawing in to do the same thing it had done the last time a bullet had pierced her body.

Magic would protect its host. That was why witches stayed alive so long. Magic healed the ravages of age, illness, and foolishness. It didn't undo death or disability, but it cured illness and injury.

Bullets are harder to heal, Dr. Jemison had said the first time they'd met.

Didn't mean to get shot, Scylla had pointed out back then. She'd done nothing wrong, but innocence didn't always protect a person. Wrong place, bad time, worse man. *Just like now.*

Vaguely, it occurred to her that whatever they'd used had fragmented inside her body. Shards of the bullet or shell or whatever it was had scattered, slicing deep into many places at once. The last time, it had been one bullet.

One that woke my magic.

This time, as Scylla's magic snapped back to her, the barrier wobbled. It was going to fall. She felt it as surely as she felt the ferns brushing against her cheek as she crawled across the ground.

Hand pressed tighter to her belly, as if she could staunch the wound through pressure alone, Scylla fought to stay awake. *Moss,* a tiny memory that sounded like Dr. Jemison urged. And as the feet of her potential killers crossed into the nonmagical world, headed far away from her, Scylla grabbed a handful of moss and tried to pack it into the wound.

A hob appeared. Then another. Then a third.

"The barrier is down," she told them. "I need . . ."

They vanished again.

". . . help," she finished.

Maybe they went to handle it. Maybe they didn't. All Scylla knew for certain was that she was suddenly alone again in the forest with a bleeding bullet wound.

8

Prospero

Not long after sunrise that morning, Prospero jerked open her door to find Ellie standing there.

"I need to check the rift," Ellie had announced. "What if they undid all my repairs? I almost went in the middle of the night, but I thought you'd overreact. So, come with me now."

"Good morning, Ellie."

"Hi. I need you to come in case I pass out again—unless you would rather I ask someone else?"

"Obviously, I'll be there." Prospero stepped aside to invite her in, but Ellie shook her head.

"Let's go. It feels urgent." Without another word, Ellie pivoted and headed toward the woods.

Prospero mutely followed her, grateful to avoid another session of interrogation but not sure what to do with the brusque way Ellie was acting. In the few days that they had been in their sham marriage, Prospero was already certain that it would not last.

This solution will not work. I need to talk to Walt. There has to be a better way to keep her here!

The Congress of Magic wasn't pleased with Ellie Brandeau. They didn't want her to be so obstinate, so outspoken, so argumentative. They certainly hadn't wanted her to escape Crenshaw. Ellie had broken the first and foremost law of Crenshaw: no witches may travel to and stay in the Barbarian Lands.

And I wasn't reason enough for her to stay.

Only a few days ago, Prospero had been pursuing Ellie and Margaret in the Barbarian Lands. Now, she was Ellie's jailer, trapped in a sham marriage, a forced punishment for Prospero and a way to keep Ellie under observation after she had escaped Crenshaw. It was the sort of ingenious torture that the Congress could impose.

Ellie stalked through the woods. And though Prospero understood why Ellie was angry, she couldn't quite erase her own feelings of betrayal.

She left me.

She hadn't cared enough to fight for me.

She hadn't even tried to talk to me.

Prospero watched her faux wife cut through the forest with the anger of a rampaging bear. It was as if trees bent out of her way and the path unfurled in front of her, sweeping itself of debris. Maybe Ellie didn't notice what she was doing, but Prospero did. Her heart quickened at the sight of the beautiful, powerful, furious witch who held Prospero's heart.

Even angry, Ellie would still do what she agreed to do.

Prospero caught up to her under the shadow of the trees where the rift was. If not for the foul scent and deadly consequences of the rift, their walk through the forest would be lovely, if a bit gloomy. The rift, however, was the source of the toxins in the air and water of their magical home. The New Economists had carved furrows deep into the earth. The furrows cut so far down that they spilled the toxins in the ground from centuries of their own decaying dead and refuse mingled with toxic runoff from factories in the nonmagical world. The result was a virulent sludge that weakened witches, and unless they had enough magic to heal faster than the sickness grew, killed them slowly.

At Prospero's side, Ellie wound through the trees with surety. Maybe her sense of direction was particularly good or maybe the trace of the magic she'd used there at the rift worked like a summons. Either way, Ellie slipped between trees, away from thorny undergrowth and over rocks and divots with a sure stride.

Prospero was nowhere near as fast or agile. She was sure of foot, but not at this speed. "Wait, please." Prospero tugged her sleeves away from a briar. "I am not—"

"The witch who can fix this?" Ellie finished cruelly.

That, of course, was not the sentence Prospero intended to say. She caught up to Ellie again and corrected, "No. I am not, but I *am* the witch you asked to join you here."

"Fine." Ellie sighed. "I'm just . . . pissed off."

"I know." Prospero couldn't change the past; even magic was useless there. "It's complicated."

"Well, then un-fucking-complicate it, or get out of my life." Ellie met her gaze again. She never seemed afraid to do that, even though she knew what Prospero was capable of doing.

What I did to her . . .

She couldn't explain that since Ellie did not *choose* this marriage, did not *choose* her, Prospero couldn't bring herself to touch her. To do so would be criminal.

And maybe, if she were wholly honest, Prospero could admit that part of her hesitation was also about protecting her own battered heart. Ellie recalled only the days before her departure—their time together intimately, their flirting, Ellie's decision to stay in Crenshaw to be with Prospero. She no longer remembered her escape or imprisoning Prospero. She no longer recalled that she had demanded to be siphoned, even if it meant death, rather than be in Crenshaw with Prospero.

And yet here we are.

The guilt was eating at Prospero as much as the hurt over being so easily dismissed.

Ellie had widened the serpents' nest and created a cage of sorts around them to protect any witch from getting too close to the rift, to inadvertently poisoning themselves. Now she stepped through the bars of that cage as if they didn't exist. The bars were solid under Prospero's hand, but to Ellie, they might as well be no more than smoke. Overhead, the hissing serpents undulated as if they were alive, and Prospero wondered briefly if she ought to approach or not. Ellie's creations were an extension of her will and magic, and right now, Ellie was obviously still angry.

The tallest of the serpents had begun to grow branches, as if the tree it had been when Ellie shifted it into something terrifying decided to push back. The wood-wrought creature vibrated in the air, body shivering with small motions. Its fanged mouth opened to flick out a forked tongue that was coated in the purple slime from the rift. Now, however, the serpent's swaying was accompanied by a rustling noise as the branches sprouting from the creature whipped through the air like an exclamation.

The ground around the serpent started to mound up as Ellie stared at it. Like water from an underground spring, it burbled to the surface around the place where the serpent's coils were resting on the ground.

After more than a century, magic had long since stopped seeming overwhelming. Prospero moved between worlds, lived with hobs as staff, aged *technically* by years, but her body remained as it had been a century ago. Magic simply *was*. Yet when Prospero watched Ellie create, the awe that had long since vanished returned with a vengeance. Ellie bent reality to her will with nothing more than her belief that it ought to be reshaped. To a casual observer, it might look like she was making things out of nothing, but Ellie had so far *transformed* existing items rather than creating from emptiness. The transformations, to date, were permanent. Not illusion but complete reformation.

"You're a frightening woman, Elleanor Brandeau." Prospero gazed at her with awe, letting the twist of fear and wonder show in her voice and face. Power was sexy, and Ellie was power personified when her magic rolled through her.

Ellie paused and sent a flirtatious smile over her shoulder at Prospero. "Don't you forget it."

Before Prospero could reply, her head hob appeared in a flour-dappled apron. "*Bernice?*"

"Scylla is in the woods," Bernice interrupted. "Near the barrier."

A feeling of dread settled over Prospero. Something in Bernice's expression was ominous, though Prospero wasn't certain what it was yet.

"Scylla shouldn't be in the woods at this hour." Prospero took a too-deep breath. There were few people she counted as friends. Scylla was one. "Take Ellie home."

"No! I can help you. Whatever it is, I'll help," Ellie said, moving away from the interrupted reparations around the rift.

Prospero glanced at Bernice, and then looked at Ellie. She was the person who mattered most to Prospero, the person who was integral to saving Crenshaw. "I need to know you are safe. Take her to the castle, Bernice."

Before Ellie could reply, Bernice took Ellie's arm and transported her away.

Away from repairing the rift.

Away from any possible threat lurking in the wood.

Away from whatever had kept Scylla in the forest this late.

9
Prospero

In a wobblier than usual lurch, Prospero tried to teleport to the barrier, but . . . *nothing* happened—which made no sense. She'd popped there on more occasions than she could dare count. The barrier was one of the markers that she used when she went between Crenshaw and the Barbarian World. It was her landmark.

Why can't I teleport to the barrier?

She tried again, feeling for the unique magic that rippled over the edge of their world. *Nothing.* The well of magic she usually could call upon did nothing at all. Prospero was standing exactly where she had been a moment prior.

Although there was a magical repulsion on the barrier, causing non-magical people to turn away, Prospero, of course, was not affected by it. She should have been able to transport herself to it. She'd done so literally hundreds of times. She couldn't transport to a person in this world, but she could transfer her presence between landmarks. It was a magic that she was especially adept at. She had only to visualize the space around her focal point and will herself to it.

And the barrier was a spot as clear as her own home.

Today, though, she could not move herself to the barrier. Prospero's alarm built closer toward panic as she stayed exactly where she was. It made no sense.

Visions of the dead witches who had been found in the woods and in the fields over the prior weeks crept into Prospero's memory, accompanied by snippets of Mae's panicked words over the way the poison from the rift had stolen their lives. *Had Scylla fallen ill?* She was the head of her house, the strongest illusionist in Crenshaw. Surely the illness couldn't strike her.

If it could fell her, they were all looking at imminent death.

Prospero tore toward the barrier, unmindful of the trees lashing her face and arms as she pushed saplings and new branches aside. She stumbled over large, fern-hidden rocks, and she slammed to the ground at least twice. She continued forward, though. Somehow, the forest undergrowth seemed thicker today, although logic said it was simply impatience because Prospero had to run rather than transport herself there. Thorned branches snatched at her cloak; leaves crunched underfoot as she moved faster and faster.

"What good is teleporting when I can't get to where she is?" Prospero muttered, scanning for her missing friend as she got closer to the barrier.

Wisely, Prospero slowed her pace in case of alerting anyone or anything with her crashing noise. *Could there have been a predator? A bear?* That made more sense than a sudden sickness. Prospero kept her mouth closed as she approached where the barrier—and the witch who maintained it—ought to be.

And of all the possibilities, what she saw had not even been the possibility of a thought. The barrier was simply not there. The space where the illusion of rock and bramble had been for over a century of Prospero's life was wide open, as if the door of a house had been torn away.

Now, instead of the illusion that hid Crenshaw from nonmagical gazes, there was nothing but air. Beyond their home, the road they took to the town was plainly visible—which meant that anyone standing there could walk right into their hidden home.

I need to tell Walter!

Before she could leave, a sound drew Prospero's gaze away from the vast nothingness. Someone or something was cloaked by the tangle of shrub and fallen leaves to her left. She followed the noise. There, Scylla was motionless on the blood-soaked ground. Her eyes were closed, and her chest did not appear to be moving. Her hands were clutched on her belly where a mound of bloody moss was.

"Scylla!" Prospero dropped to her knees, feeling for a pulse in Scylla's throat. *Nothing.* "No, no, no. Witches aren't to die this young. Come on, Scylla. Please . . ."

Prospero scooped her into an awkward embrace and transported them directly into the infirmary. She'd done so for plenty of new witches, including this one once upon a time. It had never been quite as terrifying.

"Mae! I can't find a pulse." Prospero stumbled toward a bed, but she didn't know how to lower Scylla to the bed without falling on her. "Mae! Help me!"

Dr. Mae Jemison appeared almost at the same instant as Prospero called for her. She was well used to remedial witches arriving in sorry states.

"Are we expecting a—" Her words died abruptly. "*Scylla?* Bring her here."

"Trying," Prospero bit out.

Mae took a deep breath, steadying herself before launching into whatever medical magic she controlled. In the next moment, sparks rippled over Scylla's body as Mae gathered her own information from Scylla's state.

"How? Who would hurt Scylla?" Mae helped Prospero lower Scylla onto the bed, as if the magic radiating out of her in a glittering shower required no effort.

"No pulse," Prospero started.

"It's still there. Faint. She's alive, not by much." Mae continued to run her magic over Scylla. The sparks were now illuminating the whole room like an invisible fire burned and flashed, leaving behind only the waterfall of shimmering magic.

The simple truth that Scylla was not dead was enough to make Prospero feel like some weight fell from her shoulders. It didn't fix the barrier, but once Scylla was healed, *she* could fix it. *Everything will be fine. Scylla will be fine.* Prospero stared down at her oldest friend. *She has to be.*

"If you hadn't got her to me now . . ." Mae let the words dangle, not giving voice to the fate that could have befallen the unconscious witch. Sometimes when she was healing, Mae seemed to be only half-aware that she was speaking. It was one of her many charms. She stared at her patient, magic zinging around her like a stellar show.

"But you *can* fix her . . . ?"

"I can try." Mae looked up at Prospero briefly and demanded, "What do you know? Who did this? Where? With what? Tell me." The doctor made a gesture as if she could pull the very words from Prospero's mouth.

"Her abdomen. There's moss on a wound." Prospero wasn't sure of the who or why. She had theories, but theories wouldn't help Scylla. "I don't know what they used. Maybe a—"

A scream ripped through the room.

Scylla, even unconscious, flinched and yelled as Mae removed the moss from her stomach without an audible word.

"Bullet." Mae paused, glaring at Scylla's abdomen. "Get water. Hot enough to hurt."

Prospero flinched in empathy, but she knew that Mae's magic was guiding her. They'd been in such places more often than Prospero wanted to recall. Strangers, new witches, had bled and vomited and screamed as Mae repaired them well enough to stabilize them.

And Prospero had assisted her too often.

Most of them survived.

Scylla will survive.

Medicine wasn't her magical strength, but she was adept enough to be useful. And as the proximity to death seemed to be the spark that awakened a witch's magic, Prospero had carried in plenty of witches who were approaching death's door. A handful were beyond recovery, but most of those witches were patched and spackled and medicated to the point of health. Then the magic took over.

Scylla has to survive.

Prospero opened one of Mae's cabinets and unerringly retrieved the purified water. Things were in the same places they'd been for years, although the water wasn't always bottled. Familiarity created expediency, and speed was essential in such moments.

Prospero's hands shook as she poured purified water into a vat and heated it as she carried it over to Mae.

"She's going to be unconscious a while with the blood loss and pain," Mae said, as if the jerking of Scylla's body weren't already proof of that. Mae tipped a sachet of various herbs she'd drawn from one of her apron pockets into the vat, and the scent of boiling tincture made Prospero's stomach clench.

The vat visibly cooled under Mae's touch, and then she poured the water over Scylla's stomach. It sizzled like acid, and Prospero reminded herself that she could trust Mae.

Mae heals, not hurts.

Still, when Scylla's eyes opened briefly, locking with Prospero's, it took effort not to shove the doctor away. Prospero's hands balled into fists when Scylla lurched sideways, as if to escape the agony. The look of rare betrayal was one Prospero hoped never to see again on her friend's face, especially aimed at her.

"Mae will fix you," Prospero promised. "I brought you to Mae. You're safe. *Safe,* Scylla."

But Scylla still tried to escape.

"Grab her!" Mae ordered. She was shaking from whatever magic she was still using, and Prospero hoped that she was strong enough to fix this. Once or twice, Mae's magic was not enough.

The battery. We need Monahan.

But Prospero couldn't go get him. Not yet. Right now, Prospero's hands were firm on Scylla's shoulders, and she bodily blocked her from escape as she took a wide-legged stance and braced. Scylla was taller and stronger.

"Your magic," Mae snapped.

And Prospero felt a fool for not thinking it sooner. She slid into Scylla's mind, looking for the emotions for this moment, plucking them from terror to calm. She let her friend see her, know that it was not an enemy's arms that held her still, and as she did so, she felt Scylla relax. In the privacy of her friend's mind, she selected a long-ago conversation between them and pulled it forward.

The two women sat in Scylla's home. A bottle of wine that Prospero brought as a birthday gift sat on the low table to Scylla's side.

"You're not as much of a coldhearted thing as Sondre warned me," Scylla said mildly. She glanced over the rim of her half-filled glass and held Prospero's gaze.

"Says you. I make an excellent enemy if I am inclined."

"Indeed." Scylla's expression shifted into a wide smile. "I don't think you want me as an enemy."

Prospero sighed. "I suppose we'd best be allies then."

"The word is 'friend,'" Scylla corrected, lifting her glass.

"Call it what you will. I have your back, Marie." Prospero still slipped and used her birth name, her before-magic name. "I had it when you arrived, and I have it now that you are head of House Scylla. I will always have it unless you betray me."

"Same, girl. Same."

As Prospero nudged the memory forward, reminding her friend that she was protected, Scylla opened her mouth and said, "Never betray you, P. *Look.*"

Prospero went back into Scylla's mind, diving toward today's memories. Prospero saw her walk into the woods, saw the capture, saw her free herself.

Scylla pressed her hands against her belly, as if she could keep the blood inside.

"It's not personal," Jaysen whispered. "We were just getting you out of the way, dude."

"This wasn't the plan," Jenn muttered.

"It was a hope of mine, though." A man's voice was close enough that Scylla could smell fetid breath, a mix of vomit and alcohol. "Never did like you. That felt good."

Him. *He was the one with the gun.*

As Prospero shoved through the memory, noting that Aggie was there, she tried to see the other faces. *Who did this? Who was he? Who shot Scylla?* She recognized three of the witches desperate enough to take a life, to tear down the barrier, to destroy everything. Jaysen. Jenn. Aggie. Someone would have answers. Unfortunately, the New Economists believed that they should be allowed to be in the Barbarian Lands, so finding the villains to get any answers or stop disasters from coming was a lot harder now that they were in a place with billions of nonmagical people.

Then Scylla went limp, knocking Prospero toward the floor as she was forcefully shoved out of Scylla's memories. Prospero caught herself on a nearby stretcher, scraping her arm as she slid past it, and hit the hard edge of a rolling cabinet. A glance up revealed Mae jabbing two fingers inside the wound on Scylla's belly.

"She passed out," Mae said through gritted teeth. "Come here, you bastard."

Prospero's eyes widened. They weren't friends, but that was an uncharacteristically harsh thing to say. Then Mae jerked her hand out of Scylla's belly.

"Got you." She held up a tiny piece of metal. *The bullet.* Mae's hand was blood-slick, and she was wavering on her feet, but she was smiling in victory. "Now, I can heal her. Her heart kept trying to stop, and the bleeding wouldn't."

Mae wobbled and muttered, "Sorry. All out of juice."

Prospero leaped up as Mae started to crumple. "Shit!"

Then she was standing with a bloody doctor and an unconscious patient. She hefted Mae onto the next cot over and then she yelled, "Hob!"

One of the castle hobs appeared, glanced at the witches on the cots, and said, "They aren't dead. I only take dead bodies."

Prospero swallowed the words that wanted to escape her mouth and instead ground out, "I need witches from Dr. Jemison's house, ones she trusts, to look after them. Please, fetch them now."

The hob gave her an unimpressed once-over. "You have a bit of blood just there. . . ." He gestured at her from foot to face. "You might want to fix that."

Then the hob popped out, still scowling, only to return and leave repeatedly in less than a minute until Prospero was left with four witches.

She wiped her hands as they watched.

"Keep them alive and *safe*. No one enters unless I'm with them." Prospero straightened her shoulders, resisting the urge to touch her hair in case there was still blood on her hands. "Dr. Jemison's depleted herself. Lord Scylla was shot."

Grim expressions came over them.

"The door will be warded," Prospero added. "Should anything befall either of them, badgers won't be your fate."

"The law for infractions is badg—"

"Do I look like the *law* is my priority today?" Prospero asked softly, marking each of their faces in her memory. "Keep them safe or die. Those are the options."

The witch nearest to her backed up a step.

At least one of the witches responsible was Agnes, House Grendel's head. Hers was a house of violence, and Prospero had no doubt of the odds of successfully facing such a witch.

And the witch who shot Scylla.

There will be blood.

There were currently at least two dangerous witches in the Barbarian Lands. A lot more than Prospero's own safety was at risk now. Everything would be lost if they were exposed, their safety, their home. If non-witches invaded Crenshaw with their guns and machines, the violence could be dire.

Would I die for Crenshaw? It had never been a question, but for the first time, Prospero thought there were reasons to try to stay alive. *One reason, actually. Ellie.*

"Keep them safe and alive" was all Prospero said abruptly before leaving the infirmary in search of the headmaster.

Crenshaw Castle had to be locked down. The students needed to be made safe, and they weren't the only ones. Ellie would need to be looked after. And, of course, the two unconscious witches in the infirmary. Plans swirled in her head as she stomped through the castle, mindful of the gasps of those she passed.

Bloody.

Furious.

Exhausted.

And it wasn't even midday.

10

Sondre

Sondre was on the third floor of the castle attempting to turn an unused classroom into the headmaster's office. His existing office was no longer meeting his needs since he'd decided to move all of his magic-related books and supplies out of his castle living suite. Having a completely nonmagical teen living in his quarters now had Sondre feeling like he had to reduce the threats.

So here Sondre was, trying to sort through a tower of textbooks, many obsolete, rather than leaving these in the reach of a belligerent teenager.

"Why do I still have all these books?" Sondre muttered as he looked at textbooks that hadn't been used in several decades. Each headmaster added to the library that their replacements would have for reference, but the result was that there were duplicates of several texts. Magical textbooks were replicated and revised, and in his possession he had no less than four versions of *Basic Magical Skills for the Remedial Witch*. He wasn't even sure they used that book currently.

"Headmaster." Her voice entered before she did, but even if she hadn't spoken, Sondre would know that the intruder was either his wife or Prospero. And Maggie wouldn't call him "headmaster." That left his former nemesis. There was no one else foolhardy enough to barge into his private space.

"How did you even find my new off . . ." His words faded as he turned around and saw Prospero. Her clothes were ruined. Streaks of blood on her cheeks and throat made it hard to look at her. Sondre stared at her. "What *happened* to you? Why is there blood . . . are *you* hurt or is that someone else's?"

"Not mine." Prospero paused briefly.

Sondre had an abject terror that the blood was Maggie's or Craig's or—

"Scylla," Prospero said, interrupting his mental listing of the worst possible answers. Her voice was dry and cold, and he was certain she was in shock. "Scylla was shot, and the barrier is down. I need the school secured, Headmaster."

"Is she alive?" Sondre dropped the stack of books on the desk, and tiny clouds of dust from the pages released a not-unpleasant scent of old paper. When Prospero didn't speak or move, he repeated, louder now, "Is Scylla alive?"

"So far." Her voice was a flat rasp, and that alone was reason for him to pause. Prospero was not the most emotional person he knew, but she certainly wasn't this cold. Their unfortunately intertwined interactions of late had led to an understanding that made it harder to hate her.

"She's with Mae?" he prompted in a gentler voice.

Prospero sighed, like she was starting to deflate, and said, "She's with Mae's people. Mae is unconscious. She saved Scylla so far, snatched her back from death, and then collapsed on me."

"Of course she did." Sondre smiled, despite the dire news. Few people in Crenshaw could outpace Mae for selflessness or kindness.

Prospero's hands were folded tightly together, as if she were trying to hide the blood from her own sight.

"The barrier is down," she repeated. "We need to . . . I don't actually know what we need to do. *I* need to tell you, then Walt, the Congress, and . . . Ellie. I should tell Ellie. And . . ." Prospero stood there looking like she was one wrong move from falling apart.

"How can I help?" Sondre asked when Prospero's words drifted into nothingness.

"Keep the castle secure. Tell the hobs. Doors and windows sealed. Don't let them out, Sondre. None of them. If the barbarians come . . ." She shuddered slightly, as if envisioning that regular folk—nonmagical folk—would start flooding Crenshaw and attacking.

It was that fear that divided them, had done so for years. Some witches were Traditionalists. They believed the worlds must stay apart, or else doom would come. Others, the New Economists, wanted to tear down the barrier and meld the worlds.

It hit him then.

It was us. My side. We . . . almost killed Scylla.

Sondre swallowed back the bile threatening to rise. How had their differences come to this? They'd created the rift that was killing witches in Crenshaw. *Weeding out the low magic,* Agnes had called it. Now, they'd moved to attempted murder.

And they told me nothing of the plans.

Why?

Admittedly, he had waffled in his commitment after the rift, even considered telling Prospero or the chief witch what he knew, but some of his associates were dangerous. Agnes, head of House Grendel, had transitioned from a witch whose house was focused on justice to a witch craving violence. Sondre had seen it in the army; some soldiers were there for violence, not for a *cause.* There were those who were lesser threats.

And there were days he'd understood that impulse. The danger of being able to disconnect from his own fears and guilt over taking lives did something to him. The doctors, back when he lived over there, had still called it "shell shock." These days, it was PTSD or something. Whatever it was, though, he'd felt it more years than not. The itchy feeling that led to starting fights, the satisfaction of a good brawl, the paranoia . . . He understood why Aggie was so off-kilter, and maybe that was why he'd initially agreed with them.

"Who?" His voice was a thin sliver.

"Aggie. Jaysen. Jenn. They were there. . . ." Prospero looked angrier as her voice faded. "Someone else, too. The one who pulled the trigger."

"*Not* Aggie?"

Prospero shook her head. "I don't know her two lackeys very well, but . . . they will have a name of the other witch. I'll find him. I'll find all four of them."

Sondre could practically taste her rage, not magically but because she was vibrating with it, and *that* he understood. "Jaysen? He's harmless—"

"He was there with those who shot my friend."

"Yes . . . Have you checked if Allan is still in Crenshaw?" Sondre was done, ready to full-out confess what he knew. It was one thing to have different opinions, but bullets? Shooting the witch who kept Crenshaw hidden? That changed everything.

"Not yet."

"I didn't know what they were planning," Sondre blurted out. "Whatever your spy said, I wasn't—"

"My spy said nothing," Prospero interrupted. She pierced him with a look. "He didn't *know what they were planning.*"

Sondre stared at her, hoping he misunderstood. "*Me?* I'm the spy?"

She nodded. "You aren't a bad man, Sondre. You get a spell of guilt, confess to me, and then I erase your memory of doing so."

"The fuck?" He took a step back. "How many times? I'm going to get dementia from your meddling in my brain."

Prospero looked at the ceiling as if she could find divine guidance above them. "Look. We can go through that argument later. I didn't muddle your brain. That's not how my magic works. What we need to do right now is figure out how to keep our world safe. Find Aggie, Jaysen,

Jenn, and whoever else was with her. Magic loose over there? You've seen it. Chaos is coming, and we need to stop it."

Sondre stepped out from around the desk. "Don't erase my memory this time."

She leveled a look at him. "*They* don't trust you anymore, Sondre. You're no use to me as a spy . . . and honestly, spying is no use. They shot her. They could've just left. They could've just walked out. We would still need to go after them, but . . . they *shot Scylla*. They shot her just to expose all of us to discovery."

Whatever shock she'd experienced was letting go, and Prospero's seeming numbness was giving way to something more familiar to him. This was the frigidly angry woman he was used to seeing. It was strangely comforting, hearing that knife's edge slide back into her voice. Briefly, Sondre was glad that they *hadn't* told him their plans. He enjoyed a brawl, but he didn't want to be in their shoes when they faced Prospero. For all her flaws, she had equal strengths. No one was more loyal than her.

"I'll go after them as soon as we locate them," he offered. "You stay with Scylla, and I'll go bring them back."

"I need to talk to Walt first. See if Allan is here. Get . . . permission." Prospero pulled her shoulders back. "I appreciate revenge, Sondre. On that we are in accord, but we need a plan to protect our citizens first. I need to be sure Crenshaw is secure. I can't have Ellie in peril, too."

At those words, Sondre looked at her with more sympathy than he typically thought she deserved. He held her gaze. "Your wife will be safe within the castle, but we both know how deadly she can be. Take her."

"She has classes and—"

"She's not any more likely to sit by idly than you are." He swallowed, hoping he wasn't about to have an emotional woman on his hands. Prospero never saw reason when Brandeau was the topic. He wouldn't blame Prospero for striking out at someone, but that didn't mean he wanted to be the target. He certainly didn't want to be the one to comfort her. Even now, they weren't actual friends, merely occasional accomplices.

Prospero's expression gave nothing away. After a moment, she said only, "She is integral to Crenshaw, Sondre. Keep her safe. Keep them all safe. I will speak to you once there is a hunting plan."

Then she whirled away and left with not another word.

He was grateful that he hadn't had to deal with either her rage or tears, and for a moment he wouldn't admit later, he felt sympathy for her—and gratitude that he wasn't on her hunting list.

11

Prospero

Prospero had stopped outside Crenshaw Castle, pacing there as if she were a surly guard dog. The agitation roiled under her skin. *I am stronger than this.* She actively shoved her panic into that cold place deep inside that she had been using to store emotions since she was a young woman unwillingly wed.

I do not break.

She needed to talk to Walt. To decide what to do about Ellie, but she was in one of the remedial-magic classes right this moment—which seemed ludicrous, because she was far from remedial. Bureaucracy was eternal, though.

Is Sondre right? Do I take her with me? She's not as dangerous as everyone thinks . . . She trapped me. No one else has done that. But Ellie could only do that because I was distracted by my heart.

Prospero was ready to march through the castle and jerk Ellie out of class, so the sudden tingle of magic from the Barbarian Lands was a welcome distraction when it washed over her.

"Need the headmaster already?" the hob called before his body appeared. When he did materialize, he stood atop a finial on the staircase of the castle like a miniature statue.

"No. He's busy. Tell Sondre where I've gone, and if you could tell . . . Walt, I suppose?" Prospero scowled at not having a clear protocol for retrieval now. Criminals were taken to Aggie for justice, or to Mae if they were injured. Right now, Prospero couldn't go to the infirmary *or* consult Aggie.

I'll figure it out.

She closed her eyes for a long blink and let her body follow the tug of magic. It was a singular feeling to not know where she'd be upon arrival. Often, she appeared at hospitals or grisly accidents. A few times, she'd arrived as the fallen witch was being beaten or stabbed. Those were the hardest ones.

She shoved old memories and thoughts of Ellie away as she opened her eyes.

Unexpectedly, Prospero realized that she was standing in a bookshop. There was no doubt that there was a witch in this building, though. Well, either that or someone had been gardening in the wrong place entirely. The center of the shop, where only the hip-high display tables of books were, had become a swamp. At her feet, black water swirled, and various waterlogged books floated by like leaves in a stream.

Prospero's heart tightened at the thought of wasted books. Sure, there was an informational library in Crenshaw, but fiction? That was harder to find. She glanced down at the floating books, admiring the glossy covers that still hadn't been ruined. She fished a couple out and put them in her pockets to take home. *Maybe Ellie could repair them for me.* A longing rose up; sometimes Prospero wanted only simple pleasures, like curling up with Ellie and reading for hours.

Something less book-like swam by, and Prospero wondered what creature was under the swampy water. The few people in the store were crouching on tables, so she suspected the thing under the water wasn't something she particularly wanted to encounter. Reptile? Rat? Where *was* this bookshop? All she could say for certain was that the majority of the titles on the nearest tables were in English, but that detail was not a particularly helpful clue. There were English-language books in a lot of places.

With one last pining look at the plethora of books all around her, Prospero strode through the knee-high water toward a staircase that was currently covered in what looked like poison-ivy vines. Trying not to touch the toxic vines, Prospero climbed up the leaf-strewn steps to the second floor of the building.

Whichever witch this was, they were affiliated with the agricultural house, Dionysus and Jörd. *Was* Allan the man with the gun?

As Prospero turned around a shelf on the landing of the second floor, she saw a witch sitting on a giant marshmallow with a tower of books sticking out of the fluff.

"Jaysen?" Prospero stared at him as she approached.

He looked up. "Why are you all bloody?"

"Because you people shot my friend, Jaysen."

"Didn't do it. I'm, like, an innocent bystander." Jaysen had his hair in a long braid, the end tail of which was caught in the fluff. He looked more stressed than threatening. "I just came along for information. Well, that and Allan said so. He's the head of house, you know?"

Prospero eased closer. "Did Allan shoot Scylla?"

"Yeah . . . Jenn couldn't. I couldn't." Jaysen shrugged. "She was in the way."

The wash of rage that filled Prospero made her feel like her vision tinted red. *No magic. No magic. Do not kill him.*

Mindlessly, Jaysen kept talking. "I was thinking about a hydroponic cannabis warehouse. Everyone's so angry all the time. Do you know they don't sell seeds at the farm shops here?" He grabbed a handful of fluff that was also his chair and popped it in his mouth.

"So you had no issue *shooting Scylla and exposing our world* so you could come here and plan to grow drugs?" Prospero's hand balled up. She could punch him. Surely, that was fine. Not magic. Just a solid hit.

"Herb. Yes. If we had it at Crenshaw, everyone would stop fighting," he explained earnestly, sucking the sticky marshmallow from his fingers.

"So you joined the *enemy* in pursuit of drugs? Allan shot Lord Scylla."

"Yeah . . . totally uncool of him," Jaysen said, frowning. "It's bad energy to spill blood, and it's not *drugs*. It's herb."

"Where's Agatha? Allan?"

Jaysen shook his head. "The old witch and her left-hand man skedaddled."

"And Jenn?"

"Don't know. Dionysus, though? He's wild, you know?" Jaysen laughed awkwardly. "Has an *agenda*."

"He. Shot. Scylla."

"Right, but I'm not him. I just wanted to figure things out to help at home, you know?" Jaysen gave her a wide-eyed look like he was a daft toddler. "I'm not a bad guy, you know?"

"Not . . ." Prospero wanted to punch him in the throat. "Did you see what you *did* to this place? You cannot use magic over here. There are laws."

"I didn't use *much* magic. I just wanted a snack, a comfy chair, and to be left alone. I'm not hurting anyone." He tore off another piece of fluff and held it out to her. When she ignored him, he popped it in his mouth and mumbled, "I ruined a chair. So what?"

"Aside from working with treasonous bastards who shot my friend, you flooded the first floor. There's poison ivy on the steps—"

"I *wanted* to be left *alone*," he reiterated. "I didn't hurt anyone."

Prospero wasn't in the mood to keep arguing. "Time to go home."

She snatched hold of his wrist, and she let the pressure to return to Crenshaw hook under her ribs. When she released Jaysen, he was still seated in his mound of sticky fluff, and the books were still in it. Now, however, he was at the door of Walter's cottage.

When Grish, Walt's chief hob, opened the door, he made a sound somewhere between a gargle and a word. His expression of disgust spoke loud enough. Then he vanished.

Walt stood in the doorway a moment later. "What in Henry's horny hump is that?"

"An escaped witch. He has no idea where Aggie is. He confirmed that Allan shot Scylla." Prospero stepped away from Jaysen, who gave Walt a sheepish smile.

"Hey, Chief Dude," Jaysen said.

Prospero paused to enjoy Walt's expression before adding, "I'm sticky and itchy, and there's no one at the helm of House Grendel, and Allan—fucking weasel that he is—shot Scylla." Prospero gestured at Jaysen. "This one's your problem. I need to go back to the castle."

Walt scowled. "You couldn't take him to the infirmary?"

If I stay here, I'll injure him, she almost admitted.

Instead, she said aloud, "He's not injured. Yet. Mae's busy with actual patients."

Prospero glanced at Walt and pushed her emotions down. In a more rational tone, she said, "He created a flood, covered steps with poison ivy, and he went along with Agnes and Allan *while they shot Scylla and exposed Crenshaw. He ought to be siphoned or badgered."

Then Prospero teleported away as she could feel the itching from the magical poison ivy creeping up her ankles. She was covered in blood, marshmallow, and poison ivy. All she wanted at the moment was a bath.

And vengeance.

Deeper down in that morass of feelings she tried to keep contained, she wanted to set fire to a few people. The urge to use her own magic over there and hunt them pressed on her nerves. There were *billions* of humans, though. There was no way to find three witches—not until their magic leaked—and being over there would mean her magic leaked.

Becoming a monster to hunt a monster wouldn't fix anything. Letting her baser urges reign would only bring more trouble. Randomly roaming would mean spilling more wild magic in the Barbarian Lands.

But I'll be there the moment you slip, you bastards.

12

Ellie

When Ellie returned to her spartan living quarters, she did not expect to see her wife pacing outside her door.

"Hi . . . ? What are you—" And then Ellie saw the blood. "Are you hurt? Should we go to the infirmary?" Ellie's hands slid over Prospero's bloodied cheek. *No cut there.* Then Ellie felt her sides and stomach. *Not even a tear in the fabric.* She couldn't stop herself. "Where is it? Seriously? Where are you in—"

"Scylla's blood. Not mine." Prospero caught Ellie's wrists, still standing on the threshold of the room. Her voice was more vulnerable than Ellie recalled ever hearing as she added, "I need your help."

"*Scylla?* Lord Scylla? Is she dead?"

"So far, no." Prospero's expression shifted into something terrifying in its grief, and any doubt that Ellie had about her wife's ability to love deeply vanished. "If she dies . . ."

Ellie dragged Prospero into the room and closed the door. "Look, whatever else there is between us that's fucked up, I am still here." She shoved the cloak from Prospero's shoulders and stepped back. "What happened?"

"She was shot," Prospero muttered, not quite focused. "She is near death. I thought . . . I couldn't find her pulse."

At a word from Ellie, the tub started filling.

"She'd not dead, though, right?" Ellie said, half question and half statement.

"She can't die." Prospero's jaw tightened. "I have to—"

"You have to wash away the blood." Ellie started unfastening her wife's vest. Prospero didn't object. That alone was proof that she needed Ellie's kindness just then. "Is that a rash? Are you allergic to *blood*?"

"No. There was poison ivy, too, after . . . after I delivered Scylla to Mae." Prospero's voice wobbled. "I had to go retrieve one of them, the witches who hurt Scylla, and when the next witch slips—"

"You can't go anywhere in this shape," Ellie said gently. "Let me get Bernice to—"

Prospero's hob popped into the room. She took one look at Prospero and vanished again. No more than a moment later, some of Prospero's clothes appeared as if they were falling from empty air.

". . . get you some clean clothes," Ellie finished as she scooped up Prospero's unbloodied clothes and put them on a nearby chair.

Without another word, she unbuttoned Prospero's blouse.

Prospero made a pained noise and stepped backward, out of Ellie's reach. "I need to handle the fallen barrier, and talk to Walt, and—"

"Yes, and I'll help you after you aren't dressed in blood," Ellie said, thinking about how horrible it would be to wear clothes soaked in a friend's blood. "A quick rinse. That's all. Just wash away the blood. Five minutes won't make or break the world."

Prospero bowed her head, so she wasn't looking at her. "I need privacy, Ellie. I don't need help with bathing."

Ellie froze. It stung. She took a washcloth, dipped it in the water, and wiped the blood from Prospero's cheek. "I'm not going to take unfair advantage of you."

"I don't ever want to take advantage of you, either," Prospero said, voice somehow even more raw. "I want to, but I will not."

And something about that admission sliced to Ellie's heart.

"Turn so I can be sure your back is okay," Ellie insisted, not looking anywhere but Prospero's face. Then she motioned to the tub. "Get the blood off. I'll change clothes. Then we'll go see Walter. Unified front and all that. Maybe he needs a reminder that I can leave here if he's not going to let you tell me what I've forgotten."

"Ellie . . ."

"He ordered it, didn't he? Ordered you to make me forget things?" Ellie pressed. Maybe it was time to remind all of them that she was not, in fact, a remedial witch now. She might have been a *reluctant* witch, but she was not someone to be trifled with.

Afterward, when Prospero was dressed in something not soaked in blood, Ellie reached for her arm. "Let's go. Off to see the wizard . . ."

"Chief witch," Prospero corrected absently.

And Ellie made a mental note to catch Prospero up on a few pop-culture references when they weren't midcrisis, but then they were suddenly standing outside a very modest cabin in the village.

"Please do not provoke the chief witch," Prospero murmured as she held Ellie briefly.

Ellie looked at a small cottage. Whitewashed exterior, thatched roof. The tiny house reminded her of the ones she'd once seen in Ireland or Scotland.

Prospero wrapped a firm arm around Ellie's middle. "He's dangerous."

"So are we." Ellie closed her eyes, leaning her forehead against Prospero shoulder briefly while the hornets in her stomach from teleporting settled. Then she stepped back and said, "But I will attempt manners. For now."

"Thank you." Prospero rapped on the door, and it swung open so quickly that it seemed as if the hob on the other side had been waiting for their knock.

"C.W. is coming," the wizened hob pronounced. He wandered off, trailing a knitted scarf in a clash of colors.

"C.W.?" Ellie asked quietly.

"Chief Witch."

Ellie nodded. She didn't recall being here before, but she should've been. Her wife regularly had business with the chief witch. They were surrounded by the scent of peat fire, but it brought no memories of being here previously.

They waited in the kitchen until they were more or less greeted by an irate old witch.

"Took you long enough," he muttered, glaring at Prospero. "Just the three of them to retrieve: Allan, Aggie, and that young 'un, Jennifer. I expect you'll fetch them."

"Walt—"

"I handled Jaysen. He'll likely be siphoned." Walt stayed in the doorway, barely glancing at them. "You need to retrieve the others. Mae will fix Scylla. That one can work miracles." He shook his head; the edge of a smile touched his lips for a flicker and was gone. "For now, I have Scylla's bunch working on repairs. How is she?"

"Bullet's out, but . . ." Prospero shrugged. "Mae wasn't sure."

"Oh, for the love of Fergus!" Walt threw up one hand dramatically. His other tugged on his beard as if it were a comfort object. "Guns and fallen barriers and missing witches. Someone else needs to be chief witch. Scylla'd be damn good at it. You would, too, but you have too many infernal enemies, girl."

Prospero tensed.

Ellie resisted the urge to defend her. Instead, she stared at him. "Right, well, hand-waving and drama aside . . ."

"*What* did you say?" Walt leveled a glare at Ellie that was impressively intimidating.

"Everyone here knows guns are stupid, right?" Ellie looked at Prospero and then back at the chief witch. "What are you doing other than leaving all the actual *work* to my wife? Ordering people to do what they're already doing?"

Prospero visibly winced.

"Put a leash on her, Lady Prospero," Walt said in a low voice.

Ellie idly took his knitting and started transforming it into shackles. "Try it. Please. Try forcing me to do anything. I am only in this world for *her*."

"We cannot find the others until they use magic," Prospero said, stepping in between them. "This is no different from a new remedial witch. Until there is magic used or leaked . . ."

Walt looked suddenly old. "This is the problem with not being a villain, a killer, a despot, any of that. Good people try to live by their ideals, and sometimes that means we just wait."

"Fuck that," Ellie said.

Walt leveled a steely look at her. "Ah, to be so young and stupid . . ."

Ellie flashed her teeth at him in a feral scowl. "We don't need to *just wait*. Prospero has already got Lord Scylla to the doctor, and she brought back the first of the escapees. I can work on fixing the barrier. Maybe interrogate the one who was brought here. . . ."

Prospero said nothing as she glanced back over her shoulder at Ellie quizzically.

"Interrogate?" Walt echoed.

"Why not? I feel like I could use some practice at extracting answers." Ellie smiled tightly. "Are you going to try to tell me *you've* never done something awful with magic? I don't know, ordered altering a mind?"

"Ellie . . ." Prospero said warningly.

Walt simply stared at Ellie for a long moment.

Ellie felt a nudging from her temper rise. *I could make him listen, confess, just like I could make the witch Prospero brought back talk to us.*

The chief witch was speaking to Prospero as if Ellie were no longer present. "Maybe there's one of them that might make a good temporary house head . . . ?"

"No." Prospero sounded pained. "Scylla *will* recover."

"Their illusion might hold until Scylla's up." The chief witch gestured toward the general direction of the barrier.

And Ellie knew that was what he was motioning toward. Her thoughts of interrogation fled as an image of the barrier filled her mind.

How do I know where it is? What it looks like?

She frowned at that thought. Maybe she remembered from when she arrived here? She could picture it, though, even the path to it. She was fairly sure she could find it—and knew what waited outside the barrier.

"Take me there," Ellie told her wife, ignoring the chief witch now. He gave her an unpleasant feeling. She turned so she was looking mostly only at Prospero and said, "I don't think I have the energy to fully *build* a wall, but I can weave some vines or something. . . ."

Ellie didn't miss the way her wife glanced at Walter questioningly, as if she were asking permission for something. Ellie kept the old man in her peripheral vision, and his answering nod made fear trickle over her.

Why did Prospero look at him that way? Does he know what I forgot? What does the barrier have to do with it? Why does she obey him?

With the same surety that warned her when someone lied, Ellie knew that asking was dangerous. Her *wife* was dangerous. Prospero might be vulnerable right now, and she might genuinely want and care for Ellie, but Prospero made no secret of the fact that she would live, die, or kill for Crenshaw.

"Well, go on with you," the chief witch ordered with obvious exasperation. "Even I can't tell you where Aggie and the other two went until magic leaks or is used. You and the headmaster will feel it, too." Walt made shooing motions at them, as if they were errant hens rather than grown women. He stepped closer and shooed again.

Prospero paused. Then she finally spoke. "I need permission, Walt."

"For?"

"Justice," Prospero said tightly. "Allan *shot* Scylla. Aggie—a head of house—was involved. We know that. I saw it in Scylla's memory."

"We will need a new head of house then." Walt reached past her and opened the door. "Sondre's the next in line for House Grendel. I'll get a new headmaster figured out soon, and—"

"I don't give a damn about who heads the house. I won't be bringing back three badgers. Tell me I have sanction to do so. To question the next one and deal with the other two. Aggie and Allan are *heads of house.*"

Walter sighed. "I know. It makes their treason worse. You may . . . handle Agnes and Allan as best you see fit. There will be no consequences to you—" He paused and glanced at Ellie. "—*either* of you or the headmaster if they can't be brought back."

Prospero bowed her head respectfully. "Consider it done."

With that, Allan's and Agnes' death warrants were just sealed. Prospero had permission to kill. There was a slight chance that Walt meant siphoning, but that was as good as murder for a witch who was powerful or old or both. Two heads of house would die for their actions.

And Prospero would be the one to deliver that death—at her own request.

13
Dan

Dan had decided to use the hidden library at Crenshaw Castle as his personal meeting space. Technically, the students ought to still be unaware of its existence, but Dan had been sharing the knowledge of it with other witches. Today there were roughly a dozen witches in the library with him, and it made Dan feel pleasantly rebellious to have let that many people know about it. Knowledge ought to be freely accessible, and only a corrupt soul would lock away books.

Maybe Dan was wrestling with his own sins a little, and maybe telling others about the library was a little bit of salve on his guilty conscience. Still, he was pleased that others were happy to be here. So far, the vast space was occupied solely by remedial witches, but the library was more and more active every week—although no faculty came here, and no one from the village visited. No hobs, either.

Axell, his sort-of, maybe, kind-of boyfriend, asked, "Are you okay?"

Dan nodded. It was the truth, more or less. He was "okay," but since he'd done a Bad Thing to witches he'd been trying to make into his friends, he never felt quite "okay."

It was that or risk being booted out of Crenshaw. It was that or have his friends face near-certain death. Dan could explain his actions away, but he still thought he'd been wrong to help enforce Crenshaw's ruling body's decision.

And I can't even talk about it with anyone.

So he hid away in the library and read up on the history of the magical world.

Inside the hidden library, floor-to-ceiling bookshelves, complete with rolling ladders, lined all the walls, creating a veritable fortress of books. Circular shelves jutted out in a pattern that was a bit too much like ribs for his comfort. But the important thing was that there were tables, cushy seats, and a few desks that appeared to have translucent bubbles over them for privacy. Not exactly privacy of the "let's get naked in the library" way, but the study bubbles were great for private conversation.

If a person wanted to research, as Dan had lately, there were three of Ramelli's sixteenth-century bookwheels. He could have multiple books open at once. Nothing so far offered much in the way of explanations for the sludge in the woods, why he was able to boost magic, or even why Axell could make them invisible. The library was surprisingly low on the magical information he needed for answering his precise questions, but everything he'd read led to new ideas. So it wasn't a "topic to answer" sort of organization that he'd found in the library, more of a meandering sort of knowledge-gathering that made Dan fairly sure the library needed a team of librarians.

But he hadn't come anywhere near exhausting the information yet, and he was no longer someone Elleanor Brandeau even remembered, so he hadn't figured out how to approach her and say, "I found a library that desperately needs a flock of librarians."

A fleet?

An encyclopedia?

What was *a group of librarians called?*

A knowledge?

A catalogue?

A coven?

Dan briefly mused that maybe witch brains were all ADHD, because his own thought processes seemed increasingly nonlinear.

"Does magic rewire the brain?" he said aloud, and then he felt a vague tug in his center toward a shelf with a book called *Neuromagical Intervention.* It was tucked between a book called *Daydreaming for Divas,* which looked like a spicy romance, and a book on *Mental Magic for More Magical Ministrations,* the cover of which hinted that it was on sex magic.

Of course *that* was the one in his hand when Axell joined him.

"Perhaps a bit more advanced than where we are," Axell mused. "First we should have sex, perhaps?"

Dan's face flushed. "I wasn't . . . that was . . . I was looking at this one!" He grabbed at *Neuromagical Intervention* but instead pulled *Daydreaming for Divas* off the shelf. "I was thinking about something else, not sex."

Axell laughed softly. "Such a shame. I think you are thinking of it now, though."

"Well, you just said we should have sex."

"We should. I think if you are feeling romantic, Daniel, we can go somewhere else. . . ."

Dan glanced down at the paperback in his hand. "Damn it. Not this one." He jabbed the neuromagical book. "This. I was wondering about brain magic. This is what I was trying to grab."

"Ah." Axell nodded once. "Less fun. Like the scary witch. She is not what I think about if I want to feel like getting naked."

And Dan couldn't argue with *that.* Lady Prospero was the reason he was thinking about mental magic. Helping her erase Ellie's and Maggie's minds was probably the worst thing he'd ever done, and it was impossible to stop thinking about it.

Am I a bad witch?

Was helping her for my own gain my start to being a villain?

Could I have done something different?

Part of his mind argued that what was done was done, but examining our past was how we planned our future. He knew that without doubt. He had been faced with a choice, and he couldn't help but think he'd made the wrong one.

How will I respond next time?

He wished he could lie and say he had a plan, but the truth was that he still couldn't say. Here he was safe. Here Ellie and Maggie were safe. They *looked* happy-ish. He had rolled the details over in his mind and had no clearer sense of what he should, could, would do differently if given the same choice today.

"I need to talk to you," Dan started. If he was going to try a relationship with Axell, surely he could talk about what he did.

What if he doesn't want you? a little voice asked. Self-doubt was his thing, his gift. *Maybe that's my magic? But how?*

Before Axell answered, Dan felt like something slithered over his entire body—something from outside him. Fear? Warning? Magic? He wasn't sure what it was, but he paused and looked around at the other students in the library. Every last one of them paused, glanced around, or tensed. Whatever it was, they'd all felt it.

"Daniel?" Axell reached a hand toward him, as if the urge to vanish was instinctive. The beautiful Norwegian singer had a musical magic, but he had a secondary ability to make them vanish if they were touching.

"I felt it." Dan stepped a bit farther out of reach. Louder he asked, "Everyone feel that?"

Murmurs greeted him. Their peculiar study group had become the basis for the first real group of friends he'd had in his life. Witches, all of them.

Headed his way was Ana, a rather terrifying grandmotherly woman when they'd met, but she'd been aging backward fast enough that it was easy to forget that she was twice his age. She now looked his age.

"Call one of your hob friends," she said.

"You're awfully pushy for such a young woman." He gave her a once-over, noting that a few more years had vanished from her face. "A nice girl like you . . ."

She chortled. Her long hair was ink black now instead of the gray it had been when they'd met a few weeks ago. Back then, she looked like a lot of grannies in the Southwestern states. That long hair was braided and twisted up in a graying bun, and her brown skin was lined with wrinkles. Her gaze was eerily observant both then and now, but now her skin was without line or scar. The magic that lived in all witches had clearly already changed her age.

"Still your elder, Daniel." Ana's voice was stronger, too. Magic agreed with her. "And something is wrong. I can't feel anything outside the castle."

"You could feel outside before now?" Axell asked from behind Dan's shoulder.

"Yes." She shrugged. "I am not meant for being inside, and the earth calls me. Just like everyone else in my house. Right, Silas?"

A beefy guy raised his hand in a thumbs-up gesture. "Not now that the thing slithered over the building. Like a bug net."

Bug net? Dan wasn't too keen on being compared to bugs.

Dominique, a typically quiet student, said, "I don't feel that, but there's someone very very sick in the infirmary. I feel that more and more." She glanced at Axell. "You are not well lately. I don't know why, though. It's like being itchy?"

Axell glanced away and crossed his arms over his chest.

"Did you bring *more* things in your bag?" Dan asked him quietly. Axell's near death had been from an overdose after a concert. He had, apparently, not coped particularly well with his success. The idea that he'd use again was baffling.

"Just a little that was in my pockets," Axell whispered.

"Seriously?" Dan glared. His voice grew louder. "And you *used* it?"

As much as he was astounded that the strikingly handsome man found

him attractive, Dan was equally cautious about their budding relationship. Axell was a rock star—if such words applied to men who courted
a Viking mystique. He had a long ponytail that was always bound by a
series of silver clips every few inches. The sides of his head were shaved
smooth enough that Dan often found himself absently stroking them.
Axell's beard was long and divided into several thick braids with more
metal clips.

But under the persona, under the muscles that Dan found painfully distracting, was a man who had a level of insecurity that rivaled
Dan's own. That was the root of the addiction that seemed to linger even
though it had almost killed him.

Apparently not all illnesses are healed by magic. Disability wasn't, and so
far mental illnesses like PTSD and addiction were untouched by magic.
What magic healed were the things like aging and diseases like cancer and
heart disease. *Guilt wasn't erased by magic, either.*

"You got a second chance, and you shoved a needle in your arm
again?" Dan whispered.

"Do not judge, Daniel. You are not free of mistakes," Axell muttered.

Does he know? Dan hadn't yet told him that he been party to erasing
the memories of two of their classmates. He'd not done so on his own or
even as his own idea, but still, he was guilty. Now, he awkwardly avoided
Ellie Brandeau and Maggie Lynch because of his actions. *They could've
been friends, but now . . . they don't even know my name.* He wasn't sure
what all had been erased, so it was easier to stay away from them.

"Should we head to our rooms?" Sam, another of the remedial witches,
asked from under their usual pile of wool. They had found a drop spindle
and somehow acquired a bag of wool. It seemed an odd hobby to Dan, but
Sam toted the spindle and wool around like it was an extension of their
body. Currently, they were doing something that looked like attacking the
wool with a pair of metal-toothed brushes.

Ana began, "Maybe someone ought to see the headmaster—"

"And what would that conversation look like?" the headmaster interrupted from behind Dan. He stood in the doorway, seemingly larger than normal. He was a former soldier and a brawler.

Sometimes, he was almost Dan's friend. Today didn't feel like such a day.

"We'd ask you why I suddenly can't feel nature," Ana said without missing a beat. "It feels like a fence or closed door between me and out there."

The headmaster let out a noise that was likely a muttered cuss word. Then he looked around the room. "That feeling was my magic. I put up a shield to keep you safe from harm. No outsider can enter the castle without eliminating the magic that controls it."

Sondre did not say that he was putting his own safety at risk, but if he was the source of that magic, Dan heard the truth all the same. The headmaster was standing between them and whatever dangers were outside Crenshaw Castle. Extension magic had been addressed in a book Dan read last Thursday.

Sondre added, "You are safe *within the castle*. You can gather in the common areas and continue to enjoy the library freely since you've found it, but no one leaves the castle until I tell you that it's safe. Please notify any witch you encounter."

"Safe?" Dan echoed. "Are we expecting to be under attack?"

"Perhaps, Mr. Monahan. The barrier that hides our world was taken down this morning." Sondre paused as murmurs rippled around the library.

"How?" Dan pressed. "And what does it mean?" The barrier was obviously another case of extension magic. "If the barrier fell, is Lord Scy—"

"Hush." Sondre pinched the bridge of his nose like he could chase a headache away. "It means that you all stay in the castle in case we can't get it fixed before *they* find Crenshaw." He made a summoning gesture at Dan. "It also means I need you in the infirmary to help Dr. Jemison."

"Can't Lord Scylla maintain the barrier?" Axell asked.

"Lord Scylla is in the infirmary," Sondre said. "Her house will do what they can." Sondre's gaze swept the room, and for a moment, Dan was relieved that this man was the one who would keep them safe.

"Don't test this rule," Sondre said, voice stern in a way that made every eye in the room fix on him. "Lord Scylla was gravely injured. In case you haven't heard rumors, there are factions in Crenshaw, and one of them just declared war."

"War?" someone echoed in a strained voice.

"If any of you are considering being siphoned, now is a good time to request that." Sondre glanced at Axell pointedly, and his gaze stayed there long enough that everyone had to notice. "Some of you could be siphoned easily.

"Others could not survive it." Sondre's gaze then fell on Sam, who shrugged as if this was of no interest. "Whatever you choose, know that you are safer in the castle than out of it."

Axell reached out and took Dan's hand. Quietly, he said, "I made a *mistake*, Daniel. I am not leaving here."

Dan squeezed his hand back. "I don't want you to leave." Despite both of their insecurities, Dan thought they had a shot at a real connection. "Stay with me, and—"

"Monahan," the headmaster called out. "Let's go. The rest of you ought to be in class, not frittering in the library. Go on."

To Dan's surprise, Axell wove his fingers between Dan's and said, "I go where you go."

The headmaster looked at their hands and shrugged. "He wants to fail classes, that's on him. However, he can't go inside the infirmary. Essential personnel only. That's you, Monahan, not your boyfriend."

That was all Sondre said, though. He pushed open the library door and marched down the hall. The headmaster was often gruff, but he was exceptionally so today. The thought of *war* made Dan shiver, but knowing that Sondre was what stood between the school and threat made that fear ebb somewhat. Whatever else anyone could say about the man, he was both brave and intimidating.

"We will protect our home," Axell said, keeping pace with Dan as they trailed after Sondre. "I will be here at your side."

Dan glanced at Axell's elbow. "No more of *that*? It's not in this world, so if that's what you want . . ."

"You're all the drug I need." Axell gave him a look that was far more pulse-quickening than he ought to be able to manage. "Say the word, and I'll show you."

Face burning, Dan looked away. It wasn't that he didn't want to cross that line, but every other man who'd been in his bed had been just a hookup. What if that was because he was disappointing? What if he was too skinny? Too sickly? Too boring? He wanted to be sure that whatever this was between them, it was real.

But Axell wasn't used to rejection.

If I say yes, will his interest end?

If I keep saying no, will it wane anyhow?

The thought of this world being in peril ought to have been Dan's only concern, but neither his heart nor other parts was willing to ignore the Norwegian dilemma at his side.

14
Ellie

"I can take us to where the barrier should be," Prospero said as they stood outside the chief witch's cabin.

The chief witch had slammed the door on them, as if they were a problem, and Ellie was debating whether or not it would be painfully unwise to knock on it to say something about what an ass he was being.

Ellie didn't like him, but she shoved that thought down. "I can't guarantee much of a fix on the barrier, but . . ." She shrugged. She couldn't craft illusions, but she could make other things. *Maybe this was what the prophecy meant? Is this the thing I do to save Crenshaw?* Prophecies were notoriously muddy things, and the specifics of the prophecy weren't things she had heard directly.

"Whatever you can manage to create, any sort of shield, is appreciated," Prospero said stiffly. She extended her hands toward Ellie. "May I?"

"Oh. Right." Ellie ignored the offered hands and wrapped her arms around Prospero's waist, taking the excuse to hold her tightly. "Let's go."

"You're very forward, Miss Brandeau," Prospero muttered, tensing as she did so.

So Ellie slid her hands down to rest on the curve of Prospero's bottom. "Nice of you to notice."

Prospero smiled, not quite a laugh, but it was something. The desire to protect her, ease her moods, be there for her was springing from something deep inside. Yes, they had a problem shoving them apart, but love overcame. Of that, Ellie was certain.

In the next moment, they were standing in the wooded space adjacent to the barrier, which was entirely absent. There were about twenty guards standing around, most of whom looked more tense than Ellie was used to seeing in Crenshaw. The sight of strangers raising weapons aimed at them made Ellie freeze.

Prospero turned so her back was to the guards. Loudly, she called, "We are here to patch the barrier."

"You don't need to always put yourself between me and whatever threats there are," Ellie said as quietly as she could.

"I always will, Ellie, as long as there is life in my body," Prospero swore. "I cannot be everything you want me to, but in this . . ." She lifted one shoulder in a shrug. "I will protect you."

What have I forgotten? Can I make *her tell me?*

Ellie looked beyond Prospero to the openness that was there. It was a step between this world and the rest of the world, as if there were some barrier like those that divided nations or states. There was nothing to mark it. No walls. No fences. Simply, on this side was the magical world, and over there was the start of somewhere mundane.

On the stretch of road immediately beyond the edge of Crenshaw was a truck that looked oddly familiar. Before Ellie could stop herself, she said, "Someone ought to have the transmission checked on that."

Prospero tensed so completely that Ellie felt as if she were embracing a statue. "Why?"

"I . . . don't know. I just remember the sound of gears grinding," Ellie said softly. "The jerk of it . . . Why do I know that?"

"Excellent question," Prospero muttered, turning her head and looking away.

"You weren't driving . . . when I was in the truck. I can't *see* who was. It wasn't you, though."

"Correct." Prospero pulled away again, stepping back three paces so Ellie couldn't reach her, and suggested, "If you can work on the barrier, let's do . . . that."

Her gaze dropped to a patch on the ground that was sludgy and dark, and for a moment, Ellie thought that it was a by-product of the rift until she noticed the way Prospero's eyes turned glassy and her jaw tightened.

"Is that blood?"

"Yes." Prospero walked away, as closed down as a person could be, and it occurred to Ellie that she was scared. Despite her ferocity and problem-solving persona, Prospero was afraid.

She gestured to the guards. "Miss Brandeau needs space to work. Take ten."

"Lady Pros—"

"You can stand between us and the town, but not between her and the"—she waved her hand awkwardly—"opening."

"If the escaped witches return," a guard began awkwardly, "you'll be in the line of fire."

Prospero sighed. "And do any of *you* want to be between me and one of the witches who shot Lord Scylla?"

"Not me," one woman said. "Give a call if you need us."

The guards retreated. As a group they stepped behind Ellie and Prospero, who marched closer to the edge of the magical world.

"Do you think they'll come back?" Ellie asked, trailing behind her, startled by how loud the crunch of sticks underfoot seemed in the empty woods. There was no wildlife anywhere, no birds, no small mammals in the trees, no serpents in the path, no frogs hidden under leaves.

"They haven't left." Prospero frowned. "They're back there." She looked toward the overgrown woods behind them. "I wasn't sure how your control was, and if there were more vast serpents in wait, I thought—"

"The escaped witches. Will they return?"

"On their own? No. When I find them? *Yes.*" Prospero paused. "When there is a death, the hobs handle the body. I assume I'll bring them back, and the hobs will handle the corpses."

Ellie shivered. "So, take no prisoners and all that?"

Prospero looked over her shoulder at her. "They shot Scylla." Then she gestured at the vast open space where Scylla's illusion ought to be. "They left all of us exposed, and if the nonmagical world discovers us, so many witches will die. . . . People are often not forgiving of difference. Ask women like us over the centuries. Ask Scylla about the racial violence she knew. Look at the religious intolerance."

Ellie swallowed. Murder seemed so final, so harsh. She could deal with some violence, but premeditated murder felt too far. Carefully, she said, "You're not *wrong* to be angry, but surely, they weren't *aiming* for that when they ripped down the barrier!"

Prospero leveled a stern look at Ellie. "Is not caring that your decisions harm others really any better?"

And Ellie couldn't help thinking of racist and homophobic mindsets, religious intolerance, cultural intolerance . . . hell, basic sexism . . . people who didn't care about the well-being of others. Hapless ignorance was still deadly for thousands upon thousands of people.

"No. It's really not better." Ellie stepped up to her side, caught Prospero's hand.

Prospero started to pull away, but Ellie held fast. They could both use a little comfort. "I'm sorry. You're right to be angry and worried. She was . . . *is* your friend."

"I knew there was danger coming, but I had no idea what. Cass had no useful prophecies. All she knew was that I had to stop it."

"You?" Ellie's voice was hardly a whisper.

"Or they die. Scylla. Walt. A lot of people. This is my problem, but I couldn't just . . . *attack* the enemy. I can't even find them, not in the billions of people there, unless they use their magic. I can't save Scylla, either. I am not a fucking healer." Prospero pressed her lips together, stopping the rush of words and pausing. "I am *useless,* but the gods-damned prophecy says I have to save them."

"We'll figure it out." Ellie touched her cheek. "We will."

"If I fail . . ." Prospero started quieter now. "This is our *haven,* our collective of misfits and rebels, dreamers and romantics. We have a peace here that doesn't happen everywhere. They've put all of it at risk."

"And you wonder why I want to make our marriage work?" Ellie murmured. "You're a romantic at heart, Prospero."

"Victorian, love."

Ellie clasped her hands to her chest, determined to pull her out of this mood. "And she makes jokes. . . . Is it any wonder I'm smitten?"

Prospero shook her head. "I suspect half the people who know me believe I've blackmailed you and the other half think I'm paying you."

"Well, then, the joke's on them. I *like* you, your heart and your charm, your loyalty and your mind. . . ." Ellie stared into Prospero's eyes. "Your strength. Courage."

Prospero said nothing, simply stared at her like she was at a loss for words.

So Ellie gave her a wicked grin. "Your lovely body is just icing, you know? I realize it's been . . . an issue, but it's not my only reason for wanting us to work out. You know that, right?"

"Yes."

"So let me in, please. *Tell me what you made me forget* because I know what I want." Ellie was coming to realize that she'd had more security than Prospero'd had in her life before magic.

It was easy to avoid the dangers of being out when you were single and straight-passing. She'd never *denied* who she was, but she hadn't exactly walked around with a woman on her arm most of the time.

And if I had, it would be in a safe space where people knew me and maybe whispered at the worst. It wouldn't be the 1800s or a modern country where being LGBTQIA+ was deadly.

Prospero had nearly died for being a lesbian.

"I know how I feel," Ellie said softly.

"Right now," Prospero finally said, sounding as formal as she occasionally could. "Unfortunately, if you knew of what I cannot say, of what you forgot, what I . . ."

"Fine."

"It is not fine; nothing is." Prospero sounded exhausted, as if the things before her were insurmountable.

"First, let me create a wall for Crenshaw. Then we tackle the rest. . . ." Ellie closed her eyes and pulled upon that space in her belly.

Magic didn't live in a specific organ. It wasn't in her heart or lungs or stomach, but it *felt* like it was in her low center, in some nebulous space she couldn't name properly. *The center of me.* Wherever it was properly housed, Ellie found that energy, feeling increasingly like her entire body was being shocked as she filled to the brim with the energy that was hers and added to it magic that was not hers.

"Is that *your* magic?" Ellie whispered to Prospero. "I can feel extra magic. Not mine."

"No . . . ?" Prospero whispered back. "I don't think it's me."

Something was giving her more energy than she ought to have. Ellie let it filter into her vision, that strange seeing without looking that seemed to accompany her acts of creation. She would use this magic to build a barricade.

"The barrier used to look like thorns, right?" Ellie could picture it, could picture walking past it, stepping through the illusion with another person. There were guards who were flopping on the ground.

How do I know that? It was a memory. She was certain of that much. It was part of what Prospero had stolen from her memories.

"Yes." Prospero's voice was a rough whisper at Ellie's side, but not reason enough for Ellie to open her eyes. "*What* extra magic, Ellie? I don't feel anything. Is someone else here?"

Ellie shook away the questions her memory raised. "I can see what ought to be here, what it should look like."

Then a childhood fairy tale came to the top of her consciousness. *Sleeping Beauty, surrounded by briars.* It was a satisfying image, and Ellie begin to magically tug at a few berry bushes she'd seen nearby. The roots of the berries burrowed under the soil until new shoots burst through the ground in green eruptions near the place where the illusory briars were missing.

"Taller," Prospero whispered. "Please?"

The thread of fear in her voice was enough for Ellie to tug again at that reservoir of magic that wasn't hers. She pulled it into her body and used it to weave thorns into a ten-foot wall. It wasn't solid. A person might be able to see glimpses through it.

And a saw or modern machine could tear it down.

Despite the wall of thorns that now squatted there, it was still possible now for someone to wander into Crenshaw, but not accidentally. To come into their home would require tools and concentrated effort—but it wasn't quite enough. Ellie saw several pebbles in her mind's eye, and she pulled them across the soil. As she pulled them, she felt like she heard as much as felt the earth shaking. Her body trembled.

"I have you," Prospero assured her. She moved so she was behind Ellie, the familiar warmth of her pressed to Ellie's back. Her arms wrapped around Ellie, steadying her. "I'm right here, love."

But Ellie couldn't comment yet. She pulled on her magical well again, using the energy inside to force pebbles and stones into a conglomerate boulder that was far from pretty—or natural. It held together, though, as if heat melted it. *Like cookie dough with chocolate chips and fruit inside.* Ellie smiled as she turned the stones into a person-sized rock.

Then Ellie opened her eyes to gaze upon the thorn wall she'd constructed. "No one can get in or out without teleportation."

Prospero half released Ellie and stepped forward, so they were side by side now. "Thank you."

"It's my home, too," Ellie said dismissively. She didn't know how to say "I want to protect *you*" without frightening Prospero further away from her, so she kept the words inside for now.

Prospero stared at her, as if seeking injury or wobble. "Are you . . . well?"

"You mean, am I about to fall into a coma-like sleep like I usually do when I make larger things?" Ellie asked. "*No.* I'm not sure why . . . but it was like I had all this extra magic to . . . make stuff. I feel amazing."

The guards had returned and were staring at Ellie like she was something horrifying. Hob after hob after hob popped into existence in the woods, and as Ellie stared at them she knew exactly where the magic had originated.

Prospero took several steps away again, peering at her curiously and then staring at the stoic faces of at least a dozen hobs. Clancy from the castle was there. Bernice was, too. So was Grish, the hob who had answered the chief witch's door. They stared at her.

Their magic was what I felt!

Ellie curtsied. She wasn't entirely sure of the protocol for thanking someone for sharing magic. The guards were watching both witches and hobs.

"I couldn't have done that"—she gestured at the barricade—"without you."

The hobs smiled, as if they were of one mind, and in that moment Ellie was vaguely unsettled by their attention.

"Was that what I needed to do? Why I'm here?" she asked, because she had an ongoing suspicion that the hobs were plugged into everything that happened in Crenshaw.

"Crenshaw witches and their magic should stay in the place we built for magic," an unfamiliar hob, wizened and tinier than the others, pronounced. "Your magic is useful in keeping magic here."

It wasn't an answer, not wholly, but Ellie still felt a little better hearing the words of approval. Then each hob nodded at her and Prospero and popped away. In a few moments, they were alone at her newly made barrier with the guards.

Ellie looked at the guards, who were watching her with expressions ranging from fear to curiosity.

"No one is to come in or out," Prospero said, drawing every gaze to her. Once the guards reiterated that they were aware of the rules, Prospero extended a hand to Ellie. "Send me a message by hob if there are more attacks."

"And remember that thorns won't stop *bullets* if they return," Ellie added hastily.

15

Sondre

The sight of Scylla motionless on the infirmary cot twisted something in Sondre's stomach. Scylla wasn't his friend, but she was the force that kept their world safe from discovery.

And they shot her.

He had to be ready to go after the people he'd wrongly thought were trustworthy. *I have been a villain all along. Not a revolutionary. A monster.* He motioned Monahan forward.

"You—" He paused and pointed at Axell. "—wait out here or go somewhere else. Stay away from the infirmary door." He wasn't a bad person, as far as Sondre could tell, but he was troubled. Sondre gave the musician his most intimidating look. He had recommended him for siphoning. The problem was that he had enough magic to stay, and he was a "death risk" if he went back.

Which shouldn't be a factor in our decision, Sondre grumbled mentally.

"Come on." Sondre gestured to the door.

"I'm ready. What do I do?" Dan asked, visibly straightening himself as if he were about to walk into conflict. He might be the size of a sapling, but the boy had courage.

Sondre couldn't do much else right now other than worry and grumble, so he could wait here for a minute.

Get the boy settled.

Check on Scylla.

Report to Congress.

Maintain the fortification over the school.

Handling the infirmary is the easiest thing on the list; that's the only reason I'm staying, Sondre lied to himself briefly. But the lie felt heavy in his skin, as if the act of telling himself such things was akin to eating spoiled food.

Sondre pushed open the door and motioned Dan forward.

"I brought the amplifier," Sondre called out to the healers inside. But instead of going inside, he let the door fall shut behind Dan, creating a moment of privacy outside the infirmary with Axell.

Once Dan was doing what he must on the other side of the door, Sondre stared at Axell for several moments. Objectively, the musician was handsome, but there were a lot of handsome men Dan could get to know.

"If you jab another needle in your veins, I'll call in a favor to have you sent back," Sondre said.

"I have enough magic to stay." Axell pushed off the wall and glared back at him.

"And I have enough authority to make your magical levels not matter." Sondre prodded the other man in the fold of his elbow, where recent needle bruising was obvious.

Sondre didn't mention that there *were* drugs in Crenshaw. He considered it. He considered letting Axell know and letting the obvious thing happen. They used to try to keep the drugs out, but Aggie—who had been head of House Grendel—and most everyone else had been focused on bigger concerns of late.

"If you're chasing a high, you don't belong here. You don't deserve the magic in you. If that's what you want, be siphoned and go. Don't destroy Dan along the way," Sondre said pointedly in his chilliest voice.

Axell said nothing. After a moment of silent glaring, he turned and walked away.

Sondre sighed. It wasn't that he didn't understand the occasional race toward danger or dangerous bliss. He'd been on that route himself—not with needles but with violence. No one could change a person's self-destructive tendencies, but Sondre thought Dan had enough challenges without adding this one.

And I feel brotherly toward him.

He watched Axell walk away before he shoved the door open to see what solution the doctors had inside now that they had Dan's amplification to factor into their plans. He paused, magically sealing the door behind him. Logic said all the attackers were gone to the Barbarian Lands, but Sondre wasn't sure what other secrets the New Economists had kept from him.

Are there dangerous people still here?

Are more attacks forthcoming?

Not everyone had left. There were too many of them. *Were the others like me? Not wholly committed. Or are they here like snakes in the grass?* Caution seemed the wiser path right now. Door secured, Sondre looked around the infirmary. The shelves were orderly; sparkling vials sat in racks; ceramic pots were lined in rows. Several glass-doored cabinets had devices in them, and a basket of bandages sat where it usually did on a countertop.

He paused at the sight of the prone body of one of the strongest witches in Crenshaw. Scylla was still enough that he had to watch to see her chest rise and fall before he could look away. She had often been his opposition in matters before the Congress of Magic, but Sondre was man enough to admit that he was likely the one in the wrong on a lot of those matters. She didn't deserve this.

Did anyone? he wondered. He'd taken lives. *Was that right? Did war justify it?* He'd spent plenty of time asking that question in the dark hours when booze left him maudlin.

Did Aggie deserve it? That question was a bit more pointed. There was no way that Prospero's rage was going to be easily dismissed, and if it had been someone he counted as family—if it were Maggie or Craig—would he feel any less vengeful? That wasn't a question he felt adept to answer. Not now. He'd have to, though, because he was the witch who went to that world with Prospero. He was also the witch in line to replace Aggie as head of house.

Sondre shoved those thoughts away and focused on this minute, this place.

Several healers were scurrying around Scylla as Sondre looked on. To Scylla's side was the witch he'd wronged more than once in his years in Crenshaw. Mae Jemison was motionless. Like Scylla, her chest rose and fell as she reclined, unconscious, mere feet away from the witch whose life she'd saved.

"Does the doctor need us to do anything for her?" Dan asked one of the healers.

Before anyone else could answer, Sondre spoke. "She's exhausted, so her magic is simply healing her. Like a lake refilling after a drought."

"Poetic," Dan said, not unkindly.

"Mmm." Sondre wasn't sure what else to say, so a muffled noise was the best he could do. "Let her rest. She's more than earned it."

"And Lord Scylla hasn't?" someone asked.

"Yes, of course, she has, but as long as she sleeps, our whole world is vulnerable to exposure." Sondre folded his arms over his chest. "Ask her if she agrees with me when she wakes. I have a strong suspicion that she will—and that Mae will give me hell for suggesting she be allowed to recover naturally."

One of the healers snorted. "It'll be a strange day if you and Lord Scylla agree."

"Lord Scylla's priority is Crenshaw. So's mine." Sondre's gaze swept the room, noting who was there and who wasn't. These were Mae's people, so the witches on the cots were safe in their care. He knew that, but he still wanted to be sure of who they were.

Just in case.

He'd never imagined that Aggie would try to kill Scylla, either. He looked from eye to eye and said, "With the barrier down, we will both want the same thing, and Mae will likely need to tend more witches soon enough. Let her rest."

Dan put a hand on a healer's shoulder and stood silently as the man started to examine Scylla, scanning for more injuries in her body. Ripples of magic rolled over the room like a small thunderstorm in too small of a space as they examined her.

"Small tear in her lungs," the healer muttered after several tense moments. "Deflating air sac. That's still not mending. I stitched it again and vacuumed the blood. . . ."

Sondre looked away as blood bubbled up and spilled from Scylla's lips. It seemed wrong to see her brought low, and even though he'd been a witch for more than half a century, seeing blood pushing out of her mouth and nostrils made him flinch.

He snatched a clean cloth and wiped it away. "She doesn't need it on her face like that."

Before anyone could reply, a thunking at the door had him spin and think about possible attacks. The healers and Dan all paused, looking to him for direction.

Sondre made a "back up" motion, so everyone but one healer and Monahan moved behind him. The healer looked at him, shook his head once, and went back to whatever he was doing with Scylla.

At that, Sondre nodded at the man and then turned his attention to the door. He felt in one of his pockets for spell-loaded stones. He had several. He *always* had several, as well as assorted weapons hidden in pockets of his robes.

He wouldn't say the military propaganda he'd once believed was true.

There's no honor in ending lives. He would own the truth, though, that some causes led to wars. The senseless genocide in World War II when Sondre had been a kid was cause for military action, but to draw weapons over an opinion? It was ludicrous.

Flashes of being on the wrong side of a gun threatened to rise up in Sondre. The time he spent in combat in Korea was long enough ago that it ought to be nothing more than foggy memories, and most days it was just that. There were exceptions, though. Seeing Scylla was turning out to be one of them.

"Open the damn door, or I'll remove it," a familiar cranky voice called.

And Sondre felt the rising tension settle back into his bones. The chief witch was a pain in the ass at the best of times, but he wasn't a threat.

Unless he's here to badger me for being a part of the now-obviously trai-torous group of witches. . . .

Sondre wouldn't say he didn't deserve it. He'd been conspiring for the downfall of Crenshaw, participated in the planning to create panic and force the witches to move to the Barbarian Lands. He hadn't done this latest thing, but he was not innocent, either.

"Sondre!" Walt called, the summons in time with what sounded like a booted foot against the door. "Get yourself out here. You're not a healer. What do you expect to do? Stand around and guard them?"

Badgering may be sooner than I expected. Sondre hoped his new wife would let him stay with her. Most badgers lived rough, like the animals they resembled, but the thought of that made Sondre want to run.

Bracing for a sudden shift in height and a coat of fur wasn't high on Sondre's list of plans for the day—or ever—but if Prospero had told Walt what she knew, Sondre would have to face consequences. There was little chance of avoiding his fate.

He stepped out of the infirmary and looked down at the chief witch. "Walt."

"House Grendel needs a new head of house," Walt said without pre-amble. "You're next in line."

"Me?" Sondre blinked, half thinking that he was imagining things or misunderstanding. He'd thought about that, but he was guilty of conspiracy. Surely, they'd skip over him.

"No, the unconscious witches inside the room. Yes, *you*. Is there a problem with that?" Walt tugged on his rather inflated beard, a habit that served as a good metric for how his day was going. Based on the size of the cloud under his chin, Walt had been having a day that rivaled Sondre's right now.

"Err, you *do* realize that I have stood with the New Economists for years," Sondre said, feeling like he ought to confess to the obvious at the least. He stood staring at the older Scotsman and hoping his "*are you mad, man?*" expression was better hidden than it felt. Carefully, Sondre added, "And I am the current headmaster and—"

"You like running the school, now?" Walt scoffed.

"I don't know, but—"

"So someone else can do this. We can't have a house-head spot vacant, and Aggie's screwed up too much to survive this retrieval." Walt sighed, gaze flitting away. "We can't go around Crenshaw with *guns,* of all things." He sighed and muttered, "Guns in citizens' hands here in Crenshaw? What's the world coming to if we allow that?"

Sondre looked back at the infirmary door. Whatever all they'd disagreed on, he'd have never shot Lord Scylla. Fought with her? Brawled with her? They'd done plenty of that over the last few decades. The woman had a dirty fighting style that had landed him in the infirmary a few times.

"You can't up and shoot a person because you disagree with them," Sondre said.

"Exactly." Walt eyed him. "You still have the stones for the house of justice?"

"My *stones* are just fine, Walt. Feel free to ask the missus," Sondre said dryly.

Walt guffawed. "Might just do that next time I see her."

"I want consent to let the boy move between worlds," Sondre announced. *Now's as good a time as any.* "He can't be the only teenager in Crenshaw. He has no peers at all."

"Should've thought of that before you brought him here," Walt pointed out. "Is the woman aware that he likely has latent magic?"

"Maggie. She has a name, Walt. I think she hopes it, but . . . no." Sondre squirmed at the thought of that conversation.

"You know the only reason I didn't punish you for bringing the boy here is because I knew that she'd be able to tame you," Walt said. "I was sick of you working with those dumbasses. You're smarter than that. They exploited your restlessness."

Sondre paused. "So you did what?"

"Decided to keep the chit here for you and as a friend to that hellacious Brandeau woman." Walt looked at him like he was spoiling for a fight.

"She could be siphoned." Sondre was asking as much as stating it.

"Brandeau? N—"

"Walt," Sondre cut him off. "Maggie."

"Could? Yes."

"Then why not let her *and* Craig go back?" Sondre stared at him with a new level of awareness, one he wasn't sure he wanted to have.

"Well, then, how would I control you? Threaten Brandeau?" Walt shook his head and then raised one finger to point at Sondre. "Politics means leverage. I had none on you. Now? I do."

"Your word that Craig can go back," Sondre demanded. "I'll lie to her and say we can all be siphoned if that's what it takes to keep them safe."

"Fine. The boy can go. She stays. That's the deal. And you will go with Prospero to hunt the escapees when the time comes," Walt ordered, pulling Sondre back into the *now* crisis. "Together you're a formidable team."

Walt flinched a little as he mentioned hunting, but it was the right word for what was inevitable now. Scylla was Prospero's friend; Crenshaw was her home. The New Economists who fled had endangered everything dear to Prospero. *Except Brandeau.* If that one was under threat, too? Someone would be tasked with sedating the Victorian witch. *And I can't blame her. Not right now. Not at all if I'm honest.*

Walt tugged on his frothy beard again. "She's always been right about this, you know. Magic unleashed over there will cause problems. Try not to die. I don't want to figure out another new house head for Grendel."

"But when I'm not with her over there—"

"Yes, yes, get the boy settled." Walt gestured as if he were waving away a bad smell. Then the old witch turned and marched off through the hallway, muttering something about "boils on bottoms" that Sondre was fine not hearing.

16

Maggie

"Do you know where the headmaster is?" Maggie asked one of the assorted castle hobs. This one stared out of a tall window with a portrait of several witches in medieval garb. The characters in the stained glass shifted every so often, as if they were restless. All the while, the levitating hob stared into the distance.

"Excuse me?" Maggie tried again.

"Dark days," the hob muttered. He looked down at her. "Do you like being a witch, Margaret Lynch?"

Maggie paused. It was an odd feeling to be called by her full name, especially with such a loaded question. *Do I?* She liked parts of it, but there were issues. Her lack of memory, her worry over her son, her sense that the man she was married to was not *really* her spouse . . .

"It's better than dying in the accident," she said bluntly. "Do I *like* it? Parts of it, but I miss my career. I miss mattering. I miss music. Things here aren't perfect, but it's generally good in a lot of ways, too."

The hob nodded. "I am Norton."

"Norton," she echoed. "Are you okay?"

"No. I don't think I am." The hob sighed, glancing back out the window. "But Crenshaw will right itself. Order is like that."

For a moment Maggie wasn't sure what to say. The hobs were friendly-ish, but they had their own society and enforced a sort of line between themselves and witches. Sometimes, she could believe that there were only a few hobs around, but the hobs seemed to have multiplied today, like a nest of the tiny beings had burst from within the castle walls. They were everywhere.

"Can I help?" she asked carefully, thinking back to reluctant witnesses and trembling victims.

"Are you a rule follower, Margaret Lynch?" The hob seemed to stare into her, seeing things that she couldn't always conceal as well as she tried. "In your heart of hearts?"

"Not really."

"Be who you are, then. That's why you're a witch." The hob shook his head. "Break the rules they use to bind you. It's that or . . . despair."

Maggie's heart twinged. Sometimes, she thought she'd never learn to deal with desperate people, and right now, the hob in front of her was one of many she'd met in her life *before* Crenshaw and *within* Crenshaw. She reached out, as if to touch the hob's arm. Her hand was too big, though, so she extended two fingers and rested them on his arm.

Norton looked back at her. "We only want witches to be happy, safe, *here*."

"I don't like all of it, but I am grateful for it. For Crenshaw. For a safe place to raise my son and . . . a long life." Maggie wasn't lying. One couldn't lie to a hob or a witch very successfully. "Does that make sense?"

"It does. Grateful is good to hear." Norton patted her wrist. "Smart witch. You need to help them. The maker and the singer."

"The *who*?"

"You'll figure it out, Maggie. Break the rules, and help." Then he smiled. "You seek the headmasher, no?"

"I do."

"Walk toward the sick," Norton said, nodding toward the passage near the staircase to the lower levels where the infirmary was. "He is there now."

A thread of jealousy threatened to creep up at the thought of Sondre there with the doctor. They had history, and she was gorgeous. *He picked me, though. He's happy with me.*

The words she reminded herself with seemed hollow, but there was nothing to do. She could either cope with her moments of jealous possessiveness or she could let them poison their burgeoning romance. She vowed not to become that person, bitter and suspicious, but even as she lectured herself, she walked just a little bit faster.

When she rounded a corner, she saw him. He looked more like a warrior than a scholar, and she was grateful that he was both brawny and brilliant. *And all mine.* He smiled when he saw her, and that look, that unfiltered joy and hunger, told her everything there was to know. She had no reason to doubt his interest.

She did have reason to doubt his state of mind. He looked like he'd just been through a wringer. Maggie wasn't expecting to find her husband looking so harried, but she also wasn't expecting the rush of relief she felt upon finding him. It was as if a tight cord inside her loosened just enough that her lungs could expand the whole way.

Ask the doctor about magical anxiety medicine.

As she watched Sondre stride through the castle hall, she realized that a part of her new life here that she was not expecting was the nonstop worry over him, over Craig, over the bad-air problem, over her forgetfulness, over the general sense that everything could fall apart at any moment, and she'd be helpless to resist.

"Are you okay?" he asked as he reached her side.

"Ish. That can wait, though." Maggie stared up at his face. "What happened? You look . . . shaken."

Sondre paused before saying, "I'm starting to think I'm transparent. What makes you think something happened?"

"You were scowling to yourself, and you didn't notice me immediately." Her cheeks felt hot at the latter part of her answer, but it was true. Sondre noticed her the way a hungry person noticed a surprise dessert.

"Aggie and Allan tore down the barrier protecting Crenshaw from discovery. Scylla and M— *Dr. Jemison*—" He corrected himself awkwardly. "—are unconscious. Prospero and I need to go after the witches responsible once they start spilling magic, although she already dragged one back, and I'm supposed to become the head of House Grendel to replace Aggie."

Maggie's mouth dropped open as she listened, but when Sondre's litany of stresses paused, she stepped closer and wrapped her arms around him. "Well, fuck."

He chuckled. "Exactly."

"What do you need?" she asked from the comfort of his tight embrace.

"To make sure you and Craig are safe. I can handle the rest, but I want to be sure you're both safe." He sighed, his exhalation stirring her hair. "I talked to the chief witch about Craig's situation."

Maggie leaned back so she could meet Sondre's gaze. "He doesn't belong here. I know it."

"Maybe one day . . ."

"If he has a near-fatal accident? What sort of mother wishes for *that*?" Maggie hated feeling like the two best things in her life were at odds. "He either goes back to where he's not safe or he stays where he's not safe. What choice am I to make?"

"Prospero can erase memories." Sondre gave her a pointed look. "What if people there thought he was *not* yours or your ex-husband's child?"

"Like witness protection?"

"Yes. Some witches have needed that."

Maggie looked at Sondre. "Would I go with him?"

"I don't think the Congress will agree to that. They didn't the first time you asked." Sondre stared at her as he admitted that last bit. He'd broken rules to tell her some of what she'd forgotten—but not everything.

"Sondre . . ." She wanted to tell him about the hob, about the admonishment to break the rules, but something inside held her back.

What if he's not trustworthy? her lawyer voice whispered.

"Where would Craig go?" she asked aloud.

Sondre released his hold on her. "He could live with someone trusted . . . but visit you here. The Brandeau woman—"

"*Ellie?*" Maggie hated thinking that the one person she was not to speak to would raise her son in his teen years. *I should seek her out. Break that rule.*

"No. Her aunt. Hestia."

"Would I be a bad mother?" Maggie half whispered. She didn't want to be apart from her son, but she couldn't live *with* him without making him miserable. "Would it be better to try to be siphoned and go—"

"They will not siphon you. I asked." Sondre stared at her, face twisting in some unnamed emotion.

"You asked?" Maggie echoed. "Do you want me to g—"

"No!" Sondre swallowed. "I want you to be happy. They admitted they were keeping you here to have leverage . . . on me and on Brandeau."

"On you?"

Sondre squirmed. "They apparently knew that I . . . that we . . ."

"Fucked?" she filled in.

"Had feelings," Sondre corrected firmly.

Maggie felt a warm rush of affection. *He cared enough that they thought I would be leverage.* That thought was followed closely by a bubble of rage. *So they trapped me, endangered my son, and now . . .*

Sondre had resumed talking about Craig. "You can see him sometimes, giving him the chance at a mostly normal life and future, or you can keep him here where he is in peril and unhappy, *but* you are with him."

Maggie felt tears threaten. There was no good answer. One path would make her happier, but going to the regular world and having a normal life would make her son happier. "It's like going off to college, I guess. I'd get holidays? And he'd be hidden from Leon?"

"Yes." Sondre wiped a tear away from her cheek. "My vow on that. I made the Congress swear they'll place him out of Leon's reach and let him move back to the Barbarian Lands."

"I'll ask Craig what he wants," Maggie offered. "I made the choice to bring him here—"

"To protect him from his murderous father," Sondre reminded her.

Tears flowed faster. "Leon wanted custody. Then he tried to kill us. Then I got trapped here. I remember all those parts, you know." She gestured around her. "And *here* is deadly to him. Sometimes I feel like all I do is try to protect my son."

"He'd be safer, and you could . . . hopefully enjoy being here with me. I'm not so bad, am I?" Sondre gave her a small smile. "A fair consolation prize since you're trapped here?"

Maggie laughed even though she was crying over her son's likely departure. She wrapped her arms around Sondre tightly. "You're the best part of being a witch." She rested her face against him and whispered, "Is this a done deal? My actions won't change it?"

"Yes . . ." Sondre stepped back slightly. "What's going on?"

She offered a watery smile. "Trust me . . . ?"

"I do, but—"

"This whole meek-and-obedient thing? Not really me. I will play by whatever rules I must to keep my son safe. I stayed compliant with Leon, gave up my career, accepted the 'ask no questions' mandate here in Crenshaw . . ." She made a noise that was half laugh, half snort. "My son has always been the only way to have power over me, but I'm not terribly pleased that they decided to use me as a pawn."

"Worrying me a little," Sondre muttered.

"Good. I remember enough to know you didn't fall for a dishrag,

Sondre." Maggie paused and grinned at him. "But if the chief witch thinks he has turned me into one, he's going to be surprised. I have questions. Brandeau does, too."

"Ellie," Sondre corrected. "You called her Ellie. You were friends."

"I know. We escaped together, but . . . you *telling* me that isn't enough. You *telling* me you helped feels true, but I want the whole truth. And you weren't with me."

"Because being siphoned would kill me," he pointed out.

"Not blaming you. We barely knew each other, and as much as I think we could be the second-best thing that's happened to me . . . I need the answers. I get it if you want to distance yourself from me, but I'm—"

He kissed her, stopping her words with the sort of passion that left her shivering. "Be who you are. I'll still be right here. I made them swear Craig will be safe, but that doesn't guarantee anything for *you.*"

"Good. A hob told me to break some rules, so . . ." Maggie felt a weight slide off her shoulders. "I'll be subtle until Craig is settled. After that, all bets are off."

Sondre nodded once, but worry still pulled at his expression. "I'm not going to ask."

"Probably a smart move." She leaned up and brushed a kiss over his lips before she pivoted and headed toward her room. She had plans to make.

17
Dan

After a few hours of aiding the healers, Dan felt like a wrung-out rag. He called, "Clance?"

The little hob popped into the infirmary and looked at Dan with a proud smile. "You did well."

"Thanks." Dan yawned and slid down to the floor. By the time Dan had done what he could to boost the healer's energy, he felt like a toy that needed to be rewound. Whatever spring kept a person upright was *un*sprung. He sat on a heap on the floor of the infirmary, head tilted back onto a shelf that was as comfortable as bamboo sheets and feather-filled pillows just then.

"I need the headmaster to let me out," Dan told Clancy. "I could sleep on the floor or an empty cot, but I don't want to."

The hob left with a pop, and Dan debated just taking a little nap.

Dr. Jemison was awake-ish now, and she was standing in the position favored by drunks, fighters, and people trying to get their sea legs. Her feet were wide apart, and she stared down at Lord Scylla as if reading things that Dan couldn't see. He was completely inept at healing magic, as well as—so far—mind magic, illusion, fabrication, music, and fighting.

The doctor, obviously, could read things through her magic that seemed to be the equivalent of a myriad of machines in ordinary hospitals.

"Her blood pressure is still off, and her breathing is not clear yet. Her blood levels need refreshing . . . and there's a minor infection near her stomach we need to remove, but she's going to live," Dr. Jemison said, standing with increasing wobbliness beside Lord Scylla's bed. "She ought to be awake, though. Why isn't she awake?"

The doctor yawned widely, her own magic obviously further drained by checking the patient over again.

"And why are *you* awake, Mae?" the headmaster said from the doorway.

"Because healing people is my job," Dr. Jemison said with a smile. "Lucas lent me his energy so I could focus for a few moments."

"They're capable, Mae. And Monahan—"

"Is also half-asleep," Dr. Jemison finished. "I know my limits."

"And chose to ignore them," Sondre scolded her. The way he looked at the doctor was more protective than a married man ought to look at someone not his wife.

Protective isn't the same as lustful, Dan reminded himself.

He currently felt a little possessive-protective over the doctor, and she was 100 percent not his type. Some guys took a side detour on that side to try to convince themselves that they were able to be straight. Dan wasn't one of them. He was gold-star gay. If there was an official card, he'd carry it. He had no issue with men who'd tried out the other side— *like Axell*—or even crossed the line regularly. Some people had distinct biphobia, but Dan didn't. *However,* he had never had a bodily reaction to a woman. Ever. It was unnerving.

"Are you okay?" Sondre asked, crouching down in front of Dan.

"She's weirdly pretty right now," Dan announced. "I don't like lady bits, but her"—he gestured across his own chest—"chest is pretty. Why? *Why?* I don't *like* girl chests, Sondre. These thoughts are weird."

"They're not yours, Dan. It's because you were boosting a healer who feels that way toward her." Sondre looked around the room, even as the other healers pointedly did not look at him or at Dr. Jemison.

And Dan couldn't pinpoint which one it was. He'd boosted several of them.

"Someone in the room thinks you're a goddess," Dan volunteered with a slurred voice. Exhaustion had left him no better than drunk. He'd felt that way during medical treatments, but not from magical overuse until now. He yawned. "I'm glad it's not me, though. So so glad. That would be awkward."

The doctor laughed softly. "Especially as I'll need you here to boost Scylla's magic tomorrow, Mr. Monahan. She should be able to get the barrier back up if Prospero goes into her mind and you boost it. I think if she's able to do that . . ." The doctor yawned. "I'll explain tomorrow."

"We'll take shifts watching Lord Scylla," a woman with eerily bright eyes and ghost-pale skin offered. "Xavier and I . . . I mean . . ."

Xavier, a quiet Black man, lifted a hand with a thumb up. "On it, Mae."

"Me too," offered a white woman currently reclined on a stretcher with a rag over her face. Her short brown hair stuck up at odd angles. "I'm not going first, though."

"Dominique, one of my friends . . . she's going to be in your house," Dan offered. "Maybe she could help, too. On-the-job training or whatever."

"I'll send a hob to fetch her," Sondre said. "They're opening the rest of the rooms in the castle. We've been vulnerable moving people in. Giving them a chance to be siphoned and sent back—or to stay here for now. Your healers can have a room to rest in, and I can assign a hob to transport them in and out without unbarricading the door."

"All because of Scylla?" Dr. Jemison asked.

Sondre nodded. "Safety measures assigned by the new head of House Grendel." He squirmed slightly. "The former House Grendel head was the one who . . ."

"Tried to kill Scylla," Dan supplied when no one else did. "Who's the new house head?"

"Sondre is," the doctor said in a quiet voice. "Will you be going after Aggie?"

"Eventually. Until there's a new headmaster, I need to stay here in the castle as headmaster, too, and my family will stay here while I'm over there." He looked at all of them. "I need three healers on staff at all times, Mae. You have to get rested in case there are injuries—"

"You will not get injured," the doctor said. "Do you hear me?"

"I will do my best." He squirmed. "If I don't succeed, can you . . . would you . . ."

"If you don't return, I'll look after Margaret and the boy." The doctor gave him an unreadable look, and Dan wished that he were already outside the room instead of witnessing their awkward conversation.

"Thank you." Sondre sighed deeply, before he turned to leave.

But Dr. Jemison asked, "Are you going with Prospero?"

"I am. She has the wherewithal to do what needs to be done," Sondre said in a tense voice. He didn't glance back at her, at any of them.

"Kill them, you mean." The doctor sounded increasingly upset.

Sondre turned around. "Mae . . . I know you heal, but this may not involve you. If they survive, I will try to bring them back to be siphoned—"

"Which will also kill them," the doctor rebutted.

"Probably. I can insist it's done when you're in attendance in case Aggie can be saved. In case any of them can, but justice must be served." Sondre glared at her, and Dan felt like his parents were fighting. It was a peculiar feeling, but he had a bit of hero worship over Sondre, and the doctor had saved him.

Literally, she *cured his cancer.* So he thought she could do no wrong.

Dan cleared his throat loudly. "So, kids, I'm going to bed. There's a lot of tension in here, and I need my battery-recharging time or whatevs." He looked at Dr. Jemison. "Glad you're not dead, doc." Then he looked at Sondre. "And congrats on the new job. Don't die."

Then he stood, stretched, and walked to the door. At first, it didn't budge, but after a weird ripple of magic, the door opened, and Dan strode out of the room.

Sometimes living here felt weirder than he thought he could manage to unravel. Small town where everyone lived for centuries? More drama than he had anticipated at first. It made sense because there were a limited number of people and a lot of them worked in close quarters. *And magic seems to screw with self-control.* That was the part no one had said out loud, but he was fairly sure it was a fact.

The infirmary door flapped closed behind him, and Dan exhaled.

A hob appeared, standing atop a suit of armor around the corner. *Not Clancy.* Dan had no idea which hob it was. The tiny man put a finger to his lips and gestured for Dan to follow him.

"Man, I just want to sleep. Do you have any idea how tired I am?" Dan grumbled, but he still went in the direction of the hob, who was now standing under a giant stained-glass window. Since his arrival here, "follow the hob" had always been a good idea. For whatever reason, they all seemed to take a liking to him, and so if a hob gestured for him to follow in any way, Dan obeyed.

By the time Dan reached the window, the hob had vanished again.

Dan looked around, not seeing any hobs. He turned a corner, looking from side to side. There at the end of the hall was a door—and the hob.

The hob pointed at it, and then he vanished.

By the time Dan reached the door, he had started to think about the horrors that could lurk behind the door. He'd never been led astray by a hob, but Sondre was being supercautious and talking about war and everything felt precarious today.

I can trust the hobs, he reminded himself.

Dan still thought that this world was amazing, but there were definitely some downsides he hadn't expected to find.

In fairness, he thought, *did I ever expect to find a magical world?*

There was no way to love fantasy books and franchises as much as he did and not at least imagine it, but that was just fanciful dreaming. It wasn't an expectation. Now that he was here, living in a castle, able to do actual magic, he couldn't imagine any other future. He felt like he was *home.* It was that feeling he realized now that he'd chased his entire life. He suspected it was why people switched careers, moved, dated serially . . . the urge to find that *click* drove people, and he was no exception.

"Whatever's in here, I'll deal with it," he muttered as he pushed the door open cautiously.

Inside, the room was lit by candles, and a small wooden table was heaped with an odd assortment of food. On the side of the room farthest away from the door, in the darkest shadows where the candlelight only barely touched, was Axell.

"Daniel." He didn't stand in greeting, and it was obvious that he had taken a moment to create the whole scene. It was all about enticement, from the inviting way he was sprawled on a love seat—one arm across the back as if inviting a person to fall into a waiting embrace—to the choices of the food on the table to the candles casting a calming light across the room.

"Hi." Dan shut the door and turned the oversized key in the lock. Sure, people could teleport from place to place, but they needed to *know* where they were going, so the likelihood was that a locked door was enough to assure privacy.

"I thought you might be hungry," Axell said mildly, as if the word was only literal, but Dan knew well enough that there were other offers in that word. With him, there always were.

"How . . . ?" Dan gestured around the room.

Axell lifted one shoulder in a shrug. "I had time and wanted to do something special for you."

"Why?" Dan caught and held his gaze, even though the shadows made it harder to do so. "Why do all this?"

"I *like* you." Axell shrugged again. "You need to have food . . . and the last time you went with the headmaster you came back very sad."

Dan looked away. He hadn't told Axell everything. He couldn't tell Axell for his own safety, and Axell's, too. "This was easier than that. I just had to boost the energy of the healers."

"No helping the scary witch erase memories?"

Dan gaped at him. "I . . . we . . . I never said that!"

"Ellie and Maggie both have memory holes. They're both *married* now." Axell shook his head. "You think I am stupid because I am a singer? Just a stupid musician?"

"No!"

"Maggie no longer remembers her anger with you," Axell pointed out. "She is here thinking headmaster is a good man. They had sex before, but then Maggie was angry. And now, Ellie follows the scary witch like a sad woman. Before she was not this eager to be with her."

Dan *shushed* him. "What if someone hears you? Stop. Stop saying these things."

Axell stood and crossed the room. "*You* did this thing for them, Daniel. You did a terrible thing."

Calmly, Axell reached out and curled around Dan's slightly less-bony-than-before hip. Dan froze. He always did when Axell reached out.

"You did these very bad things, and I still am here." Axell's hand tightened. "I am still here with you. I made you a romantic date. I do not want you only for sex, Daniel. You can refuse me, and you can do bad things. And I am *still here*. Are you here with me? Do you forgive *my* mistake, too?"

Dan felt like ice had hit him, thinking about the danger Axell could be in if anyone realized what he knew. "Don't risk dying from drugs, please, and you can't tell anyone what you know, Axell," Dan whispered. "They're dangerous. Ellie was raging, fighting. . . ." He felt tears escape and race over his cheeks. "She was willing to die to get out of here. Maggie's kid was on the ground like a dead person, and there was Prospero. Sondre helped her and all, but it was her. If they know you figured this out—"

"It is done now," Axell whispered back. He pulled Dan a little closer. "I am not reckless enough to say what I know. That witch is scary, and the headmaster does not like me already. I will not tell."

Dan closed the rest of the distance between them and accepted the comfort of Axell's embrace. "I couldn't tell you about it. They said—"

"Who cares what they say? You can tell me anything." Axell stroked a hand up and down Dan's spine. "You asked why I used the drugs. It was because I thought my heart would break inside me. I could not sing. I found someone who made me feel good and alive and *real,* but then you pushed me away and I hurt."

"Axell—"

"I do not mean it is your fault," Axell said quickly. "I chose to give in to the bad feelings, but you asked why. *That* is why. You pushed me away and would not let me help you."

"If I told you, she would erase your mind," Dan said softly. "I was afraid."

"Then be afraid with me. I was afraid, too. Stop pushing me away, Daniel. I am where I want to be, where I thought you wanted me to be. Do you want to be with me?"

"I *do.*" Dan wrapped his arms around Axell. "You could have anyone you want, though, so—"

"Apparently not *any*one," Axell rebutted with a wry smile.

"But if I stop running, will you still want me?" Dan asked in a small voice.

"Yes." The word resonated with truth. "I will want you the same. More."

And Dan was glad he had finally found the courage to ask. He tilted his head slightly. "Then kiss me, please?"

Axell's mouth curved into a smile briefly before finding Dan's lips, and when they kissed, Dan was sure that this was exactly what he wanted.

This is home. He's my home.

18

Ellie

As they walked through the tiny downtown area of Crenshaw, Ellie couldn't stop herself from poking at the puzzle of the secret between them. "I can figure this out, you know? Aunt Hestia lives here without magic; that's weird. She doesn't want to be here, but I wanted her here. I have big memory gaps, and there is a *larger* secret."

The admiring looks Prospero was darting at her made her feel powerful, made her want to revel in that, but she was coming to understand that she could not. Whatever the secret was, Prospero decided that it meant that they could not cross the very lines that Ellie was near desperate to cross.

And what if she's right? What if one of us did something unforgivable?

"Tell me." Ellie glanced at her wife. "I don't want to force you, but . . . I can make you talk. I could force Walt, too. I think you are underestimating me."

Prospero shot her a look of frustration. "I am not. I know you're capable of hurting me. You've done so already."

"How?" Ellie had been listening to Prospero castigate herself, but this was new. *I was the one who hurt her?* "Why? When? How?"

Prospero stayed silent.

"Is that what I have to do to get answers? I could force you. Just tell me," Ellie begged. Her whisper was overly loud, but everyone gave them a wide berth so it wasn't as if their conversation would be repeated. Still Ellie stepped a little closer, holding Prospero's arm securely enough that her own knuckles grazed the fabric of Prospero's vest with every step.

"Things happened that I may not tell you." Prospero glanced her way before she resumed looking at every witch they passed as if there were monsters hidden in plain sight. More than half of the witches squirmed under her scrutiny, and the fear in their expressions was undeniable.

"You *want* to tell me, don't you? If I forced you, it wouldn't even be your fault. . . ."

"You aren't even supposed to know there's something you forgot!" Prospero snapped.

Ellie released Prospero and pivoted to return to the cabin they'd left. "I'll simply go back and ask Walter. I bet I can convince him to be reasonable—or maybe you can. Is that the answer, Prospero? Do I need you to slip into his mind and make him see reason?"

"Ellie!" Prospero grabbed her arm. "*No!*"

Turning back to face Prospero, Ellie folded her arms and leveled a stare at her wife. "I'll give you a choice. You either *date* me like we just met *or* I'm going to make you or him answer me. It's either start over, interrogation, or we split up. I'm done with being pushed away by the woman I am spending *my very long witchy life* married to."

All around them people were surreptitiously glancing their way.

"Ellie, you don't know what you're asking and—"

"Already established, dear." Ellie tilted her head to look up at her wife. "You cannot tell me, but I cannot live this way. So we can start over, end this, or I can force—"

"Fine." Prospero held out her hand and awkwardly said, "Hello. I'm Prospero."

"Elleanor Brandeau. You should call me Ellie, though." She took the extended hand in her own, not commenting on the way Prospero trembled. "I'd really like to have you under me, Prospero, so maybe we ought to go on a date."

For a moment, Prospero's mouth opened slightly, but no words escaped. Finally, she muttered, "You are absurd, Miss Brandeau."

"Walk me to my room, Prospero." Ellie started to walk toward the castle. "I'd be happy to come to your place and seduce you there, if you prefer. I need to plan a date and your seduction . . . things to do."

"*You* need to plan?"

Ellie gave her a look. "You may be older than me, so let me catch you up. In the modern world, both partners can lead. Dancing, seductions, dates."

"I do recall you being rather assertive in the bedroom," Prospero murmured.

"Plus I think you have a complicated task you have to address." Ellie's worry crept into her voice audibly. "If you die and miss our date hunting witches, I'll be very, *very* disappointed in you."

"Ellie . . ."

Ellie held up a hand before Prospero could explain anything. "I know you have responsibilities, but I want you to recall that you also have a reason to be careful."

"Noted." Prospero swallowed as if she was struggling to speak and then added, "I want you to know that I was at the edge of falling in love with you when . . . the things happened that you cannot recall."

Ellie could not fathom how they had fought to the point that the Congress of Magic was involved. After a moment she smiled, a bit artificially, and asked, "Are we actually married?"

Prospero cleared her throat and said, "More or less."

"So no." Ellie shot her a look.

"I *would* marry you if you could forgive me," Prospero confessed. "I offered."

"I remember that . . . but then something happened. I hurt you, but you are apologizing for things you think I cannot know." Ellie sighed. "Why can't you just break the rules? I don't see why that's such a big . . ." Her words died. "You did break rules. Or I did?"

"Both."

"What rules?" Ellie pressed. "List all of Crenshaw's rules."

"Not likely." Prospero shook her head before motioning toward a shop that had neither sign nor display window. "Come with me. Be as scary as you'd like in here. Remind us both of how frightening you can be."

Intrigued, Ellie tucked her unanswered questions away and accompanied her wife toward the blackened building a block or so away from where they'd stood. Ellie's heart quickened at the menacing energy now radiating from Prospero.

And it clearly wasn't just Ellie who noticed the shift. Anyone even tangentially in her path moved, as if there were an invisible cloud around Prospero that rolled out as she walked.

Ellie followed her at a slower pace, enjoying the look of her wife when she was being particularly frightening. Some people just had that menacing vibe to them. It wasn't about size or muscle, she'd realized, but about the willingness to cross lines. Ellie had a stray thought that this was a thing that they shared, but that made little sense. She was simply a quiet librarian who sometimes made snakes in the forest to protect her home.

And threatened to confront the chief witch a few minutes ago.

That was a bluff, she tried to lie to herself.

It was not, the wicked part of Ellie's mind argued.

Ellie stopped arguing with herself and turned her attention back to the now as Prospero spread her fingers and placed her hand on a darker section of the door. It wasn't knocking, but Ellie was sure that it was the equivalent of that.

"Welcome to Crenshaw's underground," Prospero whispered. "Just so you know, I've only ever brought Scylla here."

"Look at you, being all romantic," Ellie teased.

"Not exactly," Prospero muttered.

A moment later, the door opened.

Inside was the youngest person Ellie had seen in Crenshaw. He was sprawled atop a veritable tower of pillows. He looked like he was maybe twenty years old, but it was hard to be certain with how skeletal he was. His arms and legs reminded her of an arachnid, skinnier than they ought to be to support a body—even one that looked like dried husks. His eyes were the most unsettling part of him. The sclera wasn't white like it ought to be. Instead, there were so many red lines that his eyes looked pink around a bright-blue pupil.

"Aw, you shouldn't have, Prospy! A special trip to meet little ol' me?" the boy rasped. "I'd have met your lady love sooner or later if—"

"Enough, Howie." Prospero didn't step in front of Ellie, like she typically did when she was feeling protective. She walked deeper into the den-like space. "I need a few things."

"You do?" He pushed upward, so he was more or less sitting upright rather than flopped on his tower of pillows. "You never need things anymore."

"Today, I do."

He gave them an oily grin. "A little love potion?" He made a thrusting gesture with two extended fingers into his other hand.

Ellie gave him a dismissive look. "Howie, is it? If you think she needs a potion to satisfy a woman, you're sadly mistaken." She lowered her voice as if confessing a secret and added, "The best part of being with a woman is that a person never has to worry about being unsatisfied. With a *man*, though . . ." She shuddered exaggeratedly before glancing at her wife. "Can you imagine the horror?"

Prospero's expression was unchanged. Dryly she said, "We all have our nightmares, love."

And the spiderlike young man burst into cackles that were better suited for horror movies than anywhere else Ellie could imagine. "Your wife's funny, Prospy."

"I am aware of what she is." Prospero crinkled her nose as she looked around the odd den. "You do remember our talk."

"Sure do." Howie slid down his mountain of funky pillows, scattering a few sequins and a tassel in the process. "Haven't sold to anyone on your list of no-nos." He gave an exaggerated nod. "Only a few sleepy stones to the average witches. No weapons to the Bad Guys."

Ellie could hear the uppercase letters in that last term. "The New Economists?"

Howie side-eyed her. "They're the Bad Guys. Heard that one of 'em got a gun from the outside."

"How?" Ellie asked without thinking.

"Information isn't free, Sexy."

"Not my name." Ellie stepped forward. Without thinking, she turned all of his pillows into feathers.

"Hey!" Howie swiped at the fluffy cloud currently filling the room like snow. "That's actually cool, Builder Lady."

"Still not my name, Howard." Ellie glanced at the floor under his feet and turned it into mud.

His legs went out from under him, and he was suddenly sitting in a mud puddle with feathers all over him. He chortled. "You're a ball breaker, aren't you, Elleanor Brandeau? Back in the old days, someone would've broken you." He turned his gaze to Prospero. "I'll cut you a deal if you either loosen my restrictions or give me a favor from her."

"I do not control her favors." Prospero shook her head. "Which restrictions?"

"Let me have a crack at the new students if they find me." The previously wretched man suddenly seemed a lot scarier. "You know what it takes to be able to even find my building, Lady Prospero."

"If they do find you, I need to be told. Names and purchases," Prospero said after a longer than normal pause.

Howie clapped his hands. "Excellent. I believe you now have a long line of credit in my store."

Ellie looked around. All she saw were shelves upon shelves of tiny rocks. "What do you sell here?"

"Stones." Howie gave her an expectant look. He pulled a tiny river-smoothed pebble from his pocket and held it out. "It's a *stoner store,* get it?"

When she didn't react or take it, he frowned. "That's right. You get your happy from the monster lady, don't you?"

"Magic can be embedded in natural items," Prospero added help-fully. "Both violence aids and various other magic. Howie sells other things, but he mostly sells the basest sort. Intimate aids and pleasure stones and the like."

"Feel-*good* magic." He rolled the small pebble between his hands until it disintegrated. He stretched and made a happy noise that Ellie instantly wished she could scrub from her mind. "That was a quickie sample . . . but that's not what *you* want, is it?" He turned his pleasure-blown pupils toward Prospero. "A little violence is your taste, eh? You want blood."

"You heard about the falling of the barrier?" Prospero gave him a dark look. "*After* it happened, I presume."

"Yes, only after. Take a look in my head. No secrets from you, are there?" Howie oozed closer and tapped his temple with one of his bony fingers.

Ellie repressed a flinch of disgust. How a person covered in mud and feathers could still be so disquieting rather than pathetic was a mystery she had zero desire to contemplate. She just wanted to get out of this place—not ponder the reasons that the strange witch was so disconcerting.

"I put together a care package for my favorite monster because of the *Incident* at the barrier." Howie scurried away toward a wall that was apparently a secret compartment. He looked over his shoulder. "No need to pretend you don't know where I keep the goods. If you were less ethical, you could just rob me blind." He giggled. "Least I don't need to worry that you'll *rub* me blind."

"Just get the stones, Howie."

"She wants my stones," he quipped. He pulled out a burlap sack and held it aloft. "Some are the usual. A bit of knees taken out and bones breaking—the white stones—and a few bleeding from . . . you know, *places.* Those are the reds. A couple badgering ones. Those are the brown rocks."

Prospero nodded. "Anything stronger?"

Howie paused. "I have a few extras that I made to see if I could." He bent down and drew out a black sack. It looked like dirty oil made into fabric, not quite silk but shiny like something very similar to it. "You said I couldn't sell things like these, but I thought experimenting was okay."

Prospero strode forward. "I'll take all of those."

"Hey!" He reached forward like he was going to touch her.

And Ellie didn't even blink before she had extended a section of the wooden cabinets on the wall. The wood reshaped into wood-wrought skeletal hands that held Howie fast. He dangled from those bony wooden hands.

"I could crush your wrists with a breath, you know?" Ellie mused.

For the first time since they'd stepped into his den, Howie looked afraid, and a part of Ellie that she didn't generally acknowledge simmered. *Mine. Prospero is mine, and no one touches what's mine.* She stepped in front of Prospero, close enough that Howie could kick her if he was foolish enough to do so.

"You ought to learn to use some manners when you talk to my wife," Ellie said in a low voice. "I'm still a remedial witch, you know. I could just slip up and make a mistake. . . ." The grip on his wrists tightened a little more. "It would be an accident. No one to blame."

Howie nodded. "Message received. The monster found herself someone just as fucking scary as she is."

Prospero touched Ellie's shoulder and said, "He's not worth the guilt."

"Maybe, but if he touches what's mine, I'll find that out." Ellie stepped back, shoving her darker impulses somewhere down deep inside her where they struggled to quiet.

"Congrats on your nuptials," Howie called as they walked away from him. "Hey? Hey? I'm still trapped here. Lady Prospero? Hello? Monster Bride?"

His voice followed after them as they left the building, stepping from the darkened room into the bright light.

Prospero stopped and looked at Ellie. "Will he be trapped there?"

"No. It'll fade in about five minutes," Ellie said, plucking a few stray feathers from her wife's vest and one from her cleavage. "I guess I just . . . overreacted. I didn't like his tone, and then he reached for you and—"

"Thank you." Prospero lifted one hand to cup Ellie's face. "You made me feel like I matter."

Later Ellie could think about how she felt about her wife's planned assassination of several witches. Right now, she couldn't dwell long on that *or* on her own vicious streak. Being a witch had gifted her with a terrible power, and how well she managed that new power was a challenge no one had warned her she'd face.

For all the talk of staying or going, new houses, figuring out where she fit, protecting Crenshaw, and the why and ways of magic, the most alarming thing of all was turning out to be her own self-control. Her magic had become an extension of her will, and it was easy to see how the right—or wrong—sort of magic could be a deadly temptation.

After a lifetime without power, having it now is a heady thing.

"I suspect I may not be the scariest witch in Crenshaw anymore, love," Prospero said quietly.

"Does that truly bother you?" Ellie asked hesitantly. She didn't feel like a monster, but the drive to protect Prospero had been all-consuming. "That I can be menacing . . . ?"

"Only if you remember everything and leave me," Prospero said lightly. "Or worse. I'd hate to be your enemy, Miss Brandeau. I'm terrified of it."

"So *talk* to me," Ellie pleaded.

"I have followed the rules of Crenshaw longer than you've been alive," Prospero said. "I broke them. For you. Because of you."

"Once more then?"

"Has anyone told you that you are not one of the better angels, love?" Prospero asked wryly. "You tempt me to break every rule that I live by. . . ."

And for the first time, Ellie wondered if it might not be best that she *not* recall whatever had pushed them apart. Her temper was not traditionally monstrous, but with this power she now had . . . maybe that had changed a bit.

19
Dan

Dan looked over at the man he'd eventually fallen asleep with the night prior. Kisses had turned to touches, and touches had turned to nakedness. And as it had been every time in his life, Dan had been the passive one. Axell was the one to lead their intimacy. Dan was the one who was touched and loved. It wasn't that he didn't *want* that pleasure, but he felt vulnerable now.

Just once I want to be in charge.

I want to make the decisions.

Maybe more than just once.

The sky outside was still dark, but the moonlight was fading as sunrise crept across the sky.

Dan tried to be quiet as he stretched in the makeshift bed—a pile of blankets and pillows Axell had stacked together—in the classroom near the infirmary where Axell had prepared the impromptu date. Dan slipped on his trousers and made it to the door. He turned the lock, which was far too loud.

"Running?" Axell asked.

Dan looked back. Axell's eyes were open, and he was staring at him. Dan was a lot less comfortable than he wanted to be. He wanted to be an equal if they were going to do this . . . whatever this relationship was.

"Maybe?" Dan folded his arms. "Nervous."

Axell held out a hand, and Dan returned to the bed.

"Candlelight makes us brave, *ja*?" Axell threaded his fingers through Dan's decidedly not-long-enough hair and traced over his not-defined-enough back. Every one of Dan's insecurities felt like they were awake and speaking up this morning.

Why am I not . . . more?

This was always the issue with the morning after. When his hormones were raging and singularly focused parts of him were making all the decisions, Dan was bold enough to forget to feel self-conscious or to list his flaws. He let whatever man wanted to touch him or fuck him do whatever felt good. That had been the definition of every sexual encounter in his life. He was passive. He was compliant. He was . . . an object, often nameless, always forgettable.

And it wasn't like Dan was *unsatisfied*. He just wanted there to be more to *this* relationship, more with *this* man than the way it always had been when he went to whatever dark corner or hotel or bathroom with a man.

"I don't usually *stay* around after. . . ." Dan squirmed as Axell stared at him, and he was oddly glad to have his trousers on as they spoke. He tried again. "I typically leave. . . ."

"After sex? Same." Axell shrugged, making the gesture far more elegant than it ought to be when a person was sprawled out on a pile of blankets on a castle floor. "But this is not only sex, Daniel? Is it?"

"No . . . I don't know. I hope not." Dan looked away, staring at the room that had been lit by low lights when he'd arrived, exhausted and starving. *He took care of me,* Dan reminded himself. Axell had brought

food, a place to rest, and he'd pushed Dan backward into a nest of blankets and made him forget his self-consciousness by ways of hands and
lips.

"Do you think I changed my mind?" Axell asked the question, drawing Dan's gaze, pulling him out of his anxiety and self-doubt.

"No . . . ?" Dan managed to say again.

"Then what is this? What is happening now?" Axell was anything but
subtle, and Dan suspected that it was the very trait that made him so
alluring. He was confident. Even when Axell admitted he felt insecure,
he *seemed* to be able to ask for what he wanted.

"I can't decide what to do." Dan's face burned hot. "I want . . ."

Axell didn't ask, didn't help Dan with the words. He raised his brow
and said, "*Ja.*"

When the other man said nothing more, Dan asked, "Yes, *what?*"

"To whatever you decide." Axell shrugged again. "I say *yes.*"

"But you have no idea what I'm thinking, what I want—"

Dan's words died as Axell leaned in and kissed him. His free arm—
the one he was not currently using to do whatever contorted push-up
he had managed—wrapped around Dan so he could grab Dan's ass.
Holding him in place, as if Dan might try to flee, Axell kissed Dan
until he felt like the awkward parts of him were melting away, as if he
could disappear into Axell, as if being closer was all that mattered in
the world.

It's not just sex.

He wants me, *not just a convenient body.*

Axell paused, kissed the edge of Dan's jaw, and with his lips along
Dan's earlobe said, "I trust you. What else do I need to know to answer?
You want. I say yes."

"I . . . you . . ." Dan stuttered as Axell bit his throat hard enough to
leave a mark.

"What?" Axell asked, lips brushing Dan's collarbone now.

"It's not supposed to be this easy," Dan objected. "No one else has . . ."

"Been a witch?" Axell pulled back and looked at him. "Been a handsome pansexual man?"

"Maybe?"

"Spent a month simply trying to get you naked?" Axell peppered kisses and nips along Dan's throat between questions. "Been falling for you?"

"Yes."

"You see, Daniel?" Axell laughed. "Say yes. It is good for things to be easy."

Axell had managed to reposition them so now Dan was on top of him. Axell stared up at Dan and said, "I say yes, *ja*, please. . . ."

And Dan realized that maybe it was okay for things not to be as complicated as they felt in his mind. He had no regrets about any of the anonymous fuck-and-duck connections in his past, but he wanted to take his time to know everything about Axell.

Is this love? Is that where we're going?

Dan had never felt even the edge of that feeling before, and the thought of it was as likely as the thought of magic being real. Magic, love, men that wanted him for more than a quickie, those were as illusory as finding a life or a job where he felt like he mattered.

After saying yes, Axell let Dan take control, which helped Dan not to feel guilty about taking his time admiring and slowly kissing Axell. And it seemed like they'd connected on some nonverbal level, because every time Dan started to think he was being too slow, too selfish, too anything with his caresses, Axell said, "Yes," as if he'd heard the doubts in Dan's mind.

When eventually their breathing was harsh, Dan asked, "Stand against the wall?"

It was meant to be a question, at least, but Axell obeyed as if it had been an order. Sunrise spilled through the window as if it were falling around Axell, illuminating him like a god, as Dan kneeled in front of him and looked up.

"Yes, please," Axell said in a rougher voice now.

$$ ☽ \quad ✳ \quad ☾ $$

Later, after the awkward realization that the door was not locked, Dan felt like he had crossed lines in a race he'd forgotten he'd entered. He darted glances at Axell, who looked as satisfied as Dan had felt the night before.

Being in Crenshaw might actually be the answer to everything he'd never dared to dream. They nestled back in their pallet of blankets. And this time, Dan held Axell against his bare chest. It was a small shift in the power dynamic, and he suspected it would shift again, but in the moment, Dan liked feeling like he was in control.

Dan cleared his throat awkwardly and said, "The whole love thing you said . . ."

Axell shot an affectionate look up at him. "That I am falling for you?"

"Yeah . . . That."

"I would like us to be more than naked joy," Axell said simply. "We would share a room, and lives, and nakedness."

"Like, live together?"

"*Ja.*" Axell shrugged like it was no big deal and put his hand on Dan's stomach. "I trust belly feelings. Instinct. We are good together."

Dan blinked at him. He felt as if they had already taken a giant step, as if *he* had taken a huge step both in trust and in claiming a new part of his own sexuality. *Taking charge. Trusting someone.* And here Axell was, asking for more. It felt like they were moving at a pace that was so far outside of normal.

So instead of answering, Dan held him. *Do I want that?* The thought was both tempting and terrifying.

They drifted off to sleep, and a little while later, when they were both standing and finishing dressing, Dan tossed Axell's ridiculous skinny jeans to him. "Do you always move this fast?"

Axell laughed as he slung an arm over Dan's shoulder. "Last time I was so interested, I took them on tour. First date was to six countries."

"I don't usually date," Dan confessed. "The cancer and trying not to die and . . . I slept with a lot of men who ended up later telling me about their wives. I just . . ."

"No living together, but maybe yes on the more sex?" Axell surmised as he pulled on his clothes finally. "And yes on the dates?"

"Yes on the sex and the dates," Dan agreed. "Maybe sleeping over some . . ."

"And telling me your secrets." Axell brushed a kiss across Dan's cheek. "Trusting. Togetherness."

For a moment, Dan panicked. *Why does he want to know my secrets?* But then he calmed down. He had no secrets Axell didn't know right now. "Yes," Dan said. "I can do that."

"Good. Let us find Miss Maggie now, and make her our friend again," Axell said.

"Why?"

"Because she is funny, and you feel sad. We will fix this next."

"I want to . . . live together with you," Dan blurted. "I'm just nervous."

"You sleep in my room, and when you are needing space, you go to yours. Easy." Axell smiled and shrugged, and Dan wondered briefly if things could actually be this easy.

Is this what happens when it's right?

"Yes," Dan said. "Yes. And then—"

"No rushing. I will wait, and we will romance each other." Axell steered them toward the door of the room, as if seeking someone out and making them your friend was as simple as that.

Decide it is so, and then it becomes that way.

It was ludicrous, but honestly, it was exactly how they ended up in this situation the first time they met Maggie, and Ellie, and it was exactly how Dan ended up involved with Axell. His Norwegian beloved simply decided this was what he wanted, and so he acted as if it were already that way.

"You're a bit much," Dan pointed out.

Axell gave him a wicked smile that made Dan blush a little brighter than he wanted, but all Axell said was, "You like me, though."

And Dan couldn't help but smile and reply, "*Ja.*"

20
Maggie

Maggie was walking through the castle when someone called out her name in a way that was overly familiar. "Maggie!"

She turned to see Monahan and Axell. She felt a strange sense of panic at seeing them after the hob's elusive comments to her earlier. *Are they "the maker and the singer"*? She was working on a plan to figure out what the hob wanted her to do, but she wasn't ready to break all the rules just yet. If she was going to try to outwit the chief witch and his cronies, she wasn't going to be all willy-nilly about it.

Life seemed to come at her faster than she wanted now that she was a witch, and she wasn't quite sure what to do about it. She knew that listening to the hob she met was her plan, that figuring out what she'd forgotten was the plan, but beyond "escaped and was returned to Crenshaw" her mental gaps were pretty vast.

I rescued my son. I negotiated for his safety.

I was already sleeping with Sondre, so our relationship is not exactly a bad fate.

*I was only ordered to stay away from Ellie . . . not them.
And they clearly know me.*

Axell wasn't approaching her like she was a stranger to him. Monahan was hanging back. He was the cautious one. Axell was impetuous and bold; it made her like him. Monahan? He was cagey, but Maggie had cracked cases with more reluctant witnesses. *And Craig is safe.*

This gamble is about establishing my own place here in Crenshaw.

"Come with us. I am exploring the castle. The acoustics are good in these halls. I can sing for you." Axell closed his eyes and did just that, voice lifting in some sort of song she couldn't translate. As he did, drums thrummed from somewhere, and other instruments—not all familiar—wound around that thudding beat.

"Why would I do that?" Maggie scanned the hall for threats.

"So we become friends," Axell said intently. The braid against his head waved slightly as he nodded, looking exceptionally self-satisfied. "Better than magic."

Something about the moment felt familiar, almost like déjà vu, and Maggie took a good look at them. Monahan looked nervous, refusing to meet her gaze. Axell looked like he was defiant.

"*Were* we friends?"

"She remembers us!" Monahan said with a wide smile. "That's such a rel—"

"No, she does not." Axell leaned against the wall with one combat boot–clad foot propped on the stone wall. He looked like a model at a shoot, and she found it the most artificial thing about him. "She figured it out, *ja*? This is what happened, Maggie? You deduced?"

"Yes."

"Oh." Monahan slumped slightly. "I hoped . . . it doesn't matter." He looked over at Axell. "This is a bad idea. Do we really need to break *more* rules?"

Maggie paused. "Were you told *not* to be my friends? I wasn't told that."

"Well, no, but . . . I sorta thought we shouldn't, considering everything that happened." Monahan shrugged. He reminded her of a lost puppy. Where Axell oozed confidence, Monahan had the look of someone who was vaguely starved. Of affection or food or happiness, she couldn't say, but he had an edge to him that made her think of desperation.

He'd be a good informant back in Carolina, easy to manipulate, she thought.

Why can't he be that now? followed quickly on the heels of the first thought. She had a few questions that she thought they might be willing to answer.

"So, we were friends, but I forgot." Maggie folded her arms over her chest and leveled a stern stare at one and then the other. "Why should I believe that? Why should I *care,* for that matter?"

"You're a scary woman," Axell said approvingly. "Do you remember medical-magic class? I was the volunteer. Dan touched your shoulder while you were . . . evaluating me, and we shared much pleasure. You and me and the doctor all at once."

"No!" Her mind rejected what he just referenced. In her memory, that was someone else, but she knew that Axell's words were true. She *had* been there, and that awkward memory was her own experience.

Why was that *memory erased?*

She frowned, thinking about Sondre. *Was he jealous?* She wasn't harboring any rage over whatever thing she'd been forced to forget, but this? This had nothing to do with her missing memories of escape.

So why was it erased? Was he insecure?

Now wearing one of her practiced court expressions, Maggie let herself stare at the two men from toe to top. "Anything else you want to share?"

"Err . . . Do you remember walking to the village and grabbing a stick to use to defend yourself if there was danger?" Monahan asked, gesturing like he was grabbing something from the ground.

"I do! I was with . . . two people." She scowled, trying to bring that memory into better focus. The sense that she had to be the responsible one came rushing back. She held Axell's gaze. "That was you? Monahan?"

"*Ja.*" Axell beamed at her. "You were at the town with us, but you left the tavern with the headmaster that night. I stayed to woo Daniel."

Maggie didn't miss the smile Daniel sent Axell. The wooing had obviously worked. They were incredibly cute together, and she felt a flash of envy that she didn't have that with Sondre. Knowing that there were memories missing made her feel awkward sometimes, like she was playacting at liking him. They had chemistry, but that wasn't enough.

Although it must have been real or I wouldn't be leverage to use against him, she thought with a tiny smile.

"Could you call me *Dan*?" Monahan blurted out.

"Maybe . . . why do you want me to know any of this?" Maggie watched Dan look away sheepishly.

Axell, however, gave her the sort of look she imagined the best of teachers gave their students. "Because they are your memories. Memories make us who we are. So you should have them back. You know they stole things from your mind."

"I do. Did I . . . was I *fond* of Sondre?" she asked with a slight waver. Knowing he cared was different than having an outsider say she felt for him, too.

"Yes," Axell and Dan both said.

Relief washed over her. Magic that could change what people knew could, by extension, change what they thought or felt. Belief was a result of lived experience, so if her knowledge was false, what she felt would be, too. Quietly, she added, "Did I love him?"

"No idea, but you trusted him." Dan squirmed. "I'm not sure how much we ought to be discussing out here in the open." He looked around the hallway. "Come on."

She paused. Going with them felt like a bad idea, like taking the first step before she even had a plan. She believed in trusting her gut, but this was more impulsive than she liked. She needed to weigh and research and plan.

Break the rules, the hob had said.

Axell is obviously a singer.

"What's your magic, Dan?"

He paused. "Why?"

"Because I'm to look for a maker and a singer." She nodded toward Axell. "He sings."

"I don't make things," Dan said tensely. "I destroy things."

"Daniel . . ." Axell started.

But Dan shook his head. "I do. You know it."

After a tense moment, Axell whispered, "Ellie Brandeau *makes.*"

Then they resumed walking. Maggie followed them to a section of wall that looked uncharacteristically empty. Dan stood there, both hands flat on the wall like he was checking the castle for a fever.

"It is okay," Axell said quietly.

After several moments, the wall opened. It split as if a great silent crack was dividing the stones. At first the crack was only the width of a hand. Then the crack widened as if a section of the wall had vanished.

"What the actual fuck . . . ?" Maggie muttered.

"It is our secret headquarters," Dan said, sounding more cheerful now. "I mean, not *too* supersecret. The headmaster knows. Probably about twelve or fifteen other people know, too. We can talk here, though."

Maggie stepped inside the room; the men followed. Glancing behind her, she saw a giant wooden door that looked like it ought to be on the side of an old church. A massive ring on the door was the only fixture.

"If you pull the ring, the door opens," Axell offered, noticing her gaze. "You are not trapped in this room, Maggie. You are not trapped with us. We are safe together."

Maggie gave him a long look. For someone who appeared lighthearted and easygoing, Axell had a depth to him that made her reevaluate him.

He was canny where Dan was open. She smiled tentatively. "That was my concern. You're observant."

Axell gave her a wider smile as she studied him. "I am, and I missed your sharp mind. I missed our friendship. You are funny and frightening."

That, too, resonated as truth, and Maggie gave him a nod of acknowledgment. Then she turned away and looked around the room. The library itself was one of the most magical places she'd seen. It reminded her of both the Library of Congress and the Duke library . . . and maybe the Carnegie Library of Pittsburgh.

This room was huge and lined with floor-to-ceiling bookshelves, complete with rolling ladders. Semicircular shelves speared out from various spots like the letter "C" had been carved of wood over and over.

"Is there an upstairs?"

"Not so far." Dan stared around the room. "It shifts some days, though. So maybe later? It often shares what it—or maybe the castle? Or the hobs? I honestly don't know who *decides,* but it offers answers . . . anyhow, it or a hob or both decide what it thinks we need, but only when we need it. Like it's answering a question we were soon going to ask. I don't know why."

"A question *Daniel* was going to ask," Axell added in a soft voice. "It answers *him.* It does not answer me. The library talks to him this way, not to all witches."

Maggie wandered around the room studying the assorted tables with various workspaces—including easels and tables with chessboards inset into the wood.

"Bookwheels. Very fitting," she said, half to herself. She rotated one of them that resembled a Ferris wheel. Six books were open on the platforms, and as she skimmed the books, she realized that someone was studying mind magic. Without looking back at Axell and Dan, she asked, "Your research?"

"I didn't like that you and Ellie forgot so much," Dan said quietly.

Maggie turned in a full circle, seeking the one witch she had to avoid at all costs. "She's not here, is she?" Her voice cracked slightly. "Brandeau. I was told . . . you don't understand."

"We do." Axell reached out and squeezed her shoulder. "She was your friend, Maggie. You trusted her and—"

"And they erased it!" Maggie scowled.

"Yes . . . with my help." Dan stepped closer to her, his hands held outstretched with palms out, as if trying to show he was harmless. He didn't feel harmless, not if he was a part of erasing her memory—and Ellie Brandeau's memory, too.

Dan said, "You asked what my magic is. . . ."

The two exchanged a look.

"I amplify other magic," Dan said after a long moment. "Like when you and Axell and the doctor . . ."

"Had pleasure," Axell said.

Maggie snorted. "I was going to say got off, but your way sounds more elegant."

Axell simply smiled.

"Can we not mention that around Sondre?" Dan asked. "He already doesn't like Axell."

At that Maggie paused. She had questions there, too, but her own business was more pressing, selfish though it was. "We'll loop back to that," she said, glancing between them. "Talk to me about this amplifying thing. Can we talk about that?"

"We are alone here, Maggie." Axell opened his arms wide, as if to gesture at the expanse of the library. "It is only us. Just three friends talking among books."

The tension drained from Maggie as the truth of that statement washed over her. She was intrigued by why these two men were erased from her memory. *That* was part of the mystery that was safe to ponder, more so because it was in the shelter of a gorgeous magical library. They weren't pursuing the forbidden subject—*yet*—so Maggie thought about her backlog of questions.

"So what do you know about my escape?" Maggie settled in front of an empty bookwheel, idly spinning it. "And how do you get research books to appear here?"

As she spoke, several books appeared on the various book trays.

"Damn, where was this when I was in law school?" Maggie tapped the cover of a book. "Or studying for the bar exam?"

"Probably right here." Axell stroked the side of the wheel reverently. "Antique and magical."

"Like the headmaster," Dan teased. "Maggie has a type."

For a moment shock held back her laughter, but then Maggie barked out a loud laugh. They both joined in, and afterward, she remarked, "Everyone is probably thinking things like that, but no one else has had the balls to comment."

"Daniel has very nice balls," Axell said mildly.

"Too far." Maggie shook a finger at Axell. "File that under things I don't want to know about my friends."

"Friends?" Dan echoed.

"With you? Yes." She eyed Axell. "The jury is out on *you* so far."

"Says the lawyer," Axell murmured with a smile.

And Maggie had a strange feeling that she could be happier here than she remembered being. A man she was falling for, friends who were a shade inappropriate, and thanks to magic a secret school far away from her violent ex where her son would be safe.

Aside from the recent drama with the toxic water and whatever she was forgetting, Crenshaw offered a good life.

Once the barrier is back in place . . .

Once I figure out why they erased my memories . . .

Once they realize that I'm more than leverage to control Sondre . . .

"Do you think they are trying to keep you away from Ellie, or Ellie away from you?" Axell said lightly. "Do you know why?"

Maggie sighed. "I think you two need to tell me what you know, and then we can figure out the plan."

Dan reached out for Axell's hand. "I have terms."

"Oh?"

"You agree to help defend Axell if Sondre gets pissed off at us." Dan stared at her as he spoke. "You don't remember it now, but you're going to be angry with me when you hear what I did. And Sondre already doesn't like Axell . . . so . . . those are our terms."

Maggie nodded and said, "I'll draw up a contract."

The research table suddenly had legal paper and a pen. She glanced at it. "I could get used to this."

Then she looked at them. "Let's get started. Full names? Your terms?"

As long as Craig is safe, I'm done having anyone—especially a bunch of nameless old witches—tell me what to do, or remember, or be.

21
Ellie

The last few days had been an exercise in madness for Ellie. Prospero had decided to renew their courtship. Her wife was chivalrous, attentive, and focused on Ellie.

But still adamant that there would be no sex, Ellie grumbled to herself.

Prospero had been by the castle to visit Ellie at morning and evening meals. She had appeared at the door each time with a small gift and then asked, "Would you like to join me?"

The first day, they ate in the large dining hall where students and other witches gathered. Today, Prospero stood there holding a basket of food out and asked, "Would you like to eat somewhere more private?"

Alone with her! At last!

Ellie's ongoing desire to seduce her wife was challenging. It was as if Prospero had known that Ellie wanted to be alone with her, so she'd been as charming as possible—all while refusing any attempt to be alone together.

Today, she was *offering.* Ellie gripped Prospero's hand and marched through the castle hallway at a speed that was closer to a run than a walk.

"In a hurry?" Prospero asked quietly.

Ellie met her gaze. "You have been avoiding me, so *yes.*"

"I find you hard to resist. So I chose a tactic to assist me in that." Prospero had the grace to look a little sheepish at her admission.

"*Hmph.*" Ellie scowled and marched forward. Maybe she was rushing, but no one was going to have the audacity to comment. Half the students seemed frightened of Ellie or Prospero or both of them, and the majority of them looked at Prospero with apprehension, at the least.

And yet, I was the witch Howie found scary. Ellie shoved that stray thought away. Her self-control was a little wobbly, but that would get easier. She was sure of it. Magic was like anything else. It took practice. Her first attempts at baking scones were no better than door stoppers, so to presume magic would be instantly reflexive seemed odd.

Ellie glanced at Prospero again. *Maybe my self-control is not going to improve in* this *area, though.* Regardless of the secrets between them, Prospero was everything that Ellie craved. Beautiful and deadly. Maybe the secrecy made it more thrilling . . . or maybe it was the thrill of the hunt.

"Do you refuse my advances because it makes me chase?" Ellie asked.

"No. I am attempting to be a better person, a person who might one day be worthy of—"

"Everyone deserves love," Ellie said firmly.

"Even those who betray others?"

"So you think what happened was a betrayal?" Ellie's gaze narrowed. "Watch out!"

Prospero pulled Ellie to her as a woman walked by with a tower of boxes tall enough to completely obstruct her view.

"It's so much more chaotic in the passageways," Prospero pointed out with widened eyes as she shifted the basket of food to avoid spilling it. The castle was increasingly crowded as people from the edge of the village had been moved into the empty rooms. Ellie had obviously never visited *every* room, but all the hallways seemed longer. There was a wing on the east that she hadn't recalled existing before, either. She was not the only one thinking it. At least three students had suggested that there were two extra floors.

"It's bigger than it used to be."

"The castle simply grows sometimes." Prospero shrugged, as if buildings shifting and reshaping was a perfectly normal experience. It wasn't, as far as Ellie knew, but Crenshaw was still something of a mystery. "The Congress is moving witches in."

"What if there are New Economists in the group?"

"Every witch is given a choice to be siphoned first, so if anyone thought that going back was better, they have that chance." Prospero frowned slightly.

"What if they can't be?"

This time Prospero paused. "Only the low-magic-level witches are moving into the castle. It protects them from the rift and the rogue witches but doesn't endanger students."

Ellie paused, a stray thought wriggling up out of the depths of her mind. "Could I have been siphoned?"

Prospero's expression blanched. "Do you want to be?"

"You're avoiding the question." Ellie caught her gaze. "Could *I*?"

"No."

Ellie was certain that detail mattered, but she wasn't sure why. She stepped around a pair of students coming out of another room. There was something about this that was unsettling her wife, more so than the topics of threats and dangers, so Ellie decided to be sure they were back on track.

"No gift today for me?" Ellie teased, hoping to pull Prospero out of her reserve.

"Just me, unfortunately."

"That seems like an excellent gift." Ellie squeezed her hand. "You know I don't need *things,* don't you?"

"You wanted me to court you," Prospero said, sounding more awkward than usual. "Gifts, attention, flowers, praise. There are rules."

"I want you to *date* me." Ellie unlocked her door and pushed it open.

She felt briefly self-conscious that all of Prospero's recent gifts and notes were beside her bed, but at the same time, she wanted Prospero to notice that Ellie treasured each token, too.

Notice that I think about you before I sleep each night.

Both the click of the door shutting and then the thud of the lock being thrown seemed louder somehow, reminding Ellie that she was alone in a locked room with her wife.

"That's much better," Ellie murmured.

Prospero set the basket of food on a table. "I wanted a chance to speak to you in private."

"I'm here. . . ." Ellie stepped closer. Private time sounded perfect.

"I expect that I will have to leave tonight," Prospero told her. "There was magic, but by the time we felt it, the witch relocated. Teleported. We weren't fast enough."

"What does that mean?"

"Once a witch starts . . . leaking, it'll be easier. Something is causing the witch to be unstable. That's not likely to be Agnes, and the most logical answer is that the witch teleported. That's going to happen again, and each time the spills get bigger. We will find her, and maybe she knows where Aggie and Allan are."

"I don't like this. Let me come with you," Ellie urged.

"It's an easy thing, but I didn't want you to think I was skipping our meals together by choice if I can't come back in time."

Fear tightened Ellie's stomach so intensely that she couldn't speak. *If? If she can't come back? What does that mean?* Ellie felt her excitement shift to worry.

"If I can return to you—"

"If?" Ellie interrupted. That was twice now Prospero had used that word, and Ellie's anxiety now felt like worms writhing in her stomach. "If? What do you mean if? *If* is not okay. *If* is that I might lose you and . . . no. Not *if.*"

Prospero reached out and caught Ellie's flailing hand. "Perhaps the process will be quick. Perhaps it will go well. Retrieving the other witch was easy enough. However, we may need to pursue her if she teleports, and with a spill we need to repair whatever damage we can in their world."

"What if they shoot you like Lord Scy—"

"I am not new to people trying to kill me, love." Prospero smiled like she was charmed by Ellie's worry. "Few witches can stop me. I slip into their minds and change their perceptions, so they no longer want to hurt me. It's simple magic. I'm not expecting to be shot or killed."

"That's similar to Grendel's magic. You said she could summon fears and—"

"Walt is optimistic that this is just one of the others. There's a witch called Jenn, and Allan, too. He's simply a drunkard, and it's highly unlikely they're all together, love."

Ellie felt like clutching her. "Why you? Why can't I help?"

"If this one is spilling magic over, that's not Agnes. Plus, the headmaster will be with me. He's transferred his role here temporarily, to keep the castle safe." Prospero cupped Ellie's face in both hands. "And this is my responsibility. I retrieve witches when their magic flares, along with whichever witch is headmaster. You know this."

"I object. What if Grendel is there?" Ellie pressed.

"She's a tactician. She knows we would be less likely to find her if they stay apart." Prospero sounded increasingly exasperated. "I know what I'm doing, Ellie."

"But we can't do magic over there, so how are you to be safe?" Ellie frowned, jumbled images of a car shifting form and a diner reshaping into a cage crowded into her head. *Why do I know that?* She stared at Prospero, who looked tenser now.

Because of what I said?

She stared at Prospero. "What if you do magic and . . . what if it goes wrong?"

"You're right that magic is not as *stable* over there, but my magic is specifically designed because of the need to alter memories to bring them to Crenshaw. It's not like *other* magic because it's all internal."

"So that should be true with Grendel's."

Prospero dropped her hands. "Elleanor."

"What are the *exact* rules?"

"I don't know because *we are not to do magic there.*" Prospero's words snapped out. "That's the whole point of spell stones. It's why they were invented . . . well, that and to let witches be able to do magic larger or different from their innate magic."

"But *mental* magic works? Stuff that doesn't change the outside world? Could I manifest something internally in someone and that would be allowed?" Ellie asked, trying to make sense of the rules that governed the use of magic outside Crenshaw.

Maybe there was a detail here that could unlock her memories. *Is that what I forgot?* Ellie started to panic harder. *Did I break someone?* She felt like there was someone she'd hurt, but more . . . the thought skittered away like insects at night.

All she could ask was, "Could I do that?"

Prospero looked briefly traumatized. "I suppose. Perhaps?"

"So I could make their heart or lungs—"

"I would not ask that of you, Ellie." Prospero reached out again and stroked Ellie's cheek. "This is not your responsibility. Sondre and I will manage it. I would never ask you to take a life."

"But it's okay for you?"

"I don't relish it. I do what I must to protect our world. Agnes and Allan tried to kill Scylla and expose our world. They are an exception." Prospero's voice was colder now.

"Am I to think you've never killed anyone?" Ellie asked.

Prospero dodged the question. "Would you think less of me if I had?"

Ellie pondered. The rules were not entirely different here. Murder was still murder. Self-defense and war were still nebulous territory. *Would I forgive her all of those?* She knew the answer before she considered long.

"Self-defense is different." Ellie pulled her closer, grateful when Prospero didn't resist. "All I want is you to be safe and uninjured. I want you to be here in my arms and life and bed. I want everything to be okay, and us to be happy and Crenshaw to be safe and peaceful."

"Is that all?" Prospero's words were a half laugh against Ellie's hair.

So Ellie did the only reasonable thing. She pinched Prospero's side.

Prospero yelped and jerked away.

"Yes, that's all," Ellie said in the most serious voice she could muster. "Happy life, happy wife. I think those are reasonable goals. Seems like someone else has been working toward the same things lately. . . ." Ellie gestured to the tiny stash of gifts on her bedside table. A candle; lavender, of course. A pretty notebook. A bouquet of flowers that was beautiful, albeit slightly eggy-smelling. "Am I wrong?"

"No."

"Well, then." Ellie shoved Prospero onto the bed she'd just magically widened at the same time.

Prospero laughed. "Someone's grown confident in her magic."

"Shut up and hold me for a minute before you need to abandon me to hunt," Ellie grumbled.

"Yes, dear." Prospero pulled Ellie closer, and Ellie nestled her cheek against Prospero's shoulder.

After a blissful few moments, panic rumbled like something angry under Ellie's skin. *What if she gets injured?* Ellie couldn't imagine losing her. "I could go with you. I'm strong enough. You know I can help."

"No." Prospero stroked her hand through Ellie's hair. "We know these witches are capable of extreme violence. They *shot* Scylla. She was simply in their way, so they resorted to using a gun . . . on a witch with centuries of life ahead of her. She's still not healed. She should have been, and Mae has no idea why. The barrier won't stay up. Scylla isn't healing, and Mae is constantly drained. I'm not going to risk *you*."

"I can transform things. Gun or bullet—"

"No," Prospero said. "A blast or burst of accidental magic is one thing, but sustained magic use has consequences."

"What sort?"

Prospero was silent for several moments. She continued running her fingers through Ellie's hair, but that was the only clue that she was still awake. Finally, she offered, "It ripples things. Reality is not well suited for a lack of scientific laws. I don't know the right terms because they change . . . but physics, I guess, is the right word. There are laws of physics. Magic ignores them. And the laws of medicine. And chemics."

"Chemistry," Ellie corrected quietly.

"Yes. That. Magic has its own laws, but it doesn't *blend* with non-magical worlds. We talk about witches accused of whole fields of animals sickening . . . and while most so-called 'witches' were women who died for no crime other than failing to fall in line or speaking their minds or being bright enough to see the efficacy of herbs, *some* were actually real witches. When they woke, before there was Crenshaw, there was a ripple."

"Whole herds died," Ellie said. "That was a witch-trial accusation."

"Plagues. Fevers. Other . . . odd acts. It depends on the sort of magic." Prospero sighed. "My presence over there too long would make people forgetful."

"Agnes was head of House Grendel. Grendel was a monster, right?" Ellie wasn't sure what sort of side effect that would have.

"Yes, who was violent and wandered." Prospero's voice sounded thicker with worry. "And Allan is head of Dionysus and Jörd, a house of debauchery. And there are at least three others who went, but they are not house heads."

"I still think you ought to take me," Ellie said, propping herself up on one arm.

"No."

"Obstinate woman. I just want to take care of you." Ellie leaned down and caught Prospero's mouth in a kiss. Her free hand cupped her wife's breast, thumb flicking over the nipple hidden under both a vest and a blouse.

The hand that had been threading through Ellie's hair tightened, holding Ellie to her, and teeth and tongues clashed.

Mine, Ellie thought yet again. *Whatever we did wrong doesn't matter.*

But a few moments later, Ellie moved to undo the buttons of Prospero's trousers, and her wife's hand wrapped around Ellie's wrist, stopping her.

Prospero turned her head, ending their kiss abruptly.

"What?" Ellie asked, looking down at her.

"No." Prospero's voice was ragged, but her words were clear. "You really don't want this. Me. You don't want *me.*"

"The throbbing between my legs disagrees with you," Ellie snapped.

"I'm trying to do the right thing." Prospero rolled out from under Ellie and came to her feet. She sounded as upset and rejected as Ellie felt. "This is not easy for me, Ellie, but I care about you. I want to respect you."

"By denying me? By making choices for me?" Ellie glared at her wife. "I'm able to make my own choices, Prospero!"

"Not without all the information."

"And whose fault is that?" Ellie bit out.

"Mine. It's mostly my fault, but I won't compound it by doing this." Prospero tidied her hair and clothes, not making eye contact as she did so, and when she looked up, her mask of indifference was securely in place. "I'll see you again as soon as I am able. Please stay safe in my absence."

Prospero leaned down and brushed a quick kiss over Ellie's lips.

And Ellie decided to push the line a little more. She knew what she wanted. She wasn't sure why Prospero—who clearly wanted the same thing and was *courting* her and had already married her—was being so difficult.

Ellie unfastened her jeans and shoved them and her underwear down. "Prospero . . ."

When her wife glanced back, Ellie said, "I'll settle for thinking of you while I touch myself. If you weren't so difficult, I would invite you to stay, but I won't beg."

"Ellie . . ." Prospero stared at her. "I swear I'm trying to be a better person, and later, you'll probably understand why. I cannot take advantage of you, though."

"You cannot take advantage of the *willing*," Ellie argued.

"If you remembered why you were angry, you wouldn't be willing, love." Prospero shook her head. "I'll court you as you asked, but I can't . . . we can't . . ."

"So that's a no to *all* touch? No sex? Tell me that's not forever," Ellie begged, because maybe she was a little bit of a liar after all. She *would* beg for an answer.

"I need time, Ellie. I am asking you to give me time, to wait for me. . . ." Prospero swallowed, gaze fastened exactly where Ellie wished her wife's mouth or hand was.

Ellie was done with her wife's refusals. "Tell me you'll at least stay and watch next time. That's not going to require you to touch me, but I want you *here* with me."

"That . . ." Prospero's voice broke as Ellie folded her left leg, so she was in a figure-four and exposing herself more fully to Prospero's hungry gaze. "*Ellie.*"

Ellie held out a hand toward her, and Prospero moved toward her like she was unable to resist.

When Prospero was near enough, Ellie took her hand and directed it to her thigh. "Just hold on to me."

"Ellie." Prospero watched as Ellie widened her legs and touched herself. Her grip tightened on Ellie's leg as Ellie started to tremble under the combination of her wife's laser-focused gaze and Ellie's own quickly moving fingers.

"*I want you,* Prospero," Ellie pronounced as she hurtled toward orgasm. "And I know you want me."

It wasn't a question, but Prospero answered as if it were. "I do."

Then Prospero bent closer and kissed Ellie, swallowing her whimpers and moans as she fell into that silent bliss. Alone.

"Next time," Ellie started, pulling back just enough that her words fell on Prospero's lips, "Your turn. None of your rules would be broken by that."

"Ellie . . ."

"Say yes," Ellie whispered.

Prospero gave a single nod. "You're making my attempts to be a good person harder than they already were."

"Good." Ellie leaned away from her. She didn't again ask Prospero to stay, even though she knew they both wanted that. Ellie knew what the answer would be if she tried. She did, however, add, "Promise me you'll come back to me."

And whether or not Prospero meant it in all the ways Ellie did, she agreed. "Yes."

Prospero paused, as if she couldn't step away from the edge of Ellie's bed. Then she released Ellie's thigh, knuckles briefly trailing upward until they were pressed against Ellie's throbbing center. "I will return from their world, and I'll be here. Just be patient for me, please?"

Ellie nodded, but Prospero was already gone, teleporting herself from Ellie's room to wherever she needed to be.

"Please be safe," Ellie whispered to her empty room.

22
Ellie

When Ellie left her class—History of Magical Bonds—the next morning, she was not expecting to be greeted by the headmaster's wife and
two of her other classmates. They bustled her back into the classroom as
their professor was leaving. The professor had a towering hat, peacock
feather bouncing erratically as she looked back at them with a reproving
look.

"I'm not to talk to you," Maggie Lynch stated by way of greeting.

"Then don't." Ellie put more distance between them. The moment
felt like an ambush.

Maggie made a face that was halfway between amused and irritated.
"My son is going to live with your aunt. I thought we could try talking
since we'll be almost like distant relatives. That's not breaking the rules,
is it?"

"I don't know you." Ellie stared at her, feeling like there was clearly
more going on than she knew.

"Awkward panda," one of the men said softly.

"Monahan, right?" Ellie said.

At the same time, all three of her classmates said, "Dan." Then exchanged looks as if there was a joke there.

"Right, well, *Dan* . . . and Maggie . . . and . . ." She looked at the third student.

"Axell," he offered.

"Axell," she echoed. "Why do I feel like the three of you are up to something?"

Maggie grinned. "I'm the headmaster's wife. What could I possibly be up to? Do you know something about me that would make you think that?"

Ellie rolled her eyes. Obviously, she didn't, and she didn't love the gap in her memory making the whole conversation feel like she was the only person in a game who couldn't see her adversary's cards while hers were all face up. She shoved all her anxiety away and said, "Hestia is going to be looking after your kid? Lucky boy. She raised me, and she's amazing."

"Truly?" The bravado in Maggie's expression slipped briefly, and she looked like someone Ellie wanted to help.

"Truly." Ellie nodded her head. "I wanted her to live here, but . . ." She motioned to the window of the castle, through which dappled light cast interesting shadows on the floor. "It's poisonous out there."

"My kid's not magic. That's why he's going back," Maggie offered.

"And you?" Ellie prompted.

"They won't let me. Witches can't move back there, can't even visit long, or magic . . . spills." Maggie stared at her, seeking something that she obviously wasn't finding. "Did you know that?"

"My wife is the one hunting the witches who shot Lord Scylla and created the rift, so . . . yes, I know," Ellie hedged.

"That's the *only* reason you know?" Dan asked. "No other stray details that might cross your mind?"

"Obviously, you think you know something about me." Ellie crossed her arms. "Spit it out."

"I met you in Ligonier," Dan blurted. "I know your magic is intense. You were scary when we met. I'm really sorry for my part in everything, but it was either help the bad guys or be forced to give up my magic."

Ellie paused, staring at the three of them. "We met before I was a witch?"

"No."

"No," a second voice answered as the headmaster appeared with a hob on his shoulder, teleporting into the classroom like an angry bull. "Shut your gob, Monahan. Not a word more. Are you *trying* to get called before Congress?"

Ellie opened her mouth to reply but then realized he was talking to Maggie.

"Now, Sondre . . ." Maggie put her hand flat on his chest. "We just ran into a classmate in the passageways. No one nearby. No one—"

"Woman, there are ears everywhere." The headmaster ran his hand over his face as if to wipe away worry. "And you two. Go on. Anywhere but here." He glanced at Ellie, softened his tone, and said, "Prospero risked everything for you. I don't like her, but . . . seriously? Stay away from my wife."

Then he disappeared with Maggie.

"I don't want to get deported," Axell said. "We should go, too. Until next time."

"Deported?" Ellie echoed.

Axell paused. "Some witches can be sent back there. Siphoned and disposed. Others . . ." He glanced pointedly at her and then at Dan. "Others are too special to send away, even if they *want to* go."

"Do you want to go back?"

Axell shook his head.

Dan gave her a sad smile. "No. I'd do just about anything to stay. Going back would be a death sentence for me. Cancer. In and out of remission."

"You know what I forgot," Ellie said baldly. They had obviously been trying to suss out what she knew before Maggie was snatched away.

"Parts of it. Maggie knows *most* of it," Axell said in a very quiet voice.

The next group of students started filing into the room, darting awkward looks at her, and Ellie decided that she was going to go wherever Dan and Axell were headed to get answers, but in the moment she'd looked away, they were gone.

That leaves Prospero or the chief witch. . . .

Ellie looked for the two men as she left the classroom and wound her way through the halls. Wherever they'd vanished, they'd gone quickly. She marched to the exit and out the front doors, only to be stopped just outside the castle by a young woman who looked about as threatening as a daisy.

"If you don't go with her, she's going to get hurt," the woman said in lieu of greeting.

"And I should trust you why? Who are you? Who will get hurt? Less riddles, more facts." Ellie stared at her. "Do I know you?"

"No, but I know you, Elleanor Zelena Brandeau. I foretold your arrival and—"

"Got it. Prophecy." Ellie held a hand up in a "halt" gesture. "We make our own destinies in the world."

"So you'll risk the woman you love?"

"*Do* I love her?" Ellie countered. "Apparently, she erased my memory."

"You have to save her." The stranger offered a beatific smile that mostly just pissed Ellie off. "Or we're all doomed."

"From what?"

"Peril. Pigs. Any number of things . . . or all is lost."

I'm over cryptic warnings and strangers interfering in my life.

"Who are you?"

"Cassandra."

At that, Ellie paused. "Like the seer no one believed?"

"Yes, but you must listen, Elleanor Zel—"

"Stop." Ellie stepped around her and kept walking, calling back over her shoulder, "You'll find that I'm not a huge fan of secrecy *or* being told what to do. If you think I need to go with Prospero, tell her. Tell the chief witch. I've *tried to,* but she refused."

"I've tried, too," Cassandra snapped.

And for a moment, Ellie felt sorry for her. Obviously, Ellie offered to go with Prospero, but no one seemed willing to let her.

Because I was an escapee. That was the undeniable truth. *She doesn't want to take me over there because I was an escapee before this!*

23
Sondre

"This was the plan?" Sondre thundered at Maggie as soon as they were alone. "Court trouble in the middle of the damn castle?"

She stepped back. "I warned you."

"At least practice a little subterfuge, woman. The junkie—"

"Who?" Maggie interjected.

"The leech trying to ruin Monahan's life here." Sondre scowled.

"Oh. Axell and Dan said you dislike him," Maggie said quietly.

"Monahan could be someone. He's powerful in ways you don't even—"

"He amplifies magic," Maggie said levelly. "If memory serves, he amplified some healing magic and then Axell and Dr. Jemison and I all got off at once?"

"You remember that?" Sondre stared at her for a moment. Then he frowned before he realized what she'd done.

"No. I don't. Why is that, dear?" She crossed her arms and eyed him like he was a monster.

He had the sense to look away and mutter, "He's an attractive man. I'm older, and you . . . he . . ."

Maggie slapped his arm harder than a tap but not enough to actually hurt. "You idiot. I'm with you."

"I had an insecure moment when Prospero was—" He gestured at her head. "—meddling around in there. I want you to only want me."

She stared at him like he was a slug. "Don't ever do something like that again. I'll make you regret meeting me if you try to control me, Sondre."

He nodded once.

Then he felt a tug, a certainty that he knew was magic in the other world summoning him. "I need to go. I'm going to drop Craig off for fresh air while I'm away."

"What?"

"Craig, let's go," he called. "We were on our way over so Hestia and Craig could bond. Remember? Then you . . . a hob told me you were being reckless . . . and now the escapees." He pulled her in and kissed her soundly. "Sorry I was a fool, Maggie. You can yell at me in a bit." He glanced around the room. "Craig! Now!"

Then he grabbed the boy's arm and teleported, landing in an open-air shopping center where Prospero and Hestia Brandeau were waiting. Around them were fountains, seating areas, and plants. That told Sondre that they were in California or the Southwest.

"Slower than usual," Prospero said, surveying him. "Hestia is already inside for the car."

"Five minutes later isn't slow." Sondre watched as Craig looked around with a wide grin.

"Where are we?"

"Los Angeles," Sondre said mildly.

"Amazing," Craig whispered. "I've never been."

Although he was never entirely at ease with her, Sondre paced through a shopping center with Prospero and Craig.

He'd be safer if he were a witch. Sondre had qualms about sending the boy to school, to live with Hestia Brandeau, but it was safer and more sustainable long term.

And I can't shove him into traffic and hope he has latent magic! That thought had actually occurred to Sondre when Maggie had started crying the morning prior.

"You know she'll rent some old-lady car," Craig muttered as Hestia waved over her shoulder from inside the rental office.

"Hestia?" Prospero scoffed. "We'll be lucky if she doesn't rent a motorbike."

Craig looked back at her with renewed interest as they waited for Hestia—who was still inside the car-rental center—to finish the paperwork at the desk. Part of Craig's excitement seemed to be from the game currently on the television. Obviously, Sondre had seen televisions from time to time when he was fetching a newly awakened witch, but he hadn't *watched* one. When he'd become a witch in the 1950s, half the homes had televisions. His was one of them. Most were still black-and-white, but color sets were starting to filter out to the public. Now? They were in vibrant color, and major sporting events were broadcast live even in the lobbies of shops. It was easy to see why people missed these when they came to Crenshaw.

Before he could ask any questions, Hestia came outside, holding a set of car keys. "Convertible. Want a driving lesson?"

"No!" Sondre looked at her. "He's just a child."

"Asshole," Craig muttered.

"Oh, the horrors." Hestia patted her purse, where she currently had three thousand dollars, donated by Sondre's wife. "Should we spend it all on booze and horse races since Mr. Cranky Pants won't let me teach you to drive? What do you think, Craggy?"

"Aunt Hestia," Craig groaned, but he nudged her gently with his shoulder. "I told you to stop calling me that."

Hestia cackled. "Should've brought the girls instead. Mags and Ellie would be more fun than any of you."

Sondre glanced at them. Honestly, Craig rarely smiled this much. For a moment, Sondre actually *liked* Prospero, because she looked at Craig and asked, "Maybe, but would *they* enjoy a Major League Baseball game?"

"No way!"

"You know your mom can't come, and I need to handle this problem, so I thought it might be a good idea and . . ." Sondre shrugged as Hestia pulled the tickets out of her purse. Honestly, Sondre wished he could go— both to see the game and to try to bond with his stepson.

"Stay out of trouble," Prospero said. "Both of you."

"Spoilsport," Hestia muttered.

"I will," Craig promised. "Thank you, Auntie P."

"Don't thank me," she countered. "It wasn't my idea." Prospero nodded toward Sondre.

"Oh . . . err, sorry about the asshole remark, Sondre." Craig gave him a sheepish look.

"If the worst thing you do this week is call me a name, we'll be fine," Sondre said, thinking about finding the boy in a bar drinking with a pair of badgers two days ago.

Prospero added, "And I was talking mostly to *you*, Hestia. Stay out of trouble."

"I'll look after her," Craig said, sounding far more mature than usual.

For a moment, Sondre wondered if he ought to hug the boy or something. *What was normal dad behavior here?* But then Hestia pointed at the lot and the two went off in search of their rental car.

"They'll be fine. If she's going to raise him, this will be a good test," Prospero said quietly. She motioned for Sondre to follow her. "And we have a target."

As soon as Prospero and Sondre turned the corner of the car-rental building, Prospero's lighthearted demeanor shifted to more serious. The

Victorian witch took his hand, and in the next moment, they were standing in an alcove near a busy area with what looked like several dozen shop fronts. There was a store selling only sunglasses, another looked like a penny-candy store, a third was a two-story bookstore. A fountain and benches and . . . *fake* grass lined the space in front of the stores, and across from them was yet another series of shops. One seemed to have mannequins wearing all manners of undergarments.

"Those have certainly changed, haven't they?" Sondre gestured. "I have seen some of the newer ones when—" He stopped himself. Discussing undergarments with Prospero wasn't normal, even as their lives had grown entangled.

We aren't friends. She was the woman he'd thought of as evil for several decades. He could admit that he was wrong about her on several points, but that was as far as he could adapt. *Not friends.*

"We may have to stop in there." Prospero's pale face was tinged red, even though her expression was blank. "For research."

Sondre broke out in a loud laugh and said, "We're still not friends, but maybe you aren't *entirely* evil."

"The jury is still out on that," Prospero murmured.

Before he could reply, a badger darted out of the underwear store behind a woman who was carrying a bright-pink bag. As the woman scurried away from the store, the badger ran in the opposite direction, a pair of stockings trailing behind the furry mustelid like a plume of smoke. A scream came from the same store.

"Found one," Prospero muttered, before taking off into the panty store.

At the doorway, she dropped something tiny on the floor, but Sondre didn't pause to see what it was. The floor was a veritable field of silk and lace and whatever else these things were made out of. Reds, blacks, whites, pinks, and a surprising number of blues littered the floor like a frippery truck had exploded.

Prospero was wading through the stuff. A pair of polka-dotted translucent knickers had snagged on the buckle of her boot. It waved like a woman's fluttering hankie as she marched into the lacy morass.

Inside, people were popping into badgers all over the store. Other badgers rolled around in the bright and pastel clouds of fabric. Several badgers were panicking.

A witch called Jenn was standing in the middle of the store with her eyes wide. She looked over at him in shock. "Sondre? What are you doing here?" Jenn paused and glanced from Sondre to Prospero. "With *her*?"

"Bringing you home." Sondre stared at the dozen or so badgers running around inside the store. No one was able to open the door, so they were captives here. One badger was a baby, still wearing the tiny cap it had on as a human child. "Look what you're doing, Jenn."

"I didn't mean to badger anyone!" Jenn folded her hands together. She looked around, as if expecting to find a way past them. It was foolishness. Prospero was not a witch to underestimate, and everyone in Crenshaw knew that.

Not that I'm a pushover, Sondre thought, *but I guess she sees me that way because I put up with Aggie's ego.*

"Don't make this hard." Sondre stared at Jenn, knowing the futility of his request even as he spoke the words. Jenn was one of those overly officious people who carried her self-righteousness with her like a cloak. She decided that she wanted to keep her magic *and* be in the world she'd left behind for Crenshaw.

"I don't see why this has to be a big deal. . . ." Jenn smiled her plastic smile.

"Magic in this world has consequences." Prospero sighed loudly. "It's like you've ignored everything I've said about this for the last decade . . . or you're stupid. Is that it, Jenn? Stupidity? Or arrogance?"

"You just wanted to keep us under your control." Jenn glared across the sea of badgers and lacy clothes. "I had a career over here. Now? I'm nothing."

"Sure, perpetual health, long life, and magic are *such* a burden." Prospero couldn't have sounded less sympathetic.

Jenn made a crude gesture in reply. Then she smiled an ugly smile. "Well, *you* can't use magic over here without breaking your own rules, so what are you going to do? Those rules don't apply to me now. I'm free of—"

"I can erase your memory," Prospero interrupted. "Slip inside your head and fix—"

"Fuck you." Jenn closed her eyes, scrunching her face up as if she had to fold everything tightly together. "You cannot. Not if I don't cooperate. Aggie warned all of us. I'll keep my eyes sh—"

"And where is dear Agnes?" Prospero said in a low, calm voice, as she stepped closer to Jenn, not quite touching her.

Sondre looked at the two women, and then he scanned the store. The only other people in the store were badgers. A veritable crowd of badgers ran amuck in the piles of panties. They were obviously panicked and afraid. Sondre wasn't sure how to unbadger the people, but they couldn't be left here in this state. "Are *all* of the badgers nonwitches?"

"Yes." Jenn turned her back to them and presumably opened her eyes, because she was weaving between racks of clothes as she tried to escape. The only way to not slip on the silken mess or run into a rack was to have her eyes open.

For a moment, Prospero stayed still, as if she couldn't quite believe Jenn's audacity. Sondre watched them briefly, but then he saw two badgers start to roll around in some sort of tussle.

"Do you honestly think I was unprepared?" Prospero asked quietly. She was striding through the silk and lace piles on the floor fast enough to set the frilly things to flight a few times.

Without missing a step, Prospero flung a tiny stone at Jenn, hitting her in the calf. At impact, the stone released a spell, and Jenn crumpled to the floor with a scream.

Sondre looked at Prospero with a measure of surprise. "Spell stones?"

She glanced back at him and gave a solitary nod. "I will not commit the same crimes I'm here to stop, Sondre. I packed supplies."

"Do you want me to grab her?" He watched as the witch on the floor continued to flee slowly. Jenn was now crawling toward the door, dragging her injured leg but still moving with impressive speed. She was almost to the door.

"She's not going anywhere but back to Crenshaw," Prospero announced coolly. She was always so damned calm about everything. It made him want to ruffle her feathers.

"Should've hit the knee," Sondre muttered.

Although Prospero shot him a scathing look, she didn't reply. Instead, she turned back to Jenn and marched after the crawling woman.

"Can't teleport, huh?" Prospero taunted, nudging the fractured leg. "Maybe you could stop trying to get away . . . ? It's pointless."

"Bitch." Jenn was almost at the door. She pulled herself upright on a rack of nightgowns that were more decorative than functional.

Prospero pulled out another stone and rolled it in her fingers. "I don't feel like chasing you, Jenn. Stop, or else I'll—"

Sondre tackled Jenn. His patience had expired, so he wrapped his arms around her from behind and held her to his chest. She squirmed and kicked at him with her unbroken leg, but Sondre held her tightly. "Stop it. Do you really want to give her an excuse to keep tossing spells at you? I'm trying to keep you uninjured."

Jenn opened her mouth to reply.

Prospero slapped her palm—the one holding the stone in it—against Jenn's mouth.

"Wait!" Sondre started, but it was too late. The spell in the stone was instant. Jenn went limp like she had no pulse. The sudden drop made him feel like he was holding an unwieldy sack of beans.

He lowered the escapee to the ground and looked up at Prospero. "What was that?"

"Sleep stone." She shot Sondre a glare. "I wasn't going to let her get away. Just chase her for a minute. I had plenty of stones for if she fought back."

He glared back at Prospero as he straightened. "Sadist."

"They *shot* Scylla." Prospero jabbed a finger into his shoulder. "They risked our whole world. I'm not a sadist, Sondre. I'm *angry.*"

Sondre had no retort for that. It wasn't like he was opposed to justice. Hell, he was in Aggie's house. Jenn was in his house, too. It hit him then that his reactions were altered by that very reality.

"She's part of my house," he muttered, mostly to himself. "I want to protect her because . . . I'm assuming the head-of-house responsibility."

"I know." Prospero looked weary. "I wondered if that would make you less likely to do anything to stop her. Allan's not in yours, though, and Aggie's no longer in any house. That ought to help, right?"

Sondre nodded, feeling self-conscious. House loyalty was likely a factor in why Agnes' arguments made so much sense over the years, but that detail wasn't one he could be sure of . . . until Agnes had left Crenshaw. A lot had changed now that she'd abandoned House Grendel. He felt like he'd been swayed by the fact that she was, in essence, his supervisor. Agnes had been his veritable captain, his superior officer—to borrow the terms from a lifetime ago when he was in the army. And while Sondre might be adept at rabble-rousing, he was also the sort of man who gave respect where it was due.

How am I going to fight Agnes after years of obeying her?

He didn't want to. He'd always found the churlish old witch fascinating.

Focus on the issue at hand.

One task at a time, one disaster in a moment: that was how he managed everything. Well, that, and the occasional bar fight or tumble into bed with a willing woman. *Just Maggie these days.* He'd thought that having a wife would be limiting, but he had to admit that he felt centered by marrying Maggie rather than resentful. *Deal with this. Go home to Maggie.*

Sondre motioned at the now-napping badgers. They'd undoubtedly gone into shock at the fact that they were all tiny, furred mammals. The mind could be tricky when magic was involved and a person didn't believe in magic. "The badgers should revert to human form after we take Jenn out of here. I think . . . I've never seen accidental badgering, though."

Prospero ignored the clan of badgers and the comment. She stood looking down at Jenn with a deep scowl. "I wish I was surprised that the escapees didn't all stay together. This makes it harder. I hoped we could just scoop them all up at once, but . . . this complicates everything."

"You think?" Sondre couldn't dwell on it long without worrying. As of the last four days, they'd discovered that there were at least seven witches—six now that they'd recovered Jenn—who had left Crenshaw. Three were heads of house. One, Agnes, had been *his* head of house.

"I'll need to look around in Jenn's head when we get her home. I'll take her to the Congress building for that, so you can skip seeing it." Prospero folded her arms over her chest. They'd argued for years about what her magic did to people's minds, and Sondre had his share of worries there since he'd learned how often she'd messed with his own head.

"So the magic of their house leaks out when they're here." Sondre swallowed, thinking through the ramifications. "Aside from massive fields of badgers, what does that mean? Aggie is violent. And Allan is . . . a drunkard?"

"So fights because of Aggie and intoxication because of Allan? Maybe."

Sondre didn't think that was the worst possible scenario, by far, but he hoped it was no more than that.

"With the barrier down, I don't know if the area near home is at risk, either. Will our collective magic harm those nonmagical people nearest Crenshaw, too?" Prospero stared upward as if praying or seeking clarity.

At the same time, Sondre took in the disaster around them. *How had we been so wrong?* The effect of magic on regular people was a messy, dangerous thing. Maybe over time it would normalize, but right now, it looked like the admonishments were true. Witches needed to stay home.

"Jenn's done, though. That's two of four contained," Prospero said in what felt like a forced cheer.

"What will happen to them?" Sondre asked. "Did Walt say anything to you?"

"Likely siphoned in Jenn's case. She's not happy in Crenshaw, so . . ." Prospero shrugged, looking away at the wrecked store. "We'll siphon her and return her to this world somewhere. She's been over in ours . . . I don't know how long."

"About five years?" Sondre guessed. "She could probably go back to her original life."

"Aggie can't. Allan, either." Prospero looked exhausted for a moment. "I wish I'd been wrong, Sondre. We can't keep the magic and come back here to live, though."

"So maybe we ought to ask *everyone* about their desire to stay or go." Sondre followed her toward the counter. If he had been so very wrong about the ability to return to this world, he was going to find ways to mitigate the problems in Crenshaw.

"Suggest it to Congress. I won't oppose that idea." Prospero had pulled out a stack of cash. She smacked the cash register a few times and jabbed buttons until she managed to get the drawer open. Once she did, she dropped the pile of money in it.

"For damages and . . . a few purchases." Then she grabbed a couple bags and started collecting underwear and robes and whatnot. Without looking at him, she said, "You should grab a few things. I *bought* these for everyone back home."

"Maggie's about your size," Sondre said awkwardly. "Do you know what size that is in . . . these things?"

Prospero's cheeks were as red as the sheer thing she picked up. "This one."

After a few moments, he said, "This is a little weird. Shopping with you when there's badgers everywhere and . . . Jenn's like that."

Prospero took an audible breath before saying, "If we're sharing feelings . . . Ellie's remembering things. I'm concerned."

The hurried way that Prospero said it was the biggest clue that this was, in truth, another crisis to contend with. The magic that Elleanor Brandeau had was both impressive and deadly, and when she'd escaped, she'd had to have her memory erased.

"I thought once you did that to someone's head, it stayed changed," Sondre said awkwardly.

"Correct."

"Well, you're fucked, aren't you?" Sondre glanced over at Prospero. The woman who had casually broken Jenn's leg was currently looking at a drawer of underwear with open crotches.

"Not the only one she'll be angry with," Prospero said. "I thought you deserved a warning."

"That's incredibly . . . nice of you," Sondre said awkwardly.

She snorted. Then she tossed a pair of panties at him. Sondre caught the slip of sheer material reflexively.

"Still not friends?" she asked as she looked back at him.

Sondre shook his head. "Damned if I know anymore."

24
Ellie

A memory came crashing over Ellie. The force of the accompanying emotions made her stumble and fall.

"Ellie." Prospero took a step closer. "I'm relieved to find you."

"No." Ellie raised a hand, and the diner's floor lifted up like the asphalt serpents and the forest serpents once had. This time, though, Ellie had better control of it. It was no illusion. No accident. She stared at the woman she'd been falling in love with, and Ellie willed that black-tiled floor into a cage. She willed the silvered barstools into steel bars around it.

Doubly caged, Prospero stared at Ellie. "You're making a mistake."

"Let me go. Don't pursue us," Ellie half begged, half demanded, and then she ran out the door and jumped into the waiting car. Maggie was seated there.

When Ellie opened her eyes, her brain felt overcharged from the image of creating a cage around her wife. She'd been in the other world with Maggie Lynch, the headmaster's new wife.

Does she remember? Was that why she cornered me?

Why can't I remember her if I was running away with her?

Was I with Maggie? Unfaithful to Prospero?

It hit Ellie with a sickening force that she had apparently run away from her wife with another woman. That thing she'd forgotten? It was apparently that she cheated on her wife with another student there.

No wonder Prospero keeps rejecting me.

Ellie had more questions than she knew what to do with since she remembered jumping into a car with Maggie. It was very clearly an erased memory, not a dream. Ellie was certain of that. Ellie was unsettled by the thought that she was hunted over there—*by my wife!*—just as the current escaped witches were.

Witches aren't allowed to go to that world! I don't even know Maggie. I can't recall a single conversation we've had until yesterday. . . .

And that was the crux of the problem, though. Ellie couldn't recall it. That wasn't the same as it not happening. It was simply that Ellie had no recollection of it. *Which means Prospero erased more than a memory of whatever was happening there. . . . What else don't I know?*

Ellie walked through the increasingly busy castle. The hallways were filled with witches she didn't recognize, and most of them had carts of belongings. Some were more like old-fashioned train trolleys, stacked with trunks and boxes and baskets. A few looked more like luggage carts. One woman who seemed to have an enormous bustle under her dress was carrying a raccoon that was wearing a bonnet. Odder still, the raccoon was swaddled as if were an infant.

The raccoon, for its part, looked perfectly content to be wrapped in a baby blanket—or maybe it was simply tolerant of the witch's actions.

"Make way," the witch barked out. "If you lollygaggers wake the baby, I'll make you wish you'd never met me."

"I wish that already, Bells." An older man in a pair of overalls that had seen better days shook his head and made eye contact with Ellie. "Silly bird can't tell a forest beast from a baby."

Ignoring him and everyone else, the witch swayed exaggeratedly as she ploughed through the hall with a luggage cart in front of her like a cowcatcher on the front of a train. Her other arm was wrapped around her "baby."

At her side, the Norwegian singer from her remedial-magic classes said, "Hello, Ellie."

"Axell." Ellie eyed him suspiciously, thinking back to their recent interrupted conversation. He knew things she ought to know. Of that, she was certain. "I'm looking for Maggie."

He smiled wider and said quickly, "Maggie is your friend, Ellie. You are close, and then this last week you stopped talking suddenly. Both of you." He stared at her like she ought to be understanding his peculiar pronouncements. "You can tell this is true, *ja?*"

"Yes." Ellie's eyes looked at him appraisingly. "Were *we* friends?"

"No, but I would like that." He beamed at her. "I am Maggie's friend now. You? You are frightening. Like your wife."

They paused to let the raccoon in the bonnet run past them. The little furry fellow had escaped his swaddle, but he still had on the bonnet and what looked like pink gingham bloomers and a dress. Ellie had the distinct impression that her sense of "normal" was long gone, but even with the adjustments of a magical world, the raccoon in bloomers was still a bit odd.

"Well, grab the baby, you ninnies!" The overalls-clad witch strode past them like a warrior on a mission. "C'mere, Chester."

Axell and Ellie watched as the man used some sort of magical energy to reach out and swoop Chester the raccoon up into his arms.

"Arabella worries," he told the chubby mammal.

It chittered at him, and the man listened as if he understood. Then he frowned. "Just eat your porridge for her. I'll fix you a nice plate of eggs and crayfish when she goes out with the ladies."

If anyone had told Ellie that raccoons and badgers were often people before she'd lived in Crenshaw, she'd have thought they were liars. She glanced at the man as he came back toward her.

"Are people turned into raccoons for a different crime than badgers?"

The man in overalls stopped, scowled at her, and announced, "Chester is not a criminal, miss. He's a raccoon born and bred."

Then he carried the raccoon away as it chittered angrily at her. She didn't understand a word he said, but she knew it was angry.

"Sorry," she called after the raccoon. "I wasn't trying to be rude!"

Ellie wasn't sure what to think. Raccoons were raccoons, but badgers were people who had committed crimes . . . ? She shook her head and turned back to Axell. "Right. Maggie was my friend."

For a moment, Axell's expression was torn, as if he was weighing the risks of having this conversation.

"I won't tell anyone *who* told me."

"Come." He walked away, weaving around the new residents until they reached a door that was closed. He glanced back at her and pointed at the door. "Magic the lock."

It was an odd request, but she understood what he meant. She readjusted the locking mechanism so the door swung open. Inside the room was a stack of binders that she recognized.

"My research!" She grabbed one of her Missing files and flipped it open. Dan Monahan's face stared back at her. "I have your boyfriend's information. . . ."

"*Ja.*" Axell flopped down on the bed. "You knew about some students when you came here."

Absently, Ellie flipped the pages. There was an article about Maggie, too. Ellie skimmed it.

MISSING LAWYER

RALEIGH—The search for 44-year-old Margaret Lynch continues this week. "Ms. Lynch careened off the road. Evidence suggests the mother of one was day-drinking," local sheriff Bill Bamberg explained. "Maybe she caught a ride with someone. Maybe she planned the whole thing."

Lynch, an attorney, was last seen by her teen son, who was knocked unconscious in the crash. Several campers saw the two that weekend, but there were no witnesses to the accident. "Maggie was in over her head at work, but there were no cases likely to lead to foul play," her ex-husband explained. "I think this was her cowardice. We were in a custody discussion, and I wouldn't be surprised if she was trying to kidnap our son." Authorities are hoping someone will reach out with information on Ms. Lynch's situation.

Ellie ran her hand over the sleeve that held the newsprint article. She had been collecting the stories of the missing for as long as she could recall. She sorted them by type and resolution, updated them. These binders were the work of a lifetime.

Why are they sitting in a sealed room in a castle in Crenshaw?

Ellie looked around the room for a moment. She walked to the window and saw a tree there. Ellie felt her own magic vibrating from outside the window. She had made the tree.

This was my room, she realized.

For a moment, she remembered standing there before. Not in this exact spot, but near this tree. Maggie was there at that point, too. *"Where to next? If we're going to slip off our 'campus,' where do we go?"* That meant Maggie had been in this room, too.

But I don't remember knowing her.

"Why don't I remember reading this?" Ellie asked, pointing at the binder, which was flopped open to the article about Maggie. "Or making that?" She gestured over her shoulder this time, toward the window.

"Maggie does not remember, either." Axell held Ellie's gaze. "You both forgot many things. We are helping her know now that her son is safe."

"Does everyone know that I . . . left?"

He shrugged. "I watch the people I like, the people *Daniel* likes . . . and those he fears."

Ellie couldn't figure out what could've happened to make Dan fear her, but she suspected that with her power, fear was not a surprising reaction. She was, after all, a research librarian, and here Axell was offering himself up like a book of clues and evidence.

"Did I hurt him?"

"No."

"Did I hurt you?" she asked.

Axell smiled. "That *would* hurt him, but no."

"Did I hurt Maggie?"

"No. You didn't hurt anyone, I think. Maybe Lady Prospero." Axell paused before adding, "I was not where you were, so I do not know all the things. I think you did not, though."

As Ellie tried to think of the best questions, Axell watched her, and it struck her that he could have just told her more than he did. Instead, she felt like she was pulling the answers from him—but that he *wanted* her to do that. He obviously was trying to prompt and shape her inquiries.

"Why can't you just *tell* me?" Ellie looked down at the fruiting tree. She'd made that. Her power was to shift and create. She remade things.

For a moment, Axell looked wary. "I cannot break all the rules, Ellie. I told you: some people have power, and *some* are disposable." He looked toward the door, where voices were rising and falling. "And some people have influence. . . . You have power. I have neither power nor influence. I am a cog here."

"Oh, I'm sure you—"

"I *like* this not mattering, Ellie. I *want* to be a cog, not in the center." Axell gave her a very sad smile that seemed much older than he looked. "Over there, I was someone in the center. People watched me. It was too much focus. Here? I am a cog, but also . . . being only a cog means I can be disposed."

It was an ominous statement. *Disposed? What sort of person disposed of others?* Her mind filled in a few answers before she even finished thinking the question. *My wife. Maggie's husband. The chief witch.* It took only a fraction of a moment to have several answers.

"What's his gift? Dan's? Explain it more."

And Axell's smile blossomed widely. "Daniel . . . *enhances*. If I want to sing, Dan will make my magic larger so the whole of the castle could hear. He can make *any* magic stronger."

The import of what Axell wanted her to understand was suddenly crystal clear. Dan's magic strengthened other magic, and previously, Prospero hadn't been able to erase Ellie's memories. With Dan's help, Prospero must have done so. Whatever Ellie forgot involved Maggie, and that was the secret between them.

Ellie looked at Axell and asked, "Shall I pretend we never talked about this?"

"Maybe we say only that I removed you from the hallway where the crowds were big. That is a true thing, not lies." Axell gave her a wide-eyed, innocent look. "I was trying to be a friend, Elleanor Brandeau of the House of Thesis. It is not right what they did."

Then he was gone, and Ellie was left in what had once apparently been her room. She could see why they hadn't returned her to it. There was an entire binder on her classmates. *I thought I lost that or didn't bring it here to Crenshaw.* And there was a giant apple tree. She'd obviously climbed down that tree with Maggie.

A part of Ellie thought that it was ridiculous that she be asked to forget as much as she had. That same part of her thought that this was overreaction if the crime in question was infidelity. And a tiny voice whispered, *How far would Prospero go to keep someone powerful at her side who was completely devoted to her?*

Even without all her memories, Ellie had no illusions that her wife was a gentle soul. She was currently hunting witches who had shot Scylla and exposed Crenshaw. Prospero was a witch who evoked rightful fear in anyone who crossed her.

And I left *Prospero, caged her, and ran away with Maggie.*

Whatever the reason for those choices, Ellie had no trouble believing that Prospero had not wanted to let Ellie go . . . or that if she found out now that Ellie realized the things she had, Maggie and Daniel and Axell were at risk. They were not impervious to mind magic.

So why didn't she erase Dan and Axell's memories?

Surely, Prospero had to realize that, in time, Ellie would piece it all together.

That thought hit her like a fist to the throat, and Ellie let out a gasp. Prospero was far from careless. She had talked about having to visit multiple people to adjust memories, and yet in this case, she had not.

And she knew I researched the missing.

Could she have wanted *this to happen? Wanted me to figure it out?* Prospero followed the laws as much as she had to, but she was the queen of loopholes. Ellie was realizing that as she'd started to find ways to get her wife back into her arms.

That possibility shifted the weight of things that Ellie was starting to figure out. She had no doubt of her wife's regard or the fact that Prospero *did* desire her. Prospero couldn't act on that desire as long as Ellie couldn't remember. . . .

She wants me to figure it out! Ellie grinned to herself. Being given a puzzle to solve with Prospero as the prize at the end was a rather perfect seduction for Ellie. *So I'll figure out the rest, and in the end, we'll be okay.*

The loss of memories had only lasted a few days, but they had an eternity in front of them, and Ellie had to believe that the parts she recalled were larger than the parts she'd been forced to forget.

We can make it work.

Can't we?

Was I unfaithful?

Was it a power grab?

Was I a part of the New Economists? Running away like they had?

There were answers to be had, and her mind was steadily finding more and more of them. She wanted to work things out. First, though, she needed Prospero to come home safely.

25
Prospero

As Prospero and Sondre walked out of the shop, Prospero was relieved that no one was seriously injured. In that moment, Prospero had thought that since Jenn was contained, they had only to teleport back to Crenshaw and turn the unconscious woman over to the chief witch so she could be interrogated. And honestly, if not for how cautious she was being, Prospero would've just slipped into her mind now rather than knock her out. A few screams and pointless flailing were not the worst things that had ever happened to Prospero, not by anyone's standards.

Instead, Sondre was carrying Jenn in a bridal carry—and Prospero was prepared with the "Oh, she fell and broke her leg, the poor thing" explanation if they were stopped by any nonmagical people.

Once they were out of the area, they could pop back home.

No teleportation around nonmagical folks.

Prospero had been between the worlds often enough that it ought not be a huge issue to transport one unconscious woman. So she was unprepared when she heard an unwelcome voice say, "Oh, look, the noble heroine and her lackey."

"Aggie." Prospero stepped forward; all good intention vanished at the mocking voice. She'd heard Aggie in Scylla's mind. She'd seen the woman's joy in Scylla's pain.

Fuck the rules.

"Did the other wench wake?" Aggie asked in that same faux-friendly voice. "I wasn't sure after that bullet carved into her. Allan was too drunk to aim, though, so I wasn't sure."

"She's in recovery." Prospero tried to catch the old witch's eye, but Aggie was wearing dark black sunglasses and a hat tipped low, blocking the top of her face to prevent accidentally making the eye contact necessary to use her magic. She was obviously not a witch who typically kept her face hidden, but they were no longer bound by the politeness of both being heads of house.

Some witches lose clarity with age. She could be suffering from . . .

Prospero shoved the moment of empathy away. She didn't care *why* Agnes orchestrated shooting Scylla. Regardless of Aggie's reasons, a woman nearly lost her life simply because they disagreed. Agnes and her cronies could have left through the barrier. Sure, the law opposed it, but the law opposed *murder,* too.

And even if Scylla *had* stood in the way, even if there had been a fight, guns were not the answer. Agnes had tried to take the life of one of the few people who mattered to Prospero. And she did so with cold premeditation.

Attempted murder.

As Prospero tried to angle herself to see the older witch, Sondre was uncharacteristically silent. Out the corner of her eye, Prospero saw him lower Jenn to the ground and step over her. He stayed at Prospero's side, but he rotated slightly to keep an eye on their surroundings. He didn't comment or interject himself into the situation. He watched and waited.

Prospero had a stray thought that decades of being adversaries made them slip into partnership with ease. If they worked together, they could solve this. Seeing him, realizing that he was assessing and likely running possibilities in his mind made Prospero realize that she was being careless.

And she was grateful for his more taciturn nature.

Her first impulse was simply to knock Aggie out and drag her ass back to Crenshaw. *Liar. Her first instinct was to wish she had a weapon of nonmagical means to mow Agnes down where she stood smirking.*

However, their small group was already drawing more attention than they needed—and Aggie's magic was rolling out to wash over the nonmagical people like a chemical cloud. For a fraught instant, Prospero could feel the undercurrent of agitation, could see it in the way one man shoved another, could hear it as a woman called another person a vulgar word. The crowd was seething with a wave of Aggie's magic, and violence was coming.

If we can relocate this and—

"Asshole," one person yelled.

Another man punched a woman, and the crowd churned in rage. Anything would have elicited the wrong sort of reaction from the increasingly agitated crowd, and now that the spark was lit, fights were breaking out everywhere. The smattering of squabbles would surge into a riot if they didn't get a handle on this quickly.

"Rules?" Sondre asked in a low voice.

"No magic . . . if possible," Prospero murmured.

Could I erase all the memories here if it wasn't possible to resist? she wondered. It was conceivable, but it wasn't ideal. Nothing about this moment was ideal.

We just need to get her back to Crenshaw.

"We were wrong," Sondre said, louder now, talking to Agnes. Whatever tactic he had chosen was either logic, trickery, or appealing to Agnes' better nature. Prospero wouldn't be successful with any of those attempts, but maybe Sondre could pull it off.

He stepped forward, not quite flanking Aggie now but better positioning himself to attack her if necessary. Agnes undoubtedly realized that, but she let him ease closer.

While it left Jenn's limp body exposed, it also meant that Sondre was well out of Prospero's path if she had to throw any stones at Aggie. That surely wasn't accidental, and Prospero was grateful that he was adept at thinking of both details.

"The traitor speaks." Aggie turned to face him, ignoring Prospero entirely, as if Sondre was more of a threat than Prospero. The head of House Grendel had always underestimated her, though. Being adept at avoiding physical altercations didn't mean that Prospero was inept at violence. It was simply not her first choice, not that she ever admitted that.

Years with a husband who spoke his opinion with fists will do that, she thought before shoving the memory of her pre-witch life away. Arriving in Crenshaw with the skin flayed from bone on her face had a way of souring a person on physical conflict. *That doesn't mean I didn't learn.*

After seeing another woman die from his rage, after feeling his rage time after time, Prospero had spent quite a few years learning how to fight. She felt guilty afterward, though. That was—in her estimation— why her magic was mind alteration. Better to avoid the blood and pain, better to simply change their thinking, better to change her *own* thinking if necessary. Those had been survival mechanisms in her original life.

Now they're my magic.

Prospero fished in her pocket for the silken bag she'd picked up at Howie's den. Without looking, she couldn't be sure which stone she grabbed. It didn't matter, though. Fatal or not, the stone would stop Agnes or it would slow her down.

If I can grab her, I can teleport her to Crenshaw.

Fuck the witnesses.

Fuck the rules.

"How long were you her lapdog, Sondre?" Aggie's voice sounded more hurt than angry. "Telling us you were on our side and carrying everything back to that bitch . . . Tell me: did you laugh at us? Mock us?"

"It wasn't like that. . . ." Sondre was telling the truth. Prospero could hear it, any witch could. Lies felt wrong. So that ought to have been enough answer to buy time.

It wasn't.

The staff in Aggie's hand writhed like the serpent it could become. A glint of eyes peered through the wood, and Sondre stared at them. He had a strange fear of slithering things, which Aggie surely knew. He'd nearly died from a snakebite; it was how he'd become a witch.

"Just biding your time to steal House Grendel, then," Aggie continued. "Was that it? You thought you could take what's mine?"

"Aggie . . . Grendel is . . . was . . . I had no eyes on taking the house." Sondre had spent his entire witchhood under Agnes' foot. He motioned to multiple fights in the courtyard outside the shops. "You see the way they react to your magic. You're *leaking* it."

He took his gaze off her, gesturing to several more fights and outbursts. One woman in beige trousers and a blue blouse had picked up a chair. As Prospero glanced at her, the woman tossed the chair into a shop window. Glass and the tower of sunglasses in the display rained down.

"Weak-willed sheep." Aggie's mouth twisted in disgust. "It's no fault of mine that they let their rage out. Violence simply *is*. Look at this world. Look at yourself." She laughed, sounding a little crazed. "How many bar brawls have you begun, boy? Violence is a *necessity.*"

It's not, Prospero thought, but she didn't speak the words. She was willing to let Sondre have a chance at talking to Agnes. That wasn't Prospero's preference, but she could understand his urge to do so.

"Come home with us. We can work this out." Sondre stepped closer, and Agnes pivoted.

"So that old man can badger me?" Agnes eyed Sondre. "Did I teach you nothing? Do I look like I'll surrender? I won't go back there to be reduced. . . ."

Prospero couldn't disagree with that impulse. Being badgered, being a small mustelid that was left lapping mead from the tavern floor, was no fate for a warrior. She'd rather die than be left as an object of scorn or pity again. Agnes made more sense to her than Prospero liked.

Sondre held out his hands in a placating gesture as he took another step forward. "You know I mean you no harm, Mother Grendel. We were wrong about magic in this world. It's not harmless . . . and . . ."

Prospero rolled her eyes. She still couldn't get the attention of the older witch long enough to slip into her mind. *One moment,* Prospero thought as she stared at her. *I just need one moment to connect to her mind.*

Casually, Prospero rolled the stone in her hand. *Not knowing what it would do wasn't that irresponsible, was it?* Agnes had shot Scylla. She was making all these people fill with rage and destruction. *Aren't I entitled to lash out?* A lifetime of propriety, of keeping her feelings in order, of restraining herself seemed to be filtering away.

My anger is justified.

Attacking her is better than standing here.

I should just—

Then Aggie glanced at her and winked. "You feel it, don't you? Remember how he beat you? How he killed her . . . what was her name? The one you love?"

"Ellie," Prospero whispered. She could see her beloved on the floor now. Her eyes were staring at nothing. Her mouth was open as if to speak. He'd killed her. Her only crime was that Prospero was falling in love with her. That was the fate of women like them: be miserable or be dead. To be hated for being born as a person who loved women made no sense, and yet that was her fate.

Ellie wasn't born when I was, Prospero thought briefly, but her mind's eye saw her there. Her neck was twisted unnaturally, and her eyes were sightless. *He killed my Ellie. She didn't even really love me. We didn't have time. And now she's dead.*

"You killed her." Prospero looked at her husband, standing there like he had the right to dole out deaths. "Wasn't breaking me enough?"

"Prospero . . ." Sondre reached out. "Come on. She's lying. Shake it off."

"Because it's so hard for you to think someone could love me?" Prospero felt tears on her cheeks, or maybe it was blood. Sometimes she couldn't tell. He beat her so often that it could be either one. She stared at him as he menaced her and said, "Just because you couldn't love me, that doesn't make me unlovable."

"I'm not him." Her husband's voice sounded wrong.

Prospero closed her eyes tightly. Her head throbbed, probably from being hit so often.

"Prospero!" he said.

"That's not my name. . . ." She looked around, trying to make sense of where they were. The people were dressed so oddly. One woman was in trousers that clung to her legs, and that woman . . . *Why is that woman on the ground?*

The man put a hand to his chest. "I'm Sondre. We're friends, Prospero. I'm not whoever she's trying to make you think I am!"

"He's jealous. You excluded him, rejected him, refused his touch, and then *she* had caught his eye, too. He looked at her, didn't he?" Aggie's voice was so soothing as she explained what ought to already have been obvious. "You saw it. How he looked at her with vile thoughts in his mind. That's why he killed her. He hated that she rejected him, too."

Prospero heard a keening animal noise and realized that it was her. Her husband stood there in his arrogance, looking at her as if she were something foul.

"Do you remember how he looked at her all the time?" Aggie murmured. "Were her skirts rucked up when you saw her—"

"Agnes. Enough." Sondre strode forward, closing the last of the gap between him and the old woman. *Who is she? Agnes. This is Agnes. We were coming to see her.*

His hand grasped Agnes' arm.

He snapped his fingers at Prospero. "Ellie is alive, Prospero. She wears denims, for goodness' sake. Shake this off. Whatever you're thinking isn't real."

Prospero looked at him. He was too far away to punch her this time. *Wait. Sondre. Her husband was different. This was . . .*

"Help me," Aggie begged, drawing Prospero's gaze.

The old woman is in danger! She opened her eyes wide, and Prospero remembered that she had wanted to see those eyes for some reason, but she wasn't sure what it had been. "Your poor face, Prospero. I can see the bone. He did that to you, his own wife. It must ache so. What will he do to a frail old lady like me?"

And Prospero realized that she hadn't even noticed how fragile Aggie was now. Her body was trembling as she leaned on her cane. *Men like him are deadly,* Prospero thought. Her hand reached up as if to touch the flesh that was flapped open on her face. *Will I lose my eye this time?*

Her vision blurred as she stared at the poor old woman.

"You have to stop him. Save me. You couldn't save *her* or yourself, but you can save me." Aggie's voice broke in fear. "His sort assaults women. He's assaulted me so often that—"

"I have not." Sondre's sharp voice cut into Prospero's mind. "You both know better than that!"

The old woman is lying about that. Prospero knew it the way all witches knew when words were false. She held the stone in her palm. *A spell stone . . .*

"I swear to you, Prospero. I have not ever sexually assaulted a woman . . . Agnes! Seriously?" He reached out to grab the woman's other arm, the one with the cane. "Prospero. Listen to me. I'm telling the truth."

He was, and the lie in Agnes' words cracked something in her magical hold on Prospero. *Ellie is alive, too.* The woman who died was killed by a man. *My husband.* That man was not Sondre. *And Ellie is alive.*

Prospero threw the stone, and Aggie lunged forward. Her staff shifted into something reptilian that sank teeth into Sondre's arm. It clung there as if it were a natural snake, not a magical piece of wood.

Sondre stared at it in horror. His fear of snakes was as genuine as her fear of her long-dead husband had been.

And all that was left of Agnes was the lingering edge of her laughter as she teleported away. The stone had not even glanced off her. Instead, it landed on Jenn.

The unconscious witch began to sizzle like meat on a grill. Her entire body writhed as if she were filled with things trying to get out, and in mere seconds, she was reduced to ash and a scorched mark on the pavement.

The scent of burning flesh lingered even as the crowd started to come back to clarity. The madness of the crowd was not fully gone. Most of the fights were fading, though, and people were pausing to help strangers to their feet. They looked afraid, and Prospero was about to go start adjusting memories until Sondre made a noise.

"Are you okay?" he asked in a strained voice.

"Not really, but it's not physi—" Her words cut off as she saw Sondre's hand. It was swollen and ghastly pale. She glanced up to see his expression and noticed that he was dripping sweat. His breathing was labored.

"I don't think I am okay at all," he muttered.

"Damn it!" Prospero surged forward to his side. In the next instant, she almost collapsed under the weight of him as he dropped onto her like a felled giant.

Fuck witnesses, she thought briefly as she teleported them to the infirmary.

26
Maggie

Sondre had been furious that she'd sought Ellie out, and Maggie understood that she'd been a little reckless. She didn't want to burn her relationship down, but she also figured that if she was important enough to *also* be leverage on Ellie . . . well, it only made sense to rekindle their friendship.

The only issue Maggie really had was that it seemed that her actions were sparking actual conflict with Sondre. Her recent time with him had been idyllic, although she did recall her arrival in Crenshaw and their initial sparks. Lately though, everything had felt perfect—and here she was trying to rattle him.

Her heart of hearts said that full truth was what she needed and wanted. Craig was safe. With that detail sorted, her ability to ignore the blatant misuse of power that the Congress of Magic had used was . . . absent.

Now she was sitting in her suite of rooms, replaying memories with Sondre, looking for any other fracture in the reality she currently knew—because he'd erased something utterly unrelated to Ellie. That small detail changed her acceptance of everything.

"I don't deserve your trust or your loyalty, but I tried to protect you," Sondre said. *"If I could free you from me—"*

"I like you. You keep me and Craig both safe." Maggie curled into his embrace. *"I have you both in my life. No ex to deal with. No shared custody with the man that tried to kill me. Why would I want to leave you?"*

"I'll do my best to keep you safe, to love you, and to take care of your needs," Sondre had started to say. He paused. Then he stared at her. *"But if you start talking to Elleanor regularly, I can't protect you. Hestia is fine, since she's nonmagical like Craig, but Ellie is dangerous to you—"*

Maggie shook her head. He was always so serious about everything. "Now, *let's discuss these needs you plan to take care of . . . Are you sure a man of your age can—"*

He had done just that.

Now Maggie was left wondering how to get all her memories, not just the ones he or the Congress decided she could keep. No rational soul would fault her for wanting answers. Still, Maggie resolved to be more cautious the next time she sought out Ellie.

A knock on the door interrupted her musing. So few people came to the door that she hesitated before opening it. The lack of a peephole to see who was there went on the list of things to correct.

"Hello?" Maggie called.

"Hello," a woman's voice echoed.

Maggie cracked the door slightly. Ellie Brandeau stood at Maggie's door. That was not exactly subtle—and honestly, Maggie respected it. That didn't mean she could invite Ellie inside.

"Sorry, the headmaster is out." Maggie kept the door partially shut, leaning on it to prevent Ellie from pushing it all the way open. "He has a new office on the main floor, though. This is not a place that students are to visit now."

"I'm not here to see him," Ellie said. "Could I come in?"

"No. I'm sorry, but I'm busy and—"

Ellie leaned forward and kissed Maggie. It was awkward and un-expected, and it felt weirdly like kissing a relative. Ellie held on to the back of Maggie's neck and deepened the kiss, which made it even more awkward.

Maggie jerked away. "What the actual fuck was *that*? Aside from super inappropriate?"

"A test." Ellie shrugged. "I have memories of you . . . we climbed down an apple tree."

"Is that a euphemism for something?" Maggie kept her voice low, glancing into the hallway to be sure there were no witnesses. "Look, I don't have any issues with women being with other women or whatever, but I am not going down an apple tree or whatever that means."

"A literal tree, Maggie. I remember leaving the castle with you, and I remember being in a car with you."

"That's not possible. I didn't know you over—"

"You can't drive stick—*not* a euphemism. Literally, you can't drive a stick-shift car." Ellie tacked the last bit on quickly. "You're actually a hellish driver in general."

"Okay . . . well, I can't explain why you know that. Don't care, either." Maggie shook her head. Everything that Ellie said just now rang as true, but Maggie didn't care. "You can't be here. Do you not know that? I can talk to you about it later, but not now. Not here."

"Did you or did you not seek me out?"

"I did, but you need to go away." Maggie could see someone walking this way. "Later, Ellie. I swear, we can talk later. Elsewhere."

"We are in this together somehow. You know that," Ellie insisted.

"Fine, but not *here*. Did you miss my angry husband bustling me away?" Maggie glared. "You make me seem like the levelheaded person. Also, no kissing me. You can't just—"

"I needed to know if you . . . if we . . ." Ellie flushed.

"Could have asked. Seriously, you aren't my type. I like men. Strong, dangerous men," Maggie grumbled at her. "I'll find out what I can and send Axell to you to set a meeting."

Then she shoved her back with a burst of unexpected magic and closed the door firmly. It wasn't a slam of the door, but it was final. Maggie wasn't going to be stupid about her decision to investigate. Right now, she had everything going for her.

Just need to do a little sleuthing. . . .

Decide what all she knows.

Figure out how to share what I know.

Maggie leaned her back against the door and thought about the weird situation she was in. She trusted Sondre, but it was a strange feeling, because on some level she knew that her love for her husband was manufactured. Theirs was an arranged marriage. He'd told her that much.

She was still leaning there an hour later when a hob appeared.

"Miss Maggie needs to come now," Clancy, the ever-dapperly dressed hobgoblin said. His voice appeared before his body finished appearing, so at first, there was only a voice and a pair of well-polished shoes. By the time the second syllable of her name was out, Clancy's legs and torso were visible.

By the time his hat—a smart red fedora today—was clear, he'd grabbed her ear and popped them to the door of the infirmary.

"What?" Maggie managed, reaching out to steady herself on the doorframe. "Is Craig—"

"No." Clancy gave her the sort of look she once had to give to clients who were going to lose a case.

"Where is he?" She leaned against the wall.

"With AuntHestia," Clancy said. "They're safe."

The fact that the hobs had all taken to calling the only other non-magical residence of Crenshaw *AuntHestia* as if it were one word seemed to be the least peculiar detail of the moment. Maggie glanced at the door of the infirmary.

"Sondre?"

The hob vanished, leaving Maggie standing in the hallway alone.

She pushed the door open to see the infirmary more active than she'd like. Scylla was still stretched out on one bed. The curtain beside her was pulled closed, and on the other side, she heard Sondre's voice.

"Get it off me," he yelled.

The curtain sagged as someone launched or fell against the dingy drape. A crash of metal onto the castle floor followed. And the doctor's voice almost at the same time. "Stop thrashing, Sondre."

Maggie walked past the woman in the first bed and peered around the curtain. Sondre was not a very cooperative patient at all. He flailed, trying to shake something off his arm. "Get. It. Off. Me," he repeated louder. "I don't care what your theories are. I want it gone."

"Hey . . ." She met his gaze then. "What's going on here?"

"It hurts." He glared at the snake stuck on his arm. "And no one is helping make it stop."

As Maggie got closer, she could see that the snake's jaw was latched onto his arm like a suckling babe. *Not a cottonmouth or rattlesnake.* Detailed black and brown patterns covered the snake, and she was relieved not to see either the edge of a white mouth or the telltale rattle at the end of its tale.

Regardless of what it was, the snake had pumped venom into Sondre's body. His arm was swollen, red, and mottled.

"What kind is it?"

"Magical," Prospero offered.

"So I'm not sure how to treat this, and until we can get it to release . . ." Dr. Jemison lifted her hand to jab at the hinge of the snake's jaw. "How long has it been?"

"Ten minutes . . . ?" Prospero said.

Maggie had never heard of a snake not letting go after this long. It wasn't thrashing. It was simply curled around Sondre's arm like it was hugging him. The serpent's body wrapped around Sondre's arm from wrist to shoulder. It resembled an oddly raised tattoo.

"We could cut it off." Prospero picked up what looked like a meat cleaver.

"His *arm*?" Maggie asked, ready to step in and stop her.

Prospero shot her an incredulous look. "The *snake*."

"Where did it come from?" Maggie moved closer so as to stand by Sondre's head. She picked up a cloth and wiped sweat from his brow. He was clearly in pain, features drawn and eyes tightened.

"I'm sorry I couldn't bring Craig home. I sent some hobs—"

"Hush." Maggie kissed his forehead. "I'm not worried about *him* right now. I trust the hobs."

"What if I clean the wound?" the doctor asked. "Maybe . . . if I pour the right mixture . . ." She walked away, still talking, and started putting together some sort of chemical and steaming water.

"It's the staff of your own house, Sondre." Prospero stood across from Maggie, on the opposite of the bed. "I think it was part of the house before Aggie . . . so it's *yours* now."

"Don't. Like. Snakes."

"The snake seems to like you," Maggie pointed out. Snakes don't wag, but this one flicked the end of its tail side to side like an excited puppy. "Can we call the head of house to negoti—"

"He's right here." Prospero pointed at Sondre. "So negotiate."

"You want me to *talk* to it?" Sondre sounded like they'd just suggested kissing the snake. "Do you see my arm right now? It's killing me."

"It's accepting you," a rough voice said from the other side of the curtain.

"Scylla!" Prospero practically launched over everyone to pull the curtain back. "You're awake. Mae!" She called toward the doctor. "Scylla's awake again!"

Maggie was caught off guard seeing the tense Victorian woman looking so emotional. The usually intimidating witch moved to Scylla's side and gently touched her forehead. Then Prospero helped her sit a little more upright. She was almost maternal.

"The staff is the symbol of your house, Sondre." Scylla winced as she apparently shifted upright too much. "Accept whatever you're refusing so as to take over the house from Aggie, so it can let go of her last command." Talking so much seemed to cause her pain, but Scylla stared at him. "Do it."

"What does that even mean?" Maggie stared at him.

"I don't want it. I hoped Agnes would see reason and—"

"And the snake knows it," Prospero surmised. "It's conflicted between accepting you and not, because you are rejecting it. So I think it's using both the teeth Aggie ordered *and* embracing you."

Sondre looked horrified, staring down at the now-vibrating reptile. "I don't want an embrace from a snake."

"Agnes is not dead yet?" Scylla asked, meeting Prospero's gaze.

The silence was fraught for a moment before Sondre finally said, "Prospero tried to kill Aggie. I tried to talk to her. We *both* underestimated Agnes."

Then Mae returned with a simmering pot of what looked like plain water. "This will hurt. Someone . . . maybe a couple of you . . . need to hold him steady."

Maggie crossed to that side of the bed and took hold of his hand. "Now what?"

"Can you hold his biceps, Prospero?"

The Victorian witch said nothing as she returned to the side of the bed and gripped Sondre's arm. "Ready."

"Is that boiling?" Maggie asked.

"Not much," the doctor muttered—which was not a very comforting answer—and then she dipped an old-fashioned soup ladle into the water and poured it over the serpent's head and Sondre's purplish arm.

Sondre's skin sizzled, and he arched his back off the bed. As the water sluiced to a bucket on the floor, Sondre said, "A little g'damn warning, Mae."

"You came here to get treated," the doctor snapped. "You're getting treated. There's magical venom in your arm. I'm cleansing it."

Obviously, the boiling liquid did something to the snake. As the liquid flooded over it, the snake opened its mouth wider than any real creature could. In that split instant, the serpent's head looked a perfect circle with bloody teeth and a long, narrow throat visible. Then it seemed to let out a sigh of relief and uncoil so it was a long, wooden stick that leaned against the bed. If not for the oddity of a stick with serpent's eyes, perhaps it would have seemed less menacing. The oblong pupils watched Sondre attentively, reminding all of them that it was not merely a staff.

"That was harsh, Mae." Prospero gave the doctor an appraising look.

Dr. Jemison shrugged. "Salt water to nullify Aggie's last magic. I think you were right that the poor thing got caught between Aggie's orders and wanting to obey Sondre since he's taking over House Grendel. Magic talismans aren't deep thinkers."

"Neither is Grendel," Scylla chimed in. "You need to sort out whatever you're worrying over, though, Sondre, or that staff is useless to you."

"I liked you better when you were unconscious," Sondre told her.

"Ha! We're roomies now, Grendel Junior." Scylla flashed him a remarkably friendly smile.

Sondre looked at the doctor. "Mae—"

"Don't start," Dr. Jemison snapped with a shake of her head. "I'm not exactly pleased to have either of you taking up a bed here." She glanced at Lord Scylla. "And if you end up unconscious again, I will slap you. Seriously, heal faster. And you"—she turned back to Sondre—"stop being so trusting. Did marriage make you soft?"

No one spoke for a moment, and Maggie tried not to linger long over the flash of possessiveness she felt. Dr. Jemison was a professional, and Sondre was a smart man. Maggie had no reason to worry. Logic said so.

Still, she leaned close to him and whispered, "Should I be worried about leaving you here?"

Surprisingly, Sondre didn't look away from Maggie as he said, "Can someone close the curtain? I want to be alone with my wife."

"Privacy from noise, too," Scylla muttered. "I don't want to hear any of that."

Maggie's cheeks flamed briefly, but she stayed where she was at Sondre's side. The sliding sound of the curtain rings on the overhead bar was followed by the sound of absolute silence. Then Sondre slid to the center of the mattress. He held his uninjured arm out and widened his legs, so she could curl into his side and nestle one of her legs between his.

"I don't want to hurt you," she whispered. "I don't want to fight, either. Later when you feel better . . . but not right now, okay?"

"Good." He beckoned with his outstretched hand. "Then come here and let me hold you. I was worried I wasn't going to get to do this with both arms anymore, or at all after you were so angry earlier."

"I'd still be here. Arm or no arm." Maggie carefully climbed into the bed and rested her head under his chin so that her cheek was on his chest. His uninjured arm tightened around her waist, holding her to his side even as he was both exhausted and injured. For the first time since the hob came to fetch her, Maggie felt the knots in her body loosen.

"I want exactly one woman in my bed or even on my gurney, Maggie."

"Yeah?" Her heart sped at that. This felt more real. A fight, a make-up. Talking it out. "You want me here?"

"Yeah." Sondre kissed the top of her head. "I have this wife, you know? Terrible temper. Mediocre cook. Great mom."

"She sounds like a real prize," Maggie said dryly.

"She is. She's brave and smart and beautiful," he added. "And when I was falling all I could think is that I had to figure out how to get home because I didn't want to lose you or Craig."

"Both of us?" She hated how insecure she felt, but her son and her spouse were blending about as well as bleach and ammonia. Having a surprise new family hadn't sounded terrible, but the result was veering near to poison when the two male members of her tiny family clashed so constantly.

"You're a package deal," Sondre said mildly. After a pause, he added, "And he reminds me of a younger me. Question every rule. Sure you know the best way. Ready to fight over anything."

Maggie glanced up at him. "Sounds like you now, too."

He dropped a kiss on the tip of her nose and muttered, "Kettle, meet pot."

At that Maggie laughed. "Fair." She snuggled closer. "I think I'm ready to talk to him about living with Hestia."

"He'd be safer there. He can come home for holidays," Sondre said after a wide yawn.

"Tonight, though, maybe a nap . . ." Maggie murmured, feeling unexpectedly drowsy now that the adrenaline of seeing him in pain had faded. "I'll be more careful if you are."

"Deal." Sondre held her nestled close.

They stayed that way, nestled together until Maggie was almost asleep, and then Sondre said, "I'm not sure I want to be head of house. I think being headmaster is wiser."

"Can you refuse?"

"Let them try to stop me," he grumbled. "I am the headmaster. They gave me this damn job, so it's where I'll be."

"No more hunting escapees?" Maggie asked.

Sondre didn't answer that one at first, and if he eventually did, she didn't know because she had drifted off to sleep nuzzled against his side.

27

Prospero

Prospero sat on the edge of Scylla's bed in the infirmary and looked over at her friend. *She's fine. Sondre's fine. I'm fine.* Scylla's eyes were drawn tight, and her lips were cracked as if she had been too long in the sun. Magic usually healed such things, so it was unusual to see any witch looking like the basic stages of unwellness were plaguing them.

Absently, Prospero touched the back of her hand to Scylla's forehead again.

Scylla swatted her away. "Not your patient. Bad enough that Mae and her crew are patting and potioning me."

"I was just checking your temperature." Prospero handed her a glass of fresh clean water. The town had reserves for the infirmary. If a person's magic was struggling to heal them, it didn't need to counter the bad water, too.

"We're lucky people aren't considering injuring themselves to get the good stuff anymore." Scylla drank several sips. Her hand was shaking again. "Your woman's patch seems to be working. The water the other day was almost tasteless again."

"Ellie's magic is remarkable." Prospero had been cautiously optimistic a week ago. Ellie was back in Crenshaw. The rift was steadily getting repaired. Things had looked promising, and then Aggie shot Scylla and ripped down the barrier. "Now we just need to thoroughly hide Crenshaw again."

"We will." Scylla sounded calm. That was, perhaps, the heart of their friendship. They weren't the sort of women to go hat shopping or sip tea at the town center, but they were both implacable. Plus, Scylla had a wry sense of humor, and her courage made Prospero wish that she'd joined them in the Barbarian Lands.

Unfortunately, Scylla had been too busy being tucked into a bed in the infirmary, healing from the bullet that had fragmented inside her.

Aggie should've died for the pain that she caused.

"I failed you," Prospero said.

Scylla had the uncanny ability to boil the matter to the bone. "*How?*"

"She pulled upon my memories of the day I became a witch," Prospero confessed, trying to push her own shame away. At some point she'd need to talk to Sondre about what he now knew. "She made me think then was now and—"

"No. Not how did you fail me—because honestly, you didn't—but how is not stopping her *yet* a failure? So you were outsmarted by Agnes in her madness and affinity for violence. It happens. I was being a smartass because I thought you knew better." Scylla gave her a thoughtful look. "You are smarter than this, P."

"I should have—"

"As I may have mentioned a few times over the years, you are still *human* no matter how much that detail upsets you." Scylla closed her eyes and leaned her head back on the cot. "I'm exhausted since she shot me, but am I blaming myself?"

"No."

"Exactly. So stop it." Scylla stretched, as if there were a way to make the infirmary cot more comfortable. "You're being tedious. It's bad enough that I can't do my job or hunt Agnes, but I don't want to listen to you try to lie to yourself, too."

"I feel like I'm going to let everyone down," Prospero whispered. "That damn prophecy . . ."

"Well, I'm not dead or planning on dying so get on with the rest." Scylla gave her a look. "Talk to Cass if you need, or just keep that wife of yours near. She's what keeps you alive, according to Cass."

"I can't take Ellie to—"

Scylla laughed. "Woman, she *bested* you when she escaped Crenshaw. She can go toe to toe with you. Only other witch I know who can do that is temporarily in the infirmary."

"Sondre?" Prospero teased.

"As if. That man is nicer than either of us." Scylla swatted at her. "And I can't help you, so that leaves Sondre who is in the infirmary, or your wife, or Walt, who is ancient. Take the woman with you."

"You sleep. I'll sort it out," Prospero promised. As much as she understood Scylla's perspective, the upshot of today's events was that Agnes was still in the world spreading violence.

And she's not the only escapee.

And Sondre is injured.

And Scylla is still healing.

And I don't want to take Ellie into danger.

Prospero sighed. No one ought to be trying to do magic when that same magic was necessary to heal them. "If the barrier attempts are draining you, you could pause on that. Ellie twisted some vines and things over the open space."

Scylla smiled but kept her eyes shut. "Of course she did."

"What does that mean?" Prospero stared at Scylla more freely now that the other woman had closed her eyes. They were not the most affectionate of people, but sometimes that seemed to be the basis of their friendship, too. "And what can I do to make you more comfortable?"

Scylla's eyes opened. "Feel any better after studying me?"

"I have been here studying you most every day," Prospero confessed. "It isn't helping a damn thing." She took a shaky breath. "There was a bullet in you, and you weren't moving. And then today Sondre . . . he just fell over. I should've been stronger-willed and seen through Aggie's magic."

Scylla rolled her eyes. "Agnes is more dangerous now that she's unleashed. We knew that, Prospero. *You* knew it." Scylla sighed, and then promptly put her hand on her stomach. "That still hurts. Is Mae unwell?"

A scoff nearby made clear that the good doctor was listening.

"She keeps faltering. You know she was in the cot beside you at first?" Prospero pointed out. "She saved your life and then toppled over. She keeps doing that." She glanced over at Mae. "I am forever in her debt."

Mae came over. "Debts aside, I'm not as strong as I should be yet. Neither is Scylla." She frowned, as if the words themselves were things she could glare into submission. "It's as if I am not accessing all of my magic, and neither is Scylla or she'd be well by now."

"Perhaps the bullet was poisoned?" Prospero suggested.

"What sort of poison can *magic* not cure?"

"Magical poison . . . ?" Prospero thought about Howie and his shop of questionable wares. *Was he a part of this?* She'd searched his mind often enough that she thought she'd know, but perhaps that was arrogance.

"The Dealers Den?" Scylla guessed. "I thought you had that boy on a leash."

"Perhaps Howie is not as easy to manage as he used to be," Prospero mused. "I'll pay him a visit, and I'll send Sondre's amplifier to help all three of you. Too many injuries over this fiasco for my taste so far."

"So the visit over there was no use at all?" Mae prompted.

Admitting the whole of it was far outside Prospero's comfort zone. Her own weaknesses had been used against her, as had Sondre's serpent fears. All she admitted was "We underestimated Agnes, but Jenn has been nullified."

"Dead?"

Prospero nodded once. "Aggie's interference resulted in Jenn's death." Prospero tried to push away the memory of Jenn's combustion. The scent of it would linger in her memory far too long. Guilt burbled up inside her, and she cringed at the fact that her guilt was not over the other witch's death but over how adroitly Agnes had played on her memories and emotions.

Ellie is not dead. Prospero had thought and rethought that several times. *Ellie is alive and safe.*

"I often don't like you these days," Mae announced.

"Gee, thanks."

"*But,*" Mae continued, "I know we are safer because of your loyalty to Crenshaw. No one who knows you would doubt that you did everything possible to restore order. If Agnes is not yet caught, it's not for lack of effort on your part."

"Or Sondre's," Prospero added, glancing at the curtain that gave him privacy.

Scylla gave her a strange look.

"Fine. He's not all bad, and he's been spying for me for years," Prospero blurted out. "If either of you share that detail, I'll make you think your mouths are surgically sealed so you can only speak in charades thereafter."

"There's the spiteful witch I'm used to," Mae said, but she was laughing as she said it. "My patients need rest, though, and so do you, so . . ." She made a shooing gesture. "Go away. Maybe listen to my advice and try to rest."

"You know I'll stop her," Prospero told Scylla. "I give you my—"

"Stop. You can do your best, but *only* as long as you survive it," Scylla retorted. "I want Aggie stopped, but not at the cost of your life. Remember that."

Prospero couldn't reply to that. Logically, she understood, but emotionally, she had no time for caution.

"I'll send a few guards I trust to stand watch since the headmaster cannot barricade the infirmary door." Prospero summoned Bernice as she stepped into the hallway outside the infirmary. "Guards, please."

Bernice gave a singular nod and vanished.

When Prospero looked up, she was both relieved and alarmed to find Ellie sitting there in a rocking chair that had never been in that hallway before—and, in fact, had not been there when Prospero had walked past that spot any day of late.

"Redecorating?" Prospero said lightly.

"Who's in the infirmary?" Ellie nodded toward the door.

"Still Scylla, but Sondre is in there now, too." Prospero walked forward and extended a hand toward Ellie.

She accepted Prospero's hand, stood, and then stepped past her. "You are blood-drenched again." Ellie sniffed and crinkled her nose. "And you smell of fire."

Something was obviously bothering Ellie. It didn't take magic to see that. And Prospero wasn't sure she wanted to ask, but they already had enough distance between them. For a moment, she wished that they could've met in another time and place. She wished there were an easier path they could walk toward finding a future, but wishes were pointless in this case. Prospero pivoted and extended an arm toward Ellie, uncommonly grateful when Ellie didn't flinch away.

"Are you safe?" Ellie's voice was tight with some sort of strain.

"Now? Yes."

"Tell me what happened," Ellie insisted.

Prospero said, "I faced Agnes, and it went poorly. Sondre was injured as well. The witch we were to retrieve was killed . . . also by Agnes."

"So where does that leave you?"

"In need of more information," Prospero admitted. "I need someone believable to talk to Howie." She took a steadying moment. "Any ideas?"

"Actually, I know someone . . . unless you think threatening him again would help?" Ellie sounded almost hopeful.

"Not for this. I need stealth." Prospero brushed a kiss over Ellie's lips quickly. "If I needed someone terrifying, though, I'd ask you."

Ellie laughed. "I wasn't going to hurt him."

"He didn't know that."

"Come with me, then. I have a friend who might be good at helping us," Ellie said, tugging Prospero along with her. "Then I want to go home with you."

"Is there a reason to go to the house?" Prospero asked.

"Someone watches the castle rooms," Ellie said mildly as she rested her hand lightly on Prospero's extended arm. "I'm not sure why I know that now, but I do."

Prospero glanced at her. "You used to know it."

"I figured as much," Ellie said. "I would like a private evening with you. There are no classes in the morning for some reason. First, though, follow me."

"Your wish is my command." Prospero kept pace with her as they walked.

Hopefully, the day might end better than it had been going. She wasn't expecting the sort of evening she wanted—and that Ellie had wanted of late—but today, a nice drink and falling asleep with Ellie at her side sounded like bliss.

28

Dan

Of all the things that Dan might have expected, finding Ellie Brandeau and Lady Prospero at his door wasn't on the list. He was sitting in his desk chair reading a book he'd checked out of the library, after filling a card out that vanished into wherever checked cards went, and Axell was sitting on the edge of the bed with a lute, writing a song, when there was a tap at the door.

Dan opened it and froze. Fear tangled around him as he looked at the woman he'd helped mentally erase as she was fighting to escape and the woman responsible for that heinous act. They were holding hands.

As he stood there, mouth opening soundlessly, Dan felt Axell come up behind him.

"May we come in?" Ellie asked, looking not at him but over his shoulder at Axell.

"How much danger will there be if we say no?" Axell was staring at Ellie as if Lady Prospero were not at her side.

"We come in peace," Ellie said, flashing a brief smile at Dan.

He glanced at the second witch, the one he'd amplified. "Do *you*?"

"Her idea." Prospero glanced at Ellie with a question obvious on her face. "I have no idea why we are here."

"She needs a spy," Ellie started.

Dan started, "I'm not—"

"Not you," Ellie said. "There is an underground here, a market where things can be acquired that are deadly. I need Axell."

"Why?" Axell asked.

"You can only enter if you are an addict or with *her*." Ellie gestured at Lady Prospero again. "And when I went with her, I left Howie pinned to the wall. He won't talk to me or her right now, but we need information."

Axell stared at her. "I am not using any drugs." He glanced at Dan. "I swear I am not—"

"I'm not asking you to. I'm asking you to go see if you can buy magical poison from him. Drugs or otherwise." Ellie pointedly did not look at Prospero. "You will tell him I was bragging about trapping him, and you want to bring me down."

"No." Dan and Prospero spoke at once.

"May we come in?" Ellie asked, still talking to Axell.

Axell stepped aside and motioned them in with one arm. He hadn't said no, but he had a drawn expression on his face that Dan attributed to fear. Which fear was unclear, but there were several options.

Inside the room, Ellie pulled a bit of wood and a scrap of fabric from her pocket. The fabric was patterned and looked familiar. Dan frowned at it.

"That looks like the curtains in the lower hall," Prospero said quietly.

"It is. I cut a piece off." Ellie grinned. Then she dropped both things on the floor, and in the next moment, the wood and fabric expanded, twisting and writhing into an elegant sofa. The gold-and-blue fabric was now a Victorian-style sofa, and the wood had grown into clawed feet. "It'll stay if you want it. Sometimes it's nice to have a spot to cuddle up."

Axell sat on the bed again, and this time, Dan curled up there rather than in the desk chair where he'd been earlier. They neither one had any defenses beyond Axell's ability to become invisible, which only worked on Dan if they were touching, but he wanted to be closer to him while Prospero was here.

"Only addicts can find him, and you're the only addict I know here." Ellie gave Axell an awkward look, as if she hated putting it on the table.

"There are others," Prospero said quietly.

"I do not want to be able to find magic drugs." Axell tensed.

"Look, Lord Scylla isn't healing. Without her, we have a half-there barrier I built out of sticks and rocks. . . ."

Dan bit back his three-little-pigs quip. This didn't feel like a quip-friendly moment. Instead he said, "I could boost you, amplify your magic"—he shot a look at Prospero—"and you could make the barrier stronger."

"Then how would we get in and out to bring in supplies?" Prospero asked. "We can find someone else, someone I know and trust to—"

"Ellie trusts me." Axell stared at her. "We decided to be friends. There was a raccoon."

"Chester," Prospero muttered. "That beast is not a child, no matter how often they put him in costumes."

"What is it you need?" Dan interjected. Later, maybe, he'd have raccoon-in-clothes questions, but he wanted this topic resolved and these two out of his room.

"Scylla isn't healing, so we wondered if there was poison on the bullet." Prospero sounded rattled, which wasn't the most comforting thing.

When the bad guys are frightened that means that everything has gone to shit, Dan mused. *Or does it mean the good guys are winning?* He glanced at the two women. They *were* trying to save Crenshaw. That was a definite "good guy" thing. *Maybe good and bad are relative to where you stand, what you want. . . .*

"I don't want him to have to take any strange drugs," Dan blurted out. "His body, his choice and all that, but addiction *killed* him."

Axell reached out and took his hand as he asked, "He can come, too?"

Ellie looked at Prospero, who shrugged.

"Then I will go." Axell nodded. "What do I do?"

$$\text{☽ ✻ ☾}$$

They all left the castle together and went into the village. Passing the woods made Dan pause, thinking about seeing Prospero carrying Ellie through the woods like she was a victim. Honestly, Dan still couldn't decide what he thought of either woman. They made him nervous; that was the whole of it.

He squeezed Axell's hand and whispered, "Are you sure you are okay with this?"

"*Ja.*"

"I'm staying with you the whole time," Dan said, half expecting an argument.

Axell just smiled. "To protect me."

And although Dan felt foolish at the thought that he could be at all threatening, he nodded.

From in front of him, Ellie said, "We'll be right outside. Just yell, and we'll be there. I just think . . . he's so arrogant. Get him talking. Play to his ego. Fear doesn't work as well on him."

"Fear is exhilarating to some," Prospero said lightly. "Howie can be complicated."

Ellie offered, "He liked pain."

"Also fun," Axell said with a sort of knowledge that Dan found tempting on its own. Axell glanced at him. "Fear. Power. Pain. Adoration. Many drugs we make in our own selves with emotion."

To that, Dan couldn't argue. He'd courted those natural feelings with gambling and sex. The things that were addictive were because of how they made a person *feel.* Dan squeezed Axell's hand. *Maybe his drugs were no different than my risk-taking. Maybe we are not that different at all.*

No one spoke as they neared a different part of the village. Dan had thought they'd visited all the shops already, but Prospero led them to a shop that had neither sign nor display window. The building itself had a strange look to it, as if it had been blackened by something wet and sticky and fire-tempered.

"There's no door," Dan pointed out.

"There is," Axell whispered. He spoke as if he were reading words Dan could not see. "'Place hand in the spot to knock.'"

Prospero nodded, as Axell spread his fingers and pressed his hand on a darker section of the door. Then she and Ellie crossed the street and Dan held tightly to Axell's hand as he followed him into a building that smelled of something sweet and acrid.

"Poppy and powder," Axell whispered. "They have both things. Calm and energy."

It took Dan a moment to realize that Axell meant opiates and cocaine. He could see Axell tense, whole body held taut like someone about to run. Then a voice came out of the shadows.

"Come in, my friends, come in."

Dan's stomach knotted at the sickly sweet voice, but he kept his mouth shut. He followed Axell, who glanced back and whispered, "Trust me."

Once they were inside a cavernous shell of a room, where a pallid man sprawled on filthy pillows, all Dan wanted was to carry Axell out of here, run away, and maybe torch the building.

"I wondered if you would find your way to my door." The witch zeroed in on both of them. "The gambler and the junkie. Your sort often get sent back."

"Unless someone finds us useful," Axell said, accent thicker than natural.

The dealer laughed. "You *are* a pretty morsel." Then he looked at Dan. "And you, cupcake, seem to be under the gaze of the headmaster. I didn't think he liked"—he motioned at Dan from head to toe—"that."

Dan tensed, not sure what to say. He knew that Sondre's friendship wasn't sexual. *Right? Was he planning on using me? I thought we were becoming real friends. . . .* Dan shook his head, chasing away such foolishness. He knew better. Sondre was his friend. The dealer was stirring insecurities.

"So what's your poison?"

Axell aimed a cocky grin at the man. "I like a lot of things, but tonight, I want to make someone suffer."

The words rang true, and the dealer leaned forward. "Tell Howie all about it."

"I was eavesdropping . . ." Axell glanced at Dan, who gave a nod. They'd practiced this. Literally stood away from Ellie and Prospero, who talked together but not to them so they *had* eavesdropped. Truth could be so very relative.

"And what did you learn, pretty?" The dealer patted one of the grungy pillows. "I will give you a discount if you want to convince me. . . ."

Dan's stomach twisted at the predatory tone and tried to put it in his voice. "We want to buy poison. This *bitch* was bragging about trapping you, and we thought . . . maybe you'd cut us a deal."

"Something liquid to put on a blade," Axell added.

"Revenge is silly. Pleasure, that's the good feeling." Howie cupped his crotch, and for a moment, Dan thought they were going to get an unwelcome show.

"Maybe we'd try some powder later." Axell smiled, watching Howie's hand like it was enticing. "Or molly?"

Howie shook his head. "Got things *like* molly. Get you some real hallucinations. . . ." He glanced at Dan and added, "Have a spell that is like the little blue pills, too. Keep you up for hours." His sentence was accompanied by a tug on his crotch. "Like a rock."

Axell wrapped an arm around Dan's middle. "We don't have any need for that."

"Poison, though," Dan added.

"My lover has a temper." Axell said the words like it was endearing. "Such a vicious man."

For a moment, Dan was frozen by the reality that they could not lie here; most witches could read a lie. They could twist and dissemble, but Axell was saying that Dan had a temper, and that they didn't need pills for sex, and . . . those were truths.

Was his interest in drugs for later true, too?

"Look. We just want to hurt that bitch," Dan blurted out. He didn't specify which one. There were faces of people he'd wanted to hurt, although it wasn't a thing he'd acted on as a rule, maybe the occasional petty revenge. "Some people deserve what they put out there."

"Ah, there it is." Howie rose to his feet. "The headmaster likes you because you're a Grendel like him. Vengeful boys. Maybe you want something to bulk up? Make yourself fight-ready?"

Dan didn't flinch as Howie approached. He had a moment of thinking it *might* be amazing to be able to toss people around, to overpower them, to take what he deserved. "Prospero took advantage of me. I want her to get what she deserves."

Howie stopped midstep. "No. I don't cross that one, and you won't get any poison here if she's your tar—"

"Do you have any?" Axell asked, reaching out as if to take hold of Howie's hand. "Or know where we can get any?"

"If I did, she'd already be in pain." Howie shuddered all over. "Canny thing. She'd know, and what I did have wouldn't be strong enough to take down a house head over here in Crenshaw."

Axell nodded. "Thank you."

"Doesn't mean we can't do business. . . ." Howie oozed closer. "Plenty of things to distract you. No good comes of crossing her or her wife."

"I think we should go." Dan stepped backward. "Err, thank you, though."

"You'll be back." Howie grinned wider than a human mouth ought to stretch. "Once you come here, your kind always come back. Addicts are the best customers."

Axell shook his head. "Not tonight, though."

"Bye." Dan waved cheerily and tugged Axell along with him, stumbling and looking back as if Howie would follow. He didn't, though. He was back on his pillows, pants shoved down, staring after them.

Axell shoved the door open, and they stood in the clean air. He pulled Dan in for a long hug. "Do not let me go to this village alone, Daniel, if I am sad or we have fought. Ever."

"I won't. I swear it." Dan looked back. This perfect magical world still had a flaw, and Dan wanted to remove it, to yank it out and destroy it.

Ellie's voice drew his attention away from the building. "Well?"

"Not him. Also he hates you both," Dan said bluntly.

"I'm not his biggest fan, either," Ellie muttered. She looked at Axell then, as if no one else was there. "Are you okay?"

Axell's expression was tense. He looked at Prospero. "Take this memory. I do not want to know this is here."

And Dan was impressed by his audacity. "I'll keep mine. Not to visit but because . . . I want to remember how much I hated this."

"I can do that." Prospero paused, looked at each of them, and said, "Thank you for the bravery, gentlemen."

Then she erased Axell's memory of the drug dealer's den, and Dan led his beloved to the tavern for the drink they both wanted after that encounter.

29
Ellie

Ellie marveled at the way that things so impossibly odd only a few weeks ago seemed normal now. She watched Dan and Axell walk away and said, "If it's not poison, then what?"

Prospero extended her elbow to Ellie. Her body was tense enough that Ellie could feel the muscles as firm as bone in her forearm. "I will figure that out," Prospero said mildly. "I don't have an answer yet, though."

"I feel like the chief witch puts too much pressure on you," Ellie muttered.

"He trusts me."

"He abuses your loyalty," Ellie countered. "Whatever you did to upset him isn't reason enough to allow it."

Prospero's lips pressed together as if to bite back a retort. "I visited a witch who was not yet a witch."

"I remember that," Ellie said quietly. "Is it so bad that you came to my library?"

As they walked, Ellie weighed her recent discoveries and conclusions. She still was unresolved as to what she intended to say to Prospero. The attempt to talk to both Dan and Maggie had been futile, but Ellie still now knew things she'd not known yesterday.

"I don't recall the last time I wanted something for me. Someone," Prospero said. "Then I saw you. There was a prophecy about you . . . and I knew you were a witch, but you had not yet *become* so."

"I kissed you," Ellie whispered. "I knew you were mine. I didn't know anything about magic or witches or here. I just knew that you were mine."

"Oh, Ellie . . ." Prospero glanced over at her. "Why can't any of this be simple?"

"It can." Ellie looked back at the castle that loomed behind them like a stone guardian, and for a moment, she had the sense that she'd walked this path with someone else. *Maggie.* The question was whether it ultimately mattered. Sure, Ellie wanted to figure it all out still, but the important part was that if Prospero truly hadn't wanted her to know, she could've erased the memories of those who *did* have clues.

"Do you know that Daniel Monahan and Maggie Lynch were in my Missing files?" Ellie asked.

"I did."

"I knew that before, and I know it now." Ellie glanced over at Prospero. "I think you expected me to figure everything out. All the things I'm forgetting. All the things that happened. It's piecing together, and I think that's what you wanted to have happen, isn't it?"

Prospero was quiet until they were alongside the stretch of woods beside the path. Then she said, "I did not agree with the decision to alter your memory. I just wanted . . . I wanted to talk and explain and—"

"I was in the other world. I left." Ellie felt like she'd had an espresso shot, heart racing too fast, as she was hoping she was right. Maybe Prospero *could* be trusted. Ellie barreled forward. "With her. Monahan boosts magic. He boosted yours, and you erased my memory."

"I am not allowed to tell you what happened," Prospero said after a quiet moment.

"I figured that much out by piecing things together. What I don't know is if . . . did I . . . I don't think Maggie is lesbian." Ellie took a deep breath and blurted, "I kissed her."

Prospero said nothing.

"I kissed Maggie," Ellie repeated.

"I heard you." Prospero's expression was unreadable. "Do you often kiss other women?"

"No. I had memories of her, though, and—"

"Memory of kissing her?" Prospero asked, voice as calm as an undisturbed lake.

"No. I had a memory of jumping into a car with her after I caged you in what looked like a diner . . . ?" Ellie had gone from don't-tell-her to blurting everything out. It was less of a carefully thought-out plan and more of a secrets-are-the-problem mindset. "It's not a dream. Those things happened. I left you, and I went with her. And you came after me."

"Yes." Prospero stopped and stared at her. "You were upset."

"And you won't tell me why—"

"*Can't*," Prospero corrected. "I can't tell you."

"Fine. You *can't* answer my questions." Ellie paused, looking toward the edge of the town. The streets were half-empty, a visual reminder of the dilemma before them. Witches were afraid, possibly of the escaped witches who had shot Lord Scylla, possibly of nonmagical intruders.

Ellie wasn't sure she could blame them.

"Are you angry over what you've recalled?" Prospero glanced her way, and Ellie noticed that her jaw was clenched tightly. Her voice might not waver, but the anxiety was obviously still there.

"I was angry in one of the memories, heartbroken, too," Ellie admitted. "*You* hurt my heart, Prospero. I know it was you."

Prospero nodded. "I made mistakes. I am sorry."

"So this whole 'leaving a trail so I can evade my punishment for whatever I did' is a . . . what? Grand gesture? Apology?" Ellie kept her voice pitched low as they resumed walking. No one more than a hand's width away could hear her. Even though the streets were empty, she wasn't willing to risk being overheard.

"Amends."

"Nothing is simple with you, is it?" Ellie muttered. She'd been weighing the situation. Thus far she had figured out that she had broken a major rule, but Prospero hadn't known. Maggie had gone with Ellie to the nonmagical world, and Prospero had pursued them. After being returned to Crenshaw, the memory of their escapade was erased—by Prospero, with Dan's help.

"If you only knew . . ." Prospero laughed. "You're not exactly meek, love."

"Fair."

"That's not a complaint." Prospero ascended the steps to the house. "Just to be clear."

"So I figured out most of it, but I don't know why I was upset with you." Ellie waited while Prospero let them into their house.

Inside, Prospero shut and locked the door. "I lied to you, omitting telling you things I knew."

Ellie gaped at her. "That's it?"

"They were *large* things," Prospero added as she hung up her overcoat, looking fixedly at the coat hooks rather than at Ellie. "You reacted poorly, doubted my sincerity, questioned my feelings toward you."

"I don't doubt your feeling now." Ellie put a hand on Prospero's side.

"Truly?" Prospero was motionless.

"You are rather obviously in love with me," Ellie said.

Prospero looked back at her.

"I know you lied," Ellie continued. "But I *also* know you left a trail for me to figure it out because you want truth between us . . . and you refused me because you were afraid of my reaction when I remembered."

Prospero turned the rest of the way back to face her. "You remember most of it. The majority of the worst parts."

"Do you suppose that's enough to move on?" Ellie asked hopefully. When Prospero didn't reply after several moments, Ellie felt her shoulders sag. "Go bathe. I'll fix tea."

"Wine?" Prospero asked quietly. "I don't have the answers you want, love. I feel like there are still big gaps in between us, but if I could hold you and . . . be near you to rest, I would very much like that. And maybe other things?"

Ellie's smile felt wide enough to be awkward. "That sounds perfect."

Prospero left, and Ellie gave a little spin in the foyer. She wasn't frightfully giddy by nature, but this felt like something to celebrate. Massive progress of the romantic sort. The world was still under attack, and dangerous witches had still declared war on Crenshaw. Ellie still had some holes in her recollection. The rift was better but not *fixed*. Things were far from perfect.

But she admits that she wants me in her arms.

Sometimes Ellie wondered how anything could feel significant when there was a hole in a person's heart. A hole in her memories? She could manage. A hole in her heart? She obsessed over it.

Romantic date with my wife coming right up.

Ellie felt like a thief in the kitchen. This was Bernice's territory, but the fastidious hob was absent right now. For that Ellie was grateful. Ellie pulled open the old-fashioned refrigerator. It didn't hum with electricity but with magic.

"I forgive you," she murmured aloud, testing the words for their truthfulness. The tendency to fixate on truth pre-witch was apparently a sliver of magic insisting on notice. Now, Ellie understood what it was. Magic. Plain and simple.

The words Ellie spoke ran true. She *had* forgiven Prospero. Now, she needed her wife to understand that.

Ellie walked up to their once-shared bedroom. Prospero stood in the room, staring into her wardrobe. She wore a purple dressing gown with embroidered edges. Water dripped from her hair. Beside her was a small table and chair where Ellie remembered sitting and brushing her hair, thinking about the way her wife avoided her.

Right now, Prospero was present and looked a bit desperate.

"I figured almost *all* of it out, and I *forgive* you." Ellie stared at her, not closing the distance. "Tell me why I can't love you fully, Prospero. Because right now, you have no arguments left . . . unless you simply don't want me. Is that it?"

"No." Prospero untied the belt holding her dressing gown closed. "I wanted you to remember because we'd fought. I didn't want to take advantage of you, love. I was *trying* to be a good person."

"Thank you." Ellie stepped closer. "And now?"

"Now, I just want you to touch me, let me touch you, whatever you want. I hoped . . . I *wanted* that the whole time. I was never trying to reject you." Prospero's hands folded into fists at her side. "I didn't want you to forget our quarrels—or the quarrels we'll have over the years in front of us. I *like* that my magic doesn't work on you."

"Me too. So can we never do that again? Never fight? Never turn me out of bed?" Ellie removed her shirt, dropping it on the floor. Her bra followed.

Prospero's gaze was fixed on her. "Yes."

"To which thing?" Ellie asked.

"Never again."

"Not to the fact that I'm half-naked?" Ellie teased. "Can I get a yes for that, too?"

"Always that." Prospero's voice was low and veered toward desperate. "I thought of you like this."

"When you touched yourself?" Ellie asked as she was a hand's length away from her wife.

"I didn't . . . do that." Prospero caught her eyes this time. "Not at all. If you didn't know what I did, you couldn't consent, and I needed to . . ."

"Suffer?" Ellie finished breathlessly. She dropped to her knees and parted Prospero's dressing gown. "My poor love."

Ellie kissed Prospero's thighs, and then she pushed her backward, so she was leaning against the wardrobe.

Prospero didn't resist as Ellie took her ankle and directed her to brace one foot on the chair beside the wardrobe. "Ellie . . ."

"Hush." Ellie let the warm breath of her word out in a sigh, gratified to feel the tension in Prospero's thigh. "Let me taste you."

Prospero made a sound that was somewhere between a whimper and a moan, and Ellie set her mouth to reminding Prospero what she'd been missing in their separation. After several moments of attention, Prospero was trembling. Her hands gripped Ellie's hair as if afraid she'd vanish.

"There. Please. *There.*"

Instead, Ellie paused and stared up at her. "Never lie to me again. Swear it."

"I swear. I'd swear it even if you never touched me again," Prospero promised.

Ellie grinned at her. "Such a good girl."

The sound Prospero made was the exact one that Ellie had imagined when she was alone in her bed, but tonight she wasn't alone at all. She slowly licked Prospero's folds before teasing, "Maybe we should pause. I gave you no foreplay, no kissing, no admiring looks. Maybe I was too hast—"

"Ellie," Prospero whined. "*Please.*"

Ellie chuckled. "I like the way you say that." She held tightly to Prospero's trembling hips and applied her lips and tongue to the gloriously wet juncture of her wife's thighs.

"God, Ellie. *Yes.*" Prospero's voice was raw with need. "Please please please . . . oh god, love. Love you, Ellie. I love you so very much."

Between one "please" and the next, Ellie's tongue sped up, and everything was suddenly right in her world. Her wife was begging and writhing, crying out Ellie's name, and the rest was all minutiae they could figure out later.

30
Prospero

"So . . . it sounded like you said you love me," Ellie asked a while later when they were curled up in bed together.

"I did." Prospero's hand, which had been drawing circles on Ellie's back, paused.

"Have you said that to me before?" Ellie asked, lifting her head from Prospero's chest to look at her. "Did I forget it?"

"No." Prospero felt panic swirl in her stomach. "I have thought it, but I didn't think you'd believe me."

"Because you lied to me about something, and then pushed me away?"

"Yes." Prospero swallowed her panic. Running wasn't the right answer. She knew that, but this was the part of relationships that she dreaded, the vulnerability of it all. She could handle courting, little gifts and flirting touches, and she definitely could handle the sex. Her body both ached and felt energized for having been thoroughly explored.

"What changed that you're saying it now?" Ellie sounded more curious than anything.

"When I was over there, I thought you had died." Prospero forced herself not to look away. "In my mind, you had merged with a memory of . . . my first lover because of Aggie's magic. In my mind, I saw you dead and sightless, staring at me, and the grief—" Prospero stopped herself, took a steadying breath, and added, "I wanted you to know how I feel in case I don't survive the next encounter."

"You're planning to die?" Ellie asked.

"No. I'm being realistic. Magic is unpredictable over there." Prospero held Ellie close. "I want to defeat her, come home, lock the door so I can hide away with the witch I love and ignore the rest of the world."

"So let's do that. I'm not as experienced at magic as you, but in case you didn't notice, I'm not useless." Ellie pulled away and propped up on one arm, so she was staring down at Prospero. "I have a lot of thoughts about things I want to do with you. Those require you staying alive."

"Oh?"

"We never had a honeymoon," Ellie pointed out. "I want to dance with you, walk with you, have picnics, read beside you, cook a meal—"

"Court me, then."

Ellie's smile turned wicked. "And have you naked for most of it so that we can pause to make love."

Prospero felt like her heart might beat too fast for her body to contain. "That sounds perfect, although I'm not sure about naked picnics or how well the hobs would tolerate naked cooking."

"The hobs can go somewhere else for a few weeks, have a holiday or something." Ellie shrugged. "I have plans for you."

"Most women aren't in my bed to pleasure me. I'm usually the one who—"

"Most women aren't your wife," Ellie said firmly. "So this? This is not a one-way situation."

Prospero couldn't restrain a laugh at the tone in her voice. "Where were you all my life, Elleanor Brandeau?"

"Well, I wasn't born yet for *most* of your life," Ellie said smugly.

Prospero opened her mouth to reply, but Ellie leaned down and kissed her before she could say a word.

This. This is what I've wanted for most of my life, Prospero thought.

☽ ✳ ☾

Several hours later Ellie was finally asleep in their bed, but Prospero was awake still, holding her and pondering how to retrieve a witch who could pull fears to the forefront of one's mind, a witch who lived for violence. *Strike first. Strike mercilessly.* Agnes had shot Scylla, injured Sondre, and made Prospero think Ellie was dead.

This was not the time for hesitating.

But there's no way to hunt her until she uses magic. . . .

None of that resolve made it easier when Prospero felt the alarm at her door sound, and she smothered a curse. It wasn't the most sophisticated of alarms, but Prospero always felt a visitor at the door like a hand on her shoulder.

She slid out from the tangle of limbs that was Ellie. Smiling, Prospero mused that she'd barely had a chance to sleep after several hours of bone-melting lovemaking. This was her, the person Prospero had needed for all of her life, and they were finally together, truly and fully. It was everything she'd dreamed of in a relationship, everything she'd been afraid to want.

And I almost lost it.

Prospero went downstairs and jerked open the front door with an exasperated sigh. She held her dressing gown closed even though it was tied. "Is anyone dead?"

"Always so gloomy," the tiny man, Grish, muttered. The hob was Walter's, and he was strangely quiet as a rule. Tonight, Grish had a pink-and-green-striped scarf round his neck, and the tassels of it would be touching the ground if not for the fact that the diminutive man stood in a planter beside her door. The result was that his scarf dangled over the rim of the tall, black urn. "Perhaps I'm here to ask for an egg. Or a hank of yarn or—"

"Grish. Is that a *no*?" She eyed him suspiciously. It wasn't a matter of dislike, but hobs were loyal to those they chose. Grish had been a part of the chief witch's household for the entirety of Prospero's life in Crenshaw.

"I suspect someone or several someone's lives could be in peril. I can't rightly say. The master of the house says magic's spilling over there." Grish raised his eyebrows. "Guess you were too busy to notice. What—"

"Wait." Prospero closed her eyes, feeling for the magical signature over in the other world. "Please tell Walter I'll handle it."

"With whom?"

"What?"

"Lord Scylla is bloody, and the headmasher is not well for this." Grish widened his eyes comically. "You ought not go alone, not to this. You know that."

His words felt ominous, as they often did when Cassandra shared a prophecy. Were hobs prophetic, too? Prospero stared at him and asked, "Do you know something?"

"Oh, Prospero, I know more things than a human mind will ever conceive of." He gave her a sad smile. "Tonight, what I know is that I think you should not go alone, not to this, unless you are ready to stop existing."

Prospero thought over her options. House Grendel? That used to be Agnes, and it was now Sondre. One was a villain; one was in the infirmary. Scylla would be the next logical choice. She was in the infirmary. House Hephaestus? Fatima and Omer were willing to fight if necessary. Gil, House of Charybdis, and Walter were not. That left House Dionysus and Jörd, but Allan, Dionysus, was one of the witches who had fled, so by default Prospero couldn't trust Jörd.

"I could ask Fatima and Omer, or I could speak to the sports house," Prospero mused after a moment.

"The sport-witches would have plans, at least. What would the builders offer?" Grish countered. "Might as well ask the madam . . . although prophecy isn't much use in a conflict, she has other experiences."

"It's not just about a person's type of magic." Prospero crossed her arms. "I do *mind* magic. What use am I? We are more than our magical strengths."

"True. More than our fears, too." Grish shook his head. His voice turned somber as he chided, "You know this answer, Prospero. Crenshaw has placed great trust in you for a long time. That is unchanged."

The words sounded more serious than she typically expected from hobs outside her house. "You know exactly what's happening over there," she surmised.

"We do. There are other reasons to take Thesis rather than a witch you do not trust as you trust that one." Grish gave her a sympathetic look. "It may be beneficial to you both."

"You know Cassandra's prophecy."

Grish gave a nod. "We know everything. Take Thesis."

"You don't get to decide what Ellie does."

"Neither do you," Grish pointed out before vanishing without another word.

Prospero hated the fact that she was reduced to arguing almost as much as she hated knowing that there was no other witch she could trust so wholly. She knew she *had* to take Ellie or go alone, and she didn't love either plan.

"Damn it," Prospero whispered to the empty air.

She closed the door and walked into the kitchen, buying time before she saw her moody bride. *I'm not being overprotective,* Prospero argued with herself. *I could handle this alone. I'm sure of it.*

A guilty voice rose up. *Like how you handled Aggie?*

If not for Sondre, Prospero wasn't sure what would've become of her. Her mind had swayed too easily to Aggie's magic.

"Is there a reason you are standing here alone in an unlit kitchen?" Ellie asked from the doorway.

"Arguing with myself."

"How's that going?" Ellie leaned against the doorway, and the light illuminated her bare legs. She'd obviously grabbed a shirt, but that was all. As Prospero let her gaze drift upward, she noticed that the shirt remained unbuttoned. It gaped in such a way that a long line of bare skin, from cleavage to belly, was revealed.

Prospero closed her eyes before she could see if undergarments were omitted. "I have to retrieve a witch."

"I see. And the argument . . . ?"

"Inviting you to assist me." Prospero opened her eyes and pointedly held Ellie's gaze. "It's dangerous. We can't use exterior magic, and I can't ask you to—"

"Give me five to get dressed. You might want to do the same."

☽ ✶ ☾

By the time they arrived in the nonmagical world, Prospero's emotions were no more in control than at home. Now, though, it was all worry.

I can't lose her.

I won't.

But what if . . .

"This is a terrible idea," Prospero muttered, even as she poured a handful of spell stones into Ellie's hand. "These are nonlethal."

"Who else are you going to take to do this? The headmaster and Lord Scylla are in the hospital." Ellie glared at her wife. "Do you want to try taking the chief witch? A random head of house? What about Jörd? She's already leaking magic everywhere. Oh, I know, the seer! The witch you're furious with . . ."

Prospero looked at Ellie and said, "You're obnoxious when you're right."

"Luckily, I'm also *really* invested in you coming home safely," Ellie pointed out in a kinder voice.

After debating it, Prospero took one lethal stone, wrapped in a silk bag, and slid it into Ellie's jacket pocket. "That one is lethal, love. I know you don't want to, but if it's you or them, you use it. Swear it. I don't want to lose you, so I need to know you'll—"

"I swear." Ellie stepped closer. She wrapped both arms around Prospero and said, "Now, come on. Before the witch gets away. I have things to do here at home, you know."

It only took a moment to teleport to the nonmagical world. Prospero had done so countless times to retrieve a remedial witch or modify memories.

They appeared on a college campus somewhere in the northern United States, from the look of the trees. Oak trees in bud dotted a campus that was a swath of red brick and old money. The area where they'd arrived was a green space, not quite a quad but one of those areas where there was too much ground to leave it unmanicured, but not enough to squeeze in a parking lot or building. There were shrubs, a flower bed that twined along the perimeter, three trees, and a heterosexual couple currently having vigorous sex while others cheered them drunkenly. The woman on top had her skirt around her waist like a wide belt, and that seemed to be the only clothing she had on.

Two men to the left were fondling each other. One had his jeans unzipped; the other had them shoved down to his knees. Nearby, a woman was doing a keg stand.

"So I guess we found Lord Dionysus," Ellie said mildly. Her cheeks were bright red, and she turned her gaze away from the group in the grassy lawn. "When Jörd taught one of the classes, she had this same, err, sort of magic."

"Oh?"

"I thought maybe I was just horny but . . ." Ellie shrugged. "I guess it's just their magic."

"Do I need to ask?" Prospero pushed the wave of possessiveness back.

"I admired her, touched her arm, and . . . that was all." Ellie looked around. "So, Dionysus . . ."

"He's somewhere here." Prospero cleared her throat and suggested, "Perhaps we should send you home? I can find—"

"Are you afraid my Victorian sensibilities will be offended? Oh. Wait . . ." Ellie looked at her and grinned. "That's you. This is just like we're walking through a giant porn movie. I'm fine."

"Oh." Prospero had heard that term, and it wasn't as if she was still, in fact, as innocent as she once had been. One of her two dearest friends the last few decades was the proprietress of a brothel. Admittedly, Cass' house of ill repute was not quite this acrobatic.

One woman was holding up a very large fake phallus to another woman. Prospero couldn't look away as the second woman lifted her skirt and opened her legs in invitation. That was not the sort of thing that existed in Crenshaw. "Wow."

"Not much exposure to porn, huh?" Ellie said as they walked.

"Only live shows at the brothel."

"That appeals to you," Ellie teased, looking over at the two women.

"Not *them*." Prospero didn't look away, though. She'd never seen that, never tried that. All the supplies they had in Crenshaw came from one warehouse that supplied food and clothing, *or* they had things that they made or grew.

"Perhaps we should take a shopping trip," Ellie said mildly.

Nothing Prospero could think to say seemed appropriate, so she walked in silence, trying to tune out the moans and cries all around them. Everything felt too real, too exposed, and Prospero had to remind herself that these people would not recall the worst of their misadventures.

We just have to find Allan and get him out of here, so his magic isn't spilling out and making people amorous.

31

Maggie

Since Sondre slept longer than she had, Maggie had been offered a chair by the doctor in the early hours. Maggie looked at her and asked, "Medical-magic class?"

"It was an awkward thing, but I had to tell him." The doctor gave her a tight smile. "He was already in a snit because I got back at him by having sex with Prospero."

"With . . . you? *Her?*"

The doctor shrugged. "Life is long. I get lonely."

Maggie couldn't fault the logic, other than the fact that her general impression of Lady Prospero was that the woman was a cold fish. *Not my business, though.* She held the doctor's eye. "That really happened, though? You, me, Axell?"

"It did." Dr. Jemison scowled. "Do you not remember?"

Maggie gave a single shake of her head.

"What has that woman done now? And he asked her. You know he did." She shot a furious look at Sondre. "If he wasn't sick, I'd give him an emetic. Make him spill his guts."

Briefly, Maggie thought that the doctor was her sort of person. *Clearly, Sondre has a type.* Then the doctor walked away to check on Scylla, so Maggie continued to annotate what she could piece together of her missing memories from what Sondre told her, what Dan and Axell and Ellie and now Dr. Jemison had added.

A few hours later, she was sitting there with a notepad and pencil, making plans on her next steps and keeping an eye on him, when Sondre woke muttering, "Magic."

But Sondre was half off the bed and fumbling for shoes before he was alert enough to say, "Who are you?"

"Your wife. You're in the infirmary." Maggie reached for his hand to try to lead him back to bed. His eyes were wide, and his pupils looked too large. It made her feel less angry with him, but that was more of a deferring it for later than dismissing it.

Sondre looked around, gaze darting too quickly. "I'm in Crenshaw. This *is* the castle, and you're . . . who now?"

"Your wife." Maggie pushed him onto the bed, realizing his skin was burning up. "Maggie. I'm Maggie."

"Right genius, he is," a hob muttered. "Better call the doctor."

"Dr. Jemison!" Maggie put a hand on Sondre's arm, as if she could restrain him. Luckily, he didn't resist. "Doctor!"

When the doctor came bustling over, Sondre gave her a dopey smile. "I always had trouble deciding whether I liked your bottom or your boobs more. I'll figure it out later. Got to go, though. Duty calls! Hob!"

"Dear lord," Dr. Jemison said.

"He has a fever." Maggie felt awkward, more at the fact that she was there to hear his proclamation to his ex-lover than anything else. "He woke up talking about magic and trying to get his shoes."

"He's the headmaster so he can feel a magic spill. There's either a new witch over there, or one of the escapees has done something again." Dr. Jemison tucked back a stray bit of hair that had come loose. "Either way, it'll have to wait. He's not going anywhere in this state."

"Hob!" the doctor called out.

"You *both* bellowed?" The hob, one Maggie didn't know, balanced on a water pitcher in a pose like a ballerina. Clad entirely in shades of yellow, the creature was memorable in multiple ways. Their gender was impossible to guess accurately from clothes or hair.

"Lemon." The doctor looked relieved. "There's awakened magic or—"

"Prospy has already gone to fix it. Probably want to have an empty bed for the bleeding that'll come soon. Get this one fixed, Lady Mae." The hob executed a perfect pirouette and then bowed. Then they were gone.

Maggie wasn't entirely sure what bleeding was being discussed, or if she wanted to know. Her priority was Sondre. "What do you need from me?" she asked the doctor.

"Obviously, I want all my beds empty," the doctor muttered. She rubbed her temple. "Let's get him sorted, and maybe if Scylla is staying awake this time, I can get them both out of here."

Sondre tugged on the doctor's shirt and whispered loudly, "I don't have a wife, Mae. Think I'm being held captive. She's a looker, but . . . I'd remember being married."

The doctor shot Maggie a look, and then she smiled widely. "Let me get you a drink, Sondre. Hmm? You can tell me all about it. I'll fix things right up."

The doctor sashayed her way to the other side of the curtain, and Maggie wondered if the emetic the doctor threatened was on the way.

"Knew she'd forgive me. She always does." Sondre had a smug look that Maggie wanted to knock off his face. On the other hand, he was oddly adorable in his fever state. He looked at Maggie. "Sorry . . . whatever your name is. I'm sure we had a great time, but I'm not the marrying sort. You can't trick me that way."

Maggie pointed at his ring, and then she held her hand up with the matching one. "We are married, you oaf."

"Sure, we are." He patted her butt. "I'll see you around. Maybe when

I'm not busy"—he darted a salacious look toward the curtain—"you can remind me all about our night, hmm? I don't usually forget an ass like yours."

Maggie bit back a laugh. She made a vague gesture toward the main space of the infirmary. "I'm going to go over . . . there since you're obviously in need of treatment."

When Maggie walked over to where the doctor was preparing a concoction that looked like liquid cotton candy, she paused. "That's not going to make him puke, is it?"

A laugh burst out of Dr. Jemison before she said, "Sadly, no. Oath and all that. He's actually sick. Give him a few minutes. Witches' Fever can muddle things. He'll be mortified afterward, you know. He really does care for you. Asked me to look after you and the boy if he, err, didn't survive this last trip to stop Aggie."

"*Really?*"

The doctor nodded. "Whatever he's spouting right now is nothing. He's all yours. Probably a lot more than you know, if he asked Prospero to erase your memory of our moment." She grinned. "Not that he should've. You're straight as a knife, aren't you?"

"I am."

"He was wrong to do that," Dr. Jemison said. "Don't let him off too easy for that. But this silliness? He's just feverish. He didn't mean a thing commenting on me. We've just been on and off for a few years. It's nothing real, not for him."

Maggie heard what the doctor wasn't saying: at least one of them had real feelings on the line. It just wasn't him. She kept her words simple then. "He thinks I'm going to leave him, but I'm not."

"Insecurities," Dr. Jemison said simply. "We all have them. Just wait here. You'll hear when the medicine works. Maybe you'll hear what you need to know, too."

Then she stepped past Maggie and carried the flowery-smelling pink goop toward Sondre.

"Aw, Mae. I hate that stuff." Sondre's words did nothing to make him seem more somber. He sounded drunk, in fact.

"Do it. You'll get a prize after . . ." the doctor cajoled. "Here we are. Drink up, hot stuff."

As Maggie peered around the curtain, Sondre chugged the goopy stuff and promptly flopped back, eyes closed as if he'd passed out.

Maggie waited, listening to him as the doctor ordered. She felt self-conscious eavesdropping, but at least Lord Scylla was asleep. Maggie sat on the chair next to her as the minutes ticked by and Sondre tried to flirt with the doctor.

After at least three minutes, Maggie's discomfort switched to worry. *What if he really does still have feelings for Dr. Jemison?* She knew that they had history, and Maggie was really the new person in the equation.

Then she heard an "Oh hell!" from Sondre. "I need my shoes, Mae. Maggie's probably halfway to the castle door by now. I said some stupid shit."

"Sorry I didn't catch the fever before it spiked." The doctor sounded like she was trying not to laugh. "So you remember the nonsense you were spouting . . . ?"

"Shoes. I need my shoes," Sondre muttered. "Shit. Sorry for the things I said to you, too, Mae, but I need to catch Maggie. She must be hurt that I didn't realize she was—"

"You love her." Dr. Jemison sounded slightly surprised. "I didn't know it had become a real marriage."

"I didn't expect to feel this, didn't think I was capable of it," Sondre rumbled. "She makes me feel like I want to stay at her side and watch over her, like I could be happy. . . . Being married is not at all what I expected."

"Go get her. *Tell* her."

"No. I have no intention of telling her. I've got a plan to present to Congress. She could go back, take her son, go home to the Barbarian Lands *with* him instead of staying here with my sorry ass. They are keeping her here as leverage, so I was trying to keep her away from Brandeau and not let her know I . . . love her." Sondre let out a loud sigh. "I'm going to talk to Walt again, and if I need to, I'll . . . I'll make deals with Prospero, Scylla, you, anyone I have to. If that's what she wants, she ought to be able to go. It ought to be her choice."

"You need to tell her how you feel *before* you go trying to send her back. She deserves to know how you feel, and I'm not going to deal with you being brokenhearted." The doctor's footsteps sounded as she approached Maggie's hidden spot on the other side of the sleeping Lord Scylla. The doctor paused, gave Maggie a pointed look, and carried on.

For a moment, Maggie felt worse for eavesdropping, hearing all of that, but then her temper started to simmer. He had no intention of telling her that he was still fighting for her to go back to a life without him. Simply hearing the words made her realize that she didn't want that. She was where she wanted to be, and Craig could go live with Hestia in the regular world until he was older. Afterward, he could decide if a life in Crenshaw where he was the only nonmagical person was worth it, and honestly, she suspected he'd decide to do just that.

If not, well, he could visit. The Congress had already approved Craig knowing about Crenshaw. There was no need to go to Congress, no reason to end her marriage, no reason to be anywhere but at Sondre's side. The finish-school-over-there plan would work, and she would stay right here.

With a man who loves me.

Maggie stepped around the curtain and ran into Sondre as he was rushing toward the door. He caught her instinctively before she could fall, and Maggie wound her arms around his neck. "Hi."

"I'm sorry, Maggie. I had a fever. And didn't think I could ever get married—"

"Because you didn't expect to fall in love?" she asked.

Sondre looked like she'd accused him of a crime. His expression was somewhere between guilt and denial: eyes wide, lips parted. No words escaped, though. No denial. No admission.

After a long awkward moment, he said, "Love isn't everything."

"Do you love me?" she asked, staring up at him.

"Maggie . . ."

"*Do* you?"

"I'm sorry I didn't realize we were married, and that I said those things about Mae, and—"

Maggie cut him off. "You're avoiding my question, Sondre." She pulled his head down, so they were almost lip to lip. "Do you love me?"

"Yes, but I won't trap you here. I know how important it is to you that Craig has a safe life." Sondre lifted her into a bridal carry and headed toward the door of the infirmary. "I'm a grown man, and I won't fall apart because you put him first. I lived without a wife before and—"

"Shut up," Maggie said softly. "Craig will go to school, and he'll be in a good house, in a safe place, then when he's an adult he'll decide if he wants to stay here or move to college over there. Because he was given permission to live here *and* permission to go over there, I don't *have* to leave."

"True." The door opened at his approach, and he carried her into the hallway of the castle.

Maggie leaned closer and said, "I will make sure I can see my son when he's finished high school, but I *plan* to stay with the man I love."

Sondre came to a full stop and looked at her, as if he was oblivious to the students in the hallway currently staring at them. "Repeat that."

"I love you, Sondre." Maggie had barely finished saying the words when he teleported them to their suite.

"Say it again," he said as he lowered her feet to the floor, so they were standing chest to chest.

"I . . . love . . . you." Maggie put her hands on his chest. "This is the part where you say it back."

He let out the most undignified "*whoop*" she'd heard from him, repeated the words, and pronounced, "Then, you're *not* interested in me finding a way you can leave. I thought that's why you were talking to Brandeau and—"

"I just don't like them thinking I'm a pawn. You'd have known why I was doing that, too, if you'd asked. . . ."

"I panicked."

"Yes. How about we talk instead of playing guessing games and erasing memories and plotting on our own. Be a team?" She stared up at him. "Can we do that? Talk?"

"Yes, but later? Right now, I'm about to seduce the woman I love."

"Fine. Give it your best shot." Maggie devolved into giggles at his exaggerated frown, and then she took his hand and led him toward the bed.

32
Ellie

The campus was alive with a revelry that made post basketball- or football-game madness seem tame. Ellie wasn't a stranger to seeing students in the street with cars toppled and random brawls. In her college days, she'd made the mistake of going to a basketball game between two rivals. Drunken groups of fans—some with full face and chests painted—had roamed like lost warriors. Fights broke out; fires flared to life. It was a memory she'd never forget and an event she had no desire to repeat.

This was worse. A fight in the quad had turned into a mess with what looked like a boar.

"Is that a pig?" Ellie nodded toward it. The poor thing was surrounded by students who were waving jerseys at the pig.

"We are here for the witch, love."

"But that poor pig—"

"Student," a young man interrupted. He was sitting astride a nearby statue of a giant pig with massive tusks. The tusks held a leather backpack and a hoodie, presumably the property of the young man, who looked up from his notebook. "He was a student a few minutes ago. The whole thing is fascinating. I'm chronicling it all."

"Prospero?" Ellie looked to her side for help. "He's . . . not affected."

Prospero glanced at the young man and pronounced, "Witch."

The young man chortled and then muttered, "Medieval superstitions. That's new. I wonder if the delusion comes in stages."

"He's one of us—or will be eventually." Prospero motioned for Ellie to keep walking. "We have a mission. He's not it, nor is the porcine student."

Ellie hustled to keep up with her wife. Prospero walked with an authority that made people part before her like a predator through a field of prey. Men and women separated at her approach, almost unconsciously giving her space.

And Ellie followed in her wake.

"He's behind us," Ellie said, glancing back at the young man, who had hopped down from the statue and was striding after them now.

"His life, his choices." Prospero looked around, gaze drifting over the crowds of students as if looking for something particular.

"What are we tracking?" the guy said as he caught up.

From this angle, Ellie reevaluated him closer to midtwenties than traditional college-age student, probably a grad student. No one else seemed immune to the spill of debauchery across the campus. Maybe he would be useful.

"Magic," she said.

"You're not lying," he enthused. "I know it sounds odd, but I can—"

"Tell," Prospero cut him off. "Yes, we know. It's a witch thing. You ought to take shelter somewhere until this is all resolved. Magic can be dangerous."

He shoved his notebook in his backpack and slung it over his shoulder again. "I'm in. Where to, boss witch?"

"Step back." Prospero pushed Ellie behind her just as a herd of person-sized pigs came charging through the quad.

The last few pigs stopped, and suddenly, the rest came to an abrupt halt and turned back. Within the next moment, a veritable wave of grunting and snorting pigs was running toward them.

"Steps! Go. *Go!*" Ellie called, grabbing Prospero's hand and pulling her toward a stairwell on the side of a building several yards away. "Faster!"

"Magic them!" the student who'd joined them called out. He kept pace, but he had a chivalrous streak that had him at the back. "You say you're fucking witches. Magic the damn hogs."

"Can't," Ellie huffed. "Magic is forbidden here. Up up up, Prospero."

"Tell that to them!" The man half shoved them up the steps in front of him as the pigs squealed in apparent irritation as their prey escaped.

Pigs aren't predators.

But these aren't really pigs.

And people? Sometimes people are predators.

About halfway up the flight of stairs, Prospero pulled Ellie closer to her side. "Are you injured?"

"No. You?"

"Fine." Prospero looked back at the man who'd joined them. "Look. Things are atypical right this moment. Magic doesn't stay in this world, and you are impervious to this leak because you're meant to be a witch someday."

"When?" He folded his arms, leaning against the stairwell and staring at them as if this was all perfectly normal.

"Typically, when you have a near-death experience."

A strange look came over him. "Like if I got trampled and then walked it off?"

"Fuck." Prospero closed her eyes for a moment, and Ellie knew what had happened without hearing her next words.

"*Did* that happen?" Ellie asked him anyhow.

"Yep. Then suddenly they were all pigs, and I was walking away." He shrugged. "Got a shower. Felt fine, so I went for a walk and . . ." He gestured at the chaos behind them. "Things are weird as shit around here."

Prospero looked at him and then Ellie. "He ought to go back."

"If you say I should take him, you'll end up sleeping at your desk eternally and not in *my* bed," Ellie warned. "I am here to help you." She pointed at the young man. "What's your name?"

"Ian."

"Right. Ian can stay here while we go fix this, or he can tag along. He's not *my* priority either." She looked back at Ian. "Sorry."

He held up his hands, palms out, as if to say, "No problem."

"Fine." Prospero glared back at her. "Stay here and be in peril, *but* if you get injured by roaming pigs or whatever else, I'll be furious with you."

Ellie smiled and promised, "I'll be as careful as you are." That earned her another glare. "Maybe the pigs won't follow. They seem to be angry at him, probably because he's why they're *pigs*."

Prospero glanced at Ian. "Stay."

"No." He smiled. "Take me to your wizard president or whatever the saying is."

"I swear Sondre will be . . ." Prospero paused and called, "Hob!"

Clancy, one of the castle hobs Ellie particularly liked, popped into existence on Ellie's shoulder. "Hello, Trouble Witch."

"Shit! There's a . . . there's a . . ." Ian pointed. "On your shoulder."

"Hobgoblin," Prospero supplied. "The headmaster needs to retrieve this." She pointed at Ian. "Remedial witch. He's not ready to deal with what we are here to handle, but he's trailing us like a bad smell."

"Hey!" Ian folded his arms and glared at her.

"A new student! How lovely!" Clancy clapped his hands together cheerily. "And how goes the hunt?"

"There are pigs." Prospero gestured. "We are stuck on the side of a building because *pigs*."

"Might I transport you to your field of battle?" the hob asked in a cheerful voice. "As I am already here?"

"After the headmaster is made aware of . . ." Prospero nodded toward Ian, who was trying to poke the hob's foot where it rested on Ellie's shoulder.

Ian leaned closer, as if to look at the hob's suit-clad little body.

Clancy winked, turned, and farted loudly in Ian's face before he vanished.

"Gross. What was that?" Ian scrunched up his face.

"Hob." Sondre's voice appeared before he did. He looked around at the pigs, the fights, the fire, and then met Prospero's gaze. "Why are you calling me here?" He scowled at Ian. Paused again. "Oh. I see. Remedial witch."

"Indeed," Prospero said.

Sondre gave her a look. "Are you able to handle this hunt? I can—"

"I have Ellie," Prospero said, which was sort of an answer.

"I see that. Miss Brandeau." Sondre dipped his head to her. "Is it . . . Aggie?"

Prospero shook her head. "Dionysus."

"As in the *god*?" Ian exclaimed. "Let me stay with you. I could change my thesis and—"

"Hush." Prospero rolled her eyes. "Go home, Headmaster. Take the child with you."

Sondre gave her a long look. "How did you know I wasn't going to accept Grendel?"

"You're a good man, Sondre. Go home to your family. I'll handle this one, although I may ask for aid with the last Grendel." Prospero turned her back on him and called out, "Clancy?"

"Grendel? As in from the book?" Ian sounded like all his birthdays were coming at once. "Oh. I'll be good. Let me stay! I just—" His words cut off as Sondre and Ian departed for Crenshaw.

The hob appeared again, and Prospero held a hand out toward Ellie.

Not two moments later, Ellie and Prospero were standing at the doorway of what appeared to be a biology lab—at least it *had* been a lab before House Dionysus arrived here. The room was formed in a rectangle with tall, glass windows, so passersby could look into the laboratory-style classroom. Even with the crowd, they could see the tall, black-topped lab tables with sinks in the surface. Shelves lined the back wall, still visible over the heads of the writhing, drunken, dancing crowd.

At least one window was broken, and an amorphous blob with one milky eye stared up from the glass that was littered around it like shards of ice. Whatever had been in the jar had been tossed at the window, apparently. Now there was a decaying specimen, glass, and a foul odor.

"Are you ready?" Prospero asked, pulling Ellie's gaze to her.

"No. You?"

Prospero laughed. "Use the stones. Try to avoid magic, but if it's either magic or death, use the magic. Do you hear me? We'll deal with any complications later."

"I do."

Prospero pushed open the door and they waded into the crowd.

It only took a moment to find their quarry. Allan, Lord Dionysus, was standing on a makeshift throne that had begun life mostly as a beer keg. Now, however, the whole of it was decorated with bits and pieces of things. A painting of a farm was lashed together with a houseplant to make a chair back, and the arms were fashioned of empty water bottles in vibrant patterns. Dusty silk flowers were woven onto a tangle of fabric to create the seat of the throne. The whole mess was twisted together with enormous grapevines that dripped from grape into wine that was caught in bowls and other containers around him.

The problem, aside from the whole using-magic-in-the-world, was that this room had obviously been a lab of sorts. Animals soaked in formaldehyde were spilled across the floor in a horrific mess. Rats, snakes, fish, and others she couldn't identify had been dumped out, and those same glass vessels were now being used as punch bowls for magically created wine.

"Formaldehyde and wine," Ellie muttered. "What could possibly go wrong with that?"

At her side, Prospero looked at several motionless bodies who were sprawled on the lab floor as if they were no different than the creatures in the jars. "Death. That's what usually goes wrong."

Ellie felt like the eels in her belly were swarming. *People died here because of his hubris.* It wasn't surprising. On some level, she'd expected it after the mess across campus. What was surprising was the apathy of the crowd. People stepped over the dead bodies as if they were mere inconveniences, tripping on them as they came for refills of the poisoned wine.

"No magic outside of emergency?" Ellie asked, staring at the wine. "Not even a little 'change this wine into water'?"

Prospero shook her head. "Life or death only, and even that magic will be unpredictable. He's destabilized everything, so any magic outside of spell stones is not going to react as it should."

Ellie saw a fire alarm on the wall. "Be right back."

"Allan?" Prospero called.

Ellie looked over and realized that the head of House Dionysus was wearing dark sunglasses, so that it was impossible to tell if his eyes were open or closed. He looked like an old lecher in modern clothes.

As Prospero approached the drunken man on his odd throne, Ellie wove through the crowd to reach the far wall. She pulled the alarm, and instantly, the wail blared into the existing chaos. The crowd, however, was unconcerned.

"Dance! Dance, my faithful!" Allan's proclamation boomed louder than the siren, which shifted into a song at his apparent command. Chanting voices and drums suddenly replaced the alarm, and the crowd gyrated throughout the room.

The music seemed to draw acolytes from beyond the lab, and soon the crowd swelled to double the size. *Just what we need: more bodies.* Minute by minute the crowd seemed spurred to a frenzy, moving faster by the moment, as if they couldn't stop dancing.

Several people were vomiting, and even though that foul mess was on the ground and people were nearby, no one left. No one retreated or even seemed to notice. People were still twirling as if they couldn't control themselves, bodies flailing and crashing.

Across the crowd, Ellie saw Prospero moving closer and closer to their target, and for a moment, she thought things would be resolved quickly. Then, just as Prospero was at his side, Allan turned his gaze on Prospero.

"Do you know what Dionysus had, my dear? Maenads." He smiled a vicious smile. "Would you like to meet my madwomen? If not, you need to stop this."

33
Prospero

"Can't fight your own battles?" Prospero called out, scanning the room for exits that didn't include going through a glass wall. This could get uglier very quickly if the crowd rushed the glass. Allan clearly didn't care about the lives he was endangering, though.

Prospero taunted, "Hiding behind women? Why am I not surprised?"

"I am a god. That's what you stole from all of us, you and the rest of those sanctimonious fools." Allan straightened on his grotesque throne and glared at her. "Do you think you stand a chance against our faithful?"

With his sunglasses in place, Prospero was unable to catch his eye. The danger of witches knowing her power was that they'd apparently planned to be better able to resist her. That didn't mean she was defenseless, and Ellie's gift was impossible to defend against. Prospero simply hated asking her wife to stop someone's heart or freeze their lungs.

Not the best first tactic.

"Look at them," Ellie yelled, drawing his gaze. "They're zombies.

Drunk, drugged, poisoned. Is that what you want? Come on. I barely know you, but I have to think you know you're better than this."

"Better than them," he slurred. "I am a *god.*"

"You are different from them, but that doesn't justify this madness. This is beneath you, god or witch or man." Ellie gestured as she spoke, forcing him to notice her, making herself a target.

Prospero knew Ellie's actions weren't accidental, so she took the chance and tossed several stones at Allan in rapid succession. The pebbles reflected off a barrier, as if he'd found a way to create a shield they couldn't see.

Her mind magic and her spell stones were not working. *Is the barrier physical, too?* Prospero watched to see the magic-drunk students and faculty ease close to him, but not touch him. *Maybe it is physical, too.*

He'd noticed Prospero's failed attempts to strike him.

"You dismissed me, *Lady* Prospero. Drunk Allan. Farmer Allan." He was back to staring at Prospero now, shaking his finger at her like a parent to a child. "You think you're so superior with your house of one. All the power. All the control. No sharing your division of the money with the rest of your house."

"That's what this is about? *Money?*" Prospero scoffed, despite trying to tell herself not to aggravate the drunk asshole. She was sick of it, sick of him, sick of all the New Economists' arrogance. "You had hurt feelings because I have more money?"

"Do you have any idea how many people are in my house?" Allan seethed.

"You had two shares, Allan, and a cohead to manage—"

"I didn't need a woman pretending to be my equal," he spat. "She hates me, you know. She might not say it, but I see her. I see her dismissive looks. She refuses my attention. What's the use of a cohead if I can't fuck her?"

Ellie tossed a stone at him, and like Prospero's, it bounced off the barrier. The stone and the spell in it hit a woman, who was instantly captured in a massive spiderweb. She dangled in the air and strands of magical web as thick as rope wrapped around her.

"Bitch." Another woman reached for Ellie, and Prospero reacted without thinking. She tossed another stone, which created some sort of oil slick all around her. The woman and four or five others started sliding across the floor.

"Since you like women so much," Allan said. "I'll introduce you to my maenads. *They* act like women should."

At some command of his, the men in the room started flowing out, so it was soon just Ellie, Prospero, Allan, and a group of increasingly angry, drunken women.

Allan smirked as the women started to resemble nothing more than a hive mind. When one turned to look, they all did. When one reached, they all did. They moved together almost as if they were one being with many bodies. So as the first hand extended toward Allan, a ripple carried over them all and soon it was as if waves of hands were reaching for Allan.

"I am here." He pulled off his shirt and stepped into the sea of women. Their eyes were glazed, and they watched him like he was actually a god, instead of an average pasty-skinned man. Like all witches, he was attractive in a way that magic allowed, but even magic couldn't counter daily drunken excess. Not that any of that mattered here. The afflicted women were drunk on the overflow of his uncontained magic. It had spilled across the campus, but here it was worse. He was the source of the drunken state their bodies were experiencing, and they were in his thrall.

Without magic—or in a world of magic like Crenshaw—he certainly wasn't going to get this sort of mindless worship. And the New Economists had long argued that they ought to be treated like kings or gods. Magic, however, was just a fluke of heritage. It was no different from eye color or height. Over here, though, where witches weren't to be, Allan had the rapt attention of a score or more of glassy-eyed women.

When one of the women started pawing at his trousers, Prospero had decided that this was more than enough. Naked man bits were not on the list of things she liked seeing, and even if they had been, she'd already seen enough of *that* walking across campus. It was bad enough that none of those people—men or women—had the presence of mind to consent to sexual congress. Both parties were addled, but that was little comfort. It simply meant everyone's rights were violated.

Sexual acts without consent were simply wrong. *That was why I refused Ellie. She couldn't truly consent until she attained awareness she'd initially lacked. Information I had.*

Here? Allan was clear-minded. In this moment, *he* knew what was happening, even though the women didn't, but he didn't stop it. He encouraged it. With the other situations across campus, people under magic's influence, there was no guilty party—other than him.

With these women, it was doubly wrong, as he was using his magic *and* knowingly having sexual interactions these women couldn't agree to because they were drunk on magic.

"Don't be foul, Allan. They are out of their minds with magic," Prospero pointed out, hoping against hope that he'd see his mistake before it was too late.

He grinned and stared at her as he unfastened his trousers. "They all want me. That's how things should be. In this world, I get everything. Power. Money. Houses. Cars. Women. Anything I want is *mine.*"

"It's *magic*, you raging ass-boil. They don't want *you*. Your magic is leaking. They're unable to think." Prospero swept her arm around the room. "People are dead from your chemically tainted wine, and these women are clueless. Come home, and stop this right now."

He laughed, and the sound boomed around the lab like drums throbbing to life. "Fuck you, schoolmarm.

"She wants to take me from you," Allan told the women in a thunderous voice. "These interlopers want to deny you; they want to steal my holy seed."

Holy seed? Prospero rolled her eyes. If not for the sheer danger of the moment, she would have laughed at his absurdity. Hopefully, later she could. Right now, not being killed by a mob of mentally drugged women was a more important matter.

Allan ran his hand over his chest and down to his crotch. He opened his trousers and pulled out his member like it was something impressive. Prospero had only dealt with one of those, and this one didn't look any more interesting than the last one. "She is trying to deny you!" Allan told them.

The women turned as one to glare at Prospero.

"Bring them to me!" Allan flashed an ominous smile at Prospero.

Ellie was practically hurtling herself through the crush of women. She shoulder-checked one woman who had the polished attire of faculty, or at least, she had *started* the day with polish. Currently her glasses were missing one stem and her blouse gaped open to her stomach.

For a moment, the woman's gaze cleared. Alertness was restored. Then the glazed look returned. There was something in the pain of Ellie's touch, or maybe there was another explanation. Either way, Prospero wished she had more time to ponder it.

"Plan?" Ellie asked.

"If he is shielded himself and now using them as a human shield, there aren't a lot of options." Prospero watched as the women gyrated against the debauched Allan. "They're victims. I don't want them to get hurt *more*."

"Mind zap? Can you make him think he's bored by this?" Ellie suggested as they were shoved tighter together by the now-moaning crowd of women trying—and succeeding—in pushing and pulling the two of them toward the vile man beside his throne.

"Didn't work. Sunglasses."

There were a limited number of options before them, but as things looked increasingly dire, a hob popped into the room. And with the hob was Lord Scylla. She towered over most of the women in the room, but for some reason, Allan didn't notice her or the hob who had deposited her and already vanished.

Prospero tried not to glance at Scylla as she slinked up behind him. Instead she increased her struggles against the enthralled hive mind of women, trying to keep Allan focused on her and not noticing the deadly woman who was creeping up behind him.

Don't look at her! Prospero warned herself. She also shoved the thought toward Ellie, hoping it worked.

Not staring at Scylla was a challenge, though; she had a short sword unsheathed in her hand. The pommel—at the end of hilt—was an exposed metal fist, and the blade itself was a glint of metal in the air. Because all the women were focused on either trying to touch Allan or tugging Prospero and Ellie toward him, no one noticed Scylla. Their madness was an asset in this case.

When Scylla seemingly realized the crowd was all moaning and reaching for Allan, she raised her hands and did the same. In a few tense moments, she'd reached him, as had Prospero and Ellie on the other side.

"Hey P," Scylla greeted.

In that instant, Allan's mouth gaped open, and he swiveled his head to look back at her, just as Scylla slammed the pommel of her sword into his head and knocked him out. He slumped into her arms, unconscious.

Scylla swayed under the weight of his limp body, and Prospero glared at her.

"You shouldn't be here," Prospero grumbled.

"I owed him a punch, and you were taking a while to get this done." Scylla grinned widely despite the way she obviously struggled with the unconscious man in her arms. "He should've stayed where he was. Now . . ." She gave a crooked shrug. "See you at home."

Then she and the unconscious witch were gone, and they were left with a group of confused and, in some cases, tearful women.

34
Dan

Dan was not prepared for a panicked hob to pop into his room while he was half-dressed. His shirt was long enough that it covered his boxers, but he still wasn't a huge fan of having a hob stare at his bare legs and sock-clad feet. Privacy was a rare thing in the increasingly crowded castle, but typically, he had some measure of it in the privacy of Axell's room. Dan still didn't think of it as *his* room even though they'd more or less started sharing it.

He had the rare moment of Axell being temporarily out of it without Dan. So Dan was currently sans trousers and shoes when he was startled by an unknown hob in neon-yellow overalls and a bow with bright-yellow ducks pinned in their hair. The hob blurted, "Quick! Battery needed!"

Dan darted toward a robe that was on the bed and managed to grab it. "Wait. I'm—"

The hob grabbed his ear, and they were suddenly in the infirmary.

". . . not dressed," Dan finished.

The hob was gone, and the doctor gave him no more attention than she gave anything other than her patients. He wasn't entirely sure she even noticed that he had on neither trousers nor boots. He shrugged on a robe and held it closed with one hand.

Currently, Dr. Jemison was washing a disturbing amount of blood from Lord Scylla's stomach. "You can't go teleporting and carrying dead weight and bleeding everywhere, Scylla!"

"Dragged him back like a sack of soggy cement," Scylla crowed. "Look at him."

Dr. Jemison glared at her grinning patient. She did, in fact, look over at the man who was lashed to the bed where the headmaster had been when last Dan visited.

"Sondre is all better?" Dan asked. "So you can heal people again and—"

"Excuse me?" The doctor's gaze shifted to him, and he clutched his robe tighter. "I healed *you*."

"And a hell of a lot of other witches," one of Dr. Jemison's assistants said.

Dan folded his arms awkwardly. "Seems weird that the only one you aren't healing is the one I gave you a boost to heal." He shrugged. "Just thinking about it, Dr. J."

Lord Scylla frowned. "I did feel better *faster* when he wasn't here."

The doctor scowled at her, at him, at all of it. She didn't say anything, though. Instead, she looked from him to Lord Scylla to him again. Finally, she huffed. "Damn it. Get out. Just in case it is you, get out."

Dan looked at her, mouth opening in surprise. "Seriously? You summon me here without my trousers or shoes, and then I'm just . . . to walk around out there?" He waved a hand toward the door into the castle. "Are you always this rude?"

The doctor shot a glare at him, as did an unknown witch who was sitting against a wall.

"Hey. I'm Ian." The guy lifted a hand in a wave. "Prisoner here, I guess."

"Remedial witch," Dr. Jemison muttered. "Sondre dropped him off for an exam, but then *this* one . . ."

"Retrieved an enemy," Lord Scylla finished. In a falsetto voice, she added, "Good job, m'lord. Excellent work, m'lord."

"Follow orders, m'lord. How about you try that?" Dr. Jemison snarled.

"Boring." Lord Scylla gave a wide grin.

"You are bleeding again, you stubborn witch." The doctor leveled a look at Lord Scylla that would make most rational souls quake in fear.

The illusionist witch was clearly unbothered. "If he's draining you . . ." Lord Scylla started.

"And draining you." Dr. Jemison looked him up and down. "A natural siphon? He did boost my energy. Fine." She pointed at him. "Stay a minute, but don't touch anything or anyone."

Dan bit back a remark. The only way he ever touched them was when they dragged him here. *Bare-legged under my robe.* It was chillier than he'd like, and he had the overwhelming fear that he was going to step in something gross. This was, after all, where sickness happened. He pointedly stayed clear of the bloody cloth that was dangling half out of the basin beside Lord Scylla's bed.

"Newton's Third Law states that for every action in nature there is an equal and opposite reaction," Dan suggested. It made perfect sense in a horrible way. "That's physics, but magic seems to follow *some* of the same laws. If I can *give* energy, I have to *get* it from somewhere. It took a lot to . . . do a thing I had to do at the order of a witch who outranks me, and I'm not saying I did in case I'm not supposed to say that much."

Dan grimaced at what he almost said.

Prospero was *not* one of the good guys. He was mostly sure of that. *Chaotic neutral? Lawful evil?* He couldn't quite decide what she was other than dangerous. So he wasn't about to admit to these witches that he had aided her as she erased Ellie's and Maggie's memories, but he knew that erasing Ellie's had given him a headache that had lasted for a full week.

Boosting Prospero so she could adjust Maggie required only a trickle of energy, but the magic necessary for Prospero to erase Ellie's memories was enough to make Dan glance into a mirror afterward. He felt like a husk, like everything in him had been drawn out, and he couldn't get enough food or drink or sleep for days.

"So, siphoning . . ." The doctor had a worrisome look on her face. Her cheeks were flushed, and her eyes practically glistened in excitement. "If that's the case, it would explain some things. His magic was depleted because he'd just helped Prospero blank the memory of her poor wife."

"Poor wife?" Lord Scylla scoffed. "They're meant for each other. She's so head over heels—"

"Which one?" the doctor muttered.

"Ha! Prospero. I was surprised she wasn't breaking more rules in their damnable courtship, but the both of them are fools. Ellie ought to have talked to her instead of running off." Lord Scylla made a noise like *hmph* and gave one nod as if to underline her point.

"Fair. It had to have been hard to have to try to date when she could look into everyone's mind, though." The doctor hopped up and sat on the counter, surrounded by potions and bandages.

"That's what we're calling her swath of heart-breaking the last century? Dating?" Lord Scylla rolled her eyes. "I'm grateful I don't find women attractive. Watching her roll through all of you like a bear knocking down beehives was—"

"Ahem." The doctor shot him a look. "On the matter of the siphon-battery dilemma . . ."

"Buzzzz," Lord Scylla said quietly.

The doctor sighed. He watched as she visibly pondered. He glanced at Lord Scylla, who was steadfastly staring at him.

"We need to get Sondre, probably Walt," the doctor announced. "I suspect we ought to have Prospero here." She tapped her foot in the empty air. "Brandeau, too."

Lord Scylla sighed. "Do I want to ask?"

"And can we address my lack of trousers, please? I'll do your experiment, but . . . I'm not doing anything without trousers." He gestured at his bare legs. They might be hidden under a robe, but it simply felt wrong to be here without his pants on.

"Lemon!" Lord Scylla called out.

The yellow-overalled hob appeared. "You bellowed, sir."

"Be careful, Lemon, or I'll take you home with me." Lord Scylla smiled fondly at the hob. "Take this one to his room. He needs—"

The hob flung themselves across the room like a flying squirrel and landed on Dan's head. In the next moment, he was alone in his room. *Not* the room where his boots were. Those were in Axell's room, along with the trousers he'd intended to wear.

Lemon, however, was long gone. So Dan grabbed his only other pair of shoes, a tattered pair of secondhand slipper things, and a pair of sweatpants he had been using for pajamas before he started sharing a bed with Axell, and hurriedly got dressed. This whole business of popping him in and out of places with no warning was getting tedious.

He left his room in search of Axell.

If the witches were planning on experimenting on him, he wanted someone there who cared about *his* best interests. Dan scanned the hallways, and for the first time he tensed every time he heard the telltale pop of a hob appearing. By the time he found Axell, who appeared to be composing a song in the middle of an unusually empty library, he felt like all his nerves were frazzled.

"I need you to hold on to my hand at all times today unless one of us needs the toilet," Dan blurted as he marched hurriedly toward Axell.

"Yes." Axell took his hand, pulled Dan into his lap, and said, "Now, you tell me why."

The anxiety that had been twisting through Dan lessened as Axell stroked his other hand over Dan's spine. He felt safe here, protected, even though that was foolish if he had to deal with Prospero *and* the headmaster *and* Lord Scylla *and* Ellie.

"I can siphon magic." Dan looked around. He hadn't seen the library this empty since they'd told others about it. "That's the theory. It's why I can boost it. I'm taking it from places and then putting it other places."

"Makes sense."

"Where is everyone?" Dan asked.

Axell shrugged. "The door did not open. I was locked in. Everyone locked out. Until you."

Dan hopped up. He started to let go of Axell's hand to pace, but Axell stood with him. "I am to hold your hand."

"Right. Right. I know that." Dan stood still until Axell tugged him back, and together they paced the room *slower* while Dan filled him in on everything.

When he finally stopped, Axell looked at him. "You tell them that you will not do the experiment without me there. I go where you go."

"What if they send me back, siphon me, and—"

"I go where you go," Axell repeated. "We would travel and be together there, too."

"Even when you're famous and I'm just . . . me." Dan stared at him, hating his insecurity but unable to stop the words.

"I like *just you*." Axell squeezed his hand. "Together we will be. Here. There. I know what I want."

And Dan felt like the experiment—whatever it was—would be fine. Everything would be fine. He could conquer it all, just as long as Axell held his hand.

35

Prospero

The laboratory was awkwardly silent as the magic left the women there. A few sheepishly headed toward the door. Several tried to set their clothes to rights with a modicum of success.

"You were exposed to toxic gas from a leak in the lab," Ellie said calmly to the group. "Please line up and the mind healer will examine you. Failure to be cleared will result in memory loss and vision loss. It is important that she check you for retinal damage."

Retinal damage? Prospero usually wasn't this delicate, but Ellie's excuse worked well.

Ellie smiled encouragingly as she stood between them and the door. Her authoritative voice and calm manner were undoubtedly a result of her years working in a library, but regardless of the source or the consequences, Prospero currently found it absurdly attractive.

Not the place or the time.

Shoving aside the thoughts of her wife's assertive streak, Prospero climbed up onto a tall laboratory table and watched Ellie round up the women who seemed to be trying to leave. She was managing the chaos well, even as Prospero simply wanted to curl up and ignore this part.

Ellie directed a few of the women around both the bodies and vomit on the floor.

"Oh my god," one woman said, practically breathing the words. "Is he *dead*?"

And Ellie's expression clouded. She went from capable to still in that moment. The horror of the open-eyed corpse was enough to stop her, and the calm in the room started to fade as quickly as it had arrived.

"He . . . there was . . . an incident and—"

"Yes. He's dead. You're lucky you're not." Prospero looked at her un-flinchingly and spoke loud enough that the crowd all heard. "He refused his exam, and there he is. It didn't work out well for him. Line up. Let's get this resolved so the authorities know it's safe to come in here and handle the dead."

Ellie shot her a scowl, but whether or not she approved of Prospero's blunt tactics, most of the group lined up.

One woman went over to a cabinet and pulled out several long white coats. She draped them over the three dead bodies. "Respect," the woman murmured. "No one ought to be gawked at when they're like *that*."

One by one, Prospero looked into the minds of the women, erasing memories of magic exposure, maenad madness, and male idiocy. She left just enough hints that they all knew that they had been compelled to grope Allan, but that no one had been intimately violated. She also impressed an urge to talk to a therapist about it. While she was not *actually* a mind healer, she understood—from long talks with Cass and a few other witches—that talking post-violence could help.

And it's a lot healthier than my coping mechanisms were.

Prospero wouldn't say that she had stitched all of her own cracks and panics together, but she reached more-or-less stable eventually. Therapy hadn't been a viable option in her very short nonmagical years, and it was still not popularized fully in Crenshaw.

Once the last of the women left the laboratory, Prospero stood and reached her hand toward Ellie.

"We need to sort out Aggie yet," Prospero said quietly, "but for today, I simply want to go home. She'll turn up."

"The bodies . . ."

"They are the domain of this world," Prospero said gently. "We cannot manage everything. They are covered, and they'll be found by someone here as they assess the damage across campus."

Ellie frowned. "I wonder what they'll think."

"The astounding thing about magic is that—these days—it's often dismissed with a thin excuse. To believe that it was what it was is to be declared superstitious," Prospero said. "There are places where people still believe on a large scale, but mostly, the government of advanced nations is the only place where you find unfettered belief. There are pockets, people who handle the realities of witches and missing people, but as a whole . . ." She shrugged. "The average person will rationalize it away."

Prospero looked into the now-empty hallway. The throngs of drunken people were gone. All that was left was the destruction. "Let's go home."

Ellie wrapped an arm around Prospero's middle. "Tell me how to teleport us."

"I can do it."

"You look like you're going to topple." Ellie's arm tightened, holding Prospero to her side firmly. "Implant the information in my mind."

"I can't—"

"Try. If I don't resist, maybe you can." Ellie tilted her head. "I won't resist."

"Do you typically?"

"Typically?"

"The two times I tried," Prospero clarified.

"Obviously." Ellie rolled her eyes. "Implant it or tell me."

Erasing the minds of almost two dozen women was exhausting, but Prospero tried to slide into Ellie's mind. Suddenly, it felt as if she had bodily entered Ellie's head. Prospero knew she was standing in the foul-smelling laboratory surrounded by formaldehyde, decaying wine, vomit, and corpses, but she could suddenly smell lilacs.

"Hi." Ellie was wearing a goldenrod-yellow dress, not modern in its cut or style.

Prospero reached out and poked her arm. "This feels real."

"I was researching if we could connect here," Ellie said simply. "If there are no rules here, I thought maybe we could date in ways that would . . . make you love me."

"I already do."

"I didn't know that, did I? I was going to charm you, seduce you, and make you mine." Ellie twirled, the skirt of the dress flaring out like a bell.

"Already done, love." Prospero smiled. "I need to rest soon, though. Can we—"

"Show me how to get us home."

Prospero thought through the process, taking Ellie's hand and then letting go of the way she resisted the pull back to Crenshaw. She put her hand over Ellie's stomach. "Feel that hook. Right in here. And then stop fighting it."

In the next moment, Prospero was back in the ruins of the lab. She missed the smell of lilacs and the dress Ellie had been wearing, but then Ellie put her arms around Prospero and said, "I hope I get this right."

And they were standing outside the castle. Prospero felt like she was swaying on her feet with exhaustion. "Thank you."

"Are you okay? I didn't do anything that made you sick or—"

"Just tired." Prospero gave her a wobbly smile. Over the last few weeks, Prospero had hunted down and erased Ellie's mind and the Lynch woman's mind. She'd slept insufficiently as she was trying to figure out how to live with Ellie, and then she'd been left to deal with Scylla's injury,

Aggie's attack on Sondre *and* on Prospero. And now this debacle with Allan.

"I just want to hide away in our house," Prospero admitted. "But first . . ."

They approached the main door of the castle, which swung open silently as they neared. Prospero didn't slow her stride. She never did.

"Don't use extra magic," Ellie murmured.

"I don't. I was briefly headmaster, and whatever hob or magic hides in the castle seems to welcome my visits." Prospero smiled to herself. She liked the fanciful notion that it was the castle, but in truth, she suspected hobs. They were the embodiment of magic, an unstoppable force at the best of times.

They headed to the lower level of the castle where the infirmary was housed, and Prospero felt a glimmer of pride as Ellie took her hand. No one they passed likely cared, but Prospero had felt uncomfortable about the fact that she was unable to stand with Ellie as equals, as partners, as beloveds. Even though Ellie claimed to have wanted that, it hadn't been until the night prior that they were truly able to move forward. Now, she felt permitted to touch Ellie in public.

When they reached the infirmary, Prospero was unsurprised to see Scylla in her infirmary bed again.

"Did you tear open your wound with that stunt?" Prospero asked.

"*Psh.*" Scylla gestured over at Allan, who was straining against restraints. "I punched the jackal that punched me. I am fine with a bit of bleeding. Plus, Mae has a theory we're going to test now that you're here."

Trepidation crawled over Prospero. "Dare I ask?"

Scylla chuckled. "That boy is a siphon. That's why I'm not healing. Why Mae's draining over and over. If that's the case, it's not poison we're dealing with at all, just miscategorizing the waifish one."

"Monahan?" Prospero thought about it, the side effects of boosting energy if Monahan was not an amplifier but a converter. It made sense.

"So he wasn't boosting. He was draining it from somewhere, and then when he added energy to help heal you . . . he drained from Scylla's magic. Then drained you and whomever else."

Everyone watched her as she thought it through, and it occurred to her that she was validating or invalidating their theories from before she arrived.

"What's the experiment?" she asked.

From the door, Walt, who had just walked into the infirmary with Sondre, said, "The boy will siphon Allan."

36

Dan

Everyone in the very crowded infirmary turned to look at them when Dan walked in, holding tightly to Axell's hand. Dan forced back his anxiety and asked, "Bad time?"

The chief witch, a morally gray Scotsman Dan would have liked to avoid, stood beside the headmaster. Walter had some coldhearted attitudes, and Dan realized that most of them had already come up against that viciousness. The old witch wasn't a *bad guy* in an out-to-get-you sort of way, but he didn't seem particularly concerned with the consequences of his actions or decisions on others.

In stark contrast to the older witch, Sondre's expression was uncommonly cheerful, and Dan had to hope that it was because he and Maggie were solid. Despite Dan's initial hesitations about the headmaster, he continued to be fond of the man.

Axell, however, tensed as the headmaster looked at them.

"He can wait elsewhere," Sondre started.

"Sorry, but no." Dan squeezed Axell's hand. "I'm here for your experiment, but if you want me here, he stays."

Walter raised two furry brows. "And when did anyone decide *you* made decisions in Crenshaw? I don't recall that meeting. Does anyone here?"

Dan let him growl a moment. Then he said, "Plan B is to send the both of us back to the other world. You can't summon my magic to test. You can drain it from me, or you can ask. If you're asking, that's my condition. He stays at my side."

Axell squeezed his hand when he paused, reminding him that no matter what happened here, he wasn't alone.

"I did things at your order, and I wasn't pleased." Dan glanced at Sondre and Prospero. "You lived with the consequences, but I lived with the guilt. Not cool." He took a deep breath before adding, "I did other things—helping Dr. J and Lord Scylla—that were cool. I'm tired of people ordering me to do what they think. This is *my* body, *my* magic."

Sondre gave him an approving nod. Scylla did, too. The doctor's expression was unreadable, and Prospero looked contemplative.

The chief witch made a noise like a snort before he muttered, "Always so sassy when they come into their own." He pointed at Dan. "We'll have a little chat later, Mr. Monahan."

"I'll look forward to that, Chief Witch." Dan's voice didn't crack or wobble, despite feeling like he might throw up from anxiety. He wanted this world, this life, this future, but he was done with other people trying to tell him right from wrong when their own compasses were so incredibly skewed. Dan understood justice and ethics. He thought about them constantly.

"Right, well, the plan is that you drain Allan's magic," the doctor suggested, pointing at the former cohead of House Dionysus. "Allan here participated in the attempted murder of Lord Scylla. Typically, we'd talk to the head of House Grendel, but . . ."

"I turned it down," Sondre filled in.

Dan gave him a surprised look.

"If we could focus," the chief witch snapped.

Dan walked closer to the bound man. "Can you"—he looked at Prospero—"calm his mind or something?"

"I could. I will not." She smiled viciously. "He's lucky I don't make him think he's being tortured." She leaned close to the man's face. "You do deserve to suffer, Allan. I wish you'd remember why. I wish I could drop you off in the worst imaginable place for you. I could look into your mind to figure out what you fear. . . ."

"Enough," Walter barked.

Dan reminded himself that evil was relative, that he had no reason to be afraid of her, but he was also genuinely hoping to never ever deal with her again. "Right, well, you all need to back up. I'm barely figuring out how to give magic boosts, so draining them . . . I'd hate to drain the wrong witch."

He very carefully did not look at Prospero. The scary Victorian seemed more like Crenshaw's enforcer than an average witch, so maybe fearing her was normal. Maybe they all did, but no one admitted it aloud.

To Axell he whispered, "I need my hand free to do this."

Axell released his hand. "I believe in you, but if you want to just go back over to the regular world, we can."

Returning to the other world would mean facing cancer, because the magic would be gone, but more importantly, it would mean losing this weird, wonderful world of witches. Dan shook his head. In a steady voice he said, "Let's do this."

Dan pushed past the others to stand beside the bound man's bed. "I'm not completely sure what to do," Dan admitted.

"Think of taking magic into you," Sondre told him, sounding rather teacher-ish. "You drain from other sources and repurpose it. You've been doing it all along."

"Do you remember when we had the class on illusions, Monahan?" Scylla started to sit upright, and Prospero was there in a blink to shove pillows behind her.

Ellie, who had been silent, looked at them, and in the next moment

Scylla's bed had reshaped itself into a modern hospital bed with a controller to raise and lower both the head and foot of the bed. "That ought to help," she said mildly.

Maybe the others didn't realize the wonder of an electric bed working sans electricity. Dan was impressed, though.

I want that kind of control, he thought. *And power.*

After one last glance over at Axell, who smiled encouragingly, Dan went inside himself. He wasn't sure how else to explain it, but he felt like he was traveling in a vast castle-like building, but it wasn't like Crenshaw Castle. The halls were brightly lit, and the rooms were mostly unlocked doors.

On some level, he realized he was inside his own essence. His spirit or soul or energy or whatever one wanted to call it. He looked out of a large window into the field outside. Multiple glowing shapes in different hues hovered there. One had a solid cord that was tied into Dan's castle. *Axell.* Surprisingly, another thready path twisted past several glowing shapes to a tall figure. *Sondre!*

And for a moment, Dan looked at the others and thought, *I could take some of that.* It was probably the first time he realized what Axell had truly meant when he said Dan was hungry or compared him to a wolf. There was a ravenous craving in him that wanted to consume and take.

That's my magic. It takes.

Later, Dan would ask how others were siphoned before they were sent back to the nonmagical world. For now, he concentrated on not reaching out to the witches his mind saw as glowing shapes.

"Allan. Focus on Allan." Prospero's voice echoed through the castle of his mind, sending chills over him at the thought of her entering his mind.

Dan turned his attention to the writhing, glowing shape that looked like it was levitating. It was flat where the others were standing. He reached out . . . not quite hands but a magical extension of them, as if they stretched like a pour of energy creeping toward the blue glow that was the prone witch.

As soon as Dan's energy touched the shape that he knew as Allan, his magic shifted, like a creature left off its leash finally. He felt like an invisible mouth extended from him, biting at the energy and swallowing it down in gulps.

And the more he consumed, the more he wanted.

He felt guilt at the thought of taking. He *always* felt guilt for taking, for wanting, for craving.

But I'm allowed. They want me to do this. They brought me here to do this.

And so Dan let go of his self-restraints and let himself take that glowing magic into himself as he refilled the reservoir that had been depleted by everyone's demands.

37

Ellie

Ellie watched in horror as Dan started to shake. Light stretched from him in what looked like tangible ropes. The ropes twisted across the ground, vibrating like the tips of rattlesnake tails as they pursued the people in the room.

"Is that normal?" Scylla murmured.

"No." Sondre moved forward so he was between Dan and everyone else—except Prospero. She stepped forward, too. They exchanged a glance that was easy enough to interpret.

Dr. Jemison gestured to Walt. "Help me move Scylla out of here."

"I'm not leaving." Scylla crossed her arms. "Plan, Prospero?"

For a moment, it struck Ellie that no one had asked the chief witch. Prospero was the one managing things, the one trusted to go after threats, the one the governing body leaned on and somehow also the one who had been punished by assigning her an amnesiac wife. Once the crises were all resolved, Ellie would be having words with the chief witch—and maybe the entire Congress of Magic.

But the magical cords were thrashing like living serpents now. Their serpentine motions were hypnotic to Ellie, and when one of the cords lashed out at a speed akin to a striking cobra, Ellie did nothing to resist it.

"Allan. Focus on Allan." Prospero's words were terse as she stepped between Ellie and the radiant light that was spilling off Dan's body like something inside him had caught fire.

The twist of magic released Ellie and twined around Prospero's ankle. It steadily started creeping upward.

Prospero stumbled.

Her voice taut with something Ellie couldn't identify, Prospero ordered, "Move toward the door, love. If this doesn't work, I need you to *stop* him."

Ellie realized what she meant since they had discussed ways to use her magic to stop a witch. It wasn't a thing Ellie wanted to do. Murder ought not be the first choice. This wasn't the place to say that, though, not to this assembled group.

Dan was obviously beyond hearing their regular voices, but Prospero's magic was more than words. Even as the shimmering magical cords kept seeking the witches throughout the room, Prospero stepped in front of him and grabbed his face in her hands. Staring into his eyes she repeated, "Allan. Focus on Allan."

Prospero's voice wavered, but when she stepped back, jerking her hands from Dan's now–blindingly bright body, her gaze darted to Ellie. It felt like a plea for help.

But of all the things Ellie had done as a witch, only a few had made her feel like she was dangerous. She didn't want to add to that short list. She didn't want to take a life.

On the infirmary bed, Allan made a gasping noise and stopped thrashing. Had he stopped trying to cling to his magic or had something more fatal just happened? Could a person die in front of you without you noticing?

Allan's body started to contract, like he was seizing or tensing against a strike.

Over the next several moments, his entire body shrank into itself. His hair lost its gleam. His skin began to droop with lines and wrinkles. Then the flesh shifted again, as if it were thinning and clinging tighter to the bones. In the space of several heartbeats, it became abundantly clear that Allan's vitality had been drained along with his magic.

Allan was now a mummified corpse in loose-fitting clothes. His unbuttoned shirt exposed the sunken cavern that had been his stomach moments prior. Now, it was no more than a hollow basin of contracted skin. Each rib was highlighted under the thin webbing of desiccated flesh, and as Ellie watched, the weight of his skull fell sideways.

A crackling noise reverberated in the room as Allan's head detached from his spinal column. Ellie stared at the now-empty eye sockets and then at the now-unhinged jaw. There was nothing left of Allan.

Vaguely she noticed that the foul smell in the air was gone. *He created the rift.* And with his death, his magical corruption in Crenshaw had ended, too. That at least was a comfort. Crenshaw was no longer poisoned, since Allan was dead.

Still, Dan's magic continued to try to drain magic from the withering husk of the witch on the infirmary bed.

"Daniel?" Axell called his lover's name.

"Monahan!" Sondre barked out.

"He's dead," the chief witch began. "Daniel Monahan! Stop siphoning now. *Stop.*"

Nothing was getting through to Dan. Meanwhile, the glowing rope that was around Prospero's ankle had crept up to her hips. As Ellie looked at her wife, she noticed that Prospero was breathing as if injured.

"Is he siphoning you?" Ellie asked. They'd talked about what would happen if a witch as old as Prospero were to be siphoned. Proof of that fact didn't take but a glance to the infirmary bed where Allan's crumbling remains continued to fade toward ash.

As Dan's magic started to speed faster over Prospero's body, her hair turned gray, and her limber body loosened as if decades had passed in a blink.

Death will follow. She was being siphoned, and unless Ellie did something, Prospero would die just as Allan had.

Ellie glanced again at the corpse that was cracking into pieces as every last echo of magic was pulled out of the already dead bones.

"Prospero?" Ellie whispered.

"Ell . . . ie," Prospero said, voice thready with pain and age combined.

And at that moment, Ellie no longer remembered any objection to violence or death. She was not willing to lose Prospero. Her magic lashed out as if unaware of any conscious thought or effort.

In that sliver of a moment, Ellie reshaped Dan's heart. Her magic created the selfsame vines she'd once woven together to protect Crenshaw when the barrier fell. In her mind's eye, she saw them, the thin vines taking on droplets of blood in the place of eyes. Her creation looked back at her from within the nest of his no-longer-beating heart.

And under Ellie's magic, Dan Monahan died. She stopped his life to save Prospero. There was no guilt, no hesitation. It was simple.

38
Prospero

Prospero felt the weight of every decade of her life as the moments ticked by. She couldn't force words from her dry lips. The air she'd need to do so was impossible to find, and her lungs had begun to make a strangled whistling noise. The weight of the lungs themselves was wrong, as if dirty water filled them, and a pain throbbing in her bones made tears fill her eyes.

This was it. Death. Like Allan and Monahan, she was about to end. *Ellie saved me long enough that they'd all live—Scylla, Sondre, Walt. Just like Cass' prophecy. She saved me, and in doing so saved all of us.*

Well over a century of life had seemed liked a lot once upon a time, but then she fell in love. *Finally.* After all these years of keeping her heart hidden from everyone, she'd let go of her walls.

Her gaze found Ellie, who had done something awful to stop the magical ropes that were trying to find energy to drain. Ellie's mouth was moving, and she dropped to the floor where Prospero had collapsed.

Monahan fell to the ground, slumped over.

Both Sondre and the Norwegian went to the fallen witch.

Voices were blurring as Prospero's eyes felt heavier.

"Don't sleep," Ellie ordered, all but yelling the words into Prospero's face. "Do you hear me?"

Prospero heard a door open. A new voice twined through the others in the room, and then a vibration began. Prospero forced her eyes open, trying to warn them so no one else was injured by whatever that vibration was. Her throat wouldn't work, and her lips wouldn't part.

Prospero tried to at least gesture toward the door, but instead she toppled into Ellie's lap like a cornhusk doll. She stared up at the still-young face of her bride, glad they had had one night together before this.

I want more.

The vibration grew louder until the entire room hummed as if hives of bees had been set loose in the room, but Prospero couldn't move or speak. If there were bees, the others should get to safety.

Ellie's hand threaded through the remains of Prospero's wisps of hair, but Prospero's hearing was so nearly gone that she couldn't understand whatever Ellie was saying. She stared at Ellie's mouth, trying to read the words on her lips, but Prospero's vision was fading, too.

Except the bees. I hear them coming.

But then everything went dark, as if an explosion had rocked the infirmary, and Prospero felt her body and Ellie's sail through the air. Her final thought was that she hated that Ellie was injured, that she was useless to help her, that she was too weak.

Everything stayed dark, and Prospero was not expecting to be able to lift her eyelids again. She'd barely had the energy to blink a moment ago, so she was surprised that it was painless to do so now.

The infirmary looked like a storm had tossed everything into the air and walls. Debris was everywhere, but Prospero could move again. That, too, was unexpected.

"Ellie? Love?"

"Prospero!" Hands reached for her, pulling her into a soft bosom. "You're . . . wow, you're—"

"Old. I know. I told you. I won't hold you back, though." Prospero stared into her wife's eyes, grateful she could tell her the words that Ellie needed to hear. She wasn't sure why she could speak now, or hear Ellie, but she hurried to get the words out. "I release you. You can have a life here without the burden of an old—"

"But you're *not* old." Ellie laughed. "You *were.* I thought you were dying. I wasn't fast enough. I couldn't do it. I've never killed anyone until . . ."

"You killed him?" Dan said. "That's a relief. When I opened my eyes and saw that he was ashes . . . well, mostly. There's a jaw with some teeth still in it."

"Dan." Ellie swallowed visibly. "You're . . . here."

"Did you hit your head?" Dan looked around. Louder he said, "Hey, Dr. J? I think Ellie hit her head." He scowled. "Why's everyone staring at me?"

"You were dead," the stranger who had been crouched in the corner said. *Ian.* That was his name. *Remedial witch Ian.*

Dan laughed, but when no one else joined in, he looked at Axell. "For real?"

"I killed you," Prospero said.

"Lie." Dan folded his arms. "Still a witch. I can hear lies, and that was a lie. This is not funny, guys. Telling someone they were murdered is—"

"I killed you," Ellie said softly. *Her* admission rang true, and everyone in the room had to realize it.

"Oh."

"You drained Allan until he was a husk . . . and then when Prospero started aging . . ." She straightened her shoulders. "I don't regret it. You were killing her."

Dan said nothing at first, and Prospero wondered how much she was going to have to erase from his memory. Then he shrugged. "Your wife's a scary bitch. I guess knowing I could kill her makes me feel a little better around her."

Ellie gave him a measured look. "I won't hesitate to kill *anyone* who endangers my wife." Her gaze drifted from Dan over to the chief witch and she repeated, "Anyone."

And Prospero flinched. Ellie was publicly threatening the chief witch.

Walter gave her an appraising look. "I knew you'd make a good match." He grinned like a cheerful grandpa. "Figured she needed someone vicious to love her the way she needs. Glad you're up to the task, Miss Brandeau."

Prospero's mouth gaped open.

"I assume all of your recollections are back," Walter asked.

A different sort of feeling washed over Prospero.

"Yes," Ellie said. Her voice was biting as she added, "So nice of you to meddle and announce that."

"Whatever magic the boy scooped up came boiling over when you stopped his heart." Walter looked around the room. "Your belly?"

"Healed. Barrier up at full unwavering strength," Scylla answered.

"Memories?"

The headmaster's wife said, "Intact."

"Addiction?"

Axell answered, "Cured."

"And I'm not dying anymore." Walter stood and stretched. "Feeling better than I have in centuries. Be ready to collect Aggie tomorrow." His gaze spanned the room. He paused. "Dionysus. That'll be *you* now."

The Norwegian looked stunned. "Me?"

"And you," he said, waving a hand at Dan. "You'll take House Grendel. Siphon those who need it, weigh out justice. We'll need some polish to do a better job of the siphoning, though. That attempt was a bit messier than we would typically want."

Then he walked up to Prospero, kissed her forehead, and pronounced, "I'm done being chief witch. I'll try to see to it that you get saddled with it next. Mark my words. I know it was you and"—he shot a glare at Scylla—"and you who lobbied to sentence me to it. So I'll be sure to toss this pile of dung to one of you. See how you like it."

Then he left the room, cheerily calling, "I'll summon you when I find Aggie."

39
Ellie

Ellie looked around the room. Her gaze fell on poor Ian. "Someone needs to get him settled." She glanced at her wife. "He looks traumatized. Could you . . ."

Prospero gave her a disbelieving look. "Seriously?"

Ian was staring at the ashes on the floor. Allan's bottom jaw was in his lap. "Witch boss?"

Prospero sighed, walked over to the new witch, and said, "Eyes up here. Hand me that."

He held out the partial jawbone, and Prospero called, "Hobs?"

Several hobs popped into the room, and in the next few moments, the dust and scattered pieces of bone fragments were gone. One hob paused beside Dan and whispered to him.

Meanwhile, Prospero held Ian's gaze.

A few moments later, Ian was all smiles. "So you're all witches?"

"You're in Crenshaw due to the awakening of latent magical traits," Sondre said as he approached Ian. "These traits mean that, in due course, there will be a decision whether you are to remain here or return to your home location."

They all watched as Sondre walked out of the infirmary, still talking. "As part of this process, you will attend the College of Remedial Magic, after which you will be brought to court at several points, whereupon the Congress of Magic will determine if you can remain or be siphoned safely. If you are selected to remain . . ."

The door closed behind them, ending the sound of the "welcome to witch life" speech.

Maggie looked over at Ellie. "I guess you decided to stay with her, despite everything?"

Ellie shot a smile at her wife. "Enough to break every rule, hurt anyone who tried to step between us . . ." She looked back at Maggie. "I understand why you wanted to go after your kid now. Love makes people do absurd things."

Maggie chuckled. "I'm glad you were enough of a friend to help me get to him even when you didn't understand."

Ellie felt Prospero come up behind her and wrap her arms around Ellie's waist. She put her hand over Prospero's hand to let her know she wanted her there.

"Everything I said to you stands," Maggie said, looking back at Prospero.

"I am sorry for what you had to experience." Prospero sounded stiff, and Ellie had to admit that her wife would likely never be friends with Maggie.

"Whatever. I have my kid in my life, and I'm happy *despite you.*" Maggie's smile looked more like showing her teeth in aggression. "And my friend can drain you. Useful information to have."

"Mags . . ." Ellie sighed.

Maggie shrugged. "Let's grab a drink next week. Just us. We have a kiss between us to discuss."

Ellie flinched at that, until she realized that Maggie was just trying to bait Prospero. "Sorry. I'm taken."

Maggie, Dan, and Axell all left then. And for a moment, Ellie felt a little left out. Then Maggie called, "The four of us, tavern, tomorrow?"

And Ellie reminded herself that they were all her friends, too. Tonight, her nearly deceased wife was her priority.

Prospero looked at her oddly for a moment. "The prophecy was that without you I'd die. Then a lot of others . . . Scylla, Walt, Sondre . . . you were essential. I was to save us, so I guess I'm still going after Aggie, but without you, I'd die."

"Not going to happen." Ellie gave her a look. "I don't need a prophecy to know I'll choose you. You can keep Crenshaw safe, but I'll take care of you."

Prospero smiled tremulously. "I'm not sure how good I'll be at being taken care of. I'm used to counting on myself."

"Even when I knew we fought, I still loved you. You're *mine*." Ellie cupped her face in both hands. "You can be terrifying and powerful and all the rest, but I'll still be here. And I'll still protect you."

Prospero pulled her into an embrace, holding her tightly. Then after a moment, she relaxed slightly.

"Let me tell Scylla we're leaving," Prospero whispered against Ellie's ear. "I want to go to our home."

"Me too."

Ellie watched as Prospero talked to the doctor and Lord Scylla briefly. *This is my life.* Crenshaw was hidden again, air cleaned, and water purified. That last detail gave Ellie a wonderful idea.

When Prospero rejoined her, Ellie said, "Take us home."

"With pleasure." Prospero wrapped her arms around Ellie, who leaned her head on Prospero's shoulder.

In the next moment, they were standing at the door of their home.

Ellie looked at Prospero as they stood in front of the house. "I love you. I know our wedding wasn't real, but I *would* marry you."

"I would be honored to have you as my wife." Prospero cupped Ellie's cheek in her hand. "To share my life with you. To cherish you and hold you."

"I want a ceremony," Ellie confesses. "Vows in public."

"How public?" Prospero asked.

"Small, private ceremony? Large one in the middle of the town? Whatever. Whenever." Ellie kissed her lightly. "Not tonight, obviously. After Aggie is caught."

"Should I be planning to propose or expecting a proposal?" Prospero asked.

"Yes." Ellie swept her wife up into a cradle in her arms. "For tonight, though, I give you my vow, Prospero. I will love you." She stepped up to the door, which opened at their approach. "I will cherish you and protect you." Ellie stepped across the threshold. "For as long as we both shall live."

"Witches live for centuries," Prospero reminded her.

"I'm counting on that." Ellie lowered her feet to the ground, and they twined their hands together.

"Bedroom?"

"Close." Ellie led them to the bathroom that adjoined the bedroom. The tub was stained from the bad water, so Ellie concentrated on reshaping it into a much larger black marble tub with jets.

Prospero turned the tap, and beautiful clear water filled the tub.

Ellie walked over and lit the lavender candle that rested in the alcove in the wall.

"We don't need that now," Prospero started.

"Hush." Ellie walked over and started to unbutton the vest her wife still wore. She slid it off Prospero's shoulders. It dropped to the floor.

"I can remove . . . these . . ." Prospero whispered.

"Hush." Ellie met her gaze. "I'm unwrapping my wedding gift."

Ellie unbuttoned each button on Prospero's top, and at her cuffs, and then unfastened her trousers. Item after item she dropped on the floor, and then Prospero was standing in her underwear in their bathroom.

Ellie pulled the cool piece of glass that she had stolen from the infirmary and held it in her hand where Prospero couldn't see it. She held the glass behind her. With her magic, she reshaped it, extending and expanding it until it resembled the device they'd seen the two women use on the campus—but not as large.

"In the water," Ellie ordered.

Prospero said nothing as she slid into the tub. She watched Ellie disrobe, eyes darkening as Ellie paused for Prospero to look up at her eyes.

"Focus trouble, dear?" Ellie teased.

"Not *trouble*," Prospero demurred.

Ellie slid into the water. Slowly, she dipped a cloth in the warm water and started to bathe her wife. "You scared me, you know."

After Ellie lathered the cloth, she took Prospero's hand in hers, washed it, and placed it on Ellie's shoulder. "Keep that right there for me."

Slowly Ellie washed her wife's arm, then shoulder, and repeated the process on the other arm. She dipped the cloth again, and she pulled her wife forward, parting her legs so Prospero was wrapped around her under the water.

"One night isn't enough with you," Ellie said. "Up on your knees, please."

"Ellie . . ."

"Is that a no?" Ellie asked. "Nothing you don't want. You looked interested earlier. . . ."

Prospero shifted, feeling exposed by the position.

"Such a good girl," Ellie murmured. She took the device and put it under the water. The anticipation made Prospero bite back a noise.

Ellie grinned, obviously aware of exactly what reaction she had elicited. Then she washed Prospero's chest, paying extra attention to her wife's breasts and belly while leaning in for kisses and licks and bites.

"Talk to me," Ellie urged as she slid the tip of the glass phallus inside Prospero. "Do you like it smooth like this or . . . ?" Her magic shifted it while it was sliding deeper inside Prospero, creating ridges. "This way."

"Yes." Prospero swallowed hard. "Both. More."

"Or like this." Ellie's words were barely a whisper, and the ridges started vibrating.

Prospero whimpered.

"Hands where I put them," Ellie ordered, and Prospero hadn't even realized she'd moved. "Just right there. Can you do that?"

Prospero shook her head no and looked at her as Ellie reached down and started to thrust the device in and out.

All she could do was stare as Ellie widened her legs, forcing Prospero's legs to slide farther apart. The result was that Prospero lowered deeper into the water, and the magical device Ellie had created slid deeper into Prospero's body as Ellie's finger landed on Prospero's clitoris.

"Ellie . . ." Prospero had no words left. No thoughts left. Her hands tightened on Ellie's shoulders as the pressure built.

Tremors made her shake, water rippling and breathing harsher by the moment. The first orgasm ripped through her body like a wave.

"Tell me, Prospero, do you like this?" Ellie teased as she watched her fall apart. "Or do you want more?"

Prospero felt her eyes widen. Her brain was not filling in what more there could be. "More? _How?_"

"Wider?" Ellie asked.

Prospero felt like she was filled right up to the edge of too much then.

"Or faster?"

The vibrations were suddenly so constant that it felt like one long hum, and Ellie's fingers sped in time with them.

When her free hand pulled Prospero closer, the device expanded so that the outside was longer. Ellie shifted so the edge of the device nudged between Ellie's tightly closed thighs. They both moaned then, the vibrations rippling between their bodies.

Ellie held her gaze. "I love you, Prospero."

"Yes," Prospero managed to say as she tumbled into another orgasm.

This time, she took her hands from Ellie's shoulder. She reached down and gripped Ellie's hips as the vibrations from the magical device pushed Ellie toward her own release.

They were both breathing loudly, and Prospero whispered a silent thank-you to whatever deity existed that this miraculous woman was hers.

"I love you, too," Prospero told her. "Thank you for saving me tonight."

Ellie nodded. "I'll be at your side whatever comes. Fights. Arguments. Good times. All of it. I want you."

"You have me." Prospero rested her forehead against Ellie's. "But . . . Ellie?"

"Yeah?"

"I might need help standing," Prospero murmured.

Ellie laughed. "I can do that . . ."

"And make that something I can use on you, too . . . ?" Prospero asked, as Ellie slid the now-still phallus out of her.

"Definitely." Ellie kissed her briefly. "There are plenty of things we can try if you want."

"With you? I do. I definitely do." Prospero looked over at her and stood, feeling a little self-conscious as Ellie stared as she rose from the water.

"We have a few centuries, I hear. . . ." Ellie didn't look nearly as exhausted as Prospero felt.

"Come to bed with me." Prospero stepped out of the tub and held out a hand. "I think it's my turn to exhaust you."

40
Maggie

Maggie remembered everything now. She remembered Sondre helping her escape, as well as telling her he could use their rules to let Craig come to Crenshaw. She also remembered her son sprawled out on the ground motionless—because of Prospero.

She stood in the hallway of the castle next to Dan and Axell. "Thank you for trying to help me when I . . . forgot some things."

"Do you hate me?" Dan asked.

"For trying to talk to me?" Maggie scowled. "That was his idea anyhow. I knew that." She nodded toward Axell, who shrugged.

"For erasing your memory?" Dan corrected.

Maggie looked at him, guilt plain in his eyes and frown. "I suppose they gave you a choice . . . ? It was totally voluntary?"

"No, but . . . they said I could stay if I did it." Dan crossed his arms over his chest.

"Right, help this or die? That's what would happen if you were siphoned. Whatever was killing you would return . . . ?" Maggie wasn't pleased that he'd helped, but calling it a "choice" was far from accurate.

The most important thing she'd figured out about witches was that they were just people—ones who lived long lives, often were misfits in some way, and generally had the false sense that threatening people or manipulating them was fine.

"Would you have done it?" Axell asked. He gave her a curious look, as if he wasn't sure what she'd say.

"I agreed to it. Sondre said it would mean my son was here. That was enough." She touched Dan's wrist. "We all have reasons we make the choices we make. I left because they said he was dead, and it was a lie. I came back because they said I could bring him. Sometimes, under all the bullshit, there's one true thing. One goal. One reason. For me it was love, but not wanting to *die* is a pretty valid one, too."

Dan nodded. "So we're good?"

Maggie gave him a wide smile. "I'm not sure anyone is *good* or evil."

"Not like that!" Dan objected. "I meant—"

"I know what you meant," Maggie said over him. "But if you're going to be House Grendel, and I'm going to be around arguing about the antiquated laws around here, you might want to tuck that thought in a pocket. We're going to disagree on things, Dan. That doesn't mean we can't be friends." She paused and grinned. "You might as well be my stepson or brother-in-law the way you and my husband act. He's protective of you."

"True," Axell murmured. "He's threatened me."

"In his defense, there was that whole . . . health-magic class where you and the doctor and I . . ." Maggie shrugged.

"Magic. Not by choice," Axell pointed out. "I am Dan's."

"Right . . . You are sleeping with one witch Sondre's protective over and shared orgasms with his ex *and* his wife. You're never going to be on his good side." Maggie grinned.

"Am I on yours?" Axell met her gaze.

"Yes." She looked to the end of the hallway, where Sondre had appeared. "Drinks. Tavern. Soon."

"Often," Axell amended with a grin.

The two of them walked away, and Maggie turned to look at her spouse. There were new and old memories of her time here that contained him, as well as memories of her escape. Whatever else she knew, she was certain of him.

She walked toward him, smiling slightly when he paused at a classroom door and gestured. It wasn't perfectly private; someone could walk in. Their suite wasn't either, though, not until Craig moved back to the other world.

"Hi." She smiled up at him, ignoring the ancient desks in the room as she followed him to the teacher's desk. "Are you okay?"

"I should be asking you that." Sondre opened his arms as she stepped closer.

"You helped me save my son." Maggie reached up and stroked his cheek. "You helped me escape to find him, and you proposed a plan to help me have him here where I could keep him safe from Leon."

"But I let them manipulate things, so I was married to you," Sondre pointed out.

"Was that your idea?"

"No, but . . ." Sondre shook his head.

"I'm happy right here with you." Maggie stretched up and kissed his chin. "I wasn't looking for this, for *us,* but I still want to try it. Do you?"

"Yes." Sondre's hand curved around her hips, holding her still. "I want to be yours, but I think you need to talk to Craig about the school plan first. I don't want you to resent me later if he hates it or . . ." He shrugged. "Being a parent means putting your kid first, and he's the only kid I'll ever have so that's what I want to do here."

Maggie felt like her heart was melting into goo. "How could any woman resist you?"

"Most don't," he teased. "Well, at least they didn't until I had a terrifying wife."

She mock-scowled at him. "The only one getting to be with you now is going to be me. Is that okay?"

"Very."

She pressed a little tighter to him, loving the feel of being enveloped by him. "Find us a classroom like this later, and we can play a bit of naughty schoolgirl. . . ."

He groaned. "You are incorrigible."

"You love it."

"I do. I love *you*, Maggie." Sondre lifted her up and kissed her, and she started thinking that maybe this classroom, this moment, could be—

"Gross," Craig said from the doorway.

Sondre lowered Maggie's feet to the ground and muttered, "I'm going to put a bell on him." Louder, he said, "Why are you here?"

"Dan said you were in here talking. I saw him in the hallway." Craig grinned. "Do we need to talk about hanging a sock or something on doorknobs?"

"Only on holidays," Maggie said lightly. She glanced at Sondre. "Now?"

He gave a nod.

Craig looked at Sondre. "The solution you mentioned?"

Sondre nodded again.

"You could go to a high school over in the old world, where we used to live—"

"The Barbarian Lands," Sondre interjected.

"Pennsylvania. Live with Hestia. She'd be your guardian, and you could visit me on holidays. Want to try that?" Maggie offered, trying to sound casual despite the growing fears and panic she felt.

"You'd be good with me going there? Living *not* with you?" Craig asked, looking only at her. He might be getting on slightly better with Sondre, but she was his mom. *She* was the parent he'd always looked to for answers.

"You'll visit." Maggie swallowed her burst of doubt. "It's not perfect, but it's a lot better than never seeing you because you think I died . . .

and it's better than being here where you aren't happy. Even with the air cleaned, there's no one your age. No sports. It's got to suck a little."

"A lot," Craig said. "But it's better than living with . . . Leon."

Maggie paused at Craig calling his dad by his first name.

"He tried to kill me," Craig said. "I don't think he deserves to be called Dad." He shot a glance at Sondre. "I don't know if I'll call anyone else that ever, but . . . Leon lost that right."

Maggie felt teary.

"So, let's tell the old lady you want to go to school in Ligonier," Sondre said, filling in the awkward silence. He held out a hand toward Craig.

"That hand was on my mother's ass, and who knows where else." Craig gave Sondre a look. "No thanks."

"Craig!" Maggie looked upward. "Seriously."

"We're going to need house rules when I come home on holidays." Craig wrapped an arm over her shoulders. "This is how kids end up needing therapy. Parents who act like horny teenagers."

41

Prospero

When Walt himself appeared at her door a day later, Prospero stayed in the doorway, not inviting him in. She liked him, but that didn't mean she was going to start inviting anyone into her house. When she looked down, she realized he had a badger sitting beside him.

"Cassandra would like you to know she requested badgering for going to the Barbarian Lands and putting cattle in the way of your wife's car," Walt said solemnly.

"I didn't turn her in for it." Prospero folded her arms, but it was hard to look stern when she was wearing pajamas and a robe at almost midday.

Walt nodded, the corner of his mouth starting to curve like a twitch. "Can we come in?"

"No." Ellie's voice preceded her presence, but her arms wrapped around Prospero's middle in the next moment. "We aren't entertaining guests."

"I see." Walter tilted his head as if to see her, but she was well snuggled against Prospero's back. "Well, we'll wait here while you dress. Aggie is due to be causing trouble any moment, according to the seer."

"You speak badger?" Ellie asked from behind Prospero.

"She told me *before* the badgering," Walt corrected. He paused then as Grish popped up behind him with Dan and his boyfriend. "Ah, we're all here. I will converse with the others while you find your clothing, Lady Prospero."

Prospero closed the door before she or Ellie could say something inflammatory. She turned within the circle of Ellie's arms and met her gaze. "I can do this without you or with you. It's up to you."

"Look at you. Not even trying to tell me to stay home . . ." Ellie stretched up and kissed her briefly. "Thank you, but I will go where you are. Not because I doubt you, but because I want to be at your side. You're mine, and I protect what's mine."

Prospero felt like swooning. There was no other word for it. She wasn't the sort who was used to being protected. She protected Crenshaw— obviously not alone, but she was there. Always. She shook her head. "I want to argue and also to kiss you senseless."

"Good." Ellie released her. "I'll look forward to that kiss. First though, maybe trousers if we are traveling?"

"Fine." Prospero glared at the door, thinking of the witches outside it. She had issues with Walt right now. And she wasn't entirely at ease with Monahan. He'd almost killed her, and his magic was uncontrolled. Add that to his fear of her, and it could go poorly.

Ellie can stop his heart or lungs, she reminded herself as she went to get dressed in something less comfortable.

By the time they were dressed and outside, Prospero felt the pull of magic in the other world. The last escaped witch. The one who had left Sondre in the hospital. The one who had convinced her that Ellie was dead.

"I'm ready," Prospero announced, half telling herself.

Walt gave her a look that said he understood both meanings. "I would have been helping you more of late if I hadn't been trying not to die."

"You should've told me you were so ill." Prospero gave him a surly look.

"I did, once it was resolved. Would you do differently? You're so much like me that I have trouble thinking that." He gave her a look that was far younger and more confrontational than he'd been in decades.

"Save your attitude for the enemy." She took Ellie's hand and teleported. They had no more than shown up when she heard the sound of feet landing behind her. The three other witches had arrived.

They stood in a park, and that at least was a comfort. There were few nonmagical folk here. A few people in tiny boats on a river, a few people at tents on the bank and edge of the wood, but it was not a crowded venue. That was a comfort. Wherever they were, it was more nature than city.

"What a wonderful party," Aggie said with an exaggerated cheer. "Are you here for *me*?"

"Agnes." Walter let out a long sigh. "Must we make this difficult?"

"Look at this land. Unclaimed. Fertile. We could rule all of this." Aggie stilled then. She pointed to the side. "What's that child doing with my staff?"

"You tossed it away," Prospero reminded her, not looking back. All she needed was to see Agnes' eyes. One slip of the glasses would be enough.

Maybe if I shoved her. Tackling her was not the sort of thing Prospero would typically do, but the memory of the horrible visions last time was enough to make her try new things. Unprecedented things.

"Tossed it . . . Did I *kill* Sondre then?" Aggie sounded positively gleeful. "That worked out nicely. I do hope he suffered as payment for spying for you. Tell me he and that other one are both dead."

"They're well and toasting your absence," Walt said mildly.

"Let's settle this like adults," Monahan started, drawing her attention. "You broke the rules and—"

"Fuck you." Aggie looked around at them. "Look at the lot of you. Such powerful witches. All I need is to be over here and add a pair of cheap sunglasses, and you're helpless. 'No magic around the barbarians.' Bah." She opened her arms wide. "This world could be ours. No limited space. No hovels."

"And what cost?" the Norwegian—*Axell*—asked. He was there at risk to himself to steady Monahan, so the new House Grendel head didn't drain everyone of their magic. It was either courage or idiocy. Prospero wasn't sure which, though.

"Did you see what Allan did?" Prospero asked, stepping forward to block the two youngest witches and the chief witch from Aggie's gaze.

Ellie stepped up and stood at Prospero's side. It made sense, as they were two of the only ones who could use magic to stop Aggie.

"So a few people can't handle our presence. Why is that reason enough to stay over there in Crenshaw?" Agnes shook her head.

They'd had these arguments for years, and at the center of it all was a quandary over the good of the few or the good of the many. Prospero believed that harming fewer people made sense. Aggie was of the "you have to crack a few eggs" mindset. There was no middle ground on this, and that was the sum of it.

"Monahan," she said. "It's you or Ellie."

Everyone was silent, and Prospero hated that this was where the situation had evolved. One way or the other Aggie would die here, a victim of her own beliefs. And from the look on Agnes' face, she knew it.

Walt's hand landed on Prospero's shoulder. "Give me one moment."

He stepped forward, steadily walking toward Agnes, who eyed him warily. Then he launched himself at her, knocking her to the ground. In the next moment, they vanished.

"So . . ." Monahan looked around.

Axell shrugged.

Ellie met Prospero's eyes. "Should we go home?"

Prospero was at a loss. She'd been dreading this since Aggie shot Scylla, but here they were, facing her nemesis, and Walt simply grabbed her and disappeared. "I honestly don't know what to do. I suppose we—"

Her words were lost under a noise that was somewhere between a hiss and a growl.

42

Ellie

Before they could do anything else, the chief witch was back, and in his arms was a growling badger. An angry badger that was biting and kicking and clawing. It snarled at them with a flash of sharp teeth.

"I had a talk with Dr. Jemison," Walt said, holding the badger by the scruff of its neck, keeping it at arm's length. "She suggested that badgering before siphoning might save Aggie's life."

"I can't do much with a *badger's* mind." Prospero stared at the snarling creature.

"But you needed to face her," Walt said quietly. "And I wasn't sure I wanted the boy to try to siphon her over at home." He shook the badger. "Monahan."

Dan looked over at the badger-shaped witch and sighed. "I'm sorry. I hope you survive this," he told her as he approached.

She extended a paw toward him aggressively.

And Ellie moved between Dan and Prospero. She wasn't going to risk another episode of Dan hurting Prospero, accidentally or not. She suspected that was why the chief witch brought her. He was a canny witch—bring Axell to calm Dan, bring Ellie to stop Dan's heart, and bring Prospero because there was no way she'd be calm if Ellie went without her.

They stood there, an odd collection of witches surrounding a badger at a campground. Then as the badger struggled against her restraints, Dan did the same as he'd done with Allan. This time, the witch who was being drained flailed and resisted.

But as Ellie watched, she could tell that Dan was doing something. When he stumbled back, half falling, Axell caught him.

Dan rested on his haunches. "She's unmagical."

"She knows all about Crenshaw," Prospero pointed out. She sounded confused. "I can't do anything with her mind in this shape. Do you want to transform her back?"

"No." Walt looked vicious in that moment. He held the badger up to his face. "You are powerless, Agnes, but I think I'll let you remember everything."

Ellie flinched internally. She wasn't sure what the chief witch had been like before he assumed this role, but right now, he seemed callous. She watched as he walked over to the edge of the river.

"You might want to all leave before she catches up. I don't know how fast badgers are," Walt called and then he tossed the angry badger into the shallows.

Then Walt teleported away.

"Jackass," Ellie muttered. She grabbed Dan's wrist, and Prospero extended a hand toward Axell as though she had all the time in the world. Then all four witches vanished.

They arrived at the infirmary, where the doctor was waiting at the door.

"Well?" The doctor looked directly at Prospero.

"She's a badger, memories intact, life intact, magic gone," Prospero reported. "No one died, Mae."

The doctor smiled. "It worked then. She'll be able to think about it every day."

"And that's better?" Ellie asked.

"She's alive. With life there is a chance for joy," the doctor said. "So yes, it's much better." Then she turned and went back to her infirmary, leaving the four of them alone in the hallway.

Ellie looked around. "So . . . that encounter went better than the last time."

"Yes," Dan and Prospero both said, although she realized that they were obviously referring to different "last times." Prospero's last encounter with Agnes and Dan's last siphoning were both difficult experiences in different ways.

They stood there awkwardly for a moment until Axell said, "You were a bookkeeper, Ellie . . . ?"

"No, I was a librarian."

"Yes. A keeper of books." Axell scowled. "We have a library needing a keeper."

Dan shot him a look that Ellie didn't quite understand, and Axell added, "You are moving out of the castle, *ja*? You can share."

For a moment, Dan was silent, but then he sighed. "Fine. I liked having it as our space."

"There's a library?" Ellie prompted, steering them back to the best news she'd had other than discovering that Prospero loved her. "Where? I walked through the entire village and—"

"Here." Prospero motioned around them. "The books are in the castle."

"There was a library here the whole time? Where?" Ellie tried to think of every room and hallway here. Was there a place she'd missed? An area she'd failed to explore? "Does my aunt know?"

"She used to when she first lived here," Prospero hedged. Then she laced her fingers with Ellie and walked away, pausing to scowl at the two men who were trailing behind them.

"Not scared of you," Dan whispered loudly. He was lying, which they all undoubtedly knew.

They walked through the hallway to a giant arched doorway. Pillars too wide to wrap her arms around framed the doorway. The doors were massive carved wood with iron detailing. They looked like they belonged on an old castle or cathedral.

"Was this here the whole time?" Ellie asked in low voice.

"Yes," Prospero said.

"No," Dan said.

Both statements were somehow true, but she wasn't sure how. Then Axell opened the door, and she didn't care. There were thousands of books there, and as she walked around reading spines, she found that none of them were books she'd read.

"Why isn't this available to everyone?" Ellie looked around. "That will change. We'll need a card catalogue. And staff . . ."

She continued to shelf read, scanning titles as she walked, for several moments. Finally, she paused. "Fiction section?"

Prospero shook her head. "There's some, mixed in with . . ."

Ellie held up a hand before she could finish saying that. "I'll need to reorganize."

Hobs started popping into the room, standing on shelves and tables. Every hob was smiling.

"Lady P likes fiction," Bernice said from atop a globe.

"How do we get it?" Ellie looked around at them. "Can I get some volunteers to help reorganize? I can make the card catalogue. I need some twigs."

Ellie started a mental list of things that needed to be managed to make this library fully functional in all ways.

"Friend Maggie would like a law section," another hob offered.

"These are all magic books," Ellie said, half asking, half guessing. "People need fiction, too. Plays. Poetry."

"Make a list," Axell said. "We can't stay there long, but I bet a few trips to shop . . . Perhaps we can bring albums, too."

"Yes." Ellie looked around at the hobs and witches watching her. "I have a *project*." She met Prospero's eyes. "Do you suppose you might want to help now that the conflicts are resolved?"

Prospero gave a nod, but she was smiling in a way that veered on giddy for her. "New books and music? You'll have plenty of volunteers."

Ellie's imagination was running away, and the best part was that with magic, she could accomplish it all. She let out a small squeal and wrapped her arms around Prospero. They'd build up the library, and they'd open it to the public. She could picture it.

"Crenshaw Library," Ellie said.

43
Dan

Dan wasn't sure how he felt about what he could do magically. He'd reduced one witch to ashes, and he'd left another witch as a powerless badger. He felt like there were *good* magics and bad magics, and his gift felt like both. He could take people's magic, leave them empty, but he could gift that magic to others.

He felt the weight of the magic he'd stolen from the last head of House Grendel. *Who will live and die as a wild animal.* Dan touched the wall of the castle, and a pressure inside him made him lean against the wall.

Let it go.

Let it flow into this place that has felt like home.

He closed his eyes and exhaled, and Agnes' magic rolled out of his body into the stones. As it did, he felt like pain was escaping. A weight shifted from his shoulders. He was no longer holding on to stolen magic.

Now I just need to deal with a stolen house.

He was more stressed about moving into the house that was, by extension, his now. The castle hobs were like family. Well, like a family of pranksters . . . and Agnes had felt malevolent. Her magic had made him feel agitated.

"Clance?" Dan called out. He was sitting on his bed in his room in the castle.

"Yes." Clancy appeared next to him, sprawled out on a pillow that was almost sofa-sized for someone of his stature.

"Why are the hobs so nice to me?"

"Because you belong here." Clancy looked up at him, expression uncommonly serious. "You were always going to replace the last Grendel. She was untethered. We knew."

"How?"

"Because we *are* magic, child." Clancy sat upright, legs folded crisscross, and hands held loosely in his lap. "We made this place, you know, and we knew you were ours. You'll be good for a lot of people."

"Oh."

"Some people aren't ready to be who they are. Some people are afraid of their magic. Some people want to be something else entirely. You? You are sure of yourself."

"Me?" Dan gaped at him. "I doubt everything. I feel like I think things to death. I'm anxious. I'm . . . just a guy who screws up a lot."

Clancy shook his head. "You're a person who tries. You ask hard questions. You and Thesis were needed. Now that you're ready to be what you already were, you'll help Crenshaw. That's the real secret of being a house head. You do the hard things, and you try to make the world better."

"Oh . . . well, thank you." Dan squirmed a little. "I don't want to go to that house without any hobs, or without Axell, but . . ."

"Why would you go without us?" Clancy scowled. "I picked you. You're my witch. I'll transfer to House Grendel and look after you. That was already the plan."

"I'll screw up."

"Well, of course you will. Witches are human. So they make mistakes.

Luckily, you have magic—and by magic I mean *hobs*. We always steer things back to right." Clancy stood and stretched. "Now, I need to get back to work. The house is tidy, and her things were re-sorted. Furniture shifted. Everything will be yours soon."

"Right . . . then, well." Dan looked over, but Clancy was gone. The decision to move felt better. *I can do this,* Dan tried to tell himself, although to be honest, he was still fairly sure there was a mistake. He didn't feel like he ought to be in charge of anything.

But houses were limited, and he couldn't just decide to stay in the castle. *Could I?* The last of his cohort was settled in the castle, and a few of the people from town were deciding to stay here. Other witches were moving to group houses or apartments. Everything was starting to change.

There were still at least two remedial witches who might be siphoned, and Dan could *tell* that now, but tonight they'd all been given leave to roam freely throughout the castle. It felt like a small victory to him, since he'd been doing as much since he was released from the infirmary.

Maybe I am House Grendel.

"Ana has been making liquor," Axell announced from the open door to Dan's room.

"Where?"

"Built a still in an unused classroom." Axell shrugged, as if brewing a highly flammable liquor in closed spaces was of no concern.

"Moonshine? A still? What was she thinking?" Dan gaped at him.

"It's not just moonshine," Axell said, grinning at him. "I am to be Dionysus, and she is a part of my house. We are updating the liquor options for the tavern."

"In a *classroom*?"

Axell shrugged, and Dan couldn't question the idea that the beautiful Norwegian man in front of him was well suited for the role of Dionysus. He was languid in ways that made him look like a rock star without putting any effort into it.

"I was thinking that you would need a house-toasting party," Axell said the words casually, but there was a question there, too. He wasn't pressuring, wasn't even asking if they would live together in the house that Dan suddenly had.

He knows I'm scared.

"Warming," Dan corrected absently. "*We* would have a house*warming* party."

Axell stepped into the room they'd been keeping as "Dan's" even though they practically lived in Axell's room. The door closed behind him, and Axell leaned against it. "We?"

"Do you plan to live in a tent or something like the last Dionysus? Cuddle up with badgers and whatever willing person—"

"I want a specific willing person. No matter where I sleep." Axell shook his head. "I know what I like, Daniel. I like *you*."

"Enough to live with me?" Dan asked softly. "If you had a house, too, would you still want to live with me?"

"*Ja.* Yes. Always. Yes." Axell crossed the room and crawled onto the bed, so he was sprawled on top of Dan. He leaned down, lips hovering over Dan's. "Is that what you want?"

"I do," Dan said, thinking briefly that he liked saying those words to Axell. *Maybe someday . . .*

But then Axell's lips met his, and Dan stopped thinking.

Right here, right now. This was enough.

Acknowledgments

Remedial Magic and *Reluctant Witch* were inspired by dealing with my own relationship with "magic"—which is commonly known as "medicine" outside of Crenshaw—and how even with all the healing magic (aka medicine) in the world, there are things we cannot heal. So my gratitude for this "duet" of books goes first to the doctors, nurses, techs, and pharmacists who have enabled me to live and write.

I don't want to heal my lupus—because it has shaped me and I *like* who I am—but meds (or magic) have bought back time that I can spend with my loved ones. That was the thought that started this pair of books—during the pandemic when my first worry was "can I get my meds?" before "will I get the virus?" (I got both).

In addition to the medical/magical forces that let my life keep happening, I am grateful to every person in my publishing journey, from agent to editor to publishing team to booksellers to librarians to readers. *This* time I'm a little extra grateful to all of you for coming on my journey as I pondered the cost of wellness, magic/meds, family dynamics, and finding love in the middle of upheaval.

Specific thanks to Monique Patterson, Merrilee Heifetz, and Mal Frazier for the enthusiastic responses to *Remedial Magic*.

Thank you, also, to Lisa Perrin, who created cover magic for both of these books, and Giselle Gonzalez, Jordan Hanley, Emily Mlynek, Ariana Carpentieri, and everyone else behind the scenes in marketing, publicity, and all the other essentials that make books happen.

Extra thanks to Isabella Narvaez, Max Meyers, Jeremy Parker Carlisle, Claire Beyette, and Ally Demeter, who worked magic on creating and promoting an audiobook I love for the first book—and I excitedly anticipate this one.

Thank you to my ever-patient children, my friend and the father of my children (Loch), and my wife (Amber), who have all been super supportive both when I announced I was not going to write anymore (and did quit for a couple years) and again when I wrote more books.

And most of all, thank you to the readers who gave this duet of books a chance. I know *Remedial Magic* ended on a cliffhanger—which I don't usually do—but since *this* book was already written when that one came out, the pair always felt like one long story. I hope that the wait hasn't been too long on your side!

About the Author

Melissa Marr writes fiction for adults, teens, and children. Her books have been translated into twenty-eight languages and are bestsellers in the United States (*The New York Times, Los Angeles Times, USA Today, The Wall Street Journal*), as well as overseas. *Wicked Lovely,* her debut novel, was an instant *New York Times* bestseller and evolved into an internationally bestselling multibook series with a myriad of accolades. If she's not writing, you can find her in a kayak or on a trail with her wife.

MelissaMarrBooks.com
Twitter: @melissa_marr
Instagram: @melissamarrwriting